THE PAINTING

THE PAINTING

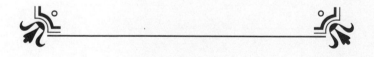

a novel by

NINA SCHUYLER

ALGONQUIN BOOKS OF CHAPEL HILL

Published by
ALGONQUIN BOOKS OF CHAPEL HILL
Post Office Box 2225
Chapel Hill, North Carolina 27515-2225

a division of
Workman Publishing
708 Broadway
New York, New York 10003

Basho haiku on page vii from *An Introduction to Haiku* by Harold G. Henderson,
copyright © 1958 by Harold G. Henderson. Used by permission of Doubleday,
a division of Random House, Inc.

Izumi Shikibu poem on page 61 from *The Ink Dark Moon* translated by Jane Hirschfield
and Mariko Aratani, copyright © 1990 by Jane Hirschfield and Mariko Aratani. Used by
permission of Vintage Books, a division of Random House, Inc.

Library of Congress Cataloging-in-Publication Data
Schuyler, Nina, 1963–
    The painting : a novel / by Nina Schuyler.—1st ed.
        p. cm.
    ISBN 1-56512-441-3
    1. Art—Appreciation—Fiction.   2. Paris (France)—Fiction.   3. Women
painters—Fiction.   4. Married women—Fiction.   5. Adultery—Fiction.
6. Painting—Fiction.   7. Japan—Fiction.   I. Title.
PS3619.C484P35 2004
    813'.6—dc22   2004051588

10 9 8 7 6 5 4 3 2 1
First Edition

for Peter and Fynn

Clouds come from time to time—
and bring to men a chance to rest
from looking at the moon.

—Basho

The Painting

JAPAN 1870

My name is Hayashi and I am someone who should have died a long time ago. Sometimes when I look at a person, I wonder, what does he think is the worst way to die? Is he frightened of raging water's hand pushing his head under? A glittering sword hurling through his heart? Poison shocking his blood? A smashing of horse hooves caving in his skull? Which way is it, I want to know.

As I sit here, waiting to be killed, I can't help but wonder how it will be for me.

Fire. For me, fire is the worst way, the lashing flames scorching the skin, the seething hiss of a blaze, smoke's smothering smell.

Fire grabbed my body when I was ten years old; it burrowed into my skin and crept under my eyelids. It plastered itself to my feet, nosing my soles.

The black smoke spilled from our burning house and snaked into the town of Chigasaki. The villagers woke to sooty grit in the spaces between their teeth. Someone shouted, Fire! and the men grabbed their kimonos and ran outside.

With buckets of sloshing water, the townspeople ran to our home. The heat! It scorched their hair and singed their eyelashes, it flashed against their skin and tore at their resolve. The heat! I heard my sister crying. The townspeople threw water on their backs and wet down their hair before they ventured closer to the spiraling flames. My mother's sobs clamored beside my sister's, and from my bedroom, hunched down on the tatami mat floor, my hands cupped to my face, a small space of air, I strained to hear my father's voice, but there was nothing.

A boy. The words crackled behind the roar of flames. Someone shouted, A boy! I put those words in my mouth and sucked. A boy, I said, telling myself I was still here. My sister's screams thrust through the wall of fire. Quickly they folded themselves into something smaller and smaller, like a sea anemone withdrawing. Lie still, I told myself, if you move, you will draw the ire of the fiery beast clawing and growling all around you. As I child, I learned when the god Izanami gave birth to the fire god, she became extremely ill. Her husband-god, Izanagi, wept bitterly, but his sorrow did not stop Izanami from descending into the Land of Yomi. Death, I understood, had a home; death, a place.

I thought I was dying, descending into the Land of Yomi.

Underneath the flames, I tried for circumspection, prayed for my father and mother, and my sister, taking refuge in Buddha, as my father had taught me. Time stretched; I felt as though I'd met infinity, and I was terrified.

The men of the village unpeeled me from the perfect kindling of cypress and bamboo. I was lying on my stomach, my arms thrown above my head, as if I were preparing to dive into the earth or up to the sky, anywhere to escape the heat. My lips were moving when they lifted the huge center post from across my legs. A man shouted, His feet! I jerked my head from the charred mass and looked down. My feet wore slippers of fire.

Water splashed on the burning pile of wood, on my face, rolled underneath my arms; it wriggled into my mouth and between my teeth. My drought-ridden insides drank and drank, expanding in the liquid. The air, watery, like someone's breath. This began my love affair with water. Water flowed into every nook and crease; each trickle, a caress, each thin line of liquid, a tender finger.

They put me in a wooden cart and rolled me for hours and hours, or maybe a handful of minutes, to the healer's house. When she lifted me from the cart, my body's heavy scaffolding fell into the soft pillow of her body. Her thin arms were cool and it seemed as if she had ten arms, her coolness all around me. For a brief moment, the fire never occurred.

She said she knew the way of fire. Ever since the Tokugawa shogunate had sent the new feudal lord to Chigasaki, the old woman had treated many burned bodies, along with people dragged from their homes and beaten, men stabbed in the chest or sliced through the neck, rope burns on wrists, on ankles, and nerves poked with needles that left chronic pain. I tried to thank her, but my lips were heavy and refused to bend. Stay quiet, my boy, she said. After her cool body, her breath was what I knew. Cinnamon, with mint. Later, I learned she sucked on cinnamon bark tucked into the soft curtain of her cheek. With my fingers, I traced her hair all the way down to her waist. Weeks later, when I could finally open my eyes, I saw it was black, with few streaks of gray, even though she was quite old. The skin on her hands, spiderwebbed with wrinkles, but her face was smooth. Each night, I watched her rub ground pearl on her cheeks and forehead, sanding off time. When she smiled at me, she revealed soft, pink gums.

My place in her home was her floor. She lived in a small hut at the edge of the village, a one-room house close to the sea. I lay on her mat with the glorious sea air wrapped around me. From my spot, I watched the woman in white tabi socks scurry from her kitchen to her Buddhist altar, where she kept lit a slender stick of incense. The smell of her home was a blend of lilac and thistle, milkweed and witch hazel, and scents I could not name. The fragrances were tucked in glass bottles that lined her shelves. Each bottle was filled with a different color of liquid. I watched the light pour through all of them. Sunlit blue. Golden peach. The purple black of blackberries. As I speak of them now, they sit immobile, lifeless, but then, as I lay on my back, they gave themselves to me so willingly, offering me a beauty that made me cling to the earthly world.

One day, she built a large flame under her cooking pot. The heat from the fire alighted my sister's and mother's shouts; they called out my name, begged me to help. I couldn't stop screaming. The old woman wrapped me in cold towels and doused the fire. From then on, she had to cook outside.

I saw through the window to the sky. I kept track of the days. They will come, I told myself; each knock on the door, my heart leaped against my ribs, the rush of questions through wide eyes, Where have you been? Why not sooner, Mother, why did you wait? Father? And to my sister, Not yet, not now, as she prepared to pounce on my chest and wrestle my limbs. When two months passed and still I had not seen my family, I stopped the steady rhythm of counting.

DAYS TUMBLED BY IN a blur. So much so I can't recall. What did I eat and dream? How did I endure those long afternoons on my back? I stared at a white wall, wondering, Why do we—Why do any of us—go on living?

Then the day I met clay. I'll never forget it. For three days, we'd had dripping hot weather, and I hadn't slept at all, my body twisting from the unbearable heat. The night lifted its curtain to another scorching morning, heavy with the scent of fairy bell lilies below the northern window. A blue dragonfly darted through the door, buzzed round and round my head. The healer frowned at me for a long time, then left, rolling a heavy wheelbarrow. She returned an hour later, blue-black clay spattered on her clothes. Working her way from my feet to my head, she grunted, slopping on the cool clay. The smell of pungent earth and deep fertility suffused the room. It took her an hour to cover me completely; I'd become a blue-black sheet of thin cloth, hideous and monstrous. Yet I slept deeply, like a tree snug in its bark. When I woke, she took a hammer and tapped on the dried mud, cracking open my chilled home. I asked for the rest of the clay and plunged my fingers into the mud, down to the bottom of the bucket, my fingers ecstatic and playful. I began to hunt for my first shape.

A crude figure of a boy. I worked the clay on top of my chest. I named the boy Jimu, and kept him beside my head. A friend, I told the silent old woman as my fingers worked furiously.

After ten months, thick sheets of shiny, pink skin covered my body, as if I were wearing new clothing. Everywhere but my feet, still black and carrying their flame.

Hayashi, she said, shaking her head as she stared at my feet. She wrapped me in a heavy quilt and set me on a piece of deer hide stretched between two long bamboo poles. She pulled me up the mountain Haguro-san. Thumping along the ground, I left my painful body by staring at the twittering pale thrushes and a swooping brown hawk owl, with its chocolate head and yellow eyes. There, the smell of pine from the crushed needles below my bedding. I tasted wood wind. I prayed to Buddha, and in my mind recited the sutras. For the second time in my life, I thought I was dying.

We reached the top. Bowed over and weary, she leaned over and kissed me on both cheeks. I thought it was my time to join my parents and sister. Why should I be spared?

She'd brought me to live with the monks. Their temple was at the top of the mountain. They were the ones who had taught her the healing ways.

I woke in a small hut. Out the window, I saw a waterfall of melted snow. The air smelled as if someone had recently wrung it out. Suddenly from my window view, an old man appeared, took off his clothes, and stood naked, a paper-thin body with no hair on his head. He stepped beneath the rush of cold water and stood there until his skin turned bright red. Then he dressed quickly and walked with the stride of a young man into my hut. He wore the strangest pants and shirt. My fingertips found silk. He told me he'd pounded the bark of a cherry tree with a hammer until it was as soft as new leaves. He smiled then; his whole face turned into a wrinkle.

Last year I climbed the mountain thirty times in bare feet, he said. He knew the way of feet. Bowing to me, he said he was going to be my healer.

I called him the cherry-bark man.

These were days marked with new smells—citrus and pine, pungent oils, and scents sweet and loamy. Slowly, my lips formed more words and my hands gained more agility. As he worked, he told me the story of his feet: On one of my hikes up the snow-covered mountain, a sojourn to find enlightenment—not yet found, he said, smiling—my feet turned a pure blue. I had three more miles to go.

What happened? I asked.

He sat down in a pile of snow and, with his mind, moved the warm heat of his body down to his toes. The snow melted around him, and he sat and sat, putting fire in his feet. When he reached the top of the mountain, he fell into a trance and found the right healing roots and herbs. You have too much fire in your feet, he said. He was doing for me what he'd done for himself, but reverse, calling the heat from my feet, returning it to where it belonged, nestled in my heart.

From my vantage point in the hut, I could see the waterfall——A most auspicious view for you, he said——and then one day two red paper lanterns appeared at its base. The cherry-bark man put them there. Red, for good luck, he said. The lanterns were made in Gifu, the ones used during the festival for the departed who return to the world of the living for three days. You've brought so many spirits with you, the cherry-bark man said, I want them to feel welcome. He knew my father. He was a great man. Your father's spirit is smoky gray, he said. I see it all around you.

One morning he stood at the edge of my bed.

Get up.

I refused.

He lifted me up by my waist. I beat on his back with my fists. I pleaded and cried. He planted my feet solidly on the floor. Neither of us moved. The room brimmed with stillness. I sunk my weight down. Through each pad of my toes, I felt the wood planks of the floor, the coolness, the roughness of an errant splinter. My legs wobbled, but there was the dizzy power of standing upright and the uncertainty of being so far above the ground. How far the descent would be if I fell. Almost two years had passed since I had stood on my feet. Everything at the ground level had become my companion, the ants and spiders, the mice and dust balls. Beneath the light, you feel as if everything above you is bobbing on the surface. But standing now on two feet, the world changed. There were people and bookshelves and brilliant, almost hurtful bright light.

Walk, he said.

For a long time, I waited. Then I lifted my right foot an inch off the floor and slowly lowered my heel, rolling through the arch, the toes. I learned this: A foot concedes to catch you at the threshold of falling. The other foot shuffled forward. I did it again. And again. It took me a half hour to walk three feet. There was pain. Immense pain. I walked to the doorway and held onto the frame. Sweat trickled down my sides. I peered outside. Rows and rows of small, stone Buddha statues. The monk had put them there and sprinkled the ground with red rice. A good luck celebration for my feet, he said. I stood under the smooth cold sky, surrounded by a sea of red and small Buddhas smiling.

The cherry-bark man said the same thing the old woman had. He'd done what he could. You cling to the dark cave of your body, he said. Perhaps you've welded yourself to it. A memory you won't release. Or maybe the injury is too grave.

I DID NOT LEAVE the mountain for another ten years. A hut and a place to do my pottery, that was all I wanted. I attended morning and midday prayers and took care of the garden, planting potatoes and daikon, daisies and wild roses. Mostly, I spun pots using clay from the mountain's stream. The same clay that had adorned my feet. The cherry-bark man still visited me. He would ask, Boy, what have you learned from your pain? It was only later that I would understand what it gave me, what it propelled me to do, and much, much later, how much it had stripped away.

JAPAN 1869

PERHAPS SHE WILL PROVIDE a distraction, he thinks, trying not to look at the once elegant teahouse still smoldering from last night's fire. Even from his spot behind the glass, he smells the bitter smoke, though he imagines he is more sensitive to it than others. And when he breathes, the gritty soot hurts his lungs. He thinks he knows who set the fire and even why; he just isn't sure what to do. He looks until his limbs quiver, his feet ache, and now he must grip the edge of the wall to steady himself.

Whatever is she doing? The way his wife is walking down the stone path in the garden, placing a sandaled foot here, arching her back, stretching over to her right and then to the center of the path, Hayashi wonders if she might be drunk. Perhaps last night upset her with the flames and smoke and panic. Her movements scare off a kingfisher. He's about to call for the maid to bring her back inside when he sees she is playing some sort of game, a silly game of not stepping on the fallen leaves. How could she possibly — of all mornings, when she must know how painful it is for him.

She's reached the small bridge that crosses over the stream and leads to the teahouse. She wears her pale peach morning kimono with images of white fortunes printed on the fabric. Her black hair tumbles from its bun, skulking down her back, and she is stunning, replete with youthful beauty. He knows that when people meet them, they wonder why such a beautiful woman is married to him.

There is fire in her body, he thinks. Look at the way the air shimmers around her. Too much desire; all she ever wants to do is paint. If she could, she'd stay in that studio for hours, painting and painting, who knows what, he's seen so little of her work. He puts his hand on the top of a chair. His feet throb, as they nearly always do, but today, they are excruciatingly painful. He can only stand on them for bits of time, his life divided up by how long they can bear his weight. He wishes she'd come back inside and tend to them.

SHE AWAKENS. FOR FOUR days, she's barely painted. There was the shopping to do and the making of a special dinner for guests, his guests, a celebration of the autumn season and his moon-watching ceremony. After the party, his feet pulsed and she worked on them for a half hour before she asked the maid to take over. And then last night, of all things, someone had burned down the teahouse. She can't imagine Hayashi has any enemies; he's such a mild, quiet man. He'll do nearly anything to keep the waters smooth. This fire, she's sure it will disrupt her plans. Everything already feels disjointed, and it isn't even midmorning. But she must paint.

Gray coats the light outside, A dull light, she thinks, rather like my thoughts. He usually sleeps at least another hour. On her way to the studio, she passes by the teahouse. Dew still glosses the grass, the night's residue. A bird calls out, slicing through the silence of the morning, and she smiles, searching for it—a long-tailed rosefinch or tree sparrow? When she first came here two years ago, she hated almost everything—the big, cold house that looms behind her, the Buddhist temple next to it, and the cemetery, where the townspeople bury their dead.

But the gardens. Oh, the gardens are lovely and expansive and she is most comfortable in the lush green, the tall willows, maples, oak, dogwood, and bamboo. Here, she can roam. And there, the smell of the rich cinnamon bark of the trees, the light dappled on the flat, shiny madrona leaves, the expanse of sky. Look! A kingfisher. Perhaps she will paint that iridescent blue, the bright orange of fire on its chest. When she first arrived, she spent all her time in the garden, wandering, sitting, sketching, until he moved his bags of clay and gave her one side of his studio.

She steps on the stone path. The maple leaves with their rough teeth edges lie in her way. She is both attracted and repelled by them. Fallen stars, she thinks, bad luck to step on one, shatter someone's dream. She moves aside. Maybe my dream. Or perhaps they are good luck, she doesn't know. She smells the teahouse from the far side of the bridge, its smoldering bamboo and reed. Her day, ruined, she is certain, by this fire.

She senses she's being watched. He is awake, she thinks, and as she turns to look, a quick glance—why is he awake—her hair comes unpinned. She turns abruptly away. He's supposed to sleep another hour. She knows it will be a difficult day for him, the teahouse burning, unfolding terrible memories, but why can't she have this small corner of time?

And now she can't erase the image of his thin limbs poking out of his sleeves, his face gaunt, and those dark, deep-set eyes, always remote, always tinged with anger and sadness. She lingers longer, watching the leaves.

She picks one up and tosses it in the air, trying to postpone when she must go and attend to him. Lately, her dreams have been about flying. She flies far from this place west of the new capital, now called Tokyo, above the rice paddies, the fields of barley and wheat, an ocean of grass racing to the horizon, above the rows of small houses, the new buildings sprouting and slanting up the hillsides, and hunts for her lover. She is no longer sure he is in Ezo, or what the new government now calls Hokkaido.

These dreams, she thinks, smiling timorously, perhaps they are a good sign. Perhaps it means he is coming, or he is here. And then she lets herself think a fanciful thought: Maybe her lover set the fire.

HE LEAVES THE KITCHEN table, tired of waiting for his wife, shuffles away from her disturbing actions, down the long hallway of the house. Along white stones, he walks to the temple, only a short distance from the house, and opens the side door to the main room. All sound is swallowed here, a pool of stillness with the focal point in the center of the room against the far wall, the contemplative Buddha, fat, golden, glimmering, and smiling, as if he has a secret. The Buddha is surrounded by the villagers' offerings, huge white bags of rice, green bottles of sake, sticks of incense, shiny coins, jars of pickled pink ginger, and dried barley. The goat that someone once brought is in the back pasture, along with a horse that needs new shoes.

He takes a soft cloth and polishes the Buddha, beginning at the base, up the legs, his rounded belly, and there—what's this—at his neck, a hairline crack. When did this happen? He studies the fragile split. Since the eleventh century, the Buddha has sat, and now, why now, this fissure? He traces his fingernail along the line and feels his eyes water.

Nothing lasts, he murmurs. And it is true, so he says it again.

He peers out the small window and a few villagers have arrived, waiting for the front doors to open. Big puffs of steam flare from their nostrils; they are slapping their hands together to stay warm and perhaps to let him know they are waiting outside.

He opens the heavy, wooden door. Please, he says. Come in.

They file in, set down their offerings, take a cushion, and sit, facing the Buddha. Today, there are only eight. A few weeks ago, more than two dozen, and the numbers will dwindle further now that the Meiji leaders have declared Shintoism, not Buddhism, the national religion. Still, the few ardent villagers come and he lets them in; still, on New Year's Eve, he will ring the bronze bell 108 times, 8 in the old year and 100 in the new year, chasing away the 108 worldly desires by the ringing sound. So smart, these new officials believe they are, thinks Hayashi. They proclaim with such arrogance they can rip asunder beliefs with a silly piece of paper.

WHEN HE RETURNS TO the kitchen, she still has not come inside.

Shall I begin, Hayashi-san? asks the maid.

Soon he will have to leave for town to report the fire. No, he says, shoving his feet into the bucket of ice. The hem of his kimono falls into the bucket and he jerks it from the freezing water and rings it out. The maid steps into the kitchen. He sits still and listens to the wind and thinks, Sorrow is a boat that only drifts backward.

Finally, Ayoshi comes inside.

I'm sorry, he says, but I must ask you—

Of course, she says and kneels before him, plunging her hands into the ice. She presses her thumbs into his arches. His hands are trembling, his jaw flares in and out as he grinds his molars. He is shaky this morning, she thinks. Perhaps she's made it worse by lingering outside. Her hands already ache from the cold. She presses and massages and for a long time, neither one of them says anything. Finally, she asks what he's going to do about the fire.

He tells her he's meeting with the government officials in town. He's going to have to walk; the horse is not yet shoed. You're welcome to join me.

I'm sorry. I have a lot of work to do, she says, averting her eyes to his feet. She pushes harder. Who could have done such a thing? she asks.

What work? he thinks. She has no work; she prefers to paint. He stares at his wife and imagines the winds of youth blowing through her. There are some mornings he is certain she'll be gone. The other side of the bed is often empty, she rises so early and rushes to the studio. For some time now, he has thought the matchmaker chose the wrong one; perhaps the matchmaker didn't know certain facts or chose not to disclose them. Of course, his wife is very skilled in the healing ways. She has hands full of energy and she moves in the spirited way. Perhaps the monks who made the arrangements with the go-between thought this was enough. Or maybe they chose not to tell him the whole story. The matchmaker guaranteed she came from a good family and that she was still pure. He knows the new leaders made her father an official representative, responsible for carving up the Hokkaido area into small plots of land for rice farmers. Before that, he was a feudal lord under the Tokugawa and adamantly against opening Japan to the West. But like so many others, he had to change his ways. Hayashi fretted about meeting her father. He assured the stiff old man with high cramped shoulders and an air of stony vigilance that he could provide for his daughter. He was certain her father would ask about Hayashi's connection to the West, whether he planned to travel there, take his daughter there, but her father stood straight as a knife and barely said anything.

He leans away from her, from the pain in his feet shooting up the back of his calves and his right shin bone. Her hands, he thinks. He often forgets how powerful they are. When she first arrived as his wife, she massaged his feet every morning without waiting for him to ask. Now he feels as if he must beg.

Her hands burn from the cold. She pries her mind from her freezing fingertips. Outside, the naked branches of the maple, each leafless line, an experiment in design. Maybe she will put them in her painting today, she thinks, but no, it has never worked that way. She hears the wind rattle the window. Last night, it whipped the flames high into the black sky, the wood crackled, the smoke billowed, and she stood at the window, enthralled. She'd never tell Hayashi this, but it looked like a festival she once attended in Hokkaido. A large bonfire, with bundles of mugwort and bamboo grass being burned for purification. The men and women dressed in costumes, dancing, singing, and feasting. A spirit-sending ceremony. A dead bear had been found and they were sending its spirit back to the god world. She watched the flames of the bear's spirit shoot up to the sky, her lover standing beside her.

Her thumb joint creaks. She begins to lose her final pocket of precious warmth. Is this working? she asks.

He nods, tasting metallic bitterness. He knows this taste comes from a lingering panic. When he was a boy, and the fire held him, swallowed up the air and the coolness, his mouth was full of the same acrid saliva. Then vomit when he smelled burning flesh. He calls out to the maid for a glass of water. She hands him a cup; he gulps it down and asks for another. As the taste subsides, he looks onto the memory of his burning house with horror, his family gone, but before that, before the flames, his proud father, his kind mother, his sister, the shameless beauty of his life; and somehow he cannot separate the two, the horror from the beauty, so closely linked, so intrinsically bound.

This is working, he says to his wife, hoping to reassure her. His grip on the edge of the chair eases.

Good. She clenches her jaw.

And it is happening, the lovely moment is unfolding. He can't feel anything in his right big toe. His left heel is disappearing to the cold and he loves this feeling, this erasure of his feet. He imagines he was once made of water. A long time ago, his limbs were plump with soft water; his skin, smooth like his wife's.

She hates his feet. The arch of each foot collapsed and blackened with streaks of dark purple, the outer edges pink with a line of bright red, the bottoms of his toes a swirl of black and dark blue, and his heels a separate color altogether, a shiny brown and black, like the streak left by a banana slug. She knows these colors too well. Several months ago, the colors seeped into her dreams. When she woke in the morning, she felt a churning in her stomach, certain they would tunnel their way into her paintings. That's when she asked the maid to take over.

She digs her fingers into his toes. Her thumb on top, her second finger below. The dent in the big toe on the left foot, he told her about it. Not from the fire. He must have been four. His family went to the seashore to escape the summer heat. He was so excited—did she have that reaction to water, he asked—he ran barefoot in the white sand and stepped on a piece of green glass. Strange, he said, how the body carries its marks.

He is sweating now, a starchy, yeasty smell. She leans away and breathes through her mouth to deny herself the odor. She knows he's almost at the point where he will no longer feel his feet. Her hands and wrists are now bright red. She presses on the crease along the center of the right foot, the puffy scar of his heels. He is most tender on the left side, the place connected to the heart.

The toes on his right foot are now numb. His left foot, along the side. He feels his breathing open. He stares out the window watching the willow tree brush the wind.

Her hands. She can barely move them now. Long, sharp spines poke into them, a punishment, but for what? What has she done? She wants to plead with someone, anyone. She closes her eyes, searching frantically for an image to take her away from the pain snaking through her body. Where is he? She has a terrible hunch that her father sent him far away. That her lover is no longer in Japan.

She pushes her thumb into the tender spot.

He sighs. He no longer feels pain.

The cold wrestles into the long bones of her arms. Her teeth chatter, her lips a pale blue, her muscles pin to her bones, and soon, very soon, she will faint if she doesn't stop. She hates the cold. She yanks her hands out, presses them into her armpits, and rocks herself.

Enough, he says. No more. You've done enough.

She shuts her eyes and wills the heat back into her hands.

Thank you, he says.

She barely hears him. The maid lifts her from the floor into a chair.

Ayoshi-san, says the maid. Let me get you hot tea.

He sits across from her, his head bowed, feeling terrible that he makes her suffer so and also deeply relieved. They sit like this in the kitchen of their home, in a room made of paper walls.

She closes her eyes again and clamps shut her jaw. When she opens them again, he is staring wide-eyed at the teahouse, his lower lip drooping haphazardly. Who did it? she asks, feeling herself despise him. He is now calm, the pain pulled from his body, only the worried expression on his face from the teahouse. And she? She is filled with cold.

He pauses. I don't know.

When he pulls his feet out of the bucket, the ice has melted, and his feet are deep red with streaks of blue. He wraps them each in a white towel.

He asks the maid to shut the window screen. The hinge on the screen squeaks, and he grits his teeth and curls his fingers into tight fists, preparing to snap at the maid, Too loud, you are too loud, but he restrains himself. He's irritable today, he thinks. He finishes his sweet rice cake and green tea.

You're not eating?

Ayoshi shakes her head. I don't feel well.

He tells the maid to wrap the cakes.

Do you think your feet will ever heal? Ayoshi asks, as though the question on her lips makes her nauseous.

No, he says, tearing away the napkin tucked in his collar, seeing the disgust on her face. No, they won't.

She looks down. The towel has fallen away from his left foot. It lies there, limp and lifeless. She feels the one sip of tea rise from her stomach and clutch at her throat.

Excuse me, she says, rushing from the table to the studio. There is a difference, she knows, between love and duty.

AT LEAST HE CAN make this trip to town worthwhile; he'll hire a builder to tear down the teahouse and a man to haul the boxes of pottery to the docks. Another large order, this time to England, and by now, he has lost track of how many boxes of vases, bowls, and teapots he has sent across the seas. These new officials are quite proud of him, in their own way, using him as a symbol of what could happen to any poor artisan or merchant or farmer. They want to like him—always the strained smiles and overly polite words—because of his busy trade with the West, but there are some things they can't ignore.

He walks with a stick, his back bent slightly forward, along the long dirt road to the town below. He knows some of these new officials, met them before the emperor's restoration to power. Young, some of them exceedingly brash, an air of jaunty indifference, many of them educated in the West. They love all things Western, indiscriminately, full-heartedly. And he doesn't disagree that the West can give Japan things it needs, but moderation, as the Buddha taught, everything with moderation.

They made him an official of the new government; he will help promote Japanese arts and meet with the Western visitors who come to the town, they said. They gave him money to renovate the house and told him to make it feel expansive so the Westerners view Japan as wealthy and powerful, a force not to be ignored. After two centuries and more of isolation, it was time, long past time, to present Japan to the world. Hayashi added three lavish Western-style rooms filled with treasures and splendor. A wife, they said, find a wife who will make the Westerners feel welcome. They sent him a matchmaker. But when the new leaders demanded he tear down the temple, he refused. After many long discussions, they finally relented, saying he could let it stand.

There, on the cliff, a bald patch in the wild wood—the remnant of the feudal lord's house. Only five years ago, this town was ruled by a brutal feudal lord. The house, a monstrous structure, once loomed above the town like a vulture waiting to ravish the dead. Now the house has been torn down, demolished by the villagers, who, at first chance, refused to live in the shadow of his home, even if the ruler was no longer alive.

The road is deeply grooved from the farmers' carts. It leads down the gentle sloping hill blanketed with cedar and willow, down to the town, which he now sees. The feudal lord, who'd been appointed by the Tokugawa shogun, used to ride this very road on a big, black horse, accompanied by a handful of samurai. He wore shiny armor with medals and ribbons and a ceremonial cap, brandishing a sword in each hand. Amid the clatter of hooves, the booming voice of the man demanded the villagers get down on their knees as he passed. As a boy, Hayashi knelt beside his father on the shop's wooden porch, his father cursing a steady rain of swear words, which would have appalled his mother, his father's face bright red, the *clickety-clack* of the horse passing by. Each morning, the shopkeepers and farmers had to place a bag of their best goods for the lord's men to take, without remuneration, without a thank-you, as if they wanted to be ruled with a swift whip and unrelenting sword. He recalls now the nights at home when there was nothing to eat, thinking of the lord's storage rooms, filled with the best rice, daikon, cucumbers, sake, and dried seaweed and fish. As a boy, he played samurai in the backyard, running around with a stick as a sword, slaying the lord's fighters as he entered the lord's house and took back the food.

He reaches the edge of town and sits on a bench to rest. Even though the air is cool, he is sweating, his kimono sticking to his back. The sun is out now, and he despises the sun's splendor. Why didn't he bring his hat?

It has been at least a month since he's been to town. Buildings are being torn down, and everywhere, the sound of hammers pounding and saws tearing through wood, the shouts of workers for another nail, another board, to move out of the way. This town was one of the earliest supporters of the new government, and for its commitment, received funding from the Meiji leaders to adorn itself in the Western style. Across the way, a sign says that a new Western restaurant is soon to arrive. Two doors down, an old grocery store is being stripped down and trotted out as a Western clothing store.

Good morning, says a storekeeper, sweeping the porch.

Hello, says Hayashi. And they exchange the pleasantries of midmorning, the weather, the beauty of fresh daikon, and the storekeeper, who sells vegetables, looks at him curiously, as many of the townspeople do, as if trying to figure out some puzzling question—Who is this man who is allowed to keep the Buddhist temple open?

Behind him is the spot where his father's green tea shop once stood. Now, only an empty lot. He used to go to the shop at the twilight hour, at his mother's request, to fetch his father. Inside the store, the shelves overflowed with bags of green tea, the scent spilling into the street.

Father? he called out tentatively. His father was often in the back, huddled in a circle with other farmers and merchants, who spoke in grave and urgent tones. He crouched in the corner and listened to the men argue over the best way to overthrow the feudal lord. One night a merchant talked about a ship. The men in Satsuma were collecting money to buy a Western military ship. The merchant held up a picture of the ship. He'd never seen such a massive thing. His father convinced the town's merchants to send them money.

Several nights later, the shop and their home were set on fire.

When the new leaders took power, Hayashi asked for the house with the stretch of gardens and the large temple.

Before he rises from the bench, he looks to the dirt road that leads to the temple. He can't see the sprawling wooden structure, or the large bronze peace bell, only the tip of the black tiled roof. He supposes it makes one curious.

He walks to the minister's building, the pain in his feet only a whisper, and as he reaches the porch, a raindrop falls on his eyebrow.

Bless the rain, he says to no one. He stands there a moment, waiting for the showers. Rain pours onto his hair. The shopkeeper is still watching him. Hayashi feels his eyes bore into him. He guesses what the man is thinking: Did you hear how his whole family died? He's the only survivor. He's heard the talk. They say he is a quiet man. A potter. When they look at him, they always glance at his feet, which they've heard are remarkable swirls of blue and black.

AYOSHI STEPS INTO THE Western room. There is the smell of the thick, musty books that line the bookshelves. Here are the polished walnut tables and red velvet sofas, the lamps with golden light and cream lampshades with gold fringe, an Italian cabinet made from tortoiseshell, a desk with a fall front.

The chaos feels vital and abundant to her; the room pulses with life. She likes to sit on the plush couch and read, and as a treat, she lets her eyes drift around the room. She has a special affinity for the painting on the left wall. A portrait of the painter's wife. The painter is looking at his wife through a window, the curtains pulled aside. She stands outside in the snow. A brilliant red scarf wrapped around her head. Ayoshi peers into the deep colors of the painting; the brownish greens and dark blues, the starkness of the white snow and the red scarf hold her eye. The woman clutches her coat around her neck. Her eyes are forlorn, as if she's been banished from her home. When she looks at this painting, Ayoshi does not feel so alone.

The Western room has a small window alcove that looks out onto the garden. She sits there, hunched over, and reads. The house creaks and sways. When the period for annulment passed, and her husband did not request it, she became more brazen. She spent more time in these rooms or painting in the studio. She did things she preferred to do; and the things she didn't, she delegated to the maid.

There is another large painting. Even now, she averts her eyes from it. The pearly blue sky, the sprite green grass and rolling hills; there's a large old oak tree on the right side, its branches providing shade for what lies in the foreground. A beautiful, young woman with straw-colored hair. She is holding a baby in her arms. Her head is tilted to the left, and she is gazing at the child with a soft, fluid look. The woman and infant are sitting on a red and white picnic blanket. When Ayoshi walks into this room where it hangs, she swivels her head the other direction, to the overstuffed orange chair or the bookshelf and finds something to read.

Now that he is gone, she heads outside to the studio and closes the door. Grabbing a brush, she finds the image waiting. Later, when the maid taps on the door, bringing her green tea and a bowl of seaweed soup, she doesn't look up, too intent on following her hand as it travels along the paper. The image before her is speaking to her; the image before her is painting itself.

HAYASHI TAKES HIS PLACE at the long stretch of polished oak table. Five other men dressed in Western clothes are already seated. Hayashi waits, sitting through the tedious agenda, staring out the window at the colorless sky. Right before the meeting adjourns, he rises from his straight-backed chair, and with his heart hammering in his ears, tells them his teahouse was burned down in the middle of last night.

The man at the end of the table clears his throat. He has a broad chest and blunt lips that seem persistently to pout. As the country changes, there is bound to be more violence, he says, diplomatically, tapping his long nails on the tabletop. Change frightens some people. Most people. They lash out to keep things the same.

We have to deal with the ignorant segments of the population who refuse to Westernize, says another.

A servant comes in and pours everyone a cup of English tea. One of the men pulls out a pack of cigarettes and passes it around the table.

There is also your father's legacy, says another, blowing smoke up to the ceiling. The man's face is dispassionate, except for the glint of self-importance that he betrays by the upward tilt of his narrow chin. Your father believed so strongly in ending feudalism, such an early supporter of restoring the emperor to power. But not everyone agreed with him. He puffs on his cigarette and blows gray smoke. Such as the samurai. Perhaps a samurai has unleashed his anger at you; it's your legacy, if you will.

The men nod in agreement.

Then there is you, says the official at the head of the table, who is clearly in charge.

Excuse me, sir, says Hayashi.

Perhaps someone felt the need to warn you.

About what?

The room is still, only the sound of cigarette ash dropping on the hardwood floor. Who can say for sure? It could be your successful trade with the

West that makes someone jealous or angry. He pauses and sighs. Or it could be the new government no longer views Buddhism as the official religion. We were quite generous when we let you keep the temple standing. As you know several of us wanted it to be torn down. But you convinced us that it is a historical building that should remain. We never dreamed you'd hold services there.

Hayashi begins to protest that he only opens the door, he doesn't lead them in prayer.

The official in charge holds up his hand, halting his interruption. That townspeople still come to pray—despite the new decree that the official religion of this country is Shintoism, which is pure Japanese. You certainly know of this decree.

Hayashi looks around the room. The men are staring at him. They already know the answer, thinks Hayashi. Why must there be more humiliation?

These are dangerous times, continues the head official. We must keep a united front or the enemies will smell weakness, like a predator hunting his prey. We must work together or we will fail. You must think again about keeping the temple open for services. The man shakes his head. Perhaps this is what the fire was about—to make you think again. The person who set the fire wants to make sure you know he is watching your decision.

SHE TAKES OUT HER notebook and writes, *It did happen. There was a man with round eyes like the full moon. With the strength of the sun. Hair on his face and chest. He was here once. So was I. We had one shadow.*

FROM THE STUDIO WINDOW, Ayoshi sees Hayashi hobble to the front door and step inside. She walks to the house and hears him shut the bedroom door. For a moment, she stands in the hallway, listening. Water is running. He is preparing for bed, she thinks. I'll paint the entire night, all morning, if need be.

She returns to the studio, takes out a new sheet of paper, and sets it on her large oak desk. Tenderly, she picks up a brush and puts the tip in her mouth, coats it with her saliva, and finds the perfect point.

The blue. What was it? Her lover adored blue.

Blue, midnight blue, angry ocean blue, bruise blue, calm lake blue, peri-winkle, the purple blue of an oyster shell, the wing of a blue jay, blue gin-ger. Her mind skips across the blues, like a flat stone on water. A brush made from the tail of her father's horse dips into a pool of bruise blue and prances across the white sheet of paper.

She paints his kimono and whittles some yellow, brown, and red from her blocks of dried ink. With drops of water, she makes the color of dried wheat.

After a while—how long, she does not know—she looks up. The first light of the morning is peering through pale yellow sky. She inadvertently glances over to his side of the studio, to his potter's wheel and clay. A big lump of brown clay sits next to the wheel, wrapped in a wet burlap cloth. What an ugly color and a messy craft, she thinks. She feels a prick of guilt, just a hint, something that can be quickly trotted back to the recesses of her mind. He is probably in the kitchen, waiting. Let him wait. There, on her pa-per, her lover is gazing at her, brilliantly alive.

Hello, she whispers. Hello, my sweet love.

HE REMOVES THE WHITE wrappings from his feet and rubs them with a towel. The maid has worked on his feet all morning. He glances to-ward the studio. A brown thrush sits on the window ledge and picks at the sunflower seeds he left out. She spends so much time in there, and yet he never hears her talk about her paintings. He has only seen a handful—rice paddies, a setting sun, the turning of a maple tree during autumn, a single twig of cherry blossom, a spray of rock azalea. They are pretty, he supposes, in their own way, but how could any of that be so compelling as to demand hours and hours?

WHAT MAKES HER GLANCE up, a stir of wind, a branch scraping against the studio window, a hum in her blood stream?—she's not sure, but he is coming. There is his strange walk, so spasmodic and jouncy, as if his legs only reluctantly give in to the task. His arms lurch forward then back, his rhythm off. She should have tended to his feet. She is a bad wife, she knows.

The black ink soaks into the white paper. She blows on it to dry it faster.

His hand is on the doorknob. It turns. She slips her painting underneath her desk. The paint is mostly dry. She covers it with another sheet.

He opens the door.

Good morning, he says.

Good morning.

He asks if she's already eaten breakfast.

No. That's where I'm off to, she says, standing. Are you here to work?

I thought I might try.

Her cheeks flush, and her eyes dart to the door. You didn't feed the fish. Should I take care of it? I can do that. If you want.

He looks at her puzzled. You never feed the fish. I thought you didn't like to. The smell of the fish food. He dismisses her offer with a toss of his hand.

There is a pause. They look at each other; he feels bold today, though he doesn't know why. I was hoping to see your painting. You've been in here so long. It must be remarkable, your painting.

She steps away, the back of her heel scrapes the door. Oh, no. It's not done yet. Maybe later. Maybe when I've finished it. But I couldn't. Not yet.

That would be nice, he says, and then just as quickly as it came, his courage leaks from him. He doesn't want to stir things up, not when he's settling down to work.

His HANDS ARE DEEP in blue clay. The other day, he had the gardener travel to the Tamagawa River and bring back buckets of this smooth mixture, so fine on the fingertips. Crushed sand, he thinks. He smells the rich earth. The wheel will sing to him, a sound that's been with him for almost thirty years. He thinks of it now as a voice. Sometimes he imagines it's the voice of the old woman healer; sometimes it's his mother's. He loves the making of the bowl. It is only later when he looks at it that he finds so many mistakes.

He pumps the pedal, which, in the beginning, only slightly hurts his foot. The wheel begins to turn. There is the hum now. He feels peacefulness wake and stretch inside, and the watery clay undulates in his hands. A beautiful bowl, he thinks, different from anything he's ever made, a bowl that makes people stop and stare, commands them to halt and forget where they are going, what was important a moment ago. Look! Look again. It will be a resplendent bowl, better than anything he has ever made.

The humming rings different today, not high-pitched, but lower, a bass tone. Who? he wonders. His fingers sink farther into the mound of clay, as if searching for the source. Then he gives a small cry. The tone, a tenor voice. His father. He rarely hears him when he works and now the clay feels too sticky. He tries to form a shape to the sound. The clay twists and contorts in his hands, like a slick animal trying to escape. The noise grows louder. The clay lashes to the right and leaps in between his fingers. And now he realizes the rumbling matches his own, the one he has been trying to ignore.

He stops pumping. The wheel's whir slows to a dullness, then stops. The angry clatter subsides, disappears. He sinks his feet into a bucket of clay to ease the growing pain.

A warning, the men said. If his father had received such a threat, he would not be sitting in his shop selling green tea or hoeing his field. He would hold meetings with the townspeople, argue over the best way to counter the attack. Repercussions for such actions, his father would say. There must be consequences. The burning of the teahouse cannot go unanswered. Nor the request to close the temple.

He looks at his wheel, the nascent shape. A mess of clay, he thinks. He punches his fist into the emerging bowl and sits, brooding. He will address it, he tells himself, but he can't ignore the other voice—how long must he go on addressing?

HAYASHI WATCHES THE BUILDER haul away the remains of the teahouse. The burned boards are gone, but the plot of land underneath is scarred, blackened by the fire. Swiping his sandal along the ground, he tries to cover up the stain. Soot rises up, and he smells the smoke and bitter ash.

The gardener rolls up a wheelbarrow full of dirt.

I'll do it, says Hayashi, grabbing the shovel. He must do something.

The gardener looks at him perplexed.

Hayashi asks for two more wheelbarrows full of soil. The gardener pauses, shrugs, dumps the dirt, then returns to the compost. Hayashi almost stumbles over as he shovels the new soil onto the black spot. The other night, when he woke and saw the flames, he stood on the cold floor in bare feet. His legs locked, paralyzed by an irrational fear of the flames; they were searching for him. Silly, he says out loud now, and tries to shake off the memory, but the image is still there; they leaped into the air, wildly and erratically, hunting for him, grazing the night sky in search of his scarred flesh.

Ayoshi comes out and stands beside him, holding work gloves. I thought I'd help, she says.

He is sweating and his face is pale. She grabs a rake from the tool shed and smoothes out the dirt, concealing the black soot. And though he nods and looks appreciatively at her, it is not from a generous spirit that she's helping; she knows if he works too long, his feet will throb, and she might be stuck the entire evening tending to him.

How often did you and your family come here to the temple? she asks.

Over in the far gardens, my father grew green tea, he says, certain he's told her this before, but grateful to talk about anything but the teahouse. My entire family almost lived here during the growing season. This house was home to about thirty monks. My father was poor. In exchange for free green tea, the monks let him use their land.

She carefully draws her rake, carving perfect lines into the dirt. If she presses too hard, there is the black from the fire. They work until there is an inch layer of new soil, the scar of the fire no longer a blight to the eye.

That night, it rains and he sleeps deeply to the sound of splashing water on the windowpane. In the morning, he stands at the window and stares, his face ghostly white, the line between his brows a deep fold. There, the black stain, the impregnable darkness where the teahouse once stood. The new dirt has washed away.

HE SITS AT HIS potter's wheel, his unfinished bowl on a shelf behind him covered with a wet cloth. Don't look yet. It's not done and you'll only make yourself upset. There is her painting desk. Small bits of color dot the wood where the brush inadvertently slipped off the paper.

I think she'll soon leave me, he says aloud, without thinking. He sits perfectly still, a clutch in his throat, held by the raw truth of this utterance. For how long he sits, he doesn't know. She walks into the studio.

I'm sorry, she says with a start and steps backward to the door. I didn't know you were still in here.

Don't go, he says. I was just thinking about something, but I'd rather tell it to you.

She nods uncertainly and sits at her desk, fumbling with her paintbrush. He grabs his Emerson book and reads from his notes in the margins.

Here, what an amazing mind, he says. When this book is finally translated into Japanese, it will change everything. He says about experience that we live in a dream. In the murk. Sleep lingers all our lifetime about our eyes, as night hovers all day in the boughs of the fir tree. Put down your brush for a moment.

She looks at him, surprised by his firm tone.

He almost stops himself, aware of his desperate effort to engage her.

> The lords of life, the lords of life,—
> I saw them pass,
> In their own guise,
> Like and unlike,
> Portly and grim,
> Use and surprise,
> Surface and dream,
> Succession swift and spectral Wrong,
> Temperament without a tongue,
> And the inventor of the game
> Omnipresent without a name;—
> Some to see, some to be guessed,
> They marched from east to west:
> Little man, least of all,

Among the legs of his guardians tall,
Walked about with a puzzled look:——
Him by the hand dear nature took;
Dearest nature, strong and kind,
Whispered, "Darling, never mind!
Tomorrow they will wear another face,
The founder thou! these are thy race.

Please be quiet, she thinks, but what about that intriguing line, the one about the puzzled look, and the little man?

Out the window, he sees a brown swallow fly from limb to limb, back and forth, as if caught in a wind current. He wants to throw himself into work and he longs for her to say something about the poem, something magnificent and worthy that will link them in this moment.

Isn't he wonderful, he says. How we live in a fog. What do you think it means?

I don't know, she says, staring at an oak leaf on the floor. It has as many colors in it as a field of wildflowers, she thinks.

Don't you think it means all we have is our own perspective? We are locked into these bodies, these histories with their circumscribed views. We can't get out, can we? It's like a prison. We need each other to get out.

She wonders why he is speaking with such urgency. I've never thought of it as a prison, she says.

No?

No. But I guess it depends on one's perspective.

Maybe, he says.

The long pause becomes awkward. His head bows with disappointment and his wheel begins to turn. The hum fills the room. She drops her gaze to the leaf, the veins, the lifeblood of the leaf.

He reaches up to the shelf and pulls down his unfinished bowl. This gives him peace, he thinks, his hands immersed in clay. What did Emerson prescribe? Muscular activity? Yes, that's it. To fill the hour and leave no crevice for repentance or approval. And so, if he could, he'd sculpt every hour of the day, and finding contentment, she could leave him, yes, she could, and perhaps he'd be so absorbed, he'd barely notice. A hiccup in an otherwise calm life. But there is a time when his hands fall silent to his side, his feet hurting too much, he must stop. She is lost in her painting. Who is she? He watches her head, the top of it facing him and her hand moving with the brush, her steady, trancelike breath, and thinks she's somewhere underneath the layers and folds. When she walked into the room, she was tucked in a dream, her eyes coated with a soft haze. She sets down her brush, raises her hands, and presses her fingertips to her temples. When she picks up her brush again, there is a red ring at the corner of her eye. He's seen that gesture before, but can't place it. He watches the redness slowly fade, still trying to recall where he'd witnessed that gesture. Only after many moments pass does he realize she is speaking to him.

What? he asks.

Shipment. The next shipment, she asks, when is it?

He's still dazed, uncertain what she's saying. He follows the words and scrapes off their sheen.

He forgot about the next shipment. Why, it's today, he says. I completely overlooked—

I'll pack the boxes, she says.

Her gesture, forgotten, as he pushes his thumbs into the clay. He is usually so organized about the shipments. If she hadn't reminded him, he'd have to wait a month to ship the boxes; the Parisian dealer who ordered his vases and bowls would probably cancel any future orders. He quickly pumps the footpad twice and grabs another handful of clay. He will make a magnificent bowl. Strong now from so many bowls, his hands bend and move the huge ball of clay. The potter's wheel turns faster.

HOURS LATER, HE IS DONE. He rises without looking at his finished bowl and announces he's going inside for lunch. He asks if she'd like to join him.

No, thank you, she says, not looking up.

He nods and almost says, Of course not; when does she ever choose to be with him? Right before he makes his safe exit, he turns and looks at his new bowl. Why did he look? How awful, he thinks. How hideous and unsightly and he must restrain himself from rushing back to his wheel and smashing it with his fist. He wills himself to open and shut the door. Not now, he tells himself. I'll come back later.

For these last hours, she has been painting around and around him. Now that Hayashi is gone, she pulls out her earlier painting. There is her lover, in a light blue kimono. He is waiting for her. She mixes yellow and red and makes peach. She begins to paint herself.

HE SETS HIS TEA cup on the kitchen table, his mind agitated. Her gesture. Her fingertips pressed so hard to the temple. At last he remembers. How long has it been since that memory visited him? How could he have tucked it away? The cherry-bark man clamped his hands to his head. He did this as if some thought just occurred to him, some horrible thought, then he collapsed and died on the floor of Hayashi's hut.

Of course, it is a painful image, he thinks, but he is relieved that he remembered, that he recovered a bit of the cherry-bark man. He smiles. A father to me, he thinks. The maid fills his wooden bucket with ice water. She hands him his Emerson book and pours more tea. He'll go back to the studio and get rid of that ugly bowl. He will soak the dried pieces in water. From the new ball of clay, the hideous thing gone, he'll begin again. Emerson probably never created anything horrible. He looks at the book cover. The Dutchman gave him this book when he was eight years old, but the fire took it. Years later, the Dutchman sent him more Emerson, and he read them at the mountain monastery. His father had met the Dutchman with pale hair in his tea shop and hired him to teach his son Western history, literature, and English. The man had pale reddish skin and pale hair on his arms. He came every Monday with a bag of books on his back.

In the West, a man can do what he wants, said his father. The way of the West is the only way for Japan.

He learned the Greek myths and the legendary figures. He wrote essays and learned English. After the tall man left for the day, the boy practiced the way the man threw back his shoulders, his chest puffed out, his chin tilted up and to the left. He chewed on his pencil and, like the man, spit out the pink eraser tip. He held his tea cup with both hands wrapped around it, as if he might crush it. As a boy, he insisted on a fork and knife and spoon. He fashioned a hat out of a piece of cloth and wrapped it around his head, like the pale man's cap. He scratched letters on a chalkboard until the chalk scorched his hand. When it was time for the Dutchman to leave Japan, he left the boy with one book, Emerson.

He heard his parents argue at night. His mother worried the boy might be injured if anyone in the government discovered what he was learning. It's against the law, she hissed. His father said he was preparing the boy for the future.

He sets his books down now. What good came from his father's efforts? What has become of him? Only a mediocre potter who can make only one bowl well—the one the monks taught him how to make so long ago. How many years has he been making it?

He is ruminating, falling deeper into sadness when the maid comes in and says there's an old man standing at the temple door knocking and knocking.

Hayashi puts on his slippers and steps outside. Excuse me. May I help you?

The man scurries toward him. My son, he says, his face lined with distress.

Hayashi freezes.

You must give my son a proper Buddhist burial.

I'm sorry, says Hayashi. But it's impossible—

The old man says his son died of a fever in the middle of the night and he was so young, only seventeen, and such a funeral would help him pass through the other side so he could quickly return.

Hayashi stands rigid with fear, hearing the echo of the government men—the threat, the smell of burning still so fresh in the air, the panic—but he thinks, Here is this poor man, look at his face, deeply creased with such desperation, and his pleas, and the way he looks at me, as if I am the only one to save his son. But it is impossible.

I'm sorry, he says. The temple is closed for such things.

He cringes as the old man looks at him, dumbly, incredulously, and wishes it were otherwise, wishes he had the courage to say, to tell the townspeople, tell this poor man the temple is open and we will hold a grand funeral for your son. But he can't; he's a quiet man who prefers his solitude, who doesn't want trouble; and the old man is shaking his head.

He tells the man to try the temple on the outskirts of town. I don't believe that one has been closed, he says, though he doesn't really know. There is a long awful pause. The man doesn't move; his face is still open with hope.

My son, says the old man again, the pleading in his voice louder.

Seconds pass; to Hayashi, it feels like hours. Finally the man turns and begins walking away, and Hayashi is flooded with regret and guilt and must fight the urge to run after him, stop him, and begin the services immediately.

Go to the other temple, he shouts.

The old man shakes his head dolefully, opens the heavy iron gate, and shuts it with a bang. Hayashi jumps at the sound and rushes back to the house.

SHE TILTS OVER HER painting and falls into the colors of memory, mixing in more red and black, wrapping the image of herself in a blood-red kimono.

They met at the fast-moving river. She arrived and stood at the river's edge, skipping stones, and before she saw him, she saw his reflection in the water, as if he were emerging from the depths, coming straight to her. Five times she visited the river. On the sixth visit, with the sun pouring down on their patch of grass at the riverbank, they leaped across the water and climbed the hill to the flowering plum tree.

His hand, a thick, calloused hand, in hers. She feels his hand now, pulling her into the painting. His fingers stroke her cheek. They are on a terraced hill above the rice fields, the place where they met in secret until they found the empty hut.

Up on this hill, they are alone. There is the farmer down below, his back bent, his head covered in a large-rimmed, straw hat, too busy with his plowing to notice them. They lie together under the plum tree, his hand haunting her breast.

A branch from a Japanese maple tree scratches against the studio window.

She looks up. The branch is stripped of its red and orange leaves. A wand waving around in the wind. Ugly, she thinks, just a line without color. Not like the flowering plum tree, with its blood-red leaves and in spring, pale pink flowers. Under the tree, they looked through the leaves to the sky, and she remembers thinking, This is what joy looks like.

She adds a soft yellow to the leaves for light.

Afterward, the grass was green, greener than she'd ever seen. And the reddish leaves, like the glow of a summer dusk. She looked at them closely, closed her eyes to memorize them, and opened them to see again. She did the same thing with him. Memorizing each detail so that she could recall this moment exactly.

The sun drops below the tree line now; she lights a candle and puts it in the lantern. By the light of a paper lantern, she finishes her painting on thin mulberry paper. In the right corner, she writes, *Beneath the plum tree even the discreet heart is seen.*

When she was young, she used to play a game with a loop of string, turning it into various forms. She called it string origami, and that's what she thinks now as she puts the shipping string around the wooden box. Inside, she's wrapped the painting around her husband's ceramic bowl.

FRANCE 1870

THIS IS A STINKING, lousy job, Jorgen mutters to himself, but where else can he go? What else can he do?

A week has eked by since he began this rotten job as a clerk, but he won't let himself complain, won't bemoan his stingy bastard of a boss, the mundane tasks, won't do any of that, though he hates it here, and certainly doesn't belong in a dusty room counting objects, his mind swallowed up by the crude details of conducting inventory.

Ignoring the pain in his leg stump, he reaches up, shoves aside a stretch of curtain, and yanks open the paint-sealed window. The cool breeze flutters over his sweaty skin. Only now, with the air on his face, does he realize he's been working for hours in an airless, hot room. And there, he looks longingly beyond the city walls to the small fires dotting the green landscape, the French soldiers' blazes—though the way the French fight, they will soon be Prussian, he thinks. Not long ago, he was out there on the battlefield, huddled next to a fire with his brigade.

Jorgen jerks the curtain shut and glares at the stacks of crates. He jimmies the nails from one that's dirty and has several cracks in the boards, reaches in with both calloused hands, and hoists the heavy bowl from the bottom. A thin paper is wrapped around the bowl. He tosses it to the dirty floor. Balancing his weight on his crutch and one good leg, he heaves the bowl on the work-table and stares at it.

A goddamn bowl, he grumbles. Damn French. There's a war going on and all they can think about are exotic, useless things. A bowl, for God's sake. A damn heavy bowl. Some rich Parisian couple probably ordered it while soldiers, good men, are fighting with guns that backfire, or some even without a gun. He turns from the bowl and looks toward the direction of his room, down the hallway, and thinks of his rifle tucked underneath the bed. The only possession he cares about, not some useless thing like a glazed bowl. He feels the urge to hold his rifle, press the cold metal to his fingertips, smell the lingering gunpowder, the remnants still nestled in the barrel. Before the war, before he arrived in France, he traded the rifle that his father gave him as a boy for a chassepot and adapted it to fire a metal cartridge, giving it a farther range. He wanted to be prepared. He wanted to be an ideal soldier. He glances at the red stamp on the crate that held the bowl. All the way from Japan.

Another fifty boxes tower behind him. Seven rooms on the second floor teem with boxes, and there are more rooms on the first floor. The house, once a brothel, has been converted into a storage facility with a small shop in front. His boss said in preparation for the war, he imported most of his inventory, but sometimes Jorgen finds a box labeled PROVISIONS FOR ARMY or addressed to MUSEUM. The room to his right holds canned goods—corn and beans and boiled mutton and beef imported from the Middle East. The room at the end stows spices, nutmeg and cinnamon and thyme wafting into every room. The perfumes—lilac and rose and jasmine, which the French women wear like bathwater—are farther down the hall. Another room teeters with lamps and kerosene; another is stacked with guns and ammunition. In the room to his left, silk and jewels, he knows only some of the names, ruby, sapphire, and moonstones; in this room, the newly arrived boxes of wine, to be sorted, and sculptures and paintings stacked on top of each other. Nothing stays very long. Soon the cans are opened and the artwork and jewels are sold to the rich.

The small window with its faded yellow curtain stingily lets in dim light.

His leg throbs—the leg that is no longer, what he calls his ghost leg—but he must scoop out the contents of twenty more boxes, jot an entry in the log before lunch. Setting his crutches against the wall, he sits and rubs his forehead. A white marble statue of Zeus stares at him.

What do you want? he asks the marble face. I have nothing for you. Nothing.

He has to pack up the statue and send it back; a hairline crack snakes down its forehead, as if it suffered a head wound. Serves him right, the rich Parisian who ordered it, he thinks. He throws a rag over the statue.

A week ago, Jorgen was in a Parisian hospital when a doctor threw back the bedsheet, glanced at the stump of the amputated leg, scribbled something in his chart, and told him he could go home. The doctor was about to scurry away—the injured men were everywhere, in cots, lying on the floor, pressing their backs against the steamy walls, and streaming out the front door—but Jorgen grabbed his sleeve.

What? said the doctor, whose drooping eyelids were underscored by heavy purplish blue circles, his skin waxy and pale.

When can I join my unit again?

The doctor shook his head, bewildered, and then laughed bitterly. You're damn lucky to be alive, said the doctor, shaking free his arm. Perhaps if you'd been brought in earlier, your leg could have been saved. He said most amputees don't live very long—the infections, the complications. His tone was matter-of-fact, too tired for the extra effort of politeness. If he lived to the end of the month, he ought to go to church every day and thank his patron saint. The doctor penned something on a sheet of paper and shoved it at Jorgen. A prescription for painkillers, which Jorgen could fill, said the doctor, if he could find someone who had any extra medication. There weren't enough medical supplies or instruments in any hospital. The doctor rushed away and Jorgen stared at the wall. A nurse set by his bedside his bag containing his few belongings—red trousers, a blue overcoat faded from years of sun and rain. One of the red epaulettes was torn off the shoulder of the coat, and his white gaiters were gray brown, splattered with mud. In a bag, the contents of his coat pocket, an extra pair of black socks, one with a hole in the heel, some francs, bullets, a Danish passport, a knotted ball of string, and a black polished stone, like a glassy eye. Next to the bag, his treasured rifle. When the nurse said they needed the cot for someone else, he didn't budge, just breathed in the stench of decaying flesh.

In the stifling storage room, he rises from the table, dispensing with the pain in his stump. Damn his leg to hell, he thinks, and yanks open another box, this one stamped AMERICA. He slides his knife through reluctant tape, and inside, shiny tin cans of meat. He pulls out a can. The tin feels cool to his fingertips. It fits neatly in his palm. He closes his fingers around it and watches it disappear. For the first time since he arrived at this stinking boardinghouse, Jorgen feels a brightening, a moment of lightness. Grabbing another can from the box, he slips them into a cloth bag and hides it behind a box. Not to eat, but to sell to a Frenchman. From each box, a little bit, nothing noticeable, just an understandable error on the part of the shipper. He'll take the money from the things he sells, and with the small pittance of a salary, he'll buy a leg and reenlist. Yes, that's what he'll do. He rips opens another box, feeling a wave of excitement at his new plan. There he finds blue bottles of perfume, and he stuffs a handful into the bag and is about to reach for another handful when the front door opens and closes. The woman calls out. Natalia is her name. Next to his cot in the hospital, her older brother lay dying. The doctors stopped attending to him; only the nurses came by, fluffing his pillow, arranging his thin blanket, and bringing him thin broth, when they remembered. Jorgen watched Natalia come visit her older brother every day. What was his name? Edgar? Edward?

Hello, hello, Natalia calls out from the bottom of the stairs.

Hello, Jorgen says, without thinking.

Come down for lunch when you are ready. I brought you some things.

Jorgen doesn't answer, wishing he hadn't said anything; if he'd been quiet, she never would have guessed he is here. And now he is overcome with a strange feeling, foreign to him, a preference, no, a consuming need for solitude. For no one to stir him up or ask questions or demand anything of him. He'll make this money, get his new leg, and leave here as soon as possible. This job has its advantages, its solitude and the extra money he's going to make from pilfering.

He hears the *tap tap* of her heels walking along the wood-paneled floor downstairs. In the past, he would have gone downstairs, flirted with her, made her blush by pointing to the freckle on the side of her neck, asking if it was a beauty mark. He knows women like that kind of attention, and he knows if he helped her unload a box or scrub the dirty dishes, she'd be so pleased, so delighted by his assistance, she'd do nearly anything for him. In the past, he would have done these things, even though he does not find this woman attractive. Her brow is too intellectual, her mouth too large for beauty, her hair dull brown, her eyes piercing, too full of expression. And that's no beauty mark, but an ugly mole. Despite this, there was a time he would have at least made her smile.

She is humming now. Plunging his hands into the packing material of scrunched up newspapers, he hears her melody through the floorboards. Now she is singing. Singing with a full voice. She is too cheery, he thinks, and he feels irritated by her noise, for the world is not the way she sees it. Not at all. He coils into himself, wishing again he hadn't answered her. He remembers with shame that night in the hospital. Natalia set her chair in between her brother's cot and Jorgen's. In his sleep, he reached for her hand and pressed it to his chest. He remembers the weight of her hand made him fall into a deeper, more peaceful sleep. He woke when she slowly removed it. At first he was uncertain what had happened, but then, as he realized what he'd done, he told himself it was unintentional. It meant nothing. He could have grabbed anyone's hand; by chance it happened to be hers. In the morning, she said her younger brother ran a boardinghouse not far from the hospital. A room had become available. She said her brother might need help in his shop. She told him her brother used to own a fine art gallery, but with the war, he turned it into a general merchandise shop. He sells anything and everything, she said. A businessman. Are you good with numbers? And he told her he was, though he wasn't at all.

She asked his name.

After a strange, elongated pause, he said he couldn't remember.

But you're not French, she said, smiling, sitting upright in her chair.

No.

Well, we'll think of a name for you.

He hadn't forgotten his name, but there were many things he was working hard not to remember, and he knew he had to be particularly careful around this woman because she reminded him of someone, not by the way she looked, but by her very being, the goodness that radiated from her. He felt it when he first met her, the way she seemed to glow. He barely spoke with her in the hospital because it terrified him, the resemblance; he wanted to be close to her and at the same time stay far away.

He tosses the newspapers on the storage room floor, and as he listens to her singing, he feels his eyelids twitch with grim apprehension.

SHE PLUCKS OFF HER large-rimmed hat and surveys the room, the shelves stocked with canned foods, water stored in beautiful midnight-blue glass bottles, fancy boxes of chocolates wrapped in dark-red cellophane. There is probably more food here than in five Parisian kitchens, perhaps even more, she thinks, trying to push away the disdain at her younger brother's plenitude. Such lavishness, such decadence, and she feels ashamed for herself, for her young brother, Pierre, then angry at his extravagance. She dismisses these thoughts quickly, reminding herself not to think badly of him. A plain biscuit, only, and coffee, no sugar, that will be her lunch.

Hello? she calls out to the back office, where she usually finds Pierre. The room answers with silence, and she is relieved. He is probably courting some customer; too in love with the war for the money it pours into his coffers, he is blind to everything else, as if someone swept his insides with a broom, removing the things that make a man noble, honorable, and virtuous. She is about to lament his poor moral condition again, but catches herself. I must do better at loving him, she chides. Not snap at him for his stinginess or when he complains that I should marry or that I am more manly than womanly. He generously gives me money or food or other provisions when needed, yet he does it with an air of superiority.

She makes herself some coffee and sinks into a chair, tired from her work. A month ago, she repaired her first rifle and the head boss watched over her shoulder, his face full of skepticism. Today, he told her she was his best worker and paid her an extra franc. All she wants is to do good, to live in goodness. When she's had too many bad thoughts in a day, she imagines a string of pearls running through her front side, down her body, looping around and coming up her spine to her skull. Over and over she runs this string, a ritual of cleansing. Lately, the pearls have stayed packed away in their box. She is so busy with her war efforts, she has so little time to think.

She stands, stretches, and pours herself more coffee. Outside, a tree stripped of its leaves; its long, thin branches scrape against the window. So beautiful, she thinks, the tree baring its essence. And this is what she looks for in people, hunts for in their eyes. In adults, there is usually only a flash, if that, and then the dullness. But in newborns, it is always there—an honest knowingness that exists beyond words. Sometimes she thinks she sees it in her eyes, a certain unmistakable glow, and she imagines her insides illuminated. But when she mentioned this light to Father Bertrand, his rheumy eyes dropped to his scuffed shoes, and he warned her she had much to learn before God came to her in such ways. He must have seen her face fall in shame because he took her lightly by the elbow and said she was a good child of God.

She hears a loud thump upstairs. She glances up and smiles. The Dane, she thinks. What name should she give him? Maybe Case, she thinks, and if he looks at her puzzled, she will say, In French, it means chest. But he probably won't recall that night, and even thinking about it now, his hand reaching for hers across the darkness, she, startled out of her sleep, the rising and falling of his warm chest, she feels embarrassed and still unsure whether it really happened.

The Dane's eyes do not burn with anything, and she has come to think he does not see or feel much at all. Locked away into himself, he seems a confusion of impatience, and there is a constant disquiet about his dark sullen eyes and perpetual frown. But there must have been a flicker of something. That one night she didn't come by the hospital, too exhausted from work. When she arrived the next morning, Edmond told her that in the middle of the night he felt overcome with thirst and called and called, but no one would come. The Dane finally sat up in his bed and grabbed a nurse by the wrist. Get him some water, he hissed. Do it now. The frightened woman quickly brought him a jug. Even now, thinking about it, she's still surprised the Dane did such a thing. He does not seem like a generous man. In the hospital, he barely spoke a word to her or her brother. They had, for the most part, left him alone.

Perhaps his name should be Donatien, she thinks, and she will say, French, my dear friend, for gift. A gift to my brother, she thinks, hopefully both brothers. She prays this arrangement works out, prayed in church this morning, but knows Pierre is not a patient or kind man. It was just luck that Pierre's assistant quit the week before to join the army. She boasted to Pierre that the Dane was a good worker, educated, and she exaggerated only slightly when she told him the Dane was fluent in five languages and excellent with numbers.

She steps into the kitchen, and as she cleans Pierre's pile of dirty dishes and her cup, she hums a tune they sang this morning at church. A lovely song, she thinks, looking out the window. "May We Rise to the Lord in the Heavens." The words flow as she scrubs the grime from Pierre's good china plate. A quick visit with the Dane, with Donatien, she corrects herself, smiling, and then she must hurry to the hospital before returning to work.

From the kitchen window, she sees a group of Parisians walk by, waving open champagne bottles and singing *La Marseillaise*. She's never heard the French national anthem sung in public. Napoléon III banned it years ago, afraid of its revolutionary associations. *Let us go, children of the fatherland, our day of glory has arrived.* Ever since the French declared war on the Prussians, Paris has felt perversely festive. She forgets herself sometimes, forgets that this mood is about war. Seeing the celebratory people, the excited mood, she feels compelled to join in. *To arms, citizens! Form up your battalions. Let us march! Let us march! That their impure blood should water our fields.* She imagines herself thrusting a French flag high in the air, leading a parade around the city. Shouts envelop her and her followers, who number in the hundreds; they sing and chant and the city becomes enlivened again, believing that God is on their side. She carries a bundle of her favorite flowers in her arms, dark red roses, white lilies, and blue peonies, and tosses them to people in the crowds that line the thoroughfares.

She watches the celebrators pass by, her head tilted to the right, her face soft, a dreamy glaze over her eyes.

THE DAMN PARISIANS ACT as if they're on holiday, thinks Jorgen, as he shambles on crutches over to the window. Someone opens a champagne bottle and white foam shoots into the air. The crowd screams with delight. An open carriage rolls by and the men inside wear goatees and red carnations. They wave a big French flag, bright green wine bottles gripped in their hands, and lying across their knees, a drunken woman, her bosom half exposed for the men to fondle. Jorgen slumps against the wall, feeling nothing as he stares at the woman's breasts, only a dullness in his senses.

Beyond the people parading down the street, the great trees that lined the Bois de Boulogne lie on the ground like fallen giants. Scrawny cats dig their claws into the flaking bark, and children with dirty faces and fingers saw off limbs for the fireplace. Next to the scavengers, men and women sit on the cement drinking champagne from a bottle. Jorgen dabs the sweat from his forehead.

Last week, when he was walking down the Bois de Boulogne from the hospital to the boardinghouse, he overheard two women discuss how the paintings in the Louvre will be saved after all. The officials removed the paintings from their frames, rolled them up, and sent them to the prison at Brest.

They are packed in boxes and marked with the word FRAGILE, said one woman, her voice excited and shrill.

Thank God. We can't lose our national treasures, says the other, aghast.

Can you imagine if we lost the *Mona Lisa*? Or if Fragonard's *The Bathers* was scratched?

The French and their obsession with beauty, he thought then, and he thinks again now, watching them celebrate. Why did he join the French army? An incompetent, ill-equipped army, disillusioned by their earlier conquests, and look at them, their frivolity, and the way the man publicly touches that woman's breast. What other country allows their rich young men to pay another, a foreigner at that, to take his place in a war? Perfectly legal, this so-called blood tax or substitution. He thinks now of the wealthy Frenchman, dressed in fox furs and a shiny black top hat, a cane for affectation, who paid him handsomely, handed him his draft notice, and told him to go as his replacement to his brigade. Jorgen couldn't believe it was legal. Quite legal, said the Frenchman. As long as I provide someone in my place, the French army does not care. He told Jorgen he was heading for the Mediterranean to sun himself until the war was over, then he would return, but only if Paris wasn't in shambles. Adieu, my friend, adieu, adieu. Appalling, thinks Jorgen, but what choice did he have? He could never fight on behalf of Prussia. The Germans killed his great-uncle in the Danish-German War. When he joined, he was certain, as everyone was, that France's superior military prowess would end the war swiftly. When he saw how unorganized, how chaotic the French army officials were, he envisioned himself soon placed in charge of a unit, in recognition of his abilities, and he'd be covered in medals, hoisted up above the shoulders of his men in a cushion of hoorays. But none of that happened, and who would have guessed he'd be standing here without a leg?

Tired of the noise, he shuts the window. He hears her come up the stairs, her voice singsong, a hello, hello ringing. He'll tell her he's too busy to talk. Look at all these boxes, he'll say. And your brother, you must know, is a difficult man. He pokes the end of his crutch at the thin paper lying on the floor, sweeping it up in one big arc. Her song is coming closer. He's about to throw the paper away, but there is something printed on it. She is coming down the hallway. He doesn't have time to look. That humming is outside the door. He plucks the paper off the end of his crutch and tucks it into his bag of goods.

Hello there, she says, peeking her head into the room. I won't stay long. I wanted to see if you were doing all right.

Busy, but fine, he says, his tone subtly defensive. He leans against his crutch and studies the toe of his black boot.

Good. My brother. He has a rather brisk manner.

I've no complaints. He closes his mouth hard and begins unpacking another box.

I'm sure it will be fine, she says, gripping and twisting her hat in her hands. I just came by to see if you needed anything.

He does not feel he owes her anything. For this job, this shelter. Happenstance, he thinks. Pierre needed a worker and he was available; he will do a fine job, and actually, her brother is getting a good deal, given the small wage Pierre is paying him.

She steps in through the doorway and surveys the boxes. A scent follows her. Not perfume, he thinks, but something slightly sweet. She tells him she's left some lunch downstairs for him.

That's not necessary, he says, bristling.

Oh, I know, she says, now twirling her hat. She steps farther into the room. It's filthy in here. Look at all that dust. How do you breathe?

She rushes to the window and opens it. There. Soon it will be autumn and the air will turn cool. I love the cold air, don't you? Most people hate it, but I don't. Well, I'm off to see Edmond. He's doing much better. Much, much better. He laughed yesterday. I forgot what I said that made him laugh, but he did. It was a wonderful sound, a melody I'd almost forgotten. Pierre and I are his only family, you know. Our parents died a while ago. Pierre never goes. I don't think he can stand to see Edmond in pain. It's too much for him.

Too busy making money or tending to his whores, thinks Jorgen. He's seen Pierre go out at night and come back with one of those women on his arm, the squeals and laughter haunting the house. He looks at Natalia's drab brown skirt, her white starched blouse, the red kerchief tucked in her breast pocket, the gold cross hanging prominently around her slender, pale neck. She is talking again about how well Edmond is doing, how soon he will be joining her for morning mass. How ignorant she is, he thinks, how blind. Such a pure, simple woman, she can't even see her brother is going to die. It'll be a shock for her when he goes, but maybe she'll grow up, and life won't seem so wonderful and she'll halt that damn humming.

She turns and is about to go. Oh yes, she says, delicately tapping her hat on her head. Did you recall your name? Because if you haven't, I've got one for you. Do you want to hear it? She smiles at him demurely.

They are about the same age, he thinks. She might be slightly younger than his twenty-six years, but she seems like such a young girl, so protected in the swathes of her innocence, abandoning herself to such silly hopes. She's grinning now, unable to contain herself, intoxicated by her secret.

Donatien, she says, her voice boasts proudly. And she tells him what it means.

No, he says, holding his temper. He's tired of her presence, wishing she would leave. He will give her this, but no more. Nothing more. He doesn't want her prying or her curiosity honed on him.

He tells her his name.

Well, Jorgen, she says, her smile slightly fading. Good, and she pulls a bright yellow scarf from her bag and wraps it around her neck. A name is a good thing to have.

She turns to go, and he hears her run down the stairs. He holds his breath, waiting for the front door to open and close, then releases a long sigh. The top of his right shoulder aches. The crutches, he thinks. He sits at the desk and stares at the boxes. A fly buzzes around his head and lands on his hand. She let it in, he thinks, when she reopened that window. Batting it away, he rises again and snatches more things from the boxes to sell. Three bottles of good wine from the south of France, a block of cheddar cheese from Holland, a ten-pound bag of walnuts, and two wool scarves because it's certain to turn bitter cold soon and someone will pay double, maybe triple for such a wrap. Looking at his pile of goods, he feels his heart race.

He reaches into the bulging bag and pulls out the thin paper. It came from the Japanese box. A painting, but on such feeble paper, as if not really a painting at all, a hint of a painting, a sketch, though it can't be because of the colors. Cryptic black lines mar the right corner. He pulls out the invoice slip. Only the Japanese bowl is noted, nothing about a painting. He smoothes the paper onto the table and studies it. Two people, a man and a woman, standing under a tree. The man is wearing some kind of strange, long dress, just like the woman. Her black hair is pulled up in a bun with two pieces of white wood holding it together. The man has black hair pulled into a ponytail on top of his head. The woman's eyes are long thin lines. How can she see? And what is the man doing? Jorgen lifts the painting up toward his face, and his hand begins to tremble. The man is parting the skirts of the woman, and there is the pink white flesh, and the groping hands.

Another thing to sell, he thinks, quickly slipping the painting between two pieces of cardboard. Some stupid Frenchman is sure to want it. And technically, he isn't stealing; her brother doesn't even know it exists. He carries the cardboard into his room and slides it under his cot.

NATALIA SITS BESIDE HER brother in the hospital. A young man moans in the same cot where Jorgen once lay. This new soldier has a bullet lodged in his side, and the one-room hospital is flooded with a fresh round of wounded soldiers, as if a great storm had washed them in through the dingy doors and strewn them against the walls, in the cots, the hallways, and in any available chair. From the flotsam, a horrible smell of stale bodies and dried blood and pungent clouds of ammonia cleaners. She tells Edmond the Dane is living in the boardinghouse, working for Pierre.

He fought for France, says Edmond. I guess that's good enough.

What do you mean? she asks, smiling at him gently. She leans forward in her chair, trying to think what else she can do to ease his pain.

Well, what do we know about him? He looks at her with clear green eyes.

She pulls her cardigan sweater tighter around her front. Whatever do you mean?

I don't want to worry you, he says. But you should be more careful. Natalia, are you listening to me?

He was kind to you, she says.

Natalia.

I think you're being overly cautious, she says, pulling her kerchief a little tighter around her neck, feeling a sudden chill in the room.

She leans over and brushes his dark hair from his sweaty forehead. Her body momentarily blocks the light shining in from the window onto his outstretched body. Almost instantly, he shivers and tells her to lean back so he can feel the sun's warmth on the heavy blanket. Without the sun, he is a block of ice.

I want to die during the night. I can't stand it sometimes. The cold.

Don't talk like that.

It's true. I'm not scared of dying. Not anymore.

Please. Stop. Let's talk of something else. Talk about the light coming through the window. Talk more about that. Or the time when we were young, and we went to the house at the lake. Remember the small rowboat, the white one with the long oars, and how early that one morning you paddled us out to the center. The mist rising off the water. So quiet. You wanted to fish for carp.

She scoops his hand and it lies listlessly in hers.

I just wonder why he would leave his country and fight for France. It makes me wonder what mess he left behind.

She lets go of his hand. The soldier behind her whimpers. I wanted to help, she says, and he needed somewhere to go. He has no one.

Why doesn't he go back to his own country? To his family?

You saw for yourself what bad shape he is in, she says. She feels her impatience, the stirrings of doubt. Maybe he doesn't want to go home because he's ashamed of his condition. Or he doesn't have the money to return. Or he's stayed to help France in any way he can.

You're too good. Not everyone is like you.

But you're good, too, Edmond. You're superbly good.

He shakes his head. I'm just asking you to be more careful, Natalia, he says, pulling the blanket up to his chin. I can't stand to be cold. Shivers are racing up and down my spine. I am so cold.

She presses a warm cloth to his forehead and tells him she will bring him more blankets. He nods and closes his eyes. When he settles into his sleep, she presses the cloth to her worry-lined forehead.

ON THE SECOND FLOOR of the storage facility at the end of the long hallway is Jorgen's room, with barely enough space for a cot and a slim chest of chipped drawers. The floor is drab, beige tile with black scuff marks, and several squares of tile have loosened. Dust balls have shuffled into crevices and hang from the ceiling. The white paint on the walls is peeling off in strips, and beneath, he sees, the room was once painted blue.

He parts the curtain and stares out the window. The fires are still burning; there are more of them dotting the countryside, many more than when he was part of the battlefield. He is mesmerized by them, their flicker and lashes at the sky, and at the same time, he can't stand to look at them. He wants to step away from the window and divert his attention to something else, but what? What is there for him to do but count and recount, unpack and shelve? How long he stands there, he doesn't know, but he feels himself slipping into self-pity and despair, and if he allowed himself to look down at his empty trouser leg, he knows he'd fall deeper into self-loathing. When there's a knock on his door, he's almost happy for the distraction.

You finished unpacking the boxes?

It's Pierre, his voice a cold clip. He lets himself in. His sharp, twitching eyes dart around the room. His bald head makes his nose seem even longer, and his ears flare out.

Jorgen tells him he will finish the rest by tonight. Pierre says he must have the inventory done by tonight to prepare for tomorrow's shipment.

I have many, many customers, he says, taking a pen out of his pocket and twirling it round and round. The war has made everyone quite hungry. You will let me know promptly if you can't keep up with the work. I can find someone else to replace you if there is a problem.

There won't be a problem.

He turns to go, but stops. I only hired you because of my sister. And even that link, I must say, is rather tenuous.

When Pierre leaves, Jorgen sits on the cot and removes his dirty trousers. Where his thigh once was, there is a smooth stump, the skin translucent pink. He runs his hand over it, barely touching it for fear of inciting the shooting pain. Pathetic, pitiful, unworthy, nothing but a stump, he thinks, removing the rest of his clothes. Reaching up to the wall, he tears off a strip of white paint. Blue, the color of cornflowers, stares at him. He quickly looks away. He jumps at the sound of cannons going off. The window rattles. His bed shakes and shimmies as never before. The war is getting closer, he thinks, the Prussians pressing toward Paris. And this is what Bismarck wants; with the defeat of France, he will have his unification of the German federation.

Another explosion reverberates. Jorgen smiles, the sounds and vibrations comforting him, for he is near the war, its dull angry roar.

He pulls on clean trousers and a shirt, grabs his crutches, and heads to the main storage room. The statue of Zeus is gone. Despite its crack, someone wanted it. Pierre must have packed it. Other things are missing, now in the homes of rich Parisians—bottles of wine, at least a dozen cans of meat, a Persian rug that was leaning up against the wall, and silverware. The bowl from Japan is gone.

When he finishes his work, he stumbles down the hallway toward his room. His heavy boot slams down on the wood floor. He stops halfway to catch his breath. Everything tires him. He almost feels the thing holding him back from the pulse of life. If he could stop himself from pushing against it, he would be fine; he could stay enclosed and what would it matter? But he can't seem to help himself. He was going to fight for France, to redeem himself, or at least lose himself in the war, to die a hero. That would have been reparations enough for what he did. And now look at him.

Night roosts in his small room, and he lights a candle, a small flicker. He reaches under his bed and pulls out the gray cardboard sheets. The light shudders, like the pain in his stump, always there, always hunting him, but he won't give in to it, though there are times when the throbbing extends to his toes, which are no longer there, or courses up the trunk of his body, sending fire flames into his brain.

He slowly removes the top cardboard. There is the painting, only from this view and in this light, it looks different somehow. He sets the candle on the cot and lowers himself so he is only an inch away. At first he thinks it's the flickering candlelight, but as he leans forward, he sees the colors pulsate; they are tugging at him, swaying in front of him, the bright green of the hilltop, the purple plums in the tree, the blue of his dress, and the woman, dressed in dark red. His heart swells and softens. It is too much, he thinks, too much. He slams down the cardboard cover and slides it under his bed.

JAPAN

OW LONG HAS IT been since he's seen her? he thinks, his chopsticks poised midair, as if caught in two opposing winds.

He hears the man working at the sushi counter say her name again, then describe her, her flash of brown eyes, her graceful walk, as if floating on warm air. He just arrived from Hong Kong, where he purchased ten cases of brandy. By the time the bottles were packed into crates, he sold them for three times the price to a rich man in London. His next trip, as soon as he's taken care of business here, is to Shanghai to buy bolts of silk for a man in Italy who makes fine women's dresses. But if it is Ayoshi, how long has it been since he's seen her? As he rises from the table, the cook behind the counter stops talking and turns toward him, as do several patrons.

Where does she live? he asks.

The cook's eyes widen in alarm.

In his haste, he forgot the decorum of politeness, something he's always despised about his native people.

Excuse me, he says, bowing low. So sorry to interrupt you. The woman. Her name is Ayoshi. Please, I have not seen her in so long.

The cook, an old man with deeply carved lines on his face and milky eyes, looks at him skeptically.

At least he remembered to remove his heavy-soled Western shoes before entering, he thinks, or the cook might have thrown him out. The cook glances at his suit and the newspaper tucked under his arm. An English newspaper. The old man's expression is blank, but his eyes are darting, as if weighing his choices.

After a long wait, the cook reluctantly gives him directions. He bows, lower than he should to a cook, and as he turns for the front door, he almost knocks over an elderly man.

The woman, says the elderly man, his voice smoky. She ran away once. Maybe more than once, I don't know. Someone found her wandering the streets, half dressed. That was right after she moved here. The coldest days of winter and she might have frozen to death. She looked wild, covered with mud, twigs stuck in her hair, muttering to herself. My wife was the one who wrapped her in heavy blankets, put her in a cart, and took her home.

This house? asks the man, anxious to be on his way.

The elderly man shakes his head dolefully. Her husband is a splendid potter, but no one knows much about him. We've heard there are many days he can barely walk. He lowers his voice. It's his feet. You should see them. Sometimes, he must lie in bed all day.

Thank you.

My wife went up there. She had a bad feeling about that house. So empty, so barren; she left as soon as she could. Something isn't right.

He thanks the old man again, grabs his bag, his newspaper, pays his bill, and heads outside.

AYOSHI RISES, STRETCHES, AND looks out the small window of the studio. The wind swoons over the leaves. There is the cold lick of autumn air. Winter is nearly here. Out by the big, ugly gates—why did Hayashi put up those horrid gates—there's an old man, his chin tucked deep into the collar of a heavy dark coat. Perhaps bringing his midday offerings, she thinks. He leans his shoulder into the gate to shut it. Not much strength left in his body.

Her mind flits to the gates. What good did they do? The teahouse burned down anyway. They make her feel like a prisoner, and she is, isn't she? Stuck here. The man is walking down the pebbled path, and she's about to head back, but there is something familiar about his gait. Not an old man's walk, but a smooth swagger, almost arrogant, as if he were not of this world, but hovering an inch above it. She steps outside onto the grass in her paint smock and watches him approach.

He didn't shut the gate properly and now it swings open and slams shut, back and forth, metal crashing against metal. She has not seen him in years. The last time must have been when she was fifteen. Her childhood friend. A rebellious boy who turned each prohibition into a license to act. Whatever is he doing here? A shiver runs along her scalp, and a pang of panic. He left for England to study, and several years later, she met her lover. She is so different now.

Sato, she says.

Ayoshi, he says. Congratulations on your fortuitous marriage. I hear your husband is a famous potter.

They walk to the house. He tells her his life is wonderful, traveling to London, New York, Paris, Shanghai, all the places they talked about when they were young, all the places they dreamed of seeing.

She steps into the kitchen. The degree to which he has aged, she thinks. The thicket of gray hairs, the crumpled, nearly emaciated body, the wrinkled suit, the lines of worry crisscrossing his forehead. A tremor ran through his hand as he pulled his handkerchief out of his front breast pocket. The water boils. She picks up the kettle and wonders what he thinks about her, what he has heard.

She turns to peek at him through the doorway and pours hot water onto her thigh. Stifling a scream, she calls out for the maid.

Are you all right? he asks from the other room.

Fine. Tea will be ready in a minute, she says. The maid hands her a cold cloth, and Ayoshi presses it to her leg. She tells the maid to see to the visitor. She must change her clothes.

He walks outside and opens the door to the Buddhist temple. The smell of burning incense jolts the air, along with the scent of reed from the tatami mats and barley and wheat from the offerings.

He turns and sees one of her paintings hanging on the wall. He remembers her paintings from years ago. Even then, she was one of the few who used shadow. This painting is particularly dark, with lots of brown and black. A face half hidden in shade. A woman's face. He steps closer. A woman stands alone under an umbrella in the evening rain. The sky steel metal, and the rain a silvery thick sheet. The woman's parasol is golden, tinged at the edges with brown, as if faded from harsh light. She wears a black kimono, the kind worn at a funeral. Her glossy hair is pulled up high with engraved ivory chopsticks. It is the expression on the woman's face that is spellbinding. On the side of the face that is lit, a swirl of haunted sorrow in the eye. And the woman is not looking at the viewer, but at something behind her, over her shoulder. She's become quite good, very good, he thinks. Exquisite. I could probably fetch quite a sum for this one. He runs through his list of clients. There's a man in England. What was his name? The tall one who soaks his biscuits in melted butter.

He hears her calling his name.

As HE WALKS FROM the south garden to the horse stables, Hayashi hears her calling a strange man's name. He is late for his meeting in town, and the gardener is waiting for him at the stables to drive him in the cart, the horse now properly shoed, bridled, and hoofing the ground. There is no way he could walk to town today. She is standing on the porch, looking out toward the forest and to the gardens. He hasn't seen her all day, tucked away in the studio. She's wearing her silk kimono; she never paints in such fine fabric. Who is she calling for?

You will be late, Hayashi-san, says the gardener.

He climbs into the cart, his feet aching; he could barely make it up the hill after feeding the fish.

He watches her pause and step tentatively into the house. Perhaps an old man from town has heard of Ayoshi's healing hands and has come to her, hoping to ease stiff joints or bad digestion. Or someone who's come to pray at the temple. The gardener drives the cart down the pebbled path. Hayashi cranes his neck to look again. No one. The gardener steps down from the cart, opens the gate, drives the horses through, then closes it. Maybe after all this time, she has finally made a friend, someone from town. But a man? Hayashi swivels around once more to see if he might see the owner of this name. She was calling for a man named Sato, but there is no one.

OVER TEA, SATO TELLS her the world is rapidly changing. She would love America, its openness, its informality, its eagerness to make a mark on the world. Brash, he says, there is no sense of history or tradition or protocol. Poor people become rich. Rich people become poor. Or maybe Paris, which is now at war, but after the war, she should go. It's teeming with artists, writers, painters; or perhaps London with its theater and a king and queen. He sips his tea and gazes out the window. Japan is poised for a tremendous transformation. It's certainly needed. How does she stand it? The silences, the politeness, the hierarchy, the pressure to conform. He shudders and hunches his narrow shoulders. That will change, he says. Fortunately. It's all about to rip apart.

How did you know I was here? she asks, lifting her gaze from her steaming tea.

He says he was passing through. He heard she lived in the area and thought he'd stop by.

She'd like to ask how long he might stay, what he plans to do. She'd like to ask what is he doing here. It's a surprise, she says, your arrival.

He sets his cup down. I remember that look, he says. That pout, the clamped jaw. You don't want me here. He looks at her closely. Her face, pale and drawn tight. She looks older than her twenty-seven years, he thinks. He has been to the drought-stricken countryside of northern China and seen the victims, their skin stretched taut. Behind the vacant look lay ravenous hunger.

No, that's not true, she says, prickling at his directness and feeling even more irritated by his presence. It's surprising. I'm surprised you're here. After so long. She sips her tea. Sato, you look so tired. Do you want to rest? Hayashi should be here in an hour or so. Why don't you rest?

I won't stay long, says Sato.

Please. Stay as long as you wish, she says, forcing a smile. And she tells him again, he is her guest. A welcome guest.

Thank you, he says. I think I will lie down and rest.

WHY HAS HE COME? she wonders, as she walks to the studio. Her delicately balanced life now feels thrown off, but by what exactly she couldn't say. Your friend, she tells herself. He is your oldest, dearest friend.

She mixes water into a bowl and sprinkles in dried red paint, stalling, not able to paint. How can she, her mind filled with the image of Sato sitting before her, with his hands now blue veined and bony. And behind the man, the young boy swelling out, the precocious boy who was selected by the government, along with twelve other boys, all of whom were fluent in English, to study abroad. Sato always loved to tell this part of his story. He'd learned English when it was illegal to do so, and he was rewarded for disobeying the law.

He wrote her letters, saying he was staying on in Europe after his school program ended, even though his parents wanted him home and so did the government. The government paid his travel expenses and his tuition on the condition that he study military science. He took business courses instead and formed his own company. He insisted she come to Europe. And how she read those letters and reread them and dreamed of joining him, not as a girlfriend, always as a younger sister; he was eight years older than she and full of advice. Oh, maybe once there was the typical girlish infatuation, but that faded when he left. *Here, you can live the way you want,* he wrote. *In the West, I see young women walking on the streets alone, working at jobs in public places, going to the cafés, smoking and drinking gin at round tables with bright white tablecloths. You would love it here, my friend. Buy a ticket—steal money from your father's purse, if you must, and join me. Japan is no place for someone like you.*

Her brush calls out for purple to deepen the red. The studio is quiet. The afternoon light will soon move across the sky and Sato will rise. He kept looking at her, as if expecting her to say something, but what, she wasn't sure. She thought the house so empty, and now, with him there, it feels crowded and confining.

She swirls her brush around and around in circles. When the brush dries, she dips it in the black paint and spills circles all over.

AYOSHI WALKS INTO THE kitchen. Hayashi is finishing a bowl of udon. We have a visitor? he asks.

An old friend. A childhood friend. You might like him. You both know a great deal about the West. And you both speak English.

Hayashi reaches down and massages his feet. She turns her back to Hayashi, trying to hide her desire to do anything but touch his awful feet. She listens to the birds outside, their calling and singing. She rises and heads for the doorway. I'll go find him.

What is he doing here? asks Hayashi.

She stops. I don't really know.

MY HUSBAND IS HOME, she says. She stands at the door frame, her hands folded in front of her.

Sato is sitting in a chair in the Western room reading a book. The light has shifted and the room is darker than the rest of the house.

I thought I heard the front door open and close, he says, smiling. So finally I will meet him.

She remembers that smile, and for the first time, she sees a hint of his former youthful elegance. When he left to study in London, she walked with him to the docks. She carried his satchel full of Western books and he lugged a huge trunk of clothes. They stood and stared at the gleaming English warship that would take him across the seas. Guns and cannons lined the deck, and from the mast, the British flag snapped in the wind. An official from the Tokugawa government was at the docks to see him off. One of the British sailors told them it was the fastest warship on the seas. Sato whispered to her that he already knew this.

He rises, smoothes out his trousers. When was the last time you visited home?

I haven't gone back. Ever. Have you?

He glances at the painting of the woman outside in the snow. Not for a while, he says. I'm surprised the government lets you keep the temple open. I walked in there and incense was burning. I'm also wondering why someone would choose to live here. The dead sleep right outside your window.

She tells him Hayashi is a big supporter of the new government. He likes it here, she says. He'd never move. I do miss the red-crowned cranes. You remember them? I'd rise early to see them fly in the morning sky. If you walked quietly, you could stand on the edge of their resting grounds.

He walks over to her. You don't love your husband, do you?

She blushes. His directness, a slap on the arm. Not a new trait, she thinks, but something she'd forgotten. I'm glad you're here, Sato. I'm glad you're here because I think it's a good sign. She looks down at her tabi socks, trying to decide whether to say anything more. He is silent, waiting. Enough, she thinks. I've said enough.

A good sign, he says. Of what? Or should I say, who?

She looks away from him. Please, my husband is waiting for you. He is honored you are visiting our home.

I hear many people, both men and women, have trouble in the beginning, he says. It's understandable. What do you know of each other when you are first married? But it'd be easier if you accepted it.

Her hard gaze strikes him, and she laughs contemptuously. That's funny coming from you, she says. You've done everything you wanted. Accepted nothing else.

I don't have those kinds of desires.

She laughs harshly. You were always so grandiose about yourself.

From what I've heard, your husband is a fine fellow. We could become the best of friends. Then what will you do?

Stop it.

We might share stories about you. The way you click your tongue to the roof of your mouth when you are nervous. Does he know that about you?

Stop.

Or rock onto your toes when you're excited.

He starts to walk out of the room, but she grabs him by the elbow. You don't know anything about me anymore. I had no choice.

Of course. Of course. The matchmaker.

She hesitates. Her eyes water and the loose strands of hair hang mournfully around her face.

They hear her husband coming down the hallway. They turn together and watch him hobble toward them. Her body bristles, and she retracts within herself, as if she were a small animal burrowing down underneath her skin. Not until now, as Hayashi slowly makes his way to them, does she realize she's dreaded this moment. How will they get along, and then she wonders, why does she care? She frantically searches for something to say, but her mind seizes, and she stands still, watching her husband. His walk, she thinks, is smoother, more fluid than usual. He seems in good spirits. But perhaps it's only a momentary change and tomorrow he will be flat on his back again. She suddenly knows what it is: She's ashamed Hayashi is her husband and Sato, with his brusque, rude manner, is her friend. They won't get along.

Sato cringes as he watches the man limp toward them. It looks as if every time he steps, something drives deep into his feet. Pitiful, he thinks, a tragic sight, feeling himself soften with sympathy for the injured man.

Hayashi bows and apologizes for not greeting Sato when he first arrived. Sato exchanges the bow and, as he stands, extends his hand. Hayashi awkwardly takes it in his.

An Eastern bow and a Western handshake, says Sato. The modern man's greeting.

Hayashi nods, smiling tentatively. When Sato glances toward Ayoshi, Hayashi studies Sato. He looks craggy and worn, thinks Hayashi. Some of his apprehension about this visitor dissipates. Still, there is the smart suit—he wears a silk scarf around his neck and Western trousers, his blouse is of the finest linen cloth with cuff sleeves, and his wool coat has a line of gold buttons down the front. And there is the full attention Ayoshi lavishes on him. He is her first visitor.

Soon the government will issue an edict about that, says Sato.

You've heard about the edicts? asks Hayashi.

Sato bows again. It's a great honor to meet you.

And you, he says.

There is an awkward moment. Ayoshi glances around. What are we doing standing in the hallway? she asks, laughing nervously. Sato has yet to see the gardens.

We shall give him a tour, says Hayashi.

They gather their coats and she leads them to the main gardens.

Everything is well kept, says Sato, motioning to the yard, the house, the temple.

Hayashi bows and says the grounds could use more tending. But any beauty you see has nothing to do with me. It's the gardener's skillful hand.

She glances nervously at Sato, hoping he does not become insolent. The wry turn of the corners of his mouth has faded, replaced by something kinder and more grave.

Do you need to sit? asks Sato.

I'm fine, Hayashi says, abruptly, waving him off. They amble toward the cluster of bamboo.

Sato hears the anger in Hayashi's response. Something solid in this man, he thinks. A strong fiber underneath the pain. Perhaps their talk will venture beyond nonsense and trivia. And the government lets you keep the temple open for services? asks Sato.

Of course, says Hayashi.

Ayoshi stifles a scoff. What about the fire, she wants to blurt out. The burning of the teahouse? Hayashi hasn't told her anything about it, but she figures it has something to do with the temple.

It's quite beautiful, the human soul striving for transcendence, says Sato. I don't have such a soul. Mine wallows in its own muck. But such a striving soul, it must be uplifting to be around. Is that why you choose to live here?

Ayoshi glances down at her hands, folded tightly in front of her, and feels her face blush.

Hayashi pauses, puzzled and slightly offended by such a direct question. He looks at Ayoshi and sees her bowed head, her reddened cheeks. She's embarrassed. I should welcome this old friend of hers; he is perfectly harmless and it's only because of his travels that he has different ways. If an old friend came to visit me, I hope she would extend a welcome, no matter the nature of my visitor. He tells Sato this morning an old woman brought three jars of pickled vegetables as offerings for the Buddha. She probably cleaned out her cupboards, and now what will she eat? he says.

I saw that kind of devotion in an English church, says Sato. Everyone got down on their knees, as if one big hand swooped down from the ceiling and pressed on their heads. What a thing to see.

They near the rock garden, the small white pebbles and large gray rocks, islands floating in a white sea. They stand there, no one saying anything.

Both of you know quite a lot about the West, says Ayoshi, hoping to ease the tension that she feels creeping into the elongated silences.

What do you like about the West? asks Sato.

Hayashi gazes at the rocks, and his mind skips back to the Dutchman. Sato's mind, his probing questions, shorn of politeness and circularity, so bold, this friend of Ayoshi. His mind is of the same fabric as the Dutchman's. Why study the myths? asked the Dutchman one day. Why bother? Hayashi was stunned. He said he should because the Dutchman told him to. The Dutchman scoffed and made him write an essay to answer the question; he can't remember now what he wrote, but he recalls how exhilarating it felt, and also how barbaric.

She watches Hayashi's face. He's trying to contain his pain, she thinks, that's why he isn't answering. Now he's gritting his jaws together, as if pushing the pain into a box for her to deal with later. They stand at the edge of the rock garden. Ayoshi has the urge to scatter the pebbles with her shoes.

Excuse me, says Hayashi. What did you ask?

I wanted to ask, What do you get for providing prayer services? says Sato.

So few people come anymore, says Hayashi. And really, all I do is open the main door.

We receive a stipend, says Ayoshi. She tells Sato they get some money for upkeep. The grounds are historical landmarks. And Hayashi receives assistance in selling his work to the West.

I didn't know our new leaders were so generous, says Sato.

No, says Hayashi, flicking a pine needle from his kimono. Not generous.

Sato raises his eyebrows, tosses his head back, and laughs. Then it must be part of the national pride campaign. I read about it in the English newspaper. He stands up tall and imitates one of the officials in a low, commanding voice, To generate respect for Japan, we will assist you in selling your ceramics. It will be good for you. More important, it is best for Japan.

Hayashi laughs and some of the stiffness in the air sloughs away.

Sato looks admiringly around the gardens, toward the house, the temple. The grounds are quite lovely. It's a good investment for the government. To preserve this. Quite old, I would think?

Hayashi shifts his weight to his heels, away from the balls of his feet, which burn now. He tells Sato the temple was built in the tenth century, a hermitage for the women of the Heian court to come and pray. It's very precious to the Buddhists.

I didn't know that, says Ayoshi.

I told you when you first came here, says Hayashi, his voice a whisper.

Lovely, says Sato.

Hayashi smiles wistfully. If you read some of these women's poetry, you discover it was also a secluded place for them to meet their lovers.

Sato takes a step toward the stone bench, hoping Hayashi will sit and rest. He thinks he sees Hayashi wince from pain, his upper lip tightening. Hayashi follows him, but stops short of the bench.

Sato tells them he's read some of the marvelous poetry of the famous Izumi Shikibu.

She lived here for a while.

Really? asks Sato.

She came here after her first husband left her because she'd taken a lover, says Hayashi.

The three of them stand underneath the pine tree.

Just one lover? asks Sato, his voice lighthearted and teasing.

Ayoshi looks away, out beyond the treetops.

You're right. More than one, says Hayashi. He tells them the brother of her lover courted her as well. He sent Izumi a gift of orange blossoms.

Hayashi walks over to the stone bench and sits, stretching his legs out in front of him. Sato sits beside him. Ayoshi stands, trying not to listen.

Fascinating history, says Sato, looking over the grounds, the house, and the temple, this time gauging their true value.

Ayoshi realizes she's been holding her breath.

Hayashi picks a dandelion and twirls it around. Izumi knew how to peer into the human heart, says Hayashi. He rises and Sato follows. Ayoshi involuntarily steps backward. She looks at Hayashi's flushed face. Strange, she thinks, how utterly left out she feels.

Hayashi turns to Sato and formally bows. Our home is yours. Please, stay as long as you like.

Ayoshi is a couple feet behind them.

Thank you, says Sato, turning around to look at her. Ayoshi has already extended the same generous invitation. It's been so long since I've immersed myself in such peace and serenity.

Hayashi glances at Ayoshi, feeling his earlier apprehension return. She did not mention the invitation. The Western-dressed man is unpleasant, really. And it's improper to have a man visiting his wife. If he had the nerve, he'd ask Sato how long he intended to stay. But he won't. Of course he won't.

Now I'm remembering one of Izumi's poems, says Sato. He closes his eyes. *I used up this body longing for one who does not come. A deep valley, now, what once was my heart.*

Ayoshi's face reddens. She bends down and picks up a leaf. The colors, she thinks, focus on the colors. The dark red in the leaf, the hint of orange. When that doesn't work, she looks up at the leaves clinging to green life.

You must know one, says Sato.

Hayashi glances up to the sky. *Although the wind blows terribly here, the moonlight also leaks between the roof planks of this ruined house.*

Wonderful, says Sato. Marvelous. He claps his hands in delight. Sato turns to Ayoshi. You must have one.

She offers a blank expression. No, she says. I don't. In fact, I'm late for the baths.

You're going to town? asks Hayashi. He steps over beside her, touches her lightly on the shoulder.

It *is* Tuesday, she says. And just because an old friend is visiting, I still need my bath.

Of course, says Sato.

If you're hungry before I return, the cook will have dinner ready for you, she says.

Ayoshi, says Hayashi, with an embarrassed laugh.

Sato leans toward Hayashi, bowing his head in a conspiratorial way, and says, That's how she was when she was a young girl. Strong willed.

And he was the older brother who tried to boss me around, she says, buttoning the top button of her coat. That was a long time ago, but not much has changed.

And everything has changed, says Sato. I tried to mold her into a proper lady, with proper manners, he says, feigning despair.

Ayoshi walks to the house. She stands on the porch looking out across the garden at the two men. They have the same short-cut hair like the Westerners. They are about the same height. Both merchants, although her husband would never call himself one. Still, all those boxes he sends. They seem, oddly, mirror images of each other, the way they are standing, face to face, nodding, gesturing, as if long-lost brothers. She hears Hayashi ask, Have you read anything by Emerson?

HAYASHI GLANCES AT THE gate and watches Ayoshi open and close it. Did she lock it? But of course not. The gardener will lock it tonight. That's caution enough, he thinks. Sato offers him a Western cigarette.

With Ayoshi gone, Hayashi closely examines this man. There is an air of enviable freedom to him, as if he's unhinged himself from rules, customs, obligations of family, culture, and even a personal history. With that comes the power to mold his life, to take it in his hands and shape something grand and beautiful. And as this refined man discusses some financial device he's never heard of, Hayashi thinks, This is what the West promises. That a man can do this, live like this, think like this. This is what his father spoke of. His face brightens. This man is his father's vision. Not abolishing religions or throw-ing out Japan's traditional customs and manners. It wasn't any of that, but what this man embodies.

Have you ever visited the Great Buddha? asks Hayashi, his voice excited.

No, unfortunately.

Hayashi tells him it's near the Enoshima Island and the Kamakura bathing beach.

You've been there with Ayoshi on vacation? asks Sato.

No, says Hayashi, feeling again his earlier irritation at Sato, his blunt questions.

Surely with your role in the government and your prestige, the govern-ment would let you move freely in the country, says Sato.

I've never been there, says Hayashi. He doesn't tell Sato that many of the monks from the mountain monastery took a pilgrimage to the Great Buddha to pray, but he could never go because of his feet. When the monks returned, their faces were weary but filled with a formidable radiance. When they spoke of the Great Buddha, their words glowed.

Why haven't you gone with Ayoshi?

Hayashi bristles. A red dragonfly alights on the surface of a willow leaf; it looks so menacing, he thinks, yet necessary, feasting on water bugs, keeping the lake clear. Sato is waiting. So sure of himself to ask such an unmediated question and expect an answer.

Hayashi bows, and, apologizing, says he must return to the house. His feet have begun to ache.

Of course. Sato follows him back to the porch. Where are you selling your work?

Hayashi turns to the man whose eyes glimmer now as he rubs his hands to-gether, as if they held precious coins. Hayashi tells him mostly to customers in England and France.

Sato stops walking. Not in America? The Americans are in love with any-thing new. Such a new country, you see. Let me sell your work.

I couldn't impose.

No, I'd be honored. They'll love your work. They've never seen this kind of beauty. The simple beauty of Japan. They've only seen the busy, cluttered beauty of Europe.

Thank you, says Hayashi. He bows stiffly. There will be proper recompense.

Oh, no bother.

I insist.

We'll find some agreeable arrangement, I'm sure.

When they enter the house, Sato tells him how much he admires the house and the wonderful architecture and artwork. Hayashi gives Sato a quick tour, pointing to the bamboo running along the wall, telling him it was grown in southern Japan, the Kyushu area. The paper walls, from a mulberry tree, a grove outside of Kyoto. The paintings over there, they come from China; the Buddhist monks imported them in the fifteenth century. I've been told they are expressions of Taoism. You see the physical landscape in the painting, the tall mountains, the grove of trees, says Hayashi. These correspond to the inner landscape of the artist's body and the celestial realm.

They wander into the kitchen.

Where are Ayoshi's things? asks Sato.

The maid brings them tea.

Hayashi looks at him curiously and slightly alarmed.

Sato tells him she had a beautiful tansu and a lovely oak writing table. I can't remember what else. Oh yes, a tall vase that sat in their hallway.

The air in the house shifts. Hayashi looks out the window at the bare space where the teahouse once stood. She arrived with almost nothing, says Hayashi.

Sato's hands twitch. Maybe I was wrong.

Hayashi smiles faintly, trying not to think of those early, dark days when she was so miserable, nothing could console her. Why wouldn't she bring her precious things? Didn't she think he was deserving? Or perhaps she thought she wouldn't stay?

The maid carries in the bucket of ice water. He tells her to set it in the bathroom. Not here, he thinks, weary of this man, Sato.

Sato scoots his chair closer to Hayashi's. I'd also like to try to sell Ayoshi's paintings, says Sato.

A shadow passes over Hayashi's face. You've seen her work?

Only the piece in the temple. Do you have any objections?

What? No. I've never said she could or couldn't sell her work.

Pain shoots up his leg. After the maid massages his feet, he will go into the studio. Distract himself with his next order. A shipment to China. Hayashi excuses himself and heads down the hallway to the bathroom. The maid brings out Sato's supper. There is a place setting for only one.

SHE WALKS TO THE baths at the far side of town. The maid, at her request, has stayed behind to tend to her husband and Sato. What does Sato think he's doing? Arrogant, bold, insistent, barging into her life to tell her what to do, and in front of her husband, reciting that awful poem; she'll speak to him later, but now, now she doesn't want to think about him. She is alone, walking in a web of tree shade. She prefers to walk alone so her mind can roam. The shadows from the trees, she turns them into shapes, a dog, a bony hand, an old woman's face, and always she sees the hands of the man from Hokkaido.

When she reaches the town, her calm is destroyed by the noise. From what she can see at the edge of town, at least five shops have been torn down and two new, taller buildings are rising up from the ground. She glances at a posted drawing of one of the new buildings. Imposing white pillars guard the front. She shudders. Men pounding nails, sawing boards, and driving in tall posts, the noises crowd her, she covers her ears with her hands. Where is the little grocery store? And the shop where she took her sandals to be repaired?

She hurries by one of the dusty, loud construction sites, ducking her head under her parasol, her eyes watery; not here, she tells herself, why should you weep about such things? Silly old buildings being torn down, but the tears hover an inch from the surface, suspended, and her chiding only makes her feel worse.

With a quickened pace, she rushes to the older of the two bathhouses. She prefers this one, over two hundred years old, surrounded by tall, thick mulberry trees and long grass. Its wood is weather stained a dark brown and black. She steps inside, closes the heavy door, and sinks into silence. Inside, old wood carvings of Buddha and bodhisattvas peer at her through the thick, watery air. She loves the bathhouse in spite of its slippery, sloped floors and warped walls and lingering smell of mold. An ancient beauty, she thinks, one that will endure forever.

Down the narrow hallway to the dressing rooms, she removes her clothing and steps naked along the wet tile to the main room, which sways with scorching steam. The sound of running water, the heat, like a cupped hand. The insides of her nostrils burn. Her skin warms and turns pink, as if she's sat for hours in the sun. Droplets of sweat gather on her upper lip. Through the mist, she sees naked women soaking in the big center bath. Occasionally, a voice drifts over to her through the thick air. A line of women are sitting on wooden stools along one wall. They are scrubbing themselves with hard brushes and throwing buckets of water on their backs. Black hair streams down their arms.

She joins the line of women and turns on a faucet. With the water running, and the mist encasing her, she suddenly collapses her head in her hands and begins to cry. For what reason? She doesn't know. She feels a hand on her shoulder. It's the woman whose husband owns the shoe shop.

Are you all right?

She nods, still crying.

I can get the masseuse, says the woman.

No. No thank you.

She has helped me many times.

No. Please.

The woman nods uncertainly and returns to washing her calves. Across the room, the old woman masseuse is rubbing a woman's back. Ayoshi watches the woman's big, sturdy hands pull and tug at the woman. Warm water drips on Ayoshi's toes. She feels soft now, after the tears, as soft as a new leaf. If someone touched her, her body would fold around the compression. Slowly something stirs inside, teetering and knitting itself tighter and tighter, growing thicker as the minutes tick by. It lurches to the right and she grips the edge of the bench. She knows what this is, though it has been a while since it felt so insistent and unyielding. Closing her eyes, she makes room in her softened, open body, shuttling her stomach up and back and cinching up her lungs. Her body feels heavy, bloated, and leaden. Sweat trickles down her sides and thighs.

The masseuse comes over and asks if she wants a massage.

No, she says. No, thank you.

The old woman touches her shoulder.

She flinches. Please. Not today.

The old woman looks at her curiously.

Please. Ayoshi wants to scream at her, push the crone to the other side of the room, repulsed at the idea of hands massaging, her mind crowded with days of her own hands pulling and grabbing his flesh. The woman shrugs and leaves. The image inside lurches, demanding that it be delivered.

SHE RUSHES TO THE studio and is about to open the door when she hears the whir of the potter's wheel. Her heart is pounding. Where can she go? She must paint. She feels as if she might burst. She opens the door. Hayashi is deep into his work and doesn't look up. She walks quickly to her desk and pulls out a sheet of blank paper. With efficient motions, she mixes her paints. The image is pressing up through her spine, spiraling down her arms. The wheel stops.

You smell wonderful, says Hayashi. Like fresh flowers. A garden of flowers.

I didn't mean to disturb you.

He asks about her bath.

Fine, she says. She can't stay here. Where is Sato?

I don't know, he says wiping his hands on a towel, frowning.

I'll go look for him, she says.

He stands and steps toward her. Lavender, he says.

No, she says. It was the usual bath. She backs away, shaken.

It's been so long. His fingers trace her waist. I am sorry for that.

His touch feels like a betrayal. No, please don't apologize. It's no one's fault.

Is everything all right? he asks.

I'm distracted. I'm sorry.

He steps awkwardly to his side of the studio. Sato is an interesting character, he says.

She feels him retreating, as if he touched a fingertip to a hot stove and now must cradle the injured hand to his chest. She doesn't care. She must hurry. Yes, she says, reaching under her desk and grabbing some paper. In her pocket, she stuffs her brushes. She's about to reach for her palette of fresh paints, but leaves it. She'll start over.

Interesting fellow. Yes, quite interesting. You knew him as a girl?

Yes. A long time ago. Yes, she says. She excuses herself and scurries to the house. With rapid steps, she walks down the long hallway, listening to the fabric of her kimono brush against her thighs, and into the Western room.

The room is filled with blue smoke. She doesn't see him at first, but when she steps farther into the room, there he is, stretched out on the plush, red velvet couch, a long pipe cupped in his hands.

She has seen men in town sunk into themselves, their bodies wrapped around their pipes. Sato, she says.

He sets the pipe down and picks up the koto and strums his fingernails through the strings, the room pulsing with haunting music.

I've been reading some of your husband's Emerson. Your husband, by the way, is in love with Emerson. Listen to this. *Every ship is a romantic object, except that we sail in. Embark, and the romance quits our vessel, and hangs on every sail in the horizon.*

Please, Sato.

He's quite charming. Your husband. You should let yourself fall in love with him. He picks up the pipe again. She sits in a chair far in the corner. He looks as if he's holding a baby, the way it's nestled up against his chest. For the first time, she notices his yellow fingernails.

He has changed, she thinks, sighing, and so have I.

Sato, she says again, not certain what to do.

He burrows farther into the cushions. Proceed with whatever you came in here to do.

She waits for a while, watching the smoke swirl above his head. Her heart pounds. She pulls out a sheet of paper, glances at him once more. Sato closes his eyes. She retrieves her set of paints from the cupboard. He does what he wants, I'll do what I want. As she mixes her colors, the room begins to disappear. She pours more water into the paint and red comes alive. In another bowl, she mixes yellow and white.

Her lover's hand begins to appear. Then the other. His body, his face, the image is coming fast, as she knew it would.

The brush blusters along the paper. Sato has fallen asleep on the couch, a gentle smile on his face, his hands folded on his chest, and now he's snoring.

Black fire, he said, as he undid her bun. He pressed into her hand a poem. *In any season, your black hair unbound, I long to touch it.*

She feels his pulse now, his scent in each pore of her skin. The heat of desire has its own sense of time.

They went down the hill and swam in the river. Her body floating in warm water under the deepening sky, the stars spilling out from the moon. Looking up, she sees him through the river's mist. She smiles, but her expression suddenly twists and fades as the current pulls at her, as if a person crept underneath. She screams. It grabs her around the ankles. Her mouth fills with brine water. He rushes over from the side of the river, jumps in, clutches her by the waist, and yanks her to the surface. She spits out water and sobs. But the current seizes her again. She wraps her hands around the back of his neck; he can't seem to release her. Frozen in this pose, the water gripping her backside, the pull of his body clutching her front. She feels like her insides are ripping apart.

She sets down her paintbrush and pushes aside the painting. It's not how it happened. What an awful image and it isn't even true. Why did he make her paint such a thing? She was pulled to the bottom, and he jumped in, swept her up, and pulled her out of the water. She was so cold. Since that day, she's always hated the cold.

A whisper of air stirs behind her. She is suddenly aware of someone else in the room. For a moment she stiffens. Sato puts his hand on her shoulder.

You're crying, he says.

She reaches up and touches her face.

He stares at her painting. Ayoshi. It's beautiful.

Don't.

She holds herself tighter.

He looks at the two figures in the painting. The woman is floating in the water. Her long black hair streaming out from her like a fan. Her kimono is falling off, her legs bare, the skin pale white. The man has wrapped himself around her like two large wings. Tall and striking, the man has a strong profile and a full head of hair. He is poised between saving her and falling in.

Is this him? The man you love?

She doesn't say anything.

Where is he now?

I don't know.

Sato is about to say something.

Don't.

FRANCE

S O LIKE HIM, Natalia thinks, finding Pierre in the hallway
gazing lovingly at a bronze vase.

What do you think it's worth? he asks, his shrewd eyes flashing. He looks
squarely at her. Silly me. Why ask you? You don't even acknowledge the material world.

How is he doing? she says, glancing discreetly toward Jorgen's office. Un-
buttoning her coat—how steamy this hallway—she's just come from the
hospital, and she won't admonish Pierre about visiting Edmond, they've
argued about it enough, and Pierre will only become irascible and refuse
to speak to her for days, or just to spite her, he'll fire Jorgen. But she knows
Edmond would love to see Pierre. He asked about him today.

I haven't decided if I'm going to keep him, says Pierre. I tell you, though,
he's an odd one. He hardly speaks. Seems almost comatose at times. Maybe
he's sipping away at absinthe, who knows? I'm usually a good judge of people, but he doesn't reveal much. He works and works, barely says a damn
thing.

He sounds like an ideal worker. How fortunate for you.

Why are you so happy? he asks, his permanently dissatisfied mouth tightening. You look like something marvelous has happened. Did you save someone's life today? Did you finally become a saint?

I'm just happy. Every day is a blessing.

He waves his hand in front of him. Please. No sermons. When I have a thousand francs in my sweaty hands from this vase, I will be very happy, and not before then.

She shakes her head and walks down the hallway, then stops. Before I forget, she says, I must ask for some extra blankets.

Pierre is about to protest.

Not for me. For Edmond.

He hesitates.

Pierre.

He sighs heavily and tells her there is a stack in the back office. He relents further and tells her to take as many as Edmond needs. And for her, too. But don't bother my new employee. I want every last franc out of him, which is my God-given right as his employer, so don't tell me otherwise.

She's almost to the inventory room, when she stops again. You know, Edmond would love to see you. Why does she insist? she wonders. Pierre will never go again. Too busy, too self-absorbed, selfish, really. After he went his one and only time, he said the stench was overwhelming, the misery too great. How stupid this war. Any war. Such a pathetic waste of lives, he said, and she held her tongue, almost lashing back, Your pathetic life, Pierre.

Pierre looks at her squarely with flat eyes and strides away.

She's about to say more, but turns and walks to Jorgen's office.

Hello, she says. Oh, don't get up. No, please.

Hello, says Jorgen.

She asks how he is doing.

He gestures weakly toward the tall stack of books; the pencil in his hand is perfectly still.

Oh, look at those terrible books. My brother must have had the work pile up before you arrived. And now he has you. What a blessing.

He perches above his carefully written numbers, each neatly situated in its column. He looks horrible, she thinks. A trace of a man. Almost as ill as the men in the hospital, and she wonders if his leg might be infected and when did he last eat? His face has become more gaunt; his sallow skin presses against his high cheekbones and his eyes appear feverish and sunken.

She wasn't planning to tell anyone what she has done. Not even Edmond, who would most likely try to stop her. Her secret, this new deed, but she feels she must do something; why, look at the way his head droops, as if struck by an insoluble, deathly question.

You mustn't tell anyone. Please, swear that you won't. She comes and stands by his desk.

He sets down his pencil.

She leans over. There's a group of women. We're training to be soldiers, and we're going to fight for France.

He shifts in his chair and strains to understand what she just said.

She leans closer and says in a hushed tone, Yesterday, two soldiers met with us and they're teaching us how to shoot. If I learn quickly, I may get to join the fighting in a week or two. She doesn't tell him how a group of National Guardsmen stood by mocking them, pretending to be hit by a stray bullet.

Her eyes are watery bright, and she tells him when she fired the gun it threw her back three feet, nearly knocking her against a stone wall, and though it was terrifying, she felt a tremendous surge of energy rip through her body. The air smelled of smoke and bitterness. Her hands, blackened from the powder.

Look, she says, extending her hands. Some of the black marks still smudge her cuticles.

He looks from her hands to her blue eyes, wide and childlike, void of life experiences.

One of the women gave her a pistol; she pulls it out of her bag and hands it to him. He turns it over and over, studies the barrel, the trigger. It does what she hoped; his eyes flicker and dart. Now he holds the gun in his palm, as if he might caress it. The hard-edged lines of his face evaporate, and his rigidly held jaw relaxes. He puts his other hand on top of it, and she can't help but smile; of course he would react this way; he is a soldier who is principled and strong, who is aching to fight again for France.

He runs his hands over the pistol, his fingertips tingling as he recalls his first pistol, a single-shot cap-and-ball pocket pistol, a gift from his father. Engraved scrollwork was etched on the barrel, a silver inlay on the finished walnut stock. When he cocked the gun, the sound was precise and final. Holding that pistol, he felt bigger and more powerful, as if he could shape things, as if he could turn and shift the world the way he wanted to, as the pistol is making him feel right now. His heartbeat quickens and he extends the gun in front of him, aiming at a box of books. He sets the pistol down, picks it up again. Maybe I can help you, he says. I can teach you.

Her face lights up, as if she's just won something grand and is proud of her effort.

Yes, she says, her bright voice insists, yes, that would be wonderful.

He nods severely.

She tells him rumors are flying that if the Prussians win, they will destroy everything in the city, all the beautiful buildings, the precious statues, and the French people will be turned into servants, she says, her voice urgent. The Prussians want to take over the world.

I don't know about any of that, he says. Dark hints of despair settle again on his brow.

Let's begin today, she says, clapping her hands together.

With blurry eyes, he stares angrily at the stack of books and puckers his lips in disgust.

She looks toward the entrance of his office, listening for Pierre. We'll get back before he notices you're gone.

He can't lose this job. Not yet. He looks again at the books, then thinks about the sound of a gun firing.

We'll sneak out. Pierre is too busy with other things.

He reaches behind his chair and fumbles around for his crutches. She grabs them for him. He hooks them under his arms, hands her the pistol, and says he'll fetch his rifle.

Wait here, she says, and, removing her shoes, walks into the hallway in her stockings. She comes back and says Pierre has gone downstairs or perhaps to the café for lunch.

Hurry, she says. She hands him his coat. He retrieves his rifle from his room, and they slip out the back door.

THE SUNLIGHT SHOCKS HIS eyes; it has been so long since he's been outside. The warm air strokes his face, and it feels as if he's been in a deep fog. They walk down the sidewalk to Burty's, behind the horse market. Soldiers and people throng the streets. They turn right at the first corner. An old woman cranes out the window and yells to a man down below, Come up, but only if you have a pastry or a bottle of wine.

I don't want to be a servant to the Prussians or to anyone, says Natalia. She is babbling, she knows, but she is excited and thrilled he offered to help her.

I wouldn't believe everything you hear.

She is walking beside him, her pace slowed to match his. If you don't think the Prussians are bad—

I'm not saying bad or good. I'm saying don't believe everything.

But why did you leave your country to fight for France? It must be because you love France and all that she stands for.

He directs his gaze at his black boot, scarred from wear. She glances at him, waiting for him to respond, but he's tipping his face to the sun and there are the smells in the warm air, the horses, the grass, the bakery, and the fires, always the smoke. The shutters on most shops are nailed shut, signs announcing their closure. They pass by the butcher's shop and overhear one woman in the long line say the only thing available today is horse meat. She heard they killed the tiger in the zoo. Down on the street corner, a woman sings, Vive le guerre. A carriage goes by carrying more wounded soldiers and Natalia crosses herself.

She bends down, picks a lone, shimmering buttercup, and tucks it behind her ear. She feels almost giddy and he looks so much better, the grip of whatever held him loosening, and he is looking around, engaged in something other than numbers and boxes. Who cares if Pierre finds him gone? If her brother had his way, he'd chain Jorgen to the desk and give him one dull errand after another.

They walk by a group of soldiers in dirty red trousers and filthy blue overcoats. She studies them, the way they hold their guns and wear their hats, pressed down, covering half their foreheads. One of them has a Prussian epaulette at the end of his bayonet. Oh, she says, pointing it out to Jorgen. She is happy to be alive, and she looks over at him and smiles. With his help, she will soon be able to stand up for something she believes in. Her life already feels bigger, more grand.

I can't thank you enough for doing this.

He nods.

She tells him the other day at the hospital, one of the nurses asked about him. She hoped you were doing better and said for you to come by if you needed anything. She gave me this to give to you. Natalia hands him a business card. A doctor named Whitbread, who is supposed to be very good at making artificial limbs. She tells him he's from England. He came to Paris to help and his office is across town.

He glances at the card and puts it in his pocket. This Dr. Whitbread, how much do you think he charges?

Natalia tells him what the nurse said.

That's what the nurse said?

Yes, says Natalia. She's the one with the light brown hair.

That's a hell of a lot of money.

Do you remember her?

No.

She felt bad for you because had the doctors treated you earlier, she says they could have saved your leg.

His expression remains blank.

Why did they wait so long to bring you in?

He shrugs.

It seems a pity. A terrible pity.

He stops and turns to her. I don't need anyone's pity.

I didn't mean—

That's the last thing I want. Pity. Goddamn pity. Everything that's happened, I deserve.

You deserve? she echoes, her lips pulled inward, frightened.

I deserve, he says again, feeling sorry for himself as he looks down at his empty trouser leg. Anyone who pities me is a goddamn idiot.

Red nudges up her cheeks and her eyes tear. It came out wrong, she says. I didn't mean it that way. She pulls out a handkerchief and dabs her eyes.

And now look what I've done, he thinks. She's a good-hearted woman, the least you can do is not make her cry. She is quivering now, her shoulders shaking, and tears are about to run down her face. Don't, Natalia. Please don't. His ghost leg sears with pain and he feels the blood rush to his face, thinking of his callousness. You let me in on your secret, he says, and now I'll tell you one.

She looks at him with tear-hung lashes. He tells her he was hit by a Prussian bullet. But the French officers who found him thought he was a spy. They questioned him for hours and hours before transporting him to the hospital.

She flinches and nods, as if both frightened and comprehending.

He watches her expression. It isn't true, what he just told her, but she stopped crying, and he briefly swells with pride at reassuring her. Her chestnut hair looks lighter, he thinks, almost golden red in the sunlight. Then he recalls the truth of what happened, which is so humiliating, he'd never admit it to anyone.

The truth is he got hungry one night. The others in the camp were asleep, and he wandered alone into the woods, hunting for a rabbit or a squirrel. His empty stomach drove his legs underneath him. Such an idiot to walk so far from the other men, he thinks now. He didn't know how far he hiked away from camp, driven by how good the rabbit would taste roasted over a small fire, so much better than the horrible mixture of sawdust added to the bread dough or the days with nothing. Surely he'd see a small jackrabbit just around the next turn. As he crossed into a small valley, he stumbled and fell. A shot rang out in the night air. His leg felt as if he stepped into a trap, the jaws of it clamped around his calf, ripping off the lower part of his leg. His fall had fired his gun and the bullet drove through his knee. No one found him for nearly two days.

Are you a spy? she asks, peering up at him.

What do you think?

She touches him lightly on the elbow. No, she says, laughing anxiously. No, of course not.

And she is convinced, for the most part, but why did he hesitate revealing his name? And Edmond's voice haunts her; he has always watched out for her. She feels a small part of herself receding, pulling back from the man beside her, watching him, though she wants to trust him, wants to trust and believe in the goodness of everyone—it is what she's been taught by the nuns. But some people fall too far from the goodness, she knows this, too. This man, though he is not Prussian, he has such a gloomy nature, his edges dark and mysterious, his disposition solemn and guarded. She wants to tell him he should only think about the highest, brightest, and most noble of things. He should feel blessed that he is alive.

He points to a park bench and says he needs to rest.

They sit and she watches a group of soldiers practice formations, and alongside, children imitate them, armed with broomsticks and mops. She turns to him. He looks down at his empty pant leg folded against the park bench.

Tell me what happened, she says. These French officers. What did they think you'd done?

He says nothing for a while. I can't remember all the things they asked. But when they finished, they threw me on a stretcher, dumped me in a cart with a bunch of other injured soldiers, and hauled me back to Paris. By then, I'd lost so much blood, I was delirious. He hesitates only a moment, then nods, marveling at his ability to lie.

I'm so sorry, Jorgen.

She reaches for his arm and he slides out of her grasp, walking. She sidles up to him. A horrible idea, she thinks, to ask him to do anything for her. Everything she says and does is wrong; he doesn't enjoy her company, and look at his long, solemn face.

They arrive at an empty lot. Along the back fence, soldiers have painted targets for shooting practice. Not far away, there is an open-air restaurant with the tricolor flags tied to the trees. Men and women are eating at small tables with white tablecloths. The smell of roasted chicken fills the air. A woman laughs, the shrillness quivers in the air, along with the clink of a wine glass, a fork against a plate. Cannon and gunfire periodically rupture the idyllic scene.

He sets up a target for her, a piece of plywood, and carefully draws a big black circle in the center with a piece of charred wood.

Perhaps this isn't a good idea, she says, her voice soft.

Why? he asks.

She bites her lower lip.

Let me show you how to insert the cartridge, he says. He opens the top chamber of the rifle, inserts the metal cartridge, and pushes the bolt forward then over to the right. He hands the gun to her. She hesitates.

I wouldn't have offered if I didn't want to teach you, he says.

She looks at him, then takes the gun.

He tells her to let it rest on her shoulder. Feel the weight of it.

The gun glues onto her shoulder and it rises and falls with her breathing.

The gun is moving too much. He feels her excitement and remembers when his father first taught him how to shoot when he was a young boy, out in the snowy woods hunting deer, how a fierce current ran through his body, and he could barely keep his hands from shaking; he was so thrilled. His father, usually so disappointed with him, calling him weak spirited, disowning him, You are no son of mine, but not this time, with a rifle in his small hands, his father looked on proudly and claimed him as his own. When the first flash of a deer bolted by, he missed, and he missed again. He had to kill a deer. Had to. The third time he missed, he heard his father swear. When he finally hit one, he didn't let his father see the tears as he ran over to the deer, placed a hand on the warm animal's dull fur, and saw its big glassy eyes filled with fear, looking right at him.

He takes the gun and rests it on his shoulder. See?

He hands her the gun. She puts it on her shoulder.

Better, he says.

He tells her to gently place her second finger on the silver cock and her thumb on the trigger. When her body is relaxed, and only then, pull the trigger.

She does as he says, firing the gun, hitting the dead center of the circle.

She looks at him, her eyes wide, her face flushed with awe and fright. She wants to hug him, tell him he is so patient; she's surprised to discover he's such a good teacher. The Parisians at the restaurant stand and clap and shout and raise their wine glasses in the air. She turns to the crowd and bows.

She will save Paris! someone yells. Long live our French women.

Well, it won't be the National Guard.

Everyone laughs.

She turns to him with a big grin.

Good, he says, a hint of a smile.

He has her try it again. And again. Then faster. From the gun by her side, the gun on the ground, in a bag, slung across her shoulder. Clumsy at first, as the hour progresses, she picks up speed, and she has patience, something he never had. And her strength, he underestimated it. He knew women could be unflinching and brimming with resolve, but he thought it was only about women things, about marrying a certain man or purchasing a particular fabric for a new dress. Never about doing a man's job or fighting in a war.

At the end of the hour, she thrusts the gun toward him.

Your turn.

He shakes his head. My balance is off, he says. His good leg is trembling. He needs to sit down.

I'll help, she says. I'll hold on to your arm. She is giddy with her quick advancement, and how much he seemed to take to this endeavor; it is the first time she has seen him care about anything.

Not now.

Come on.

He pushes her hand away. Can't you see? They chopped off my fucking leg.

WALKING BACK TO PIERRE's boardinghouse, neither one says anything for a while. Finally, she says, In the hospital, you called out a name in your sleep.

He looks straight ahead.

You said the name Agneta. Who is that?

I don't know.

Natalia is quiet, waiting for more, but the silence drags on. His leg throbs and now he can't look at her. He turns to the park instead, to the stumps of trees and the scavengers, who have stretched canvases and sheets over branches, impromptu rickety shelters. A gang of children run by barefoot, wearing ragged, dirty clothes.

Around the corner is the boardinghouse. He is suddenly adept on his crutches, moving as fast as she normally walks, eager to get home.

THE NUMBERS SKITTER AROUND the page. Her name, Natalia said her name. He feels her presence in the stale air of the office; how did she find him here, thousands of miles away; she followed him here, and now her small hand is pressing down, making it difficult to breathe. He rises from his desk and shuffles down the hallway to his bare room, nearly collapsing onto the cot, as if he forgot how to stand.

NATALIA PULLS OPEN THE heavy, wooden door of the old church and steps inside. She stands still, as she usually does, savoring the interlude between the busy street and the quiet of the church. She closes her eyes, leaving behind the pushing and selling, feeling something inside stretch out, like a taut ribbon.

Footsteps echo in the high-ceilinged church, and when she opens her eyes, she breathes in the candles, incense, safety, and silence. And then it happens. Her best self steps out of its shell, and it is shining and luminous; though it's always there, tucked behind her other self—the one that thinks so many critical thoughts about her brother, her neighbors, the world—here her highest self unfurls and subsumes everything else. It is a perfect moment.

She bows her head and enters the womb of the church. A few people sit singularly on benches, their heads bowed, hands clasped tightly, some desperately, in prayer. There's a gathering of old men in worn overcoats holding prayer books. People look beautiful in that pose, she thinks. Humble in the face of God.

She walks down the tiled aisle and slips onto a polished wooden bench. An old man tilts his head her way, discreetly, his white hair a puff of cotton. He smiles, his eyes watery and yellow. Kneeling on the oak plank, she bows and prays to God and Christ hanging on the crucifix at the front of the church. She knows she is glowing right now; the old man glances at her again. He must see it, she thinks, the luminosity, her best self, the one united with God.

With the ringing of the gun settling to the bottom of her brain, she calls up those in need of a prayer. What will become of that poor woman on the street corner selling herself for one franc? And the old women shuffling around the park looking for firewood? She prays for them, Our Father and Hail Mary, prays for their souls. For Edmond, who is doing so well, for Jorgen, who is so much more generous than she originally thought — Forgive my earlier stinginess. And after a while those thoughts drift away, and so do her worries about Jorgen and Edmond, her precious brother.

She prays with such concentration and pleads with Mary and Jesus and her patron saint, Saint Natalia, beheaded for openly practicing Christianity, and also her favorite, Saint Joan of Arc; her fear and excitement from this morning augment the fervor of her prayer. I must serve, she prays, I must fight for France. She has waited for a true purpose all her life, and here it is, so she must rise, rise up with her best self and fight.

Please give me a sign, she whispers. A sign that I will be chosen.

The bench creaks, the old man slowly rises and walks down the aisle. The light streams in through the stained-glass window, fracturing into red, purple, and yellow. The purple falls on her hands and she almost gasps. Purple, the color for penitence and mourning, she thinks, and also for royalty. A way to cleanse my sins and also to be my highest self. Here, this light, now caressing both her hands. She looks to the front of the church, to Jesus hanging from the cross, and bows her head in gratitude.

As if the world knew what just happened to her, a young infantryman walks to the melodeon organ and begins to play *Immaculata Reprisa Suprisa*. When she comes back from the war, they will honor her by playing that song. She sees herself standing at the front of the church, the priest telling the audience of her bravery. His voice booms out, She put herself in front of the devil in order to save us all. No, it won't be like that. It will be Edmond standing beside her in front of the congregation. Edmond, fully recovered, will join her in the war, and they will return together, victorious. The congregation lines up in the aisle and slowly makes it way up toward them. She bows her head and they kiss her cheek or pat her hand. Thank you, they whisper, some of them crying, pushing gifts into her arms, sweetbreads and bottles of wine, pictures of the crucifix, and handwoven cloth. Thank you.

I did it to serve God, she says.

She raises her hands. The congregation quiets. She wants to say something, but she must put this delicately. She has always felt there was something special about herself. For years, I sensed there was something else for me on this earth, something extraordinary, other than the normal duties of a woman, of becoming a wife, of bearing children. She says this, her head slightly tipped in humility, and tells them her role in the war was God's design and she carried out His will. The priest stands by, his arms crossed in front of his corpulent frame, and Edmond, too, looks on and admires this reception; the choir sings a glorious, uplifting song, the music pours over everyone, and something opens for her at that moment. A sense of walking through to another plane. She has known something exists parallel to the earthly world. She's read about it, the place beyond the body, and prays she will someday step into it. It is heavenly. There are no needs, no desires; it is a unified state where there is a beauty that could only be called sublime. Sometimes when she prays hard, as she's doing now, she can feel this other world crackling.

SMOKE SATURATES THE LATE afternoon sky, seeps into his room, and rouses him. Jorgen's first thought, The Prussians have invaded Paris and they are burning it down. Grabbing his crutches, he hops over to the window, and there, across the road in the park, it is not the Prussians, but a huge bonfire, with Parisians tossing into the flames couch cushions, shutters, legs from tables and chairs, and cloth lampshades.

What does France have to be proud of now? he thinks, watching the blaze and the people with their warmed red faces, the ashes twisting and blustering in the air like a swarm of black insects. He jerks open the window and cold air rushes in. The first cold of early autumn. A man tosses in a carved rocking chair; a woman pulls her red scarf tighter around her neck. An old woman drags something heavy—what is it?—a painting, a large one that once must have filled an entire wall. One corner of the painting trips along the ground.

They help her heave it onto the fire, and the small gathering shouts its approval. It is a picture of a curvy naked woman with long brown hair reclining on a sofa. The flames tear through the canvas and devour the image. The burning paint sends colorful flames, blue and purple and green scalding the air.

Downstairs, the front door opens and closes. The bell rings out, and Pierre calls up to Jorgen that he has a visitor.

Jorgen hobbles down the hallway and stands at the top of the stairs, and there is Svensk, a friend from home. He's leaning against the baluster, a big grin on his face, his hands shoved in his pockets, his fair hair longer; he is bouncing from foot to foot. Now he is bounding up the stairs, his expression buoyant, but halfway up, Svensk's upturned lips fall and his step slows. He stops and looks down at Jorgen's empty pant leg.

Natalia, says Svensk. I met her and she told me you were here.

Jorgen grips the top of the stairwell, shaky from Svensk's intense scrutiny of his missing leg. Svensk walks the rest of the way up the stairs, the liveliness emptied from his step. Jorgen leans forward and clouts him on the back, a gesture from a former time. Pierre is at the bottom of the stairs scowling, and Jorgen turns, leading his visitor down the hallway and outside, onto the back balcony. They stand awkwardly.

What happened? asks Svensk.

Jorgen steps over to the railing and looks out to the backyard. Svensk follows him.

Jesus, she didn't tell me nothing, says Svensk.

Jorgen barely hesitates, telling him the same lies he told Natalia, and as he speaks, Svensk looks down at his hands with false absorption.

Goddamn the French, says Svensk. You? A spy? Makes me damn angry they did this to you. Svensk clenches his hands into fists. Makes me want to get them back.

Jorgen feels slightly dizzy. Next to Svensk, his body is ancient flesh. Svensk goes on and on, how they should come up with some plan to get them back, those French, and as he talks, his eyes dart back and forth, down to Jorgen's ghost leg, back up to Jorgen's face.

It's not contagious, says Jorgen.

Svensk blushes and stammers.

Jorgen motions to the bench. He asks Svensk how he met Natalia. Svensk says he was watching the women train the other day—A damn funny sight, if you ask me—and he's about to say more but stops.

You know about that, right?

Jorgen tells him yes, and if he didn't, he'd know about it now. Svensk smiles sheepishly.

Never could keep quiet about anything, says Jorgen.

Svensk's smile widens and he sits up straighter, as if vitality has found its way into his body again. She heard me speak Danish, he says, so she comes up to me and asks if I know a man named Jorgen. I said I sure did. And so, that's how I come to be here now. Funny, isn't it?

Jorgen watches Svensk settle into his skin again, his complexion rosy and his hair a blond halo around his head, though he is no angel. They used to go to the pub in Copenhagen, leaving only when the place closed. Women loved Svensk, his soft curly pale hair and dark eyes, and he loved them back, indiscriminately. Svensk pats him on the back and tells Jorgen it's sure good to see him. Jorgen forces a smile.

Remember the fish? Svensk holds his hands up. Never thought I'd get rid of that goddamn smell.

They worked together at a fishery, and at the end of the day, they'd head to Neil's Pub on the corner of Gothersgade and Oster Sogade and drink and play cards. The floor was sticky from spilled beer, and an old coal stove warmed the place during the cold winters.

Have you been to the Parisian cafés? The women. Geez. They come right up to you. Sit right in your lap.

How about a drink? asks Jorgen.

Sure.

Jorgen pushes himself up from the bench, clutches his crutches, and sees Svensk wince. As he heads toward his room, he feels irritable, not wanting to reminisce, to walk through the stinking old hallways of his life. He steps into his room and nervously glances around, seeing it with fresh eyes, with Svensk's eyes, who looked at him with pity when he saw his leg missing, could not stop staring at him, as if he were a monster. The room is a goddamn cell. No bigger than that, and his unmade bed, dust everywhere, nothing on the walls, a balled-up pile of dirty clothes, his rifle propped up in the corner. He opens the closet door, pulls out a bottle of wine, finds a corkscrew and two glasses. He steps outside, hands Svensk a glass, and tells him he's got to get back to work soon.

Svensk says he met Pierre downstairs. Looks like a real son of a bitch. That pointy nose and those beady little eyes. Svensk tells him he came to Paris to join the war; there was nothing but farmwork—milking dairy cows or plowing cornfields—and he was sick of that. And he wasn't about to go back to that fucking fishery.

Thought I'd join the war, he says, but I met a real good-looking woman and she had some money. She paid for damn near everything, rent, food. She even bought me three new shirts. A good deal, until she kicked me out, but I keep finding women at these fancy French parties. Rich women. You should come with me.

Jorgen nods.

Svensk struts one of his furtive, charming smiles. I didn't even know you were here, says Svensk. You just disappeared. One day you were in Copenhagen. At the university, right? The next, vanished. Even your mother, she didn't know nothing about where you went off to. Just up and gone, that's what you did. Did you rob a bank or something? Svensk drinks deeply and smiles, not waiting for an answer. Best thing I did was leave Denmark. You wouldn't know a war is going on in some parts of this town. You should come with me. These parties, he says, shaking his head, as if he can't believe what he's done and seen. What do they call them? Soirees? Lot of rich people who get together and eat and get drunk and sleep together.

Jorgen drinks his wine. You said there's a lot of rich people?

Sure. You should see the gowns and jewelry on these women. And the food. Some of the best wine I've ever had. I'll bring you to the next one. You'll see.

All right.

They sit for a while, and Svensk shifts uncomfortably. Jorgen watches the trees sway and bend in the wind. Pierre has kept a big backyard with squat bushes lining the periphery. Two trees are still standing, though the lower branches have been chopped off for firewood.

Whatever happened between you and that girl? asks Svensk. He leans forward and places an elbow on his knee.

Jorgen sits motionless for a moment. Which one?

Which one, he echoes, laughing. You know. The one. The one you swore me to secrecy. The beautiful one. Young, if I remember right. Real young.

Jorgen sits still.

She was a real beauty.

Jorgen gathers into himself and barely breathes. Oh. She wanted too much. Jorgen does not move.

Oh, says Svensk.

Jorgen says he should get back to work. Pierre, he says, gesturing toward the house.

Svensk tips his head back and finishes his wine. Jorgen rises and walks him down the hallway to the staircase. Svensk leans his weight onto the railing and turns to go. Jorgen feels words catch in his throat. He looks briefly at Svensk then down to the bottom of the staircase to the darkly lit foyer.

What happened to her? Jorgen asks, feigning casual interest.

Who?

That girl.

Svensk shrugs and lets a light smile glide over his lips. I think she might have married. I'm not sure.

Jorgen grips the banister to steady himself. She married? Who?

Not sure. No, wait. I think maybe that old minister in town. That old guy with the wart on his cheek and the white spittle at the sides of his lips. She got pregnant. That was the scandal of the town. Her parents threw her out and the minister let her stay in that small cottage behind the church. I think he ended up marrying her.

Svensk slaps him on the back. We'll go to one of those fancy parties. You'll see what I mean about the women. He turns and leaps down the stairs.

Jorgen limps to his room, unlocks the closet door, and lifts the blanket from the bag. There, the stolen canned food, a string of pearls, a block of hard cheddar cheese. He picks up a carved belt buckle made from the tusk of a walrus and runs his finger over the intricate carving: an emaciated man scooping water from a river with clawlike hands. Such detailed work, he thinks. Such precision. He holds it up to the light. The sunlight turns it golden. That gold, the gold of her hair.

You said the name Agneta. Who is that?

Agneta, Agneta, Agneta, he says.

He smells her honeysuckle scent. Afterward the residue of flowers all over him. He sets the carved buckle down in the box and looks at the dusty corner of the room. Don't think about her; not going to think about her; and he covers the box with the blanket and locks the closet door. But she's found him and now he must leave Paris. Who can he sell his stolen goods to? Maybe these rich people at these parties.

He steps over to the bed and pulls out the painting. The sunlight brightens the colors, it hurts his eyes, and the woman, she is more brilliant now in her vivid clothing, her black hair, silk gloss. He puts his hands up to his face and weeps. He feels the young girl from Denmark, Agneta, says her name in a room where he thought she'd never find him, where he thought he'd escaped, traveled far enough that those lithe arms would never again wrap around his neck, her lips never find his, her bright green eyes never stare into his, never, never, because that life, he didn't want that life. He pushes the painting underneath the bed, snatches up his crutches, and walks down the hallway to the dark office, hunting for order and routine.

JAPAN

MORNING, MORNING, SAYS SATO, his voice staccato as he charges into the eating area. What shall we do today? Ayoshi taps her fingertips on the windowpane impatiently. She is not going to plan his day for him, not going to entertain him. Nor is there any desire, absolutely none, to argue with him. Always bringing up her husband. Why must he harp on something he knows nothing about? He's never married, nor will he, and look at him, chewing on his fingernails.

Sato plops himself at the table and covers his face with his hands. The smell of opium drifts across to Ayoshi. He spreads his fingers and grins at her through the spaces. Well, he says.

She sits at the table and hands him some paper. Make something, she says, swallowing her annoyance. She folds a piece of paper in half. Sato watches her run the side of her hand along the paper. She glances up. Don't you know how to make anything at all?

No. He tosses the paper at her. You're the artist, he says, standing and pacing around the room, and I'm the merchant. Even with the feudal walls crumbling, you will most likely remain who you are. You've shown a certain stubborn affection for it so far.

As have you, she says. If her husband stays too long in the studio, she will go into their bedroom and paint. She will close the door and push a stone against it.

He slides next to her at the table, flattens both palms on the tabletop, and places his face a foot away from hers. Certainly you don't intend to stay locked up in that damn studio today. It's not good for your health.

She sets her paper down and sighs. There are herbs and teas that could help you, she says. They remove the longing for opium.

Does it work for past loves?

She returns to her creased paper, thinking she despises him right now.

He picks up a piece of paper, crumples it into a ball, and bats it in the air. His wild, frenetic energy lashes like flash lightning in a summer storm. His volatility frightens and excites her, as if that lightning might sear through her life, burning a hole, letting in an entirely new life. What would it look like, this new life? What would she like it to be? She closes her eyes to imagine.

He pinches her arm. Am I putting you to sleep?

She snaps open her eyes and glares at him. Why do you do it? she asks. It can't be good for you.

His face lights up into a broad smile and he thrusts his hands in front of him, waving them as he talks. Think of your most pleasurable moment. Think of it extended through time, perhaps eight, ten hours. Perhaps longer.

She sets down her half-formed lantern. Your life doesn't give you that?

He drops his arms to his side. Does yours? He looks at Ayoshi, her small, bony, birdlike frame. Those eyes, he thinks. Dark tunnels that burrow down to a damaged heart.

Your husband wants to take you on a vacation, he says.

She sits motionless for a moment.

He told me so, but he said you wouldn't go.

Strange.

Why?

He's never asked.

Gazing out the window, he imagines Hayashi hobbling up that hill alone,

as he did the other morning, and that nearly impermeable aloneness that surrounds him like thick, gray smoke. And Ayoshi. Look at her now with her little colored squares of paper, quietly tucking herself away.

What did you do with that painting? he asks.

She twists in her seat. The paper falls from her hands. What?

The painting. The one with you and your lover.

Her mind seizes. She fixes on a small drop of soy sauce staining the table.
He saw it? How did he see it? No one sees those paintings. She wraps them
around her husband's bowls, shuttles them onto a ship, and with that sends
them out of her mind. They are scattered around the world. A stranger may
see them, but that's different. What did Sato see? Yes, of course, he was in
the Western room with her. His body contains the image, tucked inside, next
to who knows what else. How could she have been so careless?

You look worried, he says. Your secret is safe with me.

We need to go to town today, she says, her voice forcefully measured. Perhaps there is fresh yellowtail.

I still see the woman floating in the river, he says, standing. Is she drowning? I think she's drowning.

She sits there stonily.

Or maybe she's stuck in the river and can't get out. Sato jumps onto the
edge of the counter, his legs swinging. But she doesn't want to get out, does
she? She wants to soak in that river and stay floating, unable to move, unable
to do anything else with her life. Only dream. Dream a perfect life, a perfect
love, while her real life, the life happening now, is rushing by her.

With a trembling hand, she tries to balance the finished paper lantern on
the table. It falls and falls again.

He comes straight at her. I am one of your oldest friends, he says. I am de-
voted to you, to your happiness. Why are you making yourself miserable? Do
you really think he's coming for you? Let me tell you, he's not coming. It's
been over a year, isn't that right? He's not coming.

She holds her face still. He is relentless and cold, she thinks, blaming her
for everything, her life, the way it has turned out. She picks up a chopstick
and stabs at her hand, watching the small pricks turn red and then fade. What

do you know about it? she says. What do you know? Why won't he leave her alone? Her eyes turn teary and she stabs her hand harder.

I've something for you, he says, his voice soft and urgent.

I don't want anything from you, she says.

Please, he says, gently taking the chopstick from her hand. I have a gift for you.

You're here to make my life miserable, that's all you're doing. Bullying and badgering me.

No, he says. No. It's not true. Is it true? Oh, no. Please, then, let me make it up to you. Come and let me give you my gift.

After more coaxing, she reluctantly relents. They walk to the Western room. He pulls from one of his bags tubes of paints. She twists off the top and spreads a little blue on her finger.

So bright, she says, mesmerized.

He tells her they come from Europe. Aniline dye.

I must paint now. I don't care what you say.

And I'll sit here and dream alongside you, he says.

She pulls out a sheet of paper and her brushes. He sits in a chair over by the window where he can see the garden. She dabs small spots of the new paint onto a palette.

They are vibrating, she says.

And so am I, he says.

The haze from this morning is lifting. Already she is leaving this drab, ordinary existence behind, feeling the strong pulp of a beginning. The white paper, the first dot of new paint. She whirls off the couch, away from the humming Sato, let him say anything now, she doesn't care. She is traveling to her heartbeat, falling into his image.

SHE WAITED FOR HIM underneath the red arch of the Shinto shrine dedicated to the god for traveling. A hundred or more pairs of geta and wooden shoes lay scattered on the ground, flung up into the tree branches, past offerings for a safe trip. The sun flared and a charge rang through the air, as if the world tilted, poised for something tremendous to happen.

When he arrived, his eyes were bright. He said he had a surprise. Today they would walk beyond the river and into the nearby nesting fields. At that moment, they heard a high-pitched sound and saw a V of whooper swans flying overhead.

Her brush stops.

Ayoshi searches the Western room. Is that the way it happened? Or did they see the swans on another day? She said, Look! White ribbons tossed up against the blue sky — was that what she said? Her paintbrush hovers in the air. There was something in the sky, wasn't there? A configuration of the white, puffy clouds? Or maybe the branches of the pine tree, their curves and sculpted shapes? She pointed out shapes to him, or did he show them to her?

A blob of paint falls from her brush and splatters the painting, destroying his kimono and the bottom of his face. What happened on that day? Panic surges through her, tightening her shoulders. Her brush sways precariously and another drop of paint drips on his figure, turning the bright colors garish and harsh. She can't remember. What else can't she remember about him? She sets down her brush and crunches her painting into a ball.

Sato looks up from his pipe.

He's scattering her memories, she thinks, smearing them into a dirty mess. That odious smoke from his pipe. She tentatively unfolds the crinkled painting. The drop of paint has spread, smearing her lover's face. Shade and dark edges, she thinks. What was the texture of his skin? The exact color of his eyes? She rips the painting into pieces, and when she is done, her hands are shaking, her breathing thin and rapid. Above Sato is that horrible painting. That mother holding her infant, that loving, soft look on the mother's face, her gaze only for the baby. And the baby looking at the mother, the soft, pink cheeks and red ribbon lips, a penetrating look, as if they could never be separated, as if they are the same person, as if the mother will grow old and watch the baby become a child, a young girl, a woman. As if the baby will never die.

She stands abruptly and runs down the hallway, wavering and jagged. Without thinking, she heads to the temple. She steps inside. What is she doing here? She grabs a cushion and sits on the floor. For a long time, she stares at the weave of the tatami. The quiet bears down on her. Sato is not to blame, she thinks. It is she, her shortcomings, her failings; she has not been diligent with her painting, her way of visiting him. She has been disloyal to him, and he senses it, he is slipping away. She sits and takes a handful of hair, rubs it against her lips, feeling its smoothness, trying to calm herself.

Sato strolls into the room.

When she doesn't say anything, he sits beside her. When is the last time you saw this man? he asks.

Her face darkens and she drops her head. Why hasn't he ever come for her? she thinks. Is something wrong with her? What is wrong with her?

Ayoshi?

And when she tells Sato, she almost gasps. Two years.

You've never told me his name.

She is silent for a long time, staring at a bag of rice. The sound, two years, beating like a heavy heart.

Urashi. His name is Urashi. She's about to say more. Her stomach tightens, something grips her throat. She feels dazed, falling.

Sato retrieves a bottle of sake from the pile of offerings, along with two sake glasses. He pours the sake. We can put this to better use, he says.

She drinks it all, pours herself another. They sit this way for a while, feeling the burn of the rice wine on their throats. She looks at all the twirling dust in the air. There, the circular flow of this dust, she thinks. Round and round, rising to the ceiling and coming back down. There is her hand. She knows the dust is there, on her palm, but why can't she feel it?

Perhaps it will all work out, he says, his tone tender.

I was going to have a baby, she says. But my father—

He watches her face. It looks like putty and her mouth is doing something strange. She bites her lip as if to hold it still.

Urashi's.

He touches her shoulder.

She lowers her lids. I wanted to keep. The child. I wanted. The child. To marry Urashi. Did I tell you he is Ainu?

Sato feels his face drain of color. Who would marry her after such an af-

fair? he wonders. An Ainu, an untouchable. Her father must have been en-
raged. Such shame to the family, such dishonor to their name. Sato smiles
gently.

She watches another swirl of dust.

What happened to the child? asks Sato.

She knots her hands tightly and sets them in her lap. After a long while,
she tells him. It died.

He takes her in his arms and she leans her face onto his shoulder. He feels
her relinquishing, her body softening, surrendering. He rocks her, gently
kisses the top of her head. He puts his hand on her head and strokes her hair.
Rocks her in his jittery arms.

HAYASHI FINISHES HIS BOWL. It's the same design he's sculpted for
the past seven years. Inert, he thinks, stagnant. But he doesn't know what else
to make.

He quickly washes his hands and steps outside. The clouds are stringy and
the air is cold. The long grass bends and the branches scratch the bluing sky.
He didn't sleep well last night, anxious about having that man, Sato, in the
house. What does he want? Shouldn't he be on his way? He looks toward the
big house. They're probably in there, their heads bowed, laughing and talking over breakfast. She seems so at ease with him. Maybe they're making their
plans for the day, or inventing a silly game. He's about to walk to the house,
but stops. What will he say to them? They'll look at him, expecting something from him—what does he have to give them? He feels a sudden unend-
ing emptiness.

He turns to the studio, but the thought of the bowl repulses him. How
long he stands there, he does not know. The clouds whirl by, the birds, the
wind, he stands rigid, as if frozen. Gradually, he becomes aware of someone
staggering toward him. A figure clad in the familiar brown robe, the thick
twine around the waist. A monk, walking slowly, his legs hesitating before
each step, as if weighing whether to keep going.

Hayashi rushes toward him and bows deeply. When he looks into the
young man's face, he is shocked by his beauty. Despite the look of despair and

exhaustion, there is a deep glow to his smooth skin. Small black stubble sprouts on his cheeks and once-shaved head, and there is dried spittle at the corners of his mouth. His robe is matted with dirt. But beneath the layer of dirt and weariness, the monk's body seems muscular and powerful and full of a certain dignity. Hayashi bows lower, and as he rises, he decides the monk looks like a Western sculpture of a god made of rose marble.

I heard of you, says the monk.

The monk wobbles and nearly falls into Hayashi. He takes the monk by the arm and leads him slowly to the moon-viewing porch. The monk sits and lets his chin drop to his chest. He tells Hayashi he's been walking for three days without food.

I came down from the mountain monastery and got lost, he says.

Hayashi's face turns pale.

I was told to go to you. My teacher knew of you.

The monk folds in half, as if the last of his resources were used up by speech. Hayashi lifts the monk up and, holding onto his arm, helps him to the house. The monk insists on going straight to the temple. To pray, he says.

THE MONK SITS IN front of the Buddha and begins to chant. After a short spell, his throat becomes too dry. He rises to find some water. Exhaustion slows his gait as he shuffles outside, crosses the path to the house, and enters through the side door. He hears pattering in the hallway. A soft, graceful sound, only a whisper. Such a slight human being, he thinks, perhaps a boy, or a frail elderly man. He almost runs into her. She is walking so rapidly, her eyes red and puffy, as if she was crying. But what does he know, he's never seen a woman cry. Perhaps something was in her eye, or she just chopped a bushel of wild green onions.

As she rushes by him, he stammers an apology. When she disappears behind a door, he glances at his arm, certain it is on fire. He returns to the temple, terribly shaken. His teacher did not say Hayashi had married. A wife. He can barely remember his mother, and his sister was only a baby when he left at the age of four. His teacher's words of warning reverberate in his head: Women are distractions, they lead you astray. The young monk clenches his jaw, sits with his legs folded on the floor in the temple, and with more determination, resumes his sutras.

Hayashi cracks open the temple door and watches the monk. For the first time he lets himself feel his fear: It's dangerous to let the monk stay. His fingers nervously twist his earlobe. What will the government officials do? What harm is he inviting? His concerns deepen: What if the monk wants to hold a regular prayer service? The government officials will find out. Maybe the monk won't ask. And if he does? He doesn't want to think about it right now because he's not sure what to do.

How can he turn him away? There is the sound of the monk's low voice slinging off the walls. Water music. He closes his eyes, leans his head against the door frame, letting the water pour over him. How long has it been since he's heard such a full-bodied voice chant the sutras? A pure sound, a beautiful sound the monks recited in the early morning, midday, and in the evening. And now that music is here, as if he never left the monastery.

He'll tell the monk he can't wear his robe, though he wishes otherwise, wishes he could please the monk, not upset him. That's what he'll do. And if the leaders ask, Who is the new member of your household? A houseboy, he'll say. He smiles. Yes, a houseboy. Someone who tends to things, and he'll gesture toward his feet.

As he closes the temple door and walks toward the main house, he sees in his mind the monk's face. The striking beauty, only slightly smudged with a bitter experience, though what it might be, Hayashi can only guess. In the kitchen, he finishes preparing the monk's lunch, chopping up some pickled carrots and beets.

The maid scurries into the kitchen and stands awkwardly beside Hayashi, not sure what to do.

Surprised to find me in the kitchen? says Hayashi, laughing.

Well, yes, sir, she says. Should I take over?

No, no. Please. We have an honored guest. A most honored guest.

Fine, sir, she says. She tells him that Ayoshi and Sato left for town to buy more food and supplies. Ayoshi-san said I should work on your feet.

I feel fine, he says.

She stares at him in disbelief. Are you sure? You've worked all morning in the studio, and I thought—

He laughs again. Go, go, he says. My feet are fine.

She hesitates.

He smiles. Please go.

She nods uncertainly and leaves. There is sharp pain in his left foot, and his toes sting, but he must return to the music, which is still coursing in his body, vibrating his teeth and gums, rattling his thin bones. He carries a tray with a teapot, cups, and a plate of sticky rice balls and pickled vegetables. The monk, on his knees, is bowing before the Buddha, touching his forehead to the mat, over and over.

Hayashi bows low and hands the monk a cup of green tea.

Thank you, says the monk, gesturing for Hayashi to sit with him.

Hayashi lowers himself to the floor.

The monk drinks and traces his hand across the top of his head. He bows his head. I am at your service.

They sit together quietly, and Hayashi waits, putting off the uncomfortable thing he must say. He looks at the Buddha, sees the crack, and hopes the monk doesn't notice it. He must say it. To wait is absurd. He apologizes first, bowing low, then tells the monk he must wear layman's clothes. For your safety, he adds quickly.

Something flickers in the monk's eyes, a moment of stupefaction, and then it passes. Hayashi apologizes again, hanging his head, ashamed and riddled with guilt, as if it is his fault.

I have clothes for you, says Hayashi. I'm sorry, but these are difficult times.

They sit in silence. After a while, the monk turns his dark eyes to Hayashi and begins to tell him his story.

IN THE MIDDLE OF the night, I looked out the window of my hut and saw men in uniforms scurrying everywhere at once, says the monk, a hundred of them or more, running to the main temple, the garden, dashing to the ten-foot statue of Buddha in the garden. The soldiers held guns and axes and they raised a huge ladder and set it against the statue's shoulder. Two men scrambled up the ladder, and with big swings, chopped at the Buddha's neck.

Hayashi remembers the statue.

As the young monk describes watching in horror the large head of the Buddha fall from its great height, the sound of it crashing to the ground, a reverberation that shook his hut, Hayashi feels sick to his stomach. He can see it, as if he's the one standing at the hut's window—he knows exactly which hut gave the best view.

Hayashi stares at the monk and tries to numb himself to this young man's pain, to coax himself out of his reach, but their eyes momentarily meet, and he tumbles again down the dark tunnel of their gaze. He feels a heavy deepening in his own chest cavity. He must do something for this young monk. So much sorrow. Can I get you some water? asks Hayashi, shifting uncomfortably on his cushion.

The monk says nothing, as if in a trance, and then continues.

The soldiers rounded up the monks and marched them into the main room of the temple. The leaders said that under the new government, they were no longer considered monks. They must leave the monastery and find work. Civilian jobs.

I came to the monastery when I was a boy. How could I go? These soldiers were not my teachers. Why would I submit to these people?

Hayashi bites his lower lip. He is not one of these soldiers, he tells himself, but that does not stop hot shame from creeping up his spine. He is part of this new government. He is culpable.

The monks sat in a circle on the temple floor and began to chant. The leaders of these troops screamed to stop, and the soldiers stood around the periphery of the temple, holding their guns and axes by their sides, waiting for their orders. By midafternoon, the soldiers burned the small huts. They torched the ancient scrolls, shattered the porcelain bowls, and smashed the mummified bodies of sages dead hundreds of years. They set aflame the paintings of Buddha, the face of Buddha consumed by flames, and the smoke rose and choked the arch of the roof. That night, some of the monks, exhausted and weak, left the smoky temple and began walking down the mountain.

And those who stayed? asks Hayashi.

The monk swallows and tries to collect his words, but they come out in a rush. The soldiers chopped away at the temple and the walls crashed down. They died. Those who stayed died.

Hayashi feels his heart sag. The monk doesn't say anything for a long while.

I left because my teacher told me to, says the monk. I didn't want to, but he insisted. I had to obey my teacher. I had to go.

For a second, Hayashi's eyes meet the monk's, but the monk quickly looks away. Of course, says Hayashi. Of course, his voice softer.

Light drifts in and shines on the Buddha, but neither of them sees it, their heavy gaze fallen to the woven reed mats. Hayashi lifts the teapot, but his hand is shaking so badly, he sets it down again.

WHAT IS HE DOING now? asks Hayashi.

Still sitting, says Ayoshi, who is standing at the window, watching the monk who is meditating on the moon-viewing deck. He's wearing one of Hayashi's best kimonos. She presses her hand to the wall to steady herself. Like viewing a painting, she thinks. Look at how still he sits. There is a disturbing beauty to his composure, his self-restraint, the symmetry of his face. And her husband is smitten with the monk. The way he rushed to her when she came back from town, telling her to be quiet, to close the doors softly, not to run the water for a bath. They had a very auspicious guest staying with them who needs quiet and serenity.

But it's getting dark, says Hayashi, half rising, as if he planned to bring the monk inside. He'll catch a chill. He cranes his neck to try to glimpse the monk.

How long is he going to stay? asks Ayoshi.

I don't know.

She sits at the table across from him and frowns. What did he tell you?

He didn't. But he'll stay as long as he wants.

They are finishing dinner. Sato remained in town to tend to some business.

She shakes her head. Isn't it dangerous for him to stay here? she asks. What if the government finds out? What will they do to us?

I've already thought about this. Hayashi tells her his plan.

A helper? she asks, her voice incredulous. For what? What is he going to do here?

I'll make him some tea, says Hayashi, rising. He'll probably be cold when he finishes.

I don't think it's safe for him to stay.

He's halfway to the kitchen, but stops. Why are you so worried about this?

Why aren't you?

He shifts uncomfortably on his feet, as if new pain uncoiled itself.

I can do that, says Ayoshi. You rest.

Hayashi comes back to the table and sits. Ayoshi steps into the kitchen and puts the tea kettle on the fire. When she returns, she walks over to the window in the hallway and looks again at the monk's still form.

What is he doing now?

Still sitting.

I've met men like our young monk, says Hayashi. They enter the monastery at a very young age. They're like children in many ways, marveling at things we walk by without even noticing. They are acutely aware. A monk once sat with me for hours, showing me the sky, the different shades of lavender, silver, and five hundred variations of blue.

Hayashi joins her by the window.

They're very innocent in their ways, he says. Trusting. It is an endearing quality.

Maybe that's what she senses about him, she thinks. His curiosity, his open body exploring earnestly. Not a calm energy, as she expected. All his senses seem to be vibrating, alive, searching. No, not searching. Hunting. An electrical energy in the way he moves.

But our visitor will probably feel awkward around you, says Hayashi, speaking to her reflection in the window.

Why?

There are no women at the monastery, and unless his mother or sisters visited, he won't know the ways of a woman.

How strange.

Don't be surprised if he is uncomfortable with you. If he needs anything, it's probably best for him to call me.

Why did he come here? asks Ayoshi.

He tells her the monk comes from the same monastery where he once lived. The same place where I spent most of my life, he says. His face clouds over and now he must rest. He'll be in the Western room reading. Ayoshi feels him brush behind her and then he is gone. She sits in the eating room for a while longer, staring at her steaming tea, waiting for their new guest to come inside. There are things I need to get done, she thinks. I could be in the studio now. What is that man doing out there in the dark? This is absurd. He wants to make her wait, to test her in some way, though she knows this can't be true. She walks over to the window. He's standing now, stretching, and walking to the house. When he comes inside, he bows low and apologizes for causing any inconvenience.

You are our guest, she says. Excuse me, your dinner is ready.

He blushes. I'd like to speak with Hayashi. I have a favor to ask. He keeps ducking his head slightly to avoid her eyes.

I'm so sorry. My husband is unavailable.

He shifts from foot to foot. They stand there for a moment, neither one speaking. Finally he tells her, if she'd let him, he'd like to set up a small shrine in the garden. From the monastery gardens, he brought a small wooden statue.

How long are you intending to stay? she asks, and the instant after she speaks, she feels a tremor of embarrassment at her brusqueness.

He looks at the ground and fumbles with the edge of his sleeve. I'm so sorry. I won't be a bother to you, he says. I'll leave as soon as I can.

I didn't mean—

While I am here, I'll pay for my room and board with my services.

She studies his reddening face. He is so uncomfortable. She steps into the kitchen, finds a lantern, and they walk together out to the porch. There, a two-foot wooden figure, a statue of a bodhisattva in flowing robes, the hands clasped in prayer. The form is cracked and weathered, a relic from another time. The expression on the statue's face, almost like the monk's at that mo-

ment, a beautiful serenity, and a vitality and smugness that borders on boy-
ish certitude.

Hayashi steps out on the porch. I thought I heard you.

The monk bows and repeats his request. I'll leave as soon as I know where
I'm going, says the monk.

Please, says Hayashi, waving his hand in front of him, as if casting aside
smoke. We want you to stay as long as you want. Hayashi takes the lantern
from Ayoshi and the monk picks up the statue, cradling it in his arms. The
two men amble into the garden in the night air. Ayoshi is torn between stepping inside and following them into the garden. She'll stay a moment, she
tells herself, to see which spot he chooses. She walks over to them and hears
Hayashi tell the monk to choose a spot. Anywhere, he says, gesturing with
his arm to the expanse of the garden. And she can barely contain her surprise.
How animated Hayashi has become; and his walk, almost graceful; how can
that be?

The monk wanders around the garden, Hayashi following, as if this decision were the most significant event in a long time. Round and round, the
monk meanders.

Finally he sets the figure underneath the willow tree. Hayashi places the
lantern on the ground. The monk climbs down on his knees and carefully
sculpts a level clearing with his hand.

He is soiling Hayashi's good kimono, thinks Ayoshi, who returns to the
deck, snatches up a straw mat, and marches over to the monk. For a moment
she watches his hands caress the ground.

Please, she says, extending the mat to the monk.

He's fine, says Hayashi, reaching for the mat, but the monk takes it and
places it underneath his knees.

She steps back, and now she really should go inside. The maid is waiting
for her to go over the list of goods needed from town for tomorrow's dinner.
With two guests, they will need more miso soup and white rice. Maybe she
should buy something special, chicken for yakitori.

When she glances over at the monk, she sees he is watching her. His eyes,
big and astonishingly bright. Her cheeks burn. He doesn't look away. She is

the one to avert her gaze. Her heart races. Perhaps, as Hayashi said, he's never seen a woman before. She looks again. He's still staring, enthralled, it seems. How rude to stare like that. So brazen and bold. She has the urge to jump or scream, though she's not sure why. She shivers and hugs herself.

Are you cold? asks Hayashi.

Yes, she says. I should go inside. She walks briskly toward the house. When she steps inside, she sits at the kitchen table, staring at nothing. After a while, she rises and looks out the darkened window; nothing to see, only her reflection staring back. What was he looking at so intently? The front door opens and closes. Sato stumbles into the kitchen, his pupils large, his dark eyes darting.

Sleepy little Japan is waking up. I just sold a merchant in town seven bolts of silk from China.

Have you been drinking?

My new customer and I had some celebratory drinks, it's true.

We have a visitor.

He stops, dropping his jaw. Is he here? Your man from Hokkaido?

No, she says, glaring at him, and don't ever mention him in this house again.

He comes over to her. Maybe if you sit here a little longer, he'll show up.

He's breathing hard, as if he ran from town, up the hill to the house, and his breath smells of liquor. The monk and Hayashi step inside, still talking about the statue.

Well, says Hayashi, staring hard at Sato.

Sato props himself up.

Hayashi introduces Sato to their new guest and smiles, as if he's just produced something he's proud of. The monk bows and Sato stands there, slightly stupefied.

It is an honor to meet any friend of Hayashi's, says the monk.

Sato shifts from foot to foot. Yes, yes. We must drink to that.

Hayashi's face blanches as he watches Sato nearly dance in place. The maid comes out with a steaming hot plate of food for the monk.

Finally, says Hayashi, clapping his hands together.

The monk sits at the table and Sato takes a place across from him. Hayashi positions himself beside his new guest. Ayoshi stands by the doorway to the kitchen, watching the monk wolf down his food.

You have quite the appetite, says Sato.

This food, says the monk.

I'm sorry. It's nothing special, says Ayoshi, feeling alarmed by his ravenous eating. If we'd known you were coming.

You don't understand, Ayoshi, says Hayashi. After years of plain rice and barley soup, almost anything would taste good.

Then he's the perfect guest, says Sato, stepping into the kitchen.

The monk laughs, and Ayoshi is shaken by the charming sound.

Now for a drink, says Sato, raising a bottle. He tells them he bought it in town. Sake from Tateyama. Ayoshi reaches for some of Hayashi's sake cups.

No, get the good ones, says Hayashi.

The black glazed cups with small lines of crackling white. Hayashi explained to her the white lines came out so unique, so different, that these are his best cups, though to her, they all look the same. She pours them each a cup. The monk holds one in front of him, examining it.

I can see why they didn't let you become a monk, he says. The slight hint of imperfection. There at the lip.

You see it? says Hayashi.

It's a very delicate design, says the monk. You've captured the humanity of imperfection in a perfectly designed object.

Remarkable, says her husband. Not many people see the intent behind it.

My teachers taught me to look and see. That is the importance of education, I think. To learn to know where to look to see the truth.

And do you know the truth? asks Sato, pouring himself another glass, his smile slightly lopsided.

Hayashi coughs. The monk shifts uncertainly. It's what I'm searching for. I don't mean to say I know it.

I'll show you my other work sometime, says Hayashi.

I'd like to see it, too, says Sato.

Hayashi nods politely and quickly looks away.

When the monk finishes his tea, he asks if he may go to the temple.

The monk is tired, says Hayashi, placing his hand on the young man's back, gently coaxing him away from Sato, down the hallway toward the temple, where the monk told Hayashi earlier he would like to stay.

After they've left, Sato turns to Ayoshi, raising his eyebrows. Well, he says. An awkward boy, don't you think? What? You look so worried. What is it?

I think it's dangerous to have him here, she says. I told Hayashi that, but he won't hear of the monk leaving.

Your life just keeps getting disrupted, doesn't it?

It's not that. If the government finds out—

He's about to refill her drink, but she slips her hand over her cup. I'm tired, Sato, she says, standing and rubbing her eyes. Ayoshi pads down the hallway, thinking she'll go to the studio to paint, but when she steps outdoors, she walks to the front of the temple. She slowly opens the heavy wooden door, not wanting to disturb his deep meditation. He is there, lying on the floor, curled up in a ball, his head cupped into the cradle of his arms, and she listens to the sound of a man crying. What has happened? she wonders, barely restraining herself from going to him.

THE MONK CONVERTED THE main room of the temple into his home. At night, he unrolls a futon and sleeps in the corner of the room, and before the sun rises, he rolls it up again and tucks it in a closet. He diligently cleans the temple every day, dusting the Buddha, the thick molding around the floor, and the ceiling. After the temple is done, he scrubs the small bathroom located in the remote corner. These are only a few chores he would do if he were still at the monastery. Hayashi told him the temple has never been so spotless. The first time the monk opened the temple door for the villagers, Hayashi rushed over from the house, as if to stop him. The two villagers looked at Hayashi then the monk. Hayashi waited for a while, then returned to the house. This is how it's been, only one or two people. But the prayers are over too quickly and the tasks don't take very long; the monk's never had such long stretches of time, and he wishes he had more work to do. The maid chased him out of the kitchen when he walked in one morning and begin scrubbing the dishes.

In the far gardens now, away from the house, he picks up a fallen leaf and absently studies the orange and red. As he lets it go, watching it fall to the ground, the memories from the mountaintop tumble down on him with sickening vividness. They wanted to die, he thinks. The monks who stayed in the temple calmly waited for death's hand. True monks, loyal and pure, they died gracefully, with no trepidation, with conviction. And what did he do? He clutched to life and began to weep uncontrollably.

Go. The old monk would not look at him. Go.

The young monk sobbed.

Go, his teacher hissed. You are not ready.

There were only five who ran out of the temple. He led the way out the window.

The wind rustles the leaves. He looks up and sees a few green leaves still clinging to the willow tree. He can't escape this horrible thought that he is a fraud, not worthy of wearing the robe. He is only a man, he thinks. Just an ordinary man, afflicted with the same spasms of doubts. And he recalls the time he was sick for a month, how wonderful it was when his teacher excused him from his grueling, monotonous life. He spent hours in bed reading literature and drawing whatever came into view. It was a good thing Hayashi stripped him of his robe. A very good thing. Despite his deference, Hayashi must have sensed it, all his flaws, like imperfections in a poorly crafted weaving.

He must pray more. No dinner because already he finds he loves to eat too much—the sweet bean cakes, anmitsu, and red bean pancakes. And he loves to smell the grass as it relinquishes underfoot. The piney fragrance of a tree branch on his hands after brushing up against it. His teacher said he still wore a veil over his eyes. Now he thinks the elderly monk was right.

But in some strange way, he feels as if only now he's seeing the world; despite all his training to live awake and in the truth, it's as if he's never truly seen a fish, the darting sashays of color, orange, blue, red, and the one with green specks on black. Or tasted the wonderful display of flavors in food. If he could, he'd eat all day.

He walks over to a tall pine tree and lies on his back, staring at the branches swaying in the wind. It's a wonderful motion, he thinks. It's the way that woman walks. Her hips moving, as if a flame were spiraling up her spine. The same swaying swirl to her upper lip.

WHERE IS THE TEAHOUSE? asks the monk.

Hayashi hesitates. They are standing under a gray sky, the thin dull light casting short shadows. There was an accident, he says.

They walk toward the black spot on the ground and stare at it for a long time. Hayashi smells the soot in the air, puffs of it rising from the ground where the old teahouse once stood.

I could build you a new one, says the monk.

If he could have it back, thinks Hayashi, the way it was before, its simple elegance, a place of quiet refuge, perhaps it would be as if the fire never occurred. The whole problem with the officials would go away. And if that faded, perhaps the ring of his sister's call for help might disappear, the echoes, like smoky black circles bouncing inside, and his mother's screams, his father's heavy silence. His feet, the coiled gnarled toes, what if they, too, surrendered their throbbing ache? Carefully he lets himself feel the lightness of hope in his chest.

The monk tells Hayashi he did most of the repair work at the monastery. This job, he could certainly do. As repayment for letting me stay here, he says, thinking how much it will distract him from all the new temptations and pleasures of the valley below the mountain. Please, you must let me do this for you.

Hayashi bows low and tells the monk he will buy all the best materials. If the monk is busy building, he thinks, he's likely to discontinue the prayer services for the villagers. He'll be so focused on the building. Whatever you need, he says.

And now the monk is sure this is why he was sent down the mountain to this wide valley. To build something new, a grand teahouse, something stunning, something that will dazzle Hayashi and his lovely wife.

FRANCE

SHALL I TAKE YOUR bag, sir? asks the butler.

No, says Jorgen, gripping the bag to his side.

You can take my overcoat, says Svensk, handing it to the butler, a tall man with thinning brown hair.

Jorgen and Svensk stand in the front hallway, enclosed in the jingle of voices. A burst of laughter comes from the first room. White marble tile lines the hallway and a huge chandelier scatters fragments of color on the pale yellow walls. There is the distinct smell of meat cooking—chicken or beef, Jorgen isn't sure. Svensk leads the way into the next room, which overflows with elegantly dressed people drinking wine and smoking cigarettes. A cluster of people stand at a large oak table, picking at the plates of food, and two women with bare shoulders are stretched out on a red velvet couch. Lit candles flicker along the mantle and a well-tended fire burns in the fireplace.

Well, well, the Danish man arrives, says Daniel with a flourish.

Svensk laughs and tells Daniel that he is in the company of not one but two Danes. Svensk introduces Jorgen, whose head whirls from the chatter and the overwhelming stench of perfume.

I thought they tossed all the foreigners in prison for spying, says one stout man, clearly drunk, his voice booming.

That tall one is a soldier, my dear man, says a woman with a pink ostrich feather in her hair.

He fought for France, says Svensk. Wounded in the war.

Jorgen gives Svensk a nervous nod, hoping Svensk will make the introductions quickly and get on with the sale. Before leaving for the soiree, Jorgen told Svensk his plan to sell the extra inventory items. Jorgen offered Svensk a percentage, and Svensk laughed with rich delight and readily agreed to make the introductions. But Svensk is coupled already with a woman wearing a revealing black evening gown.

Where have you been hiding? asks one of the women reclining on the couch. She twists her fingers around a long string of pearls that swoop from her neck and stares at Jorgen. Next to her is another woman wearing purple satin.

Sit. Sit, says Daniel.

Jorgen sits in a big stuffed chair in the corner, and a servant hands him a glass of red wine. He sets his bag down so it touches his calf. Five empty bottles of wine crowd the table, along with caviar, bread, trout, green olives, and a platter of smoked oysters. All those boxes in the upstairs room end up here, he thinks, filling these people's rooms and bellies. He is fascinated and disgusted by these people. He puts his hand on his empty pant leg and shifts and twists in the soft chair.

We're lamenting the state of Paris, says Daniel to Jorgen. It's certainly going to fall. Those dastardly Prussians will soon be clamoring over the moat wall.

Poor France, says the woman in purple satin.

They'll be here any minute, says one of the women with impersonal eyes, smiling.

Chennevières escorted shipments of artwork to Brest, said another man, leaning against the fireplace mantle. What would France be without its masterpieces? Prussia may have the thinkers, but we have the great artists and artwork, Degas, Monet, and Manet.

What a shame, says another woman with silver bracelets lining her arms.

The whole country is shamed.

Svensk tilts toward the woman, who tosses her head back, waving her blond hair behind her, laughing at something he's said.

Jorgen studies the man leaning against the mantle. Young enough to have been recruited, he thinks. Who did he pay so he could stand here and eat this rich food and flirt with that woman with bright red lipstick? He decides he detests everyone here, and if he had a choice, he'd head home right now. Jorgen tries to catch Svensk's eye, but he is fondling a gold bracelet on the woman's arm. Jorgen reaches down and fingers the handle of his bag.

Daniel and his friends are discussing the moat around Paris and now the weaponry. A man with a big mustache tells them the Prussian cannons have a range of six hundred to eight hundred meters more than the French cannons. France could have had more power, but the emperor turned down the manufacture of Commandant Potier's cannon. Yes, Potier's cannon would have equalized the war.

A woman yawns and stares at the molded ceiling.

Our soldiers need women, says Daniel. Gorgeous French women.

Everyone laughs. Svensk turns and smiles at Jorgen, who points to the bag. Svensk nods, walks over to Daniel, and whispers in his ear. Jorgen seizes the bag, excuses himself, and shuffles down the hallway to the far end of the house. For a brief flash, he thinks of Edmond. He fought for these people, and now he's on his deathbed. What a waste. He steps into Daniel's study and there, rows and rows of books organized by subject—literature, cooking, religion, art. Jorgen traces his finger along the spines and stops on a Dutchman's journal about the Orient. He pulls out the dark red covered book and splays its yellowed pages. *This is Japan. A kindly race with courteous grace, their choicest gifts bestowing. You must leave your shoes at the front door and tread lightly on the straw mats that cover the floor.* He stuffs the book into his bag. A souvenir, he thinks, and steps into the kitchen.

The kitchen has grand windows that face out onto a garden. The evening light streams in, turning the walls a deep gold and purple. He looks out at a tree. It's been months since he's seen a tree with its full skirt of branches. The leaves are dressed up with the same gold and purple light; he's never seen such a beautiful tree. Its trunk, smooth and light brown, without any hatchet marks or open wounds. But that's not true. I have seen such a tree, he thinks, a similar unscathed tree. And it takes only a moment to recall the painting, the couple standing underneath a magnificent old tree and the branches splintering the light. The leaves, a dark red-purple.

The cook walks in, a big woman with a bright yellow apron. She's carrying a mixing bowl and a bag of flour.

Can I help you? she asks, stopping in the middle of the room.

He says he's fine. When she sees his empty pant leg, her face softens and she brings him a chair.

Thank you, he says, placing his big bag on his lap.

She sifts the flour into the bowl and the white powder floats up, into the air, then rains into the yellow bowl. There are stacks of white china on the shelves, and the glasses are shimmering. They must be crystal, he thinks. He'll ask double the price for his goods, maybe triple.

There you are, says Daniel, his face flushed with wine. Svensk told me you brought a little surprise. By now you have a whole room of eager, undiscriminating buyers. Genevieve is so drunk she almost fell out of her chair, and Charles is telling dreadful jokes.

Jorgen pushes himself up and follows Daniel back into the room booming with noise. Couples sit lazily around the room, their arms draped over each other.

The Great Dane returns! shouts a man, now with a red face from liquor. What do you have in your magic bag? Tell us. We are waiting!

Jorgen blushes and feels a sharp sting of anger. Svensk winks at him.

Genevieve was missing you, says a man. Weren't you, my dear?

Oh, stop.

My wife kept commenting on your strong shoulders. I pointed out your, shall I say, condition, and she said it wouldn't bother her a bit.

His wife places her hand on a young man's shoulder and squeezes.

Jorgen stands stiffly in the entranceway to the room.

Show us what's in the bag.

Yes. Do a trick for us, says one of the women.

Svensk laughs, grabs the woman next to him, and kisses her on the lips.

Jorgen grits his teeth, opens the bag, and pulls out cans of smoked salmon, caviar, wine, hard cheese from the north, a small ivory figurine of a girl from China. To each, they *ooh* and *ahh,* and there is more and more, which he snatched on his way out the front door. Gold bracelets and necklaces of pearl, a pair of small jade earrings carved into the shape of seashells. Cigars and rich chocolate and a bronze bell that rings everyone for dinner. He pulls out everything except the book, tucked in the folds of the bottom, and the painting. He's about to reach for it, but withdraws his hand. Not these people, he thinks. It must have a proper home.

I simply must have this, says a woman with a feathery scarf around her neck grabbing a fine bottle of wine.

I feel like we've all gone on a treasure hunt and won, says one of the ladies, who now sports a new pair of earrings. I look ravishing, don't I? She wiggles her ears.

Open those smoked oysters, says one of the men to the other.

Without the Danes, says Svensk, you wouldn't be having such a good time.

The woman looks at him with bright blue eyes. Do all the men in Denmark look like you two?

No oysters for you. Not now, says the man, hugging them to his chest. The next party. Next week.

Next week? Next week? Paris might not be standing. We must devour them now. We must live and make love and eat! Let's open those damn oysters.

Jorgen clutches his bag and moves toward the exit. Svensk saunters over to him, claps him on the back, and says he's going to stay a while longer.

Daniel accompanies Jorgen to the front door.

Good show, my friend, says Daniel. You were a smash. A big hit. You'll have to come again.

When? asks Jorgen. He's standing on the porch under a yellow gas globe light. Tomorrow?

Daniel smiles. Next week. Of course the money is there, but there is nothing to buy. This damn war better end soon or we'll all die of starvation. I haven't had a good bottle of whiskey in a long time. Keep an eye out for that, old boy. A good one.

I will, says Jorgen, feeling gloomy and regretful. He steps away from Daniel.

Daniel pats Jorgen on the back. There's a good man.

In the pale evening light, Jorgen walks down the stairs, watching the bats swoop above the dark towers of Notre Dame.

SHE BOUNDS UP THE front steps to the hospital, two at a time. The morning's gray air is wet and murky, so she wears a fine coat of mist on her hair and red coat. It should be a sunny day, she thinks, with light bouncing off everything, a splash of light over there, everything tidied and perfectly well. The previous night's target practice went better than expected, the soldiers pleased with how adept she'd become with the rifle. The officer predicted that she'd leave for the battlefield in two weeks, perhaps less. They handed her a uniform, bright red trousers, a blue overcoat, a black belt, much too large, a kepi, her regimental number, fifty-three, printed in red on a blue band. Then they gave her a bottle of champagne and told her to celebrate. She was one of the chosen.

She yanks open the hospital door. Today she will tell Edmond, and after he scolds her and warns her of danger, he will be proud of her, she's sure of it, and she will share a glass of that champagne with him. He will look at her with gleaming eyes and tell her stories of his battles, share his secret techniques, how he snuck up on the enemy, taking a Prussian soldier by surprise. When she finishes with her visit, she'll find Jorgen, tell him the good news, and thank him for the lessons. As she walks into the hospital, she thinks perhaps Edmond will be well enough by next week to come with her. He was so chipper yesterday and when she went and prayed in the church, she had that wonderful sign. Edmond, she sings his name to herself as she walks down the row of cots with faces bobbing above white sheets, contorted in pain. She passes a nurse in a little white cap, who looks at her, a mixture of alarm and stillness, and rapidly turns away.

As she comes down the aisle, she stops, beds on both sides of her. A new face in his cot. He is gone? Edmond is gone, risen from his cot, slipped on his trousers, and walked out? To where? Did she pass him on the street? Was he in the long line that snaked around a corner for the bakery? Or standing near the Seine, where water buckets are coming up on a makeshift pulley? Perhaps he was the man looking up at the sky wondering if it might rain. Why didn't he wait for her to come this morning? Certainly Pierre wouldn't have come for him. She walks down the aisle and stands bewildered in front of the bed.

Gone, says the young man with a white bandage over his ear.

What? she says.

The man who typically shouts at her is speaking to her in a normal tone. His thin pale lips moving.

Gone. Last night. After you left.

Where? Where did he go?

She grabs the arm of a nurse who is walking by.

My brother. Where is he? Where is my brother? He was here, in this cot. Yesterday, right here, and now he's gone.

The nurse scours a chart. I'm sorry, she says, her brown eyes softening, and she lowers her head.

She doesn't let go of the nurse's arm; her fingers dig into the woman's flesh.

Please, mademoiselle, says the nurse.

Natalia begins to shake the arm, and the nurse drops her tray, splattering metal and glass. A wounded soldier shouts at her and another nurse runs over, but Natalia won't let go. The answer is hidden in there, behind the white apron of the nurse's uniform. Where is he? she must know. Someone grabs her from behind, pins her arms to her side, a man's smoky breath on her neck. Another nurse comes to her. She is falling, submerged in white.

In the basement, lady, says the soldier. Packed away in a coffin.

Natalia rips out of the stronghold, runs to the back of the large room, flies down the staircase. In the dark room, everywhere, wooden coffins, rows and rows of them, stacked on top of each other. The airless room, the suffocating odor of rotting flesh. Her stomach wretches and churns. She presses her handkerchief to her nose.

You're not allowed down here, says a nurse.

Where is my brother?

The nurse grabs her arm, and Natalia shoves her away, sending her into a stack of coffins.

Where is my brother?

A man with two protruding teeth and a long face comes up to her.

I'm sorry for the intrusion, says the nurse to the man.

It's fine, says the man. He asks for her brother's name.

She shouldn't be down here, says the nurse, her voice sharp and sour. It's against the rules.

Shut up, says Natalia. You just shut up. Shut up.

Calm down, says the man. Tell me his name.

Edmond. Edmond Blanc.

He leads her to the back of the room and points to a square wooden box. His name, painted in red on the side, in bold letters. Edmond's name. She stares blankly at the box. Anyone could be in there. They are lying. She reaches for the lid. Nailed shut. Tugging and pulling, she tries to pry it open.

I'm sorry, mademoiselle, we cannot open it, says the man.

He's my brother.

We cannot, says the man. We have too much to do here, and if we make an exception for you, then we will have to do so for everyone.

The nurse stands off to the side. Natalia flings herself on top of the coffin lid, pressing her lips to the crack between the lid and the bottom of the coffin. Edmond. Edmond.

Mademoiselle.

Edmond, she sobs.

Please, says the nurse. You must go. This is against the rules.

Natalia rests her cheek on the wood. Hands pull on her shoulders, lifting her limp body, dragging her upstairs. The wood coffin shut, shut, nailed shut, and the nurse pulling her, her feet dragging, up the staircase, through the thicket of moans and cries and vacant eyes, where death haunts and takes, passing his cot. She jerks away from the nurse and tries to run back to the basement.

Someone presses something against her nose, and an acrid smell fills her nostrils. The sounds elongate, dragging across the rough surface of her mind, each letter, each vowel, its own vibration in her ear. She doesn't want to move her heavy limbs. Ever again. She will lie where he did. Find the pillow that held his head, his sweet head. Won't ever leave here. She stretches her fingers like tendrils, and closes her eyes, finding the place behind her eyelids, the world of red and black.

Strong hands lift her deflated, flattened body, shuffle her down the aisle toward the door. Someone opens the door and leads her outside. She stands stunned on the sidewalk in the flat gray light. Everything moves around her, but she is as still as a piece of driftwood buried in the sand, the wild current rushing around. The first raindrops splatter and a wailing wind blows. Someone runs into her and she crumples to the ground, as if falling back into a great sea.

WHERE IS PIERRE? Natalia stands in the doorway of Jorgen's office.

Jorgen pushes his palms against the edge of the desk and rises, knocking over the lit candle. Red wax splatters on his hand.

Jesus, he mumbles.

Where is Pierre? Her voice is monotone, a hard hand clamped down on it. The rims of her eyes are pinkish red; streaks of dirt pattern her skirt, and her hands are scraped raw.

Did you fall?

Pierre. Where is he?

I don't know. Why are your hands bloody?

He died. Edmond. He died last night.

Jorgen unrolls his sleeves down to his wrists, picks up his pencil, and puts it back down.

Her eyes brim with water, and she fights back the tears. When I went to the hospital this morning, he was gone.

Jorgen looks over to the chair in the corner and shakes his head. He won't look at her; can't look at her. Didn't she know this was going to happen? How could she remain so deceived? So blind? He has the strong urge to say these things to her, the anger unfurling inside. He feels a certain self-satisfaction; he was certain Edmond was going to die. The world is not the way she views it, and it's good for her to discover this lesson now. But he can't say these things to her. What should he say? Where is Pierre so she will leave his office? Before she entered, he felt prosperous, and for the first time in a long time, almost giddy, as he ran his fingers through the large pile of bills stuffed away in his drawer. And now, now, she is crying and a heavy shadow of despair soaks into the corners of the room.

She wraps her arms in front of her and crouches far into herself. Do you know where I found him? They put him in the basement. Stuck him in a coffin in the basement as if he were a piece of luggage or something they had to hurry and get rid of. She stops for a moment and begins to weep silently, pressing a handkerchief to her eyes.

Jorgen chews on the side of his cheek until he nicks it and draws blood. Where is Pierre? He steps toward her, wanting to find Pierre. She twitches and he stops moving.

They nailed the coffin shut. She stops again and trembles. I didn't get to see him because they nailed it shut.

Her face quivers, and her head drops as she begins to sob. Jorgen looks down at his rows of numbers, and the wind blows in through the open window and wraps strands of her hair around her neck.

Natalia, he says, and his tone is weak and constrained. Anyone else would go to her, comfort her, but a thick, black line bars his way, something as sturdy as a wall across the room. Please stop crying, he thinks. Please, I beg you. He glances down at the musty books and stands there, stiffly, awkwardly.

Natalia, he says.

Crying softer now, she steps toward him. With her right hand, she is taking the cloth of her skirt and bunching it up into a tight ball. Over and over, her hand reaching, grabbing, releasing, and now there is blood on her skirt. He knows he should do something. But what does he have to give? He's only a meager fistful of himself, nothing remaining for anyone and, really, barely anything for himself. Look at him, he's missing a goddamn leg. What does she want from him? And if, by some miracle, he made it across that divide, what would he do? He presses his thigh into the edge of the desk, hard, trying to make the moment tilt another way, and when it doesn't, he wishes again she would leave him alone. Fury surges and he clenches his jaw. He looks at his crutch.

He loved France, she says, still bunching up her skirt. He fought for his country and was such a good man. Such a good, noble man. How could this have happened?

And everything that comes to mind to say is wrong, so he stands, his hands gripped tightly together, grateful for the wide stretch of desk between him and her.

She leans against the side wall, staring out the window. Did I tell you he saved me once? It was a hot summer day. I'd taken the sailboat out on the big lake. The ducks and geese were all around. The wind picked up and the boat tipped over. I was a young girl, and I didn't know how to swim. Have you ever come close to drowning? Felt the water go down into your nose and mouth? Choking, I remember choking and sinking. Clawing at something but there is nothing to get ahold of. There is no light underwater. Edmond heard me. She begins to cry anew and it takes a while for her to speak.

He tugs on his sleeve, waiting, listening for Pierre.

Edmond saved me, she says, her eyes filled with tears. He dove into the water and raced toward me. He swam so fast, his arms were wings.

She presses her hand to her heart. The many nights she sat beside her brother, believing he was in God's hands. But he wasn't and God turned his back on Edmond, on her. All those nights and days, praying, holding her brother's hand, imagining that through her touch, he might find vitality to rise again. All the while, the man across from her brother, spewing oily vitriol at her for visiting every day. Who comes to see me? he shouted. No one, and then there is you. The sound of the whimpering ones, fallen into the state of boyhood, and the angry men who lashed out and attacked, like trapped animals. She remembers a young man's fingers curling inward as he died, as if drawing in his claws. But her brother was different; he never complained or shouted or yelled about the pain. He was blessed and should have been spared. He was honest and true and courageous. Edmond should have been spared. Shouldn't God have turned and chosen another? Why did He let her lose him? She looks at Jorgen, bewildered, and for the first time sees him standing like a rigid pole. Jorgen is still behind that desk. Why did she come here? Where is Pierre?

He steps toward her. She leans toward him, and it is more like falling, wrapping her arms around his neck; he holds her, rigidly, not smelling the lilac scent of her hair or feeling her wet tears, or her breasts rising and falling. Tries not to feel her strong back, the way she clutches him, her fingertips pressed hard into his back. A shudder ripples through her shoulders, her ribs, her hips. Natalia's body releases its grief, and underneath, the softness of a breeze.

It's too late, she cries. Too late.

Anything he could say would be wrong.

Too late.

It is she who releases him. Pierre, she says. I must find Pierre. Her hair falls limply around her face.

He feels helpless. Her eyes are deep blue, the color of a heavy rain. Her hair a beautiful shade of rich reddish brown, unleashed from its usual bun, wildly disheveled. She looks radiant and luminous, her cheeks flushed pink, as if something has washed away and left her in a lovely state. And in that moment, he sees all of her, the young girl and the grown woman, and it is too much, a terrible moment of utter honesty. She turns to the door. He drops his head and stares at the dust-covered floor. When he looks up again, she is gone. Her footsteps echo down the hallway, and then fade, and then they are gone.

Natalia, he says.

He numbly walks over to his chair, plops down and sighs with relief and agitation. He stares blankly at the numbers, gazes so long they begin to scramble and yaw, arranging and rearranging themselves over and over, turning into dots and squares and patterns of long, slithery snakes. He looks at the doorway and sees the dark hall. The front door opens and closes downstairs. He stares out the open window.

WHEN SHE ARRIVES AGAIN, she hears Pierre talking in Jorgen's office, Pierre's shrill cackle spilling from his thin-lipped mouth and the low rumble of Jorgen's monotone voice. She presses her hand to the door and enters the dimly lit room. Her brother's face is sweaty from excitement, and Jorgen sits expressionless at his desk, his hand clutching a pencil, as stiff as when she last saw him.

Our man here knows a route into the city that bypasses both the Prussians and the French, says Pierre. If our army listened to him, they'd realize there is a gap leaving Paris wide open for attack. They should be consulting his maps. Hell, they should make him a general and have him run the war. He used it to get ammunition for his men, didn't you?

She can barely look at her brother, who shrugged when she told him about Edmond's death. What did you expect? he asked. The French are the ones who declared war and we're paying the price. She stares at Pierre's hands, their grotesqueness. The dirt under his nails and the hangnails. The things they've touched, the prostitutes, the money, his stingy, wiry body. He pushes a finger into his ear, fiddles around for earwax. She shudders and takes short sips of breath, not wanting to breathe the same air as he does. She won't tell him her news. He'd just make her feel worse than she already does.

Jorgen fumbles a pencil between his fingers and stares at his row of numbers.

The food supplies in the city are extremely low, says Pierre, striding up and down the room, and will become increasingly so as winter approaches. Have you seen the lines for bread? My God, he rubs his hand over his misshapen head. And the prices? Bread will become like precious flank of steak. Hell, it's already become so. Water will be like wine. A block of cheese, glowing gold.

Pierre stops and grins at the Dane. Natalia coughs and Jorgen's gaze shifts to her. Her face is pale, her eyes weary, and before she sees him staring, he looks beyond her to the boxes lined up against the walls, filled with marvelous things for him to sell, and then beyond that, he imagines the fancy rich people in the luxurious, top-floor apartments, to the new leg that will be fitted to his limb so he can walk again, walk with the command and boldness he once had, walk right out of here.

My dear sister, the best thing you've ever done is send me this man, says

Pierre, laughing, and his eyes flash harshly with arrogance. Jorgen will get his share. I'm a fair businessman.

Jorgen absently stares at a column of numbers and adds it up in his head. He writes the number faintly at the bottom. Yesterday, Pierre fired one of the clerks who kept some of the books. Caught him stealing a can of food. My family, the clerk wept. Jorgen heard the old man crying. My little daughter is starving. Grim faced, Pierre showed him the door.

Natalia's flat eyes move to her brother and then to Jorgen.

These are good times, says Pierre. Very good times for a smart, enterprising man. Every situation creates an opportunity. War magnifies everything.

And both of you seem to be taking full advantage, she says.

Jorgen sits up in his chair. The front door downstairs opens. Pierre's eyes light up. He skips out of the room and charges down the stairs. Jorgen tenses, not wanting to be alone with her, afraid she'll begin to cry again.

She turns to Jorgen. I'm leaving for the front line.

He drops his pencil onto the desk.

I'm not sure when I'll leave, but it'll be soon.

Congratulations, he says, feeling hot jealousy rake through him.

I came by to say thank you for your help. They picked me and a handful of other women.

Do you know where you're being sent?

No. They didn't say.

He picks up his pencil again, twirls it nervously, and sets it down. You must be excited. He stands now, feeling a flutter in his chest.

Yes.

He sees again a haggard look to her face. She must have exerted herself at target practice, he thinks. How fortunate she is. She doesn't know how fortunate she is to be going.

She tells him the officers chose ten women out of one hundred. They said it's quite an honor, she says flatly.

Of course it is, he says. A tremendous honor. It will help her forget all about Edmond, he thinks. Life takes with one hand and gives with another.

Just as he has found this dreadful job has a lucrative lining. How lucky she gets picked so soon after he died. Who do you report to?

I don't know. She pauses. It doesn't matter, really.

He feels his body tighten and he shifts in his chair. Still, it's an honor.

She steps back, as if preparing to leave.

Let me buy you a celebratory drink or something. He wants to be close to her. No, not to her, but what she's brought into the room—the war, a different life, an opening to something else.

She looks at him quizzically. He grabs his crutches and they step outside. An old woman is gathering twigs off the ground. Boys run by in a pack, red handkerchiefs tied around their heads. One of them rams into the old woman, knocking her down. The boys don't stop, but glance over their shoulders and laugh cruelly. The woman swears, picks up a rock, and throws it at them, nearly striking one in the head.

Jorgen looks over at Natalia expecting her to do something. To rush to the woman, make sure she is all right, but she does nothing.

Did they give you a uniform? he asks.

Yes. And a rifle.

That's good. Very good. Jorgen is quiet for a moment. I needed some fresh air.

There's nothing fresh about this air.

It's true—above them, blue-black smoke billows into the sky, the daylight turning to murky brown. They pass by brick buildings, clock and shoe repair shops, bakeries and corner grocery stores, the fronts now wearing big bandages of white canvas with the Red Cross hospital insignia painted in bold brush sweeps.

She says she needs to sit. They rest on a park bench, the back of which is missing; someone must have stolen it for firewood. A hollow-flanked cat slips between their legs. Jorgen reaches down and pets its back. The cat's hair is sticky and balled up into mats. It leaps up on the bench and rubs its chin against her arm. She pulls her arm away from the cat.

He'd like to explain why he told Pierre anything that will help his business. How he made so much money the other night at Daniel's and how, with more goods coming into Pierre's possession, there will be more sales to the rich. But now she's hung her head, as if any minute she might cry. What's wrong with her? he wonders. Why isn't she excited? She feels all coiled up, aloof in gloom.

You're very lucky, he says. It's what I want. To fight again.

She doesn't answer.

Perhaps she is frightened to go to war, he thinks, for what does she truly know about it? About being a soldier? Of course, she is scared to go.

Did you ever have a cat? he asks, trying to draw her out.

No.

I had a cat when I was a boy. He waits for her to say something, but she stares at the houses across the street. I must go on, he thinks. I found her in the trash can. A black cat, I named her Laila. Whenever she went out at night, she got into fights. In the morning, she'd come back with scratches on her head and legs. When I came close to her, she would spit and fight, wanting to be left alone.

Why didn't you leave her alone? she asks.

The cat steps gingerly into his lap. I had to battle that cat almost every morning to put ointment on her wounds.

You should have let her be.

She would have died. Jorgen shifts uncomfortably. A group of women wearing big bows around their waists burst from the front door of a mansion, step onto the porch, and walk to the sidewalk. Natalia and Jorgen overhear them say they are going to the belt railway to stand on the top deck, where they can look over the line of fortifications and see the soldiers. Won't it be fun? says one of the women.

Natalia turns to Jorgen. If you know this special passageway, you could leave, couldn't you?

I can't without a good leg, he says.

Why not?

He glares at his empty pant leg and curls his lips into a tight mean smile. He tells her part of this entrance travels through the sewer line. It's slippery, and if you get caught in there at the wrong time, you need both legs to swim through it.

If you get this new leg, then what?

He doesn't answer for a long time. This brigade you are joining, what do you know?

She laughs darkly. I don't know anything. What do *you* know, really? She pauses and stares at nothing. I once thought I wanted to be a missionary, but the Church would not have me.

Why not?

I'm a bastard child. Hasn't Pierre boasted about this? He loves to remind me of it. I'm not pure, as he puts it. Only a half-relative. But I don't mean to tell you these silly personal things, she says. And you don't want to hear them.

He's about to protest.

The French army needs me to go, so I'll go, she says. Her voice is empty of emotion, as if reporting an inevitable duty.

He feels her shudder, and slowly, he begins to understand. She doesn't want to go. All of life seems to have been sucked from her, and it's as if she's stepped into something and is being relentlessly hurled along, as if nothing could stop it now. She shouldn't go. Not like this. It's too dangerous like this—this state of futility. Jorgen braces himself, half turning to her. You might end up like this, he says, gesturing to his body. It could happen. Anything could happen. Even worse things.

He hears the feebleness in his voice and sees her faint, cynical smile.

You once said you didn't want anyone's pity, she says, but that's exactly what you want.

He's about to defend himself, but the harsh tone of her voice vanishes as she murmurs softly, Poor poor Jorgen. He sits at the edge of the bench in the growing violet light. She's bitten off all her fingernails, down to the tender pink skin underneath. He has an overwhelming urge to take her hand and touch that sensitive part and, at the same time, to quickly walk away.

The wind blows away any warmth left in the dying day. Shivering, she pulls her collar tighter. She rises, her face almost gray, a look of dullness coating her eyes. I should leave, she says.

. . .

Let her go, he thinks, lying on his cot, staring at the ceiling. The quiet night is suddenly split by cannon fire. The metal frame of the bed rattles and for the first time the acrid odor of gunpowder pollutes the air. The Prussians have moved closer to Paris. The pain in his ghost leg flashes again. He snatches the flask in his pocket and pours some brandy into a glass. If he could get drunk, he thinks, he could numb the pain and get some sleep. He drinks a glass and pours another.

He looks down at his stump. She doesn't know what she's doing. He thinks again of her tone of voice, flat and crushed. And on the park bench, the way she looked, he remembers the slender line of her pale neck, and her small hands, her fingers, like stems of flowers.

Gunfire rips through the silence again, as portentous and as loud as the first blast, nearly startling the glass of brandy from his hand. He snatches up his crutches, and walks to the window. In the near distance, the red glow of fires. Probably Prussian fires by now, he thinks. Let her go. What does it matter? The Prussians are nearly here anyway, and the war will end soon with stiff Prussian soldiers holding immaculate guns marching in perfect rows down the boulevard.

He could go to her right now and tell her it's insane. Walk to her flat across town and ask her, How can you possibly be prepared in less than a month? The French are desperate now, throwing bodies at the enemy. And he sees again her new, cynical smile, her hardened look, and he will stand there, feeling like a failure, with nothing to say.

Forget her, he thinks. He clamors under the cot and retrieves the book he stole from Daniel. He stares at the strange letters at the front. Like the ones in the corner of the painting. *Some letters I've learned from the Japanese alphabet,* writes the seaman. Elegant black lines, perfectly balanced, like pictures. The word for wound, *kizu.* The Dutchman writes, *A wounded person left exposed to rising sun.* He studies the shape and tilt of the word for wound, then sets the book on the floor, and as he leans over the edge of the cot, he sees the painting, tucked between cardboard. Pulling it out, he lights another candle, letting the warm glow flood the couple who embrace each other, as if they will never separate. He leans closer into the painting, and what he thought previously were blue flowers clustered around her feet are not that at all. There are lines on her face, translucent blue streaks, and there, down the front of her dress. The woman is crying. She is standing in her tears. Not tears of joy, but impending departure, though he can't say why. Perhaps by the way she clutches to the man with such urgency, and the wind in the plum tree, he hadn't seen that before. The leaves are blowing in the opposite direction, away from the man. Her dress, the swing of it around the hem, is flying away from him, as if some natural force is separating the two.

He looks at the man and he's not quite sure if he's truly seeing it or if he's making it up. The same pale blue drips on his face. Why can't he hold onto her? How could he let her go?

A beetle skitters along the floor by his foot, and he recalls the way Agneta lunged for him. She knew he was leaving, sensed it without him saying a word. White hair like a child's, before the stain of adulthood, her cheeks the color of ripe peaches. The first time he saw her, long golden braids tumbled down her back. The first time he heard her laugh, a soft melody. She was sixteen. Maybe fifteen. Nights he couldn't sleep, like this one, he ached to be near her. The way the wind blew on her, he wanted to do that to her skin. The way the sunlight touched her, he wanted to do that to her hair.

He first touched her in a field of corn.

The swish of tall green stalks all around them. A curtain of private green. And again and again at night in the barn.

He left her. No wind blew him away, no strange force. He did it by his own choosing. Left her and the child that she was carrying.

He shoves the painting under his bed. His throat tightens and his hands tremble. He doesn't want to think about Agneta. Doesn't want her with him. Doesn't want her. Doesn't want anything.

The first rush of indignation rises. I'll tear that painting up, he thinks. Rip it to shreds. Get rid of the goddamn thing. I should have sold it to Daniel and his despicable friends. Why not? He pulls it out and pinches the corner, preparing to tear.

Damn it. His fingers are stuck at the corner, paralyzed. Damn it all.

He grabs his coat and rushes outside.

SHE WRAPS UP HER half-eaten scone, saving the rest for tomorrow. Cannon fire and rifle shots boom in the night, and she registers them, as if listening to birds. Running her hands along her sides, she feels her ribs punching against her skin. She hasn't eaten more than a bite all day. Her skin smells acrid and slightly rancid. Putting her hand up to her mouth, she smells her breath, stale and foul, like something decaying. In the past, she refrained from eating to attain a certain purity of vision. Now, she has no appetite and can't come up with any good reason ever to eat again.

She pulls out her mirror from the nightstand and props it on the dresser. Her white face stares back at her. Her skin, so pale, she can see the blue veins pulsing near her temples. Grabbing her long hair into one clump, she takes a pair of scissors and begins to cut. She watches herself do this, mesmerized, as if she is perched off to the side, letting someone else do this to her. The hair falls in swirls on the cold floor. Her hair. She always thought it was her one redeeming feature. Everywhere else her body and shape failed her, falling far short of pretty, and her lack of suitors proved her hunch. But her hair, a deep chestnut color that flared in the sunlight. She takes another clump and watches the strands coil at her shoe. This is the way my mother probably looked, she thinks. Ugly.

She's halfway done when she hears the front door rattle. She quickly ties a red kerchief around her head and rushes to the door. Perhaps someone with news about the departure time or one of the soldiers telling her where she will be sent. Or maybe a neighbor wanting the last of her belongings. As she reaches the door, her heart skips with her last thought, the one thought she'd never say out loud, the one she secretly wishes for, Jorgen has come. With her hand on the cold doorknob, she pauses, imagining what he might say. You must stay. What possible reason? Give me a reason, she'll ask. One reason. She turns the doorknob. Please. A reason. And he will stand there, leaning on his crutch, his body hunched over his one good leg.

Only the empty hallway, the tiles loosening from the floorboards. She shuts the door and leans her forehead against it. Edmond is gone. She weeps, with the horrible sounds of controlled crying. There is no one to save her now.

HE STEPS INTO THE café for a glass of wine. One of the few places still open. Can't sleep. Can't be in that damn room. Someone calls out to him. Pierre and Svensk are sitting at a corner table with two women.

Come here, my friend! shouts Pierre. Come join us.

The women wear heavy makeup and low-cut dresses, their bosoms half exposed, their arms bare and pale, ringed with colorful, jingling bracelets. Empty bottles of wine line the table. Wine glasses with smears of lipstick sit in front of the women.

Jorgen hesitates.

Sit! Sit down.

Pierre introduces the women, Julianne, with glossy black hair pulled into a loose bun, and Vanessa, whose brown hair falls in rolls to her plump shoulders. Jorgen nods.

Sit.

Jorgen slides into the long, rounded bench next to Julianne, who wears a dark red dress. Like the color of the dress in the painting, he thinks, and with keen interest, he looks at the cloth. Not silk but something shiny. The skin on her face is covered with small bumps, though he can't really tell because it's far underneath layers of orange makeup. But she has the same color hair as the woman in the painting, and he has the sensation he must know this woman.

My friend, says Svensk.

Pierre calls the waiter over and orders another bottle of wine, more stuffed mushrooms.

This man is a genius, says Pierre. He sniffs out money better than I can.

Svensk laughs and the women join in.

Pierre, honey. You're a sweetheart, says Vanessa. A pure sweetheart. She rubs his head as if petting a dog. You give us whatever we want.

As long as I get what I want.

The woman called Julianne titters like a bird.

Jorgen looks out the window. Nothing but darkness stares back at him. This morning he saw a bird sitting outside on the windowsill. With a chestnut brown front and wings of spotted black and white. The bird lingered;

Jorgen rose slowly, about to search for some seeds to feed it, when the bird slammed straight into the window, its downy feathers stuck to the glass. Someone hit it with a slingshot. The small body tumbled to the ground.

The woman in the dark red dress crams herself closer to him, pressing her leg against his. She reeks of cigarette smoke and sweat. She is nothing like the woman in the painting, he thinks. That woman would smell fresh and sweet and clean. He feels his leg muscles tighten and flinch as she slides her hand on his inner thigh. It has been so long. He wants to scoot away, and yet, at that moment, he becomes acutely aware of his deep hunger.

Svensk leans over and whispers, Nice to see you out here, old friend. They don't cost much.

Jorgen smiles faintly, trying to dust off his former self. If he could slip into it, put on its slight weight, he could do this and the melancholy might slough away.

Let's drink to the Dane, says Pierre, who is clearly the most drunk.

The women raise their glasses. Jorgen finishes his glass and Pierre refills it. Another woman joins them. Maria Anna or Anna or something, Jorgen isn't quite sure. Svensk sidles up next to her, smiling brightly, and pours her a drink.

Like Old Jasper's in Denmark, Jorgen thinks, with the men playing cards and drinking and the women hanging around, waiting for loose hands and money, and nobody watching their language or putting on stiff airs. Those were good times. The hand touches his other leg. He feels his appetite clamor inside.

Pierre pinches Vanessa's arm. You are well fed, aren't you? How can that be?

She laughs.

Julianne leans over and licks Jorgen's ear. Do the Danish girls do this? she whispers. I don't think they do. The French women are the best. I see you like this.

He puts his hand on her bare thigh and tries to stop it from trembling. There is a sad odor to her. Something that probably never washes off with soap and warm water.

Jorgen pours himself more wine and the woman finds his crotch. He feels the heat and a strange hollowing in his chest. Svensk has his arm around the new woman, and she is kissing his cheek.

Do you always blush, asks Julianne, or are you just getting warm? She giggles, her fleshy shoulders shaking.

Svensk hears her comment and laughs. You should have seen this man in Denmark. A lady's man. A big lady's man. Women hanging off his arms. Real beauties. One after the other.

Jorgen shifts uncomfortably.

We've got these women here to help us celebrate this fabulous bottle of wine, says Pierre, reaching over and pinching Vanessa's nipples.

Not here, doll, she says, kissing him on the lips.

Then we shall return to the boardinghouse, says Pierre, rising and pulling Vanessa along with him. The others stand and Julianne slinks up beside Jorgen. They walk to the front door.

You get along pretty well on those crutches, says Julianne.

Jorgen clenches his jaw.

Don't worry, she says. I've been with plenty of injured soldiers. I consider it my duty, she says, then bursts out with a hardy laugh, and the woman called Vanessa joins in. Svensk and the woman turn down one of the streets. Heading home for my own private party, he says.

The streets are empty, only the continual crackling of gunfire in the distance. The lamplights glow in the mist. Jorgen feels the damp night on his face and, glancing up, he wonders, Where is the moon?

They enter the boardinghouse, and Pierre grabs Vanessa by the arm and leads her into the back room. Jorgen and Julianne stand in the front room. She tugs on his arm.

Are you up this way? she asks, pointing to the staircase. He follows along, numb. Almost immediately, she is standing in his room naked. The sight of her is jarring. He has spent so much time alone in this room that it feels almost blasphemous to bring her here. He stands by the door, fully clothed. She climbs into his bed.

Come in, she says. It's cold.

He barely knows what he is doing.

Let me help, she says.

He makes her turn off the light. She unbuttons his shirt, unbuttons his pants. It is over so fast, and she immediately falls asleep. Jorgen scoots to the edge of his cot, far from her, not wanting to touch her, and presses his fingers to his temples. For hours, he lies staring at the wall, listening to the shattering bursts of shells. When he wakes, a red dawn colors the mist. She is gone, but the smell of her stains his sheets. Stripping off the bedcovers, he rolls them into a ball to clean later. He scrubs himself with soap and throws cold water over his head, then steps into his office. His head throbs and the light is too bright. Even though he washed, her smell is still on him. He feels a wave of nausea when Pierre comes into his office in a bitter mood.

That damn whore stole all my money.

Jorgen looks at Pierre's gray face.

Goddamn her. Pierre tells him how much.

She didn't take it, says Jorgen. You spent it all.

On what?

Wine. The women. Food.

Pierre studies him coldly. I have new inventory coming in today, he says. I want you to unpack the boxes and make a list of what's arrived. Pierre is about to leave. And the price for last night?

Jorgen looks up from his numbers.

The whore. I will deduct it from your wages. I'm not here to provide you with entertainment. He smiles. You should think before you spend.

Pierre leaves. Jorgen sits in the stunned silence of the morning. He feels sick, his stomach turning and quivering. Clutching his coat and crutches, he walks down the hallway, down the stairs, steps outside onto the porch and stops in his tracks. A light white frost coats the thin blades of grass, turning everything into a crystallized dreamland, as if the stars floated down to earth and covered the grass. His heart jumps. He feels as though he's looking into the true vision of something, the way the world dismantles and tumbles to reveal itself. Each thin green line shimmers in its misty greenness. He steps down from the porch and the grass crunches under his crutches, the frost holding each blade in perfect pose. He turns around to show someone.

JAPAN

WHATEVER AM I DOING here? The monk stares at the stack of boards. If he were at the monastery, he would have recited morning prayers until noon instead of pounding in nails and measuring boards. It's now midafternoon. He glances over at the temple. Today, no one came to the temple to pray. But yesterday, an old man came, collapsed on his knees, and wept, overwhelmed by the beauty of Buddha. The monk rushed over and perched his hand on the man's frail shoulder, trying to give comfort, but at the same time, feeling cut off from the man, knowing he once felt the same way about Buddha, but not since he's come down the mountain.

He chooses a piece of wood and absentmindedly rubs his thumb against the grain. So pleasurable, the texture. But just as he lets himself indulge in the fine grain, protruding behind it is the glimmering image of the old man, his face enraptured with what, joy? Yes, joy for Buddha. He sets the saw down. Where is my devotion? thinks the monk. What has become of me? He picks up the shovel and jabs it at the hard ground, trying to chase away the soft pain pushing at his ribs.

He's been working on the teahouse for five days and by now he knows any moment she will walk by on her way to the studio or to the gardens. What will I say? Every time, there is this rush of panic, the heart racing, what to say, what to say? If I were at the monastery, I wouldn't have to speak at all. Not say a word to anyone for days. How easy that life was; how hard and yet how easy to live tucked away in a monastery. He glances toward the house. What will she think of me if I have nothing to say?

HE WILL BE HERE for a while, Ayoshi thinks, as she watches the monk from the hallway window. He is building the new teahouse, his brow intense and furrowed as he paces the clearing and then drives the shovel into the ground, digging a deep hole for a post, carefully measures each board twice, sometimes three times, and bears down on the saw, as if his whole being depended on it. He wears new workman pants and a white canvas shirt—Hayashi must have sent the gardener to town to buy such clothes—rolled up to his elbows, revealing strong forearms and wide wrists. Look at how meticulous he is, she thinks; he will take his time with this project. And this thought, along with the sense that something new is coming—look at the stack of fresh wood, the color of newborn flesh—delights her and fills her with nervous fear.

Ayoshi walks into the kitchen. Sato is slumped at the table.

At least that young man knows how to do something useful, says Sato, turning a tired gaze toward Ayoshi. He picks up his bowl and slurps his steaming miso soup. The room is filled with the sound of a hammer pounding and the intermittent growling of a saw tearing through wood. But that awful pounding, he says, pressing his hands to his throbbing head.

You don't like him? she asks, leaning her back against the wall. She watches, trying to gauge his mood. He doesn't look like he's slept; his hair is splayed out in the back and dark circles lie under his eyes. She guesses he spent last night with his body tucked tightly around his pipe.

He coughs, his throat parched and dry. I've never seen much need for religion. Especially a monk's practice. A waste of a life. Look at him. A strong, strapping man like that throwing himself into self-mortification and denial. All those hours of sitting and sitting. For what? So in the next life he will return more holy?

Some people consider it noble, she says.

He looks at her, his expression wild and fierce. I've never gauged myself by what others think.

That's obvious. She stares at the flower arrangement the maid has placed on the table, cuttings from the apricot tree. I'm not sure he has the temperament of a monk, she says. She tells Sato that the other day, the monk was stretched out under a tree, humming.

Well. Good. A breakthrough. He sips his soup and pauses. He turns toward her. What do you think of him? he asks, his voice strangely apprehensive.

He seems quite happy. Which is more than I can say about you.

Me? I'm happy. Why shouldn't I be happy? I make more money in a day than most people earn in a year.

He gets up and strides over to the window, lean as a knife, his shoulders hunched, as if he planned to pounce. What does the world need with a man like him? he says, staring at the monk from the window. Tell me that. What does he produce? What does he grow? Or create? How does he help anyone? If we populated the world with men like him, everything would come to a halt.

Maybe that would be good.

If he extols the virtues of Buddhism, I'll walk away.

If you continue to tell me how to live my life, I'll walk away.

He looks at her with tender, sympathetic eyes.

Why did she tell him anything, she thinks, wishing once again she'd contained everything, Urashi, the baby, kept it tight in a strong box, as she'd done for so long.

When are you going to show me the rest of your paintings? he asks. I loved the one of the drowning woman.

The blood rushes to her face. I don't know, she says, putting on her coat. I'm going for a walk.

She steps outside and strides toward the far wavering edge of the garden. The air feels like a fine veil thrown over her face. As she passes the monk, she prepares for that brazen stare. But the monk doesn't look up, not even an acknowledging nod. Yesterday he said hello, but the days before, he only nodded. Sweat runs down the sides of his face. He places his foot on the metal shovel and tears open the dirt. She hears the scraping, his huffing, and the dumping of the dirt on the ground.

That bold stare the other night, she thinks, probably a young man's first long glance at a woman, an innocent gesture, and then he decides what he needs to know and it is over. Good, she thinks, well and good, she will have her peace. She walks down the sloping hill to the stone bench, away from the sight of the house and studio.

She sits on the bench under the willow tree. Here is where I'll paint the lavender when it blooms. And here, forget-me-nots. Over there, a pine tree, a necessary green for the eye, year round. I will sit here until I feel it. Feel the new painting. She waits and stares at the long grass, listening to the hammer. She pulls out a pencil and makes a quick sketch of the trees. A breeze plays with her hair. She senses someone watching her, but when she looks up, shyly, there is no one. She is too jittery, too distracted. For days, she has been anticipating the next painting, but nothing has come.

The hammering stops. Why did she have to find the monk in such a state the other night? The shudder of his body, the tender clutching of his hands to his own forearms, as if trying to hold himself, rock himself, find some comfort in the cradling of his own flesh. She looks up. The monk is walking toward her with something in his hand.

He nods severely.

She feels a slight flutter of her heart and restrains her arm, which seems to want to rise up and wave to him.

He waits until he is near her to speak. Good day, he says. His eyes graze over her, through her.

She stands, wipes off her kimono, and tucks her sketchbook into her obi. What to do with her hands? She crosses her arms in front of her and looks at the pail; he follows her gaze downward.

The fish, he says. I'm going to feed the fish. I told Hayashi I'd feed the fish this morning.

The fish? she says. That's his favorite task, she thinks. He must be in great pain today or so enchanted by the monk that he'd give the monk one of his greatest joys.

Yes, he says, gesturing with his head to the lake.

They stand for a clumsy moment. A skylark flies by, a flash of brown and white wings. This standing and shifting from foot to foot, she thinks, is too much, so she asks if she might accompany him. If you don't mind.

He nods rigidly, and they begin walking down the hill. He clears his throat several times, and she glances at him, expecting him to say something, but what? What can be done to step out of this seemingly endless wellspring of awkwardness? How uncomfortable this is. And then she realizes: He doesn't know what to say. What a small world he lives in; he can't think of what to say. A pity, really, and she feels herself warm to him, to his innocence.

She asks about the teahouse.

I'm thinking of using wood from the north. Hayashi-san said he would order it.

I'm from the north, she says, a lilt to her voice. I grew up in the shadow of a mountain, near an ice-cold river.

You're from the shadow and I'm from the no shadow, he says, smiling faintly, scratching his forearm. At the top of the mountain, the shadows are almost nonexistent. Or so it seemed. It's different down here.

It is good to walk, she thinks. Calmer, she is calmer. He tells her more about the teahouse, as if he was longing all this time to talk exactly about this. She glances at him as he tells her in a serious tone about the wood, how it will give a feeling of timelessness, the smell of ancient sap. His eyes are deep brown and sparked with amber. He gestures with his free hand, and his fingers are long and elegant.

The imperfections, he says. The small alcove for a shelf. There, a bowl of water, a lotus flower floating. And he explains the careful balance he wants between wabi and sabi, simple beauty and tranquility. The northern wood will bring out the wabi, highlighting the simplicity that comes with a noble poverty. The inessential stripped away, and there, only the very essence and purity. The one window will bring the sabi, letting in only the view of the garden, settling the mind into tranquility.

They've reached the blue shimmering lake. She pulls on her thumb knuckle, wondering what to say. The fish swirl in front of them, and he clears his throat again, louder, as if he's found more facts to tell her. She leans over, reaches into the pail, which he still clutches, and tosses a handful of fish food into the lake. She laughs uneasily, not quite sure why she is doing so. A brown bird flies overhead and they both watch it and its shadow passing over the lake.

The gardens are quite peaceful, aren't they? she asks.

Yes, he says.

The earlier tension is slowly dissipating, and she senses they can stand for a moment in silence. She feels a flush of vitality, and the bird—a thrush, perhaps—the glimmering lake and fish, the deep green of the long grasses, everything feels vibrant. They stand there a moment longer, watching the clouds occasionally tear, allowing the sun to shower down. Something swoops, a splash of gray wing. The teahouse design must be kept simple, he says, his tone serious and slightly defensive, as if she'd just told him otherwise.

She stiffens and clasps her elbows with her hands. Do you find the simple the most beautiful?

Some of my best teachers have been the most simple men. There's a saying: Before enlightenment, I chopped wood and carried water. After enlightenment, I chopped wood and carried water.

She drops her arms to her sides and laughs lightly. Well, then, I don't think you'd like my paintings, she says.

He sets the pail down and looks directly at her. You're a painter?

Yes, she says, jarred by his intense gaze, the pool of amber and brown fixated on her.

He shifts on his feet and touches his hand to his forehead. One of my favorite teachers was a painter, he says. He did many ink drawings of Daruma. He said they were born, not made.

That's how I paint, she says.

My teacher said they came as if the heart were speaking.

If I were given one talent, I would choose to be a painter.

You'd probably consider my paintings too cluttered, she says, reaching into the bucket and throwing another handful of pellets into the water. She points to her favorite fish. Not a simple one, she says.

He searches the swarm and finds one. That one, he says, smiling. Red and orange and black and a fine thin line of pale blue.

She laughs. Hardly simple.

He smiles, and for the first time she feels his immense warmth, as if she'd stepped next to a fire.

When they finish feeding the fish, they walk up the hill. She is suddenly overwhelmed by the need to show him her paintings. She leads him to the studio. Inside, there is only stillness. The monk stands at the doorway.

Please, come in, she says.

He steps into the studio and stands beside her at her drawing table. She pulls out a black folder. He looks at her birthmark, a pale red spot the size of a pebble on the side of her neck.

She shows him a painting of the ocean and a small fishing boat. Another one of a large seashell.

Do you know I've never seen the ocean, he says, his tone full of amazement, as if he can't believe it either.

She looks at him, jaw dropping. What a shame, she says. What a shame if you never see it.

THE NEXT DAY, THE monk is up earlier than usual. By the time Hayashi steps outside, the monk has finished digging two deep holes and pounding in the main posts.

Fine day for work, says Hayashi, picking up a handful of wooden nails and tossing them back and forth in his hands. A certain camaraderie has formed, Hayashi is sure of it. Did I ever tell you about the time I folded five thousand origami paper cranes?

The monk stifles a sigh, pulls out a slab of wood from the stack, and sets it on the workbench. He is not used to such excited chatter. With a ripsaw, he makes the cuts, then wipes the shavings from his shirt.

I made them for my favorite monk, says Hayashi, glancing over to the studio and seeing the top of Ayoshi's head. The cherry-bark man, that's what I called him. Strung them together with thread. Long chains of colorful paper birds. Good luck, they say. I hung them from his outside rafter and they flew in the wind, making a sound like bird wings. He was sick, you see, and he did get better. For a while, at least. A wonderful man.

What do you think? asks the monk.

As they stand studying the plank of wood, they hear the iron gate open and slam shut. Hayashi tenses at the sight of a Japanese man in Western clothes walking toward him with a sturdy, confident stride.

Please do not say anything, says Hayashi to the monk. You are a construction worker. I've hired you to rebuild the teahouse. Please.

Hayashi has seen the man before, what is his title? His responsibilities? Why is he here? The man has a lean, austere face and pale gray eyes, almost translucent, that look deceptively bored. His closely cropped hair is as smooth as an animal's fur. Hayashi rushes over to greet him.

Hayashi bows low, much lower than the official, and when he rises again, his face is flushed, his heart racing. What is the expression on the official's face? Anger? Judgment? Hayashi does not know. Can I offer you tea or perhaps breakfast? Such a long hike up the hill. Hayashi turns quickly to locate the monk. The monk is standing by the stack of wood.

The man looks at him shrewdly, his mouth tight. He declines Hayashi's invitation and says he is here to deliver a letter. Who is he? asks the official, nodding toward the monk.

Hayashi sees what he hasn't noticed before. The monk's bald head. Only a monk would shave his head. Why hadn't he thought of that before? How stupid of him, and now what?

A builder. I found him in town, says Hayashi. Hired him to rebuild the teahouse. You heard it burned down?

The man stares at the monk.

He seems quite competent, adds Hayashi. I'm sure he will do a fine job.

The official turns to Hayashi, and now his eyes are dark and critical.

He might have been a monk at one time, says Hayashi. I really don't know.

Hayashi feels a deep trembling, like a wound opening. He tries hard not to hang his head and stare at the ground.

The official watches the monk. After a while, he turns to Hayashi and pulls a thin white envelope from his breast pocket. He tells Hayashi it's an official notice to close the temple. No more services.

Hayashi laughs nervously, clutching the letter in his hand. So few people come here anymore. I can't imagine what harm it does to anyone.

The official studies Hayashi. These are orders issued by the emperor's cabinet members, he says, his voice steady and cold. The official doesn't wait for Hayashi to respond, but turns and heads toward the gate again.

Hayashi stands stunned. He waits until his breathing settles before he walks over to the monk. The monk sets down his measuring tool. Not yet, thinks Hayashi. Enough upheaval in my life already, in the monk's life, too. We can enjoy today, work together on the teahouse. Perhaps the emperor's men will change their minds. Yes, or I'll convince them there is no harm done—what harm, really?—and in fact, with such change, it will retain everyone's sanity to keep some things the same.

He wanted to make sure I hired the right man to rebuild the teahouse, says Hayashi, still trembling from the encounter. I assured him you would do a fine job. Now, where were we?

A white wagtail flies down and hops on a long plank. The pale quills, the quick jerk of its head, and this is so much better than thinking about that official and what he must do. How can he close the temple? Why must they make such a demand? There is the bird's alert black eye. They stare at each other in stunned silence. His lungs empty and gasp and the moment elongates as everything falls away. The bird flies to an overhead branch.

The monk resumes his sawing and Hayashi stands for a moment longer before he picks up the box of nails and searches for the strongest ones. That bird, he thinks, the gloss of its wings, the flutter of white as it flew.

When the monk finishes with the board, he pulls out his drawing. The hearth will be between the two entrances and the picture recess, he says.

The bird is sitting on an overhead branch.

Look up, says Hayashi.

The monk stops and peers up.

He's still here, says Hayashi, feeling the encounter with the official almost fade. It's trying to say something.

The monk almost speaks out, but instead, picks up a hammer and pounds in a nail.

That piece of wood with the small stain, says Hayashi, it belongs along the perimeter of the window.

The monk stops. I'm sorry, I'm not sure I understand.

Hayashi gestures to the bird. So we can see the birds in the sky.

I'm not sure that is the point of the tea ceremony.

But a lovely addition, says Hayashi. We could make the window even larger than normal to see more of the outside. Not just the garden, but perhaps the tree branches where the birds land.

The monk sets the hammer down. But the tea ceremony should be nothing more than boiling water, making tea, and sipping it. If you are busy watching the birds fly wildly by—

But the birds—

If you are watching the birds, are you truly sitting in the room drinking tea? asks the monk, watching Ayoshi step out of the studio.

Hayashi looks away from the bird and down at the handful of nails still in his palm. Perhaps you're right.

The monk picks up his hammer again.

Hayashi shakes some sawdust from his sleeve. But I think we should at least consider it.

SATO FINDS AYOSHI HUDDLED on the bench by the lake, throwing small stones into the water. Her face, grim and tight, the color of smoke. The cold wind rolls down from the higher mountains and into the garden. He buttons up his coat and sits beside her.

Aren't you cold? he asks.

She says nothing. He picks up a stone and throws it to the fish. They swim toward the plop of the pebble.

She throws another stone in the water and watches the smooth surface ripple. How many days has she been painting the same scene over and over? There she is on her back, floating in frigid water, and that current, that hideous current, dragging her to the bottom. She was sure it would be different this morning, but when she saw the same image, she felt a dead white glow in the center of her being.

I have some news that might cheer you up, says Sato. He tells her he might have a buyer for one of her paintings. A rich American who arrived in the capital the other day and is spending furiously. The man bought an ordinary painting by a little-regarded artist for three times its value. The painting was of mediocre quality of a Kabuki actor.

Oh? Which one of my paintings?

The one in the temple. The one in shadows.

She smiles faintly.

I think you'll get a lot of money for it.

No one ever looks at it.

Well, it's settled. I'll do my best to get a good price. And the person I have in mind to buy it, he'll look at it. What will you do if you become a rich woman?

Run away.

He laughs and clutches her arm. Good. You can come with me.

Of course she won't run away. What if Urashi came for her? What if he finally came and she wasn't here?

Sato watches the long green grass strands teeter on each other. Your father would be proud, he says.

Her face collapses. My father?

He probably wanted you to be a famous artist as much as you did. Maybe more. Or have you forgotten how he always provided you with the best painting teachers, the best paints and paper?

A fish rises and breaks through the still surface of the water.

She wraps her arms tighter around her shins and places her chin on her kneecaps. You always liked him, didn't you? For some reason my father could ignore your obsession with the West. I don't know why. He thought of you like a son.

Sato smiles fondly. He has always wanted the best for you.

She frowns bitterly and throws another pebble into the water. I'll never see him again and that's fine with me.

Sato pulls his coat tighter. Why?

The cattails rattle and the surface of the lake creases. The clouds come hurling over the mountains and the air chills. A shudder passes through Ayoshi. The first raindrops break open the lake.

I should get back to work, she says. She rises to go.

What happened between you and your father? Come inside and sit with me. You're cold. Look, goosebumps on your neck.

No, I can't.

Then tell me about the baby, he says.

She stiffens and throws a handful of pebbles into the lake. He waits and stands next to her.

The fish's body is a remarkable thing, she says. We're not built that way, to move so easily with each current.

He touches his fingertips to her hand.

She moves her hand away. I'm not like you, she says, beginning to feel herself unravel. You come and go when you want. You do what you please. You don't belong anywhere. Not here in Japan, probably not America or Europe or wherever you've gone.

No, you're right. I don't belong. And maybe you don't either. Has that ever occurred to you? That you're trying to swim in the wrong current?

She turns and faces him. Every day.

The rain falls steadily, releasing and recreating the tension of the lake's still surface. They stand there a long time, listening to the wind and the patter of rain.

My father, she says. There was an old woman, her back so bent and brittle. Ayoshi has never spoken of these things. The woman's breath, she says, in a half-dreaming, half-grieving state, when she stood over me, a sour bitterness seeped all over. I still remember that horrible odor. Ayoshi picks up a small twig and snaps it.

It was the middle of the night, her father woke her. With a firm grip on her arm, he led her out the front door to the sleigh. The two horses were already strapped in. Where are we going? she asked, how many times did she ask? Her father sat beside her, staring straight ahead, just the constant clicking of his tongue at the horses. Ayoshi tipped her head back and fell into the sound of the horses trotting. The stars seemed to be falling out of the sky, extinguishing their light as they approached the earth. She thought the world was dying, one star at a time.

The next day, I was emptied out, she says. She sits again on the stone bench, sinking below awkwardness or discomfort. The silence, strangely calming. I told myself there could be another, but I knew it was a lie. After that, I never saw Urashi again. Ayoshi leans over, tears off a piece of grass, and runs her fingers along the long green stretch of it. My mother threatened seppuku if I brought more shame. She wraps the grass around her wrist and tightens it. The wind blows stronger, tipping the tops of the pine trees. And the baby, she thinks, it would have been almost two years old.

The rain begins to fall harder.

Sato stands and pulls her up by the arm. She feels dizzy now for speaking of these things, as if they happened long ago, with the emotion teased out. A raindrop falls on her hand, magnifying everything. She stares at it, in a daze. Neither one says anything for a while.

I'm sorry, Ayoshi. So sorry.

She tightens her jaw.

Does he know? Sato asks.

She turns to him, slowly registering what he is asking, and then laughs bitterly. I don't think Hayashi knows anything about me. He probably knows more about that monk than me.

WONDERFUL WORK, SAYS HAYASHI. A real talent, you have.

It's late morning and Hayashi and the monk are taking their break, eating rice cakes and sipping tea. The heaviness the monk felt earlier now feels like dusk has entered his body, a shifting of day into night. His head aches. That man, Sato, he stepped out of the house and followed her down to the lake. They've been down there together for quite some time. Whatever are they doing?

He stands, wiping his hands on his trousers, prepared to walk down to the lake. Hayashi asks if he's ready to begin again.

Yes, says the monk. He turns to Hayashi, who is still eating. Please, you finish your meal. He walks over to the pile of wood and picks up a board.

You are a superb carpenter, says Hayashi.

No, he thinks, I am a monk; it's what his uncle did, and before that his great-uncle, on down the line for ten generations. And if he gives it up, what would he be? He senses, however irrational, that he would vanish. The thought makes him shudder. In the beginning, he admits he hated the monastery, he missed his family so, wondered how his mother could have left him there, but enough of that. He is a monk now. He pulls on the rope tied around his waist. He will always be a monk, and they can't take that away from him. Do you know anything about the Kencho-ji? he asks. Is that temple still standing or have they torn that one down, too?

Please don't worry. This is not what the Meiji Restoration is about. It will pass. Please don't concern yourself.

He sets the board down. What good can come of this new government? he asks. They are founding it on Buddhist blood.

I don't think—

They killed my teacher.

Please, there is no reason—

Someone must speak out.

—to act rashly. Not now, says Hayashi, his face draining of color.

I'll speak against this government.

These are difficult times. Misguided in many ways, I agree with you. But these things must be handled delicately.

The monk's face is red and his eyes fierce. Misguided is hardly the word for it.

The first raindrops fall and splatter on the porch.

Hayashi hurriedly explains the new leaders will soon offer free education for everyone, even the peasant's child will learn, but the monk is barely listening, the words fragmented, a stream of excuses. Reading. Math. Pottery.

Learn anything. If a merchant's son desires, he can become a religious man. An artisan, to a merchant. Like the West, the truth of every man.

The gray day slurs with his gloomy mood. Except if you want to be a monk, he says.

The rain comes down harder, a thick silvery sheet of metal. Hayashi gazes out to the green tea fields. I'll speak to them, says Hayashi, his voice filled with resignation. His feet now throb. He says he must step inside to rest.

A BONENKAI CELEBRATION, SAYS Sato, raising his glass to the monk, who walks in dripping wet, with his collar and the bottom of his pants frozen stiff by the cold. All day, he has worked alone on the teahouse, in the silence of the rain that eventually turned to snow. A pre–New Year's party is well under way in the kitchen. A celebration to forget the past year's misfortunes and welcome a prosperous new year.

We're celebrating early, says Sato.

The monk stands there, bewildered and overwhelmed, trying to take it all in. Two empty sake bottles sit on the kitchen table, and bowls overflow with rice crackers wrapped in seaweed; there's a plate of mochi, and the aroma of grilled fish swarms the eating room, reminding the monk of his hunger. Sato leans against the counter holding a blue bottle; Hayashi sits at the table, smiling, cutting designs out of washi paper and gluing them onto a wooden paddle. Ayoshi sits across from him, wearing a pale blue kimono with the figures of white cranes. Her face is flushed pink, her dark eyes brightly lit. She is so animated, so lively. Look! Her long hair streams down her back. He's never seen it released from its binding. It reminds him of long meadow grass.

Ayoshi hoists her design above her head and waves it. A magnificent yellow bird, its wings spread as if in full flight. Two alert black eyes stare at him.

Water trickles down the sides of the monk's face.

Hayashi turns to the monk. Hot sake for the drenched man.

The maid brings the monk a glass. Hayashi announces tonight they are making hagoita paddles for the new year.

I don't know this hagoita, says the monk.

Ayoshi laughs, covering her mouth, and the monk blushes, embarrassed that she is laughing at him. She tells him the game is what girls play around New Year's. A game for good luck.

And we need some good luck, says Hayashi, pouring himself another glass.

And we need to forget our misfortunes so the new year brings something better, says Sato. So drink up and think about all the awful things you'd like to put behind you.

You make it sound so easy, says Ayoshi.

Why not? says Sato, reaching for the sake bottle. Why shouldn't life be easy?

The house is warm, and the monk, who worked too long, can't think of anything except what floats up in front of him, the warm cup pressed against his cold, red hands, the sake in the folds of his mouth. He empties the glass and looks over at her. The bottle of hot sake goes around again, and the monk's glass is refilled.

Look at the snow, says Ayoshi, rising. Still holding her bird paddle, she stands by the window and presses her hand to the glass. Her breath makes a fogged, milky circle. I've always thought the earth had secret openings. White patches that fall into the deep center. What do you think lies at the center of the earth? she asks, turning to the others.

Gold and more sake, says Sato.

Thick, rich mud and the bones of the dead, says Hayashi. Oh, yes. She wants this evening to be fun. That's what you said earlier, right? Then gold and tubes of paint for you.

The monk is still standing by the doorway, and now he sees her feet are bare. Her toes, smooth and perfect, her toenails, milky white.

It's remarkable, says the monk. Your imagination. The bird. It looks so real.

You've brought in the rainwater, says Hayashi, pointing to a muddy puddle spreading on the floor. Hurry now. Go change your clothes or you'll flood us.

Sato gazes steadily at the monk.

The monk looks down. The puddle is running across the floor and now staining the hem of her kimono.

Let's not be serious tonight, she says. Let's not be serious ever again.

For the new year, my wish is that we all go to Europe, says Sato. We'll go to Italy. There is lush food, fruit all year round—

Wonderful, she says, laughing.

Red plums and green grapes and thick pastries with white frosting. Tomatoes as sweet as sugar. You've probably never eaten a tomato, have you? I'll order four boxes of them and we'll spend a day eating tomatoes. Sato stops and turns to the monk, still standing there in his wet clothes. Except the monk probably couldn't endure such indulgences, could you? I suppose you'll just have to stay here.

Ayoshi lets herself imagine Italy. What if she leaves with Sato, travels to these places they once dreamed about as children? She could have her freedom, and there would be no more heavy silences, no more feet that never heal, only paintbrushes and these tomatoes as sweet as sugar.

At the center of the earth, says the monk, lost souls, or maybe nothing, nothing at all.

Oh, now, don't be dismal, says Sato.

Yes, don't be so dismal, says Ayoshi. The color is still bright in her cheeks. Not tonight.

We're having a party, says Sato, who moves closer to Ayoshi. The new year is around the corner, and we don't want to make the gods angry. What would you like to forget, Hayashi?

Shinto gods, says the monk. You mean Shinto gods.

Sato turns abruptly and faces the monk. Of course, says Sato. I pray to them all or none at all. It depends on the day and time of year.

What would I want to forget? asks Hayashi, who pops open another bottle of sake.

What's so bad about Shintoism, really? says Sato. Are you aware of any of the precepts? Even I, who haven't been to a Shinto or a Buddhist ceremony in a very long time, can recall a few. Let's see. Don't be sluggish in your work. Now, what's wrong with that? You believe in that, don't you?

I think the monk is cold, says Hayashi, still smiling. Let him go change his clothes.

Oh yes, says Sato, bearing down on the monk. Here's another. The world is one family. What do the Buddhists think is wrong with that? Sato's eyes are darting and flickering.

We agree with that, says the monk, his voice firm.

Sato, says Hayashi, his smile vanishing. Let him go change into dry clothes. Look at him. He's shivering.

What's wrong with believing that spiritual forces pervade the natural world? asks Sato. Where did I read this? It was a beautiful line. Oh, yes. Sato closes his eyes and recites, *Myriad spirits shine like fireflies and every tree and bush can speak.* He opens his eyes again. Beautiful. Shintoism teaches you to love the world with its spirits. And what does Buddhism teach? All is transitory. We'll be dead soon, so turn your back to the world. Isn't that right?

Ayoshi finishes her drink and noisily sets down her glass. The Ainu believe that hanging the forepaws of a hare over the doorway wards off the spirit of demon disease.

Hayashi looks over at Ayoshi, his mouth slightly ajar.

I'm not sure how it helps anyone to think there are eight million gods floating around in this world, says the monk. If you adhere to that, you ignore the core of the Buddhist teaching.

Which is? asks Sato.

You'll suffer if you remain attached to this transient world. And that's not a philosophy. It's true. Anyone can know it if he examines his life. But I suppose you need the ability to reflect.

Sato grins at him. Is the composed monk becoming angry, experiencing emotion like the rest of us?

Please, Sato, says Hayashi.

Oh, we're just having a little fun, says Sato. Aren't we?

Shintoism is just a clever way for the government to unite the country, says the monk, biting the inside of his cheek. That's all it really is. It's a pagan belief system that says the emperor is of divine origin and everyone must obey him. It's filled with silly rituals and frivolous festivals. If I throw a coin to the rain spirit, I will win favor and receive rain. And to the sun god, I pay an extra yen to ensure enough sun. For this, they are killing monks. They are burning down monasteries.

And Buddhism isn't full of rituals and festivals? says Sato, rubbing his hands together.

The monk is about to blurt something, but forcibly stops himself, turns swiftly, and marches down the hallway.

There is a moment of awkward silence.

Please, says Hayashi, twisting his napkin in his lap. Please. I must ask you. Sato. Everyone. Please. Let's enjoy tonight.

Yes, says Ayoshi, startled at Sato's raw bluntness. And now her little fantasy of leaving with Sato and traveling to Europe shrivels up and is cast aside; ludicrous, how could she put up with his rudeness? His almost instinctual need to stir up calm waters?

You are both our guests, says Hayashi.

Sato snatches up a blank sheet of black paper and puts it back down. We were just having a little discussion, says Sato. He grabs the bottle. Now, Hayashi. What were you saying? He turns his gaze up to the ceiling. Oh, yes. What would you like to forget?

Hayashi pauses, trying to collect his thoughts and compose himself. The last bowl I made. I'd like to forget that.

Really? I thought it was rather interesting, says Ayoshi.

Tell him that again, says Sato.

It was different. But you destroyed it. You always do that.

Hayashi raises his eyebrows.

She glances down at his feet. Wrapped in white bulky sheets—the maid did it, she's sure—his feet nest in healing herbs. And there is the monk, now in dry clothes, his face composed, the earlier anger almost disappeared, but a spark still lights his eyes, and a hint of it resides in the pursing of his lips.

Come. Sit down. Join us, says Hayashi.

There are big bowls of steaming sukiyaki, tempura shrimp, and an array of colorful sliced fish. The monk sits next to Hayashi, across from Ayoshi. Sato has stationed himself at the head of the table. He opens a green bottle.

Everyone must try this, says Sato. Wine from France. He opens the bottle and pours everyone a glass. With all due respect to the monk, the French have their own form of Shintoism. They treat wine as if animated by supernatural beings. Wine is their god and they drink until they become animated.

He will only have one more glass, the monk tells himself, then he will excuse himself to say his evening prayers. His teacher once said the person who upsets you the most is your best teacher, but what can this man possibly teach him? Sato is still talking about this new drink of wine, and Ayoshi is smiling, as if applying some balm to this obnoxious man. He's not prepared to think ill will of her, but it's curious that she should have such a friend as this man. It reflects on her character, he thinks, though he's not sure how.

AFTER DINNER, THEY SLIDE open the door and step out onto the wooden deck. The moon fans itself onto the wooden panels, and the snow lights up the garden. Hayashi finds his flute and asks the monk to play the bronze gong. Together they fill the garden with haunting sounds. The night air, dazzled now with stars, makes room for the music to fall over them like a web.

Sato takes Ayoshi in his arms. This is called dancing, my friends, he says. Western style.

The monk watches Sato's hand on her narrow back. When Sato's index finger presses too hard, he has to look away. Sato swirls her around and around, and her laughter rings out in the night. After the song ends, Sato dances over by Hayashi and takes the flute from his hands. Hayashi rises and takes Sato's place.

No, no, says Sato. He pushes them together. There. That is dance. You move together, not separate bodies in space. Together. Together. Better.

Sato sits and begins again. He gestures to the monk to play a higher note.

Ayoshi's fingers rest lightly on Hayashi's back, not daring to move them from their original spot, as if she might break something. He seems so fragile, compared to Sato. Delicate bones and fragile flesh. She holds him carefully, worrying about his feet. This can't be good for them. This morning, his work on the teahouse and now this, this dancing. He's carefully rolling through his heel, his arch and ball, an acute attention to the placement of his feet.

Are you all right? she asks.

Fine, he says.

Your feet.

I said I'm fine.

She wishes he would sit down; he's too clumsy and he'll be in such pain tonight. Gradually they pull apart again. She feels the night air on her face. When the music stops, Ayoshi and Hayashi drop their arms to their sides. The monk slips into the house, excusing himself politely, and Ayoshi watches him go, surprised at what she was expecting; she thought she'd dance with him next.

Both of you need more practice, says Sato. Once a week. My orders.

Ayoshi glances into the darkness; not his feet, not tonight. She won't do it. She can't do it.

What if she began again with the plum tree, not the river? If she didn't wait for him to speak to her, but painted the tree on the paper. Maybe Urashi would find her again, the blood-red leaves scattered around her.

Listen, says Hayashi.

In the quiet they hear a sound like a squeaky door rapidly opening and closing.

A snowy owl, she says.

I haven't seen one since I was a boy, whispers Sato. What's it doing down this far south?

I've never seen one, whispers Hayashi. What's it look like?

Ayoshi tells him it's pure white with black speckles and yellow eyes. The immature females are darker. It could be a male or older female, but I think it's a female, she says. She must be in the tall cedar tree, nestled in the limbs. She likes that tree.

You've heard it before? asks Hayashi.

I heard her when I first arrived.

A straggler, says Sato.

Maybe she's disoriented, says Hayashi.

I think she's lost, says Ayoshi.

The three of them stand in the dark listening.

There she is. On the bottom limb on the right. See?

Oh, says Hayashi. Oh, my. She's like a slice of the moonlight. Stunning. Look at her wings. And the owl turns its neck around, and there are its yellow blazing eyes. I should go get the monk.

No, let the monk be, says Sato. The bird is an adventurer. That's what she is.

No, says Ayoshi, she's lost.

HIS FEET THROB.

Hayashi steps inside to find a chair, and Ayoshi, looking for another bottle of sake, follows him inside. She sees his face contort in pain. Shall I? asks Ayoshi, her voice meek, betraying her reluctance.

No. You're having such a good time. Please, go on.

Ayoshi hesitates only a moment, then returns to the porch with Sato. Hayashi calls for the maid.

Oh, says the maid, her mouth dropping open. You've stood too long, sir. They're very swollen. They must hurt terribly. She brings a bucket of ice. You shouldn't have danced, sir. He thrusts his feet into the bucket and picks up his flute and twirls it round and round, something to move his mind from the pain shooting up his calves, his knees, his thighs. When she is done, the maid wraps his feet in heavy wool socks. He asks for his boots.

Please, sir, you should rest.

He waves her off. A candle glows in the studio. Ayoshi must have left Sato and gone to the studio to paint. A walk to the garden will fill his lungs with the cold. When spring comes, he will plow the back fields and plant new green tea plants. Fields of tasseled green tea will stretch to the woods.

He's full of reverie tonight. Perhaps it's the glistening snow, he thinks, but it isn't that; it is Ayoshi's laughter ringing. She looked lovely tonight, her face lit up with smile after smile. More lovely than he's seen her in a while. She's been so happy since Sato and the monk arrived.

The light from the studio glows on the midnight grass. Perhaps he'll knock on the door and say hello. He might try to make that bowl again, the one she said she liked. What did she see in it? he wonders. Probably just being polite. But maybe if he did it again, she could point out what is redeeming.

His feet begin to speak. No, let her be.

Hayashi walks over to the construction site and picks up a nail, suddenly remembering his earlier promise to the monk. Why did he say anything? He drops the nail. He'll have to meet with the officials again. What can he say? Why would they listen to him? Pain shoots up his legs. For the first time, he wishes the monk had never come.

FRANCE

A NEW SHIPMENT IS ARRIVING, says Pierre, and the way he stands, with his chin tilted up, that ingenuous smirk on his face, Jorgen knows Pierre wants him to inquire what it is.

It is early October, the morning light seems unnaturally muted, and there is a touch of winter in the air. When Jorgen woke, he threw on his clothes, intent on finding Natalia, and he hoped by the time he reached her, he would have hacked from the block of ice inside the right words to convince her not to go. But here is Pierre, pulling on his earlobe.

Pierre shifts on the heels of his boots, unable to contain his surprise. Pigeons, he says.

Jorgen leans into his crutch. What?

Carrier pigeons, he says again with a triumphant smile.

Whatever for?

Pierre says that Paris is now almost completely encircled by Prussians. The Prussians, they are so much smarter than the French, found and severed the secret underground telegraph wire that lies in the bed of the Seine; they've already cut the overhead lines and now the government is desperate for a communication system. The balloons are so unreliable, and so, carrier pi-

geons will carry out messages and mail. I've won several lucrative government contracts, he says. They offered to pay me one hundred francs a bird,
but I got them up to two hundred.

How are you going to get them into the city?

The tunnel.

But not all of them will make it through the sewer line.

Pierre shrugs. There's more where they come from. It turns out there are
quite a few carrier pigeon breeders in Tours.

Jorgen's fingers ache from the cold air. Dirt clusters underneath his nails,
a stain of grease on his index finger. What do you know about pigeons?

Nothing. But *I* don't need to know anything. *You* do because I've just put
you in charge of them. The birds will be housed in the backyard. A cartload
is arriving any minute.

Jorgen leans his back against the wall. Housed in what?

Again a triumphant smile. You are going to build the aviaries. Today. And
tomorrow. And however long it takes.

A detonation of a cannon resounds, echoing from the Sevres and Meudon
hills. Pierre and Jorgen wait until the sound dies down.

You can use two of the clerks to help.

Jorgen doesn't move.

What are you waiting for?

I need to run an errand, says Jorgen.

Pierre stares at him, a dark gaze, his jaw clenched with uncompromising
severity. I need this done now. There are plenty of hungry men out there who
would do anything to have your job.

They stand glaring at each other. The moment drags on. Jorgen swallows
and does a quick calculation, and he can't do it, can't leave now, not enough
money. Goddamn stuck, he thinks, and this is the thing that kills a man's
spirit, he knows.

But your sister, says Jorgen, without thinking.

Pierre crosses his arms in front of him, waiting for him to explain.

He tells him what his sister has done.

The army? repeats Pierre. The French army? She is such an embarrassment to my family. She's joined the army? What a fool. It's her mother's blood, not my father's, he mutters. Her mother was a simple housemaid. He thinks about it for a moment. Well, we'll throw her a going-away party. Send her off with a big hoorah. Get her good and drunk for once.

I was going to try and talk her out of it.

How? Pierre says, half laughing, a derisive flicker in his eyes. How exactly were you going to do that? You don't know, do you? I thought so. She's too headstrong. A dangerous idealist, and at her worst, a self-righteous bore. Let her save the world. That's what she told you, right? She's joining the French army to save Paris. She will lead the march to victory, in God's name, of course. He takes a handkerchief out of his pocket and wipes spittle from the corner of his mouth. And she has such nerve to call me arrogant.

Pierre looks at him gravely. If you leave, don't bother coming back.

Jorgen leans into his crutch and grits his teeth. Neither one of them speaks for a long time. Send the two clerks, says Jorgen.

Good, Pierre says, smiling sickly. He turns to leave, and stops. Oh. For every pigeon that, shall we say, expires, it comes out of your wages. Pierre heads down the stairwell, his hard footsteps punctuating the floorboards.

Jorgen grabs his crutch, stomps down the stairwell, and flings open the back door. He picks up a stone and throws it. The two clerks step outside, slack jawed, shifting on their booted feet, waiting for instructions. Jorgen glares at them. Idiots, he thinks, and he fights the urge that burns in every muscle to walk right out.

Boss says we answer to you today, says the tall one with dark, lazy eyes.

Said to get started right away, says the other one, whose cheek bulges with a wad of chewing tobacco.

Jorgen grumbles and walks over to the stack of new wood. He leans over the piece of wood, measures it, and marks the cut lines in pencil. Here, he says, thrusting the marked wood into their hands. He tells them to saw the wood two meters by two meters. For chickens, you need a minimum of a half square meter per bird or they go crazy from being cramped up. For pigeons, probably more.

All morning, they measure and cut and pound nails. The boys follow his lead, and after a while, Jorgen's mind unhooks from its fury and latches on to work, the grip of a hammer between his ice-cold hands, and the smell of fresh cedar. Late morning, a dull drumming showers the air. They halt their hammering. Coming down the main road, the National Guard, fifty or more, carries a procession of coffins, a kepi of a soldier on top of each one. A drummer beats out a funeral march on a black palled drum. A small crowd of civilians, with heads bowed, follows, and at the end of the gathering a group of soldiers play the recorder. The music roars over the backyard, and the three of them stand frozen, watching. Blood rushes to his temples and Jorgen feels dizzy, his stomach knots up. One of the clerks takes off his hat and puts it on his chest, bowing his head. Jorgen stares at a black coffin. If she doesn't come by at lunch, he'll go by her room during a lull. He'll find her.

By noon, three lofts are nearly done. Jorgen affixes a thin dowel rod as a perch. For a nesting area, he nails a platform raised up from the floor. When Jorgen looks up again, Svensk is standing on the porch.

How about lunch, says Svensk, waving a satchel in the air.

Jorgen sets down his hammer. You brought me lunch?

Svensk smiles sweetly and bats his eyes. Would I do such a thing?

Jorgen walks over to the porch.

Natalia dropped it off.

She was here? asks Jorgen. When was she here?

Svensk reaches into the satchel, pulls out a sandwich, and begins eating. When was she here?

Svensk looks at him curiously. Not too long ago. I don't know.

Is she still here?

No. She went to her brother's funeral, says Svensk.

Alone?

Svensk stops chewing and studies Jorgen. Pierre said he was too busy. She dropped off this bag of food and Pierre handed it to me. Said we could have it because we'd be working all day and night to make these cages. He just hired me to help you. Lousy pay. The bastard.

They sit and eat and Jorgen thinks about the coffins that went by earlier; perhaps one was Edmond's. He chews his sandwich, not tasting anything.

Pierre teased her about joining the army, says Svensk.

Jorgen stares at his sandwich. What did she do?

She smiled and walked out the front door. Svensk puts down his sandwich and looks at Jorgen closely. I thought you fell for the real pretty ones.

It's not that, he says, feeling his face turn crimson. He has time, he thinks, and most likely, she won't go. Doing domestic things like making sandwiches, hardly the mindset of someone heading to war. She'll stumble onto someone in need and suddenly that will be her new mission. His face brightens a little, and he watches the birds slice the air, listening to the whoosh of their wings. And now that his worry eases, he thinks of the book he found in the office, an old copy of Irving's *Rip Van Winkle* with an author's preface. Struck by the words—they seemed to be written with him in mind—he memorized them: *So the traveller that stragleth from his own country is in a short time transformed into so monstrous a shape, that he is faine to alter his mansion with his manners, and to live where he can, not where he would.*

Do you remember that scam we did with that old man? asks Svensk.

Jorgen stiffens. He knows exactly what Svensk is talking about.

We took that idiot man for his entire paycheck, says Svensk.

Let's skip it, says Jorgen.

It was great.

Drop it.

You don't feel bad about that, do you? asks Svensk.

The man had sloped shoulders and a large, idiot forehead, his fingers thick and broad, as if they'd all been smashed in a door. Jorgen came up with the idea. They told the man if he bought their raffle tickets, he might win a year's worth of salary. When the man hesitated, they told him they had the special tickets, the ones more likely to win. Other people were selling gold tickets, but they had blue ones. Blue was better.

Well, I don't feel bad, says Svensk. That guy was stupid.

Jorgen smashes his sandwich wrapping. He wasn't right in the head.

All winter that man asked about the winning ticket. Did he win? When would he win? By spring, the man finally forgot about it and stopped asking.

Svensk finishes his lunch. You were the one who came up with the idea. I was thinking about it because of the stuff you took from Pierre.

Jorgen grabs his arm. Don't mention that again.

Jesus, I won't, says Svensk, his eyes narrowing. It just seems like we are doing the same thing, but it's even better, isn't it? We can make more money from Daniel and his friends. I wish I thought of it. Svensk rises and stomps his boots on the wooden porch. The first raindrops fall. Svensk holds out his hand. A drop splatters. Shit, says Svensk. The back door swings open and closed, and Jorgen glances over, but no one is there. She'll come again, he thinks. At least she hasn't left yet.

OUR FATHER. NATALIA MURMURS the words, trying to make sense of them. People are dressed in black and the women are crying. A funeral for so many young dead men. The trees are stripped of leaves and limbs. Soon, winter's harsh grip. Heads bow under black umbrellas. This is our horrible fate, she thinks. Off to the side, behind the widows and the children who have lost their fathers, Natalia stands motionless, her hair getting soaked in the hard rain. Edmond, Edmond, can you hear me?

Our Father. How could, why would a father allow such a thing? A good father would not, a caring father, a father of love, a divine father. And if there is no father of love? She feels her heart wringing itself into a tight knot. Have we fallen so far from grace that He's turned His back?

A little girl hugs her mother's legs. I did that to Edmond when I was a girl, she thinks. A wave of grief clutches, she breathes it in, her lungs tightening. The wind rattles bare branches. Edmond, his name written on the wood in red paint, now smearing with the rain. The red, white, and blue of the French flag weep over the wood. Where are you going, my brother? There are the church bells and the trumpet. The women weep and the children grab their mothers' knees.

You will forget, children, this day and live as if forever holds you, but they will bury your body underneath the waking world. How can I say Our Father, with head bowed, not shouting Our Father, how could you? The clumps of dirt are now falling; Edmond, who loved me. Children, you will look around at the faces and clenched hands, listen to the blood racing, the heart beating, Our Father, and you will cry out as I do, as Job did, against God, We are innocent. Edmond, sweet Edmond, was pure innocence.

SHE DOESN'T COME BY that night, but the birds begin to arrive, cages and cages of pigeons, a formidable wall of metal wiring, great towers of birds looming in the yard, fortifications of silvery black and purple and light mossy green wings. The backyard sounds like the din of women chatting. In rain-soaked pants, Jorgen sits on the porch and stares at them. Mingled with the breeze comes the strong stench of bird droppings. Something frightens them, and they toss themselves up and crash into the wire walls, a new round of shrieks cleaves the night. He wants to open their cages and be rid of them.

One of Pierre's clerks has almost completed a tall fence around the backyard so the hungry will not steal the birds.

Don't just sit there, yells Pierre from the back door. Start unloading.

With the tip of his crutch, Jorgen nudges Svensk, who is lying on the porch, half snoozing. As they approach, the pigeons jump around on the bottom of the cage. Svensk reaches into the cage and grabs a bird. It pecks him hard on his thumb.

Fucking bird, he shouts and tosses the bird into the loft.

Be careful, says Jorgen. Any of them die, Pierre said he'd dock us.

Pierre can go to hell. The damn thing bit me.

Jorgen steps inside, finds some old gloves, and hands a pair to Svensk. Jorgen carefully wraps his hands around a bird. Through the gloves, he can feel the small body's warmth, its heartbeat, a rapid pulse firing. He's never held a live bird before. Its pulpy vitality startles him.

Just grab it and throw it in, says Svensk.

With his weight balanced on his crutch, Jorgen gently lowers the bird into the loft.

What a stinking job! says Svensk, wringing his hand. This fucking one bit me, too.

In their cages, they are scrambling side to side, screaming.

You'd think we're slaughtering them, says Jorgen.

Maybe we should.

An hour or so later, they finish and stand on the porch in the dark. Svensk hands Jorgen a bottle of wine.

Look at them, says Svensk.

Jorgen drinks and passes the bottle to Svensk.

This job is all yours, says Svensk. Going to be a lot of work.

He hadn't thought of this until Svensk said it, he'd been so focused on building the lofts. A hot panic ripples through him. He'll have to trudge out here each day, three times a day, maybe more, to feed them and give them water, and who knows what else they'll want? And what if he forgets? If he chooses not to? If he sleeps in or would rather spend the day at the café? What then? He feels his life narrow into a sliver, and he grabs the bottle from Svensk and drinks.

You want this job? asks Jorgen, feeling the wine warm his tired limbs.

Svensk laughs with amusement and slaps Jorgen on the back. It's all yours. You're the nanny, not me.

Jesus, says Jorgen.

Svensk laughs louder. It won't be so bad. They walk over to the lofts and look inside. Svensk says he's read about these birds. They fly up to eight hundred kilometers in a day at about eighty-four kilometers per hour. They can fly home, from wherever they are, and no one knows how they do it.

I don't give a damn, says Jorgen.

Svensk laughs again.

Jorgen puckers up his face and turns back to the porch. Svensk gathers his things, says he'll be back tomorrow. Jorgen shuffles to his room and collapses on his cot. He is not hungry, not anymore, the wine, the exhaustion, and as the night closes down on him, he remembers he needs to feed them. He can hear them squawking from here.

Outside, they hear him coming and begin fluttering and cooing. He walks to the first cage. The birds turn their heads; orange flat eyes stare at him. Jorgen flinches and steps back. He's shot mallards and geese, watched them fall from the funnel of sky. Then on the ground, stared into their unseeing dead eyes. There was never a moment of latching on to each other, not like now, falling into the deep hole of an alert eye. Startled at the intensity of the gaze, he looks down at their feet and is amazed by the color vermilion.

Look, he whispers.

He gathers handfuls of seeds, fills their feed bins, and the birds settle down. A stiff outer feather floats to the ground. He picks it up. The white shaft feels as sturdy as a tree branch. He runs his finger along the perfect edge and watches each fine strand find its place again. He climbs the stairs again and feels exhaustion dig deeper. On the night table, he grabs a notebook and writes, *Vermilion feet on the metal wire, and an eye unblinking. Show her this and this and the painting, too.*

I CAN'T BELIEVE MY sister is a soldier, says Pierre. What happened to love and marriage and babies?

They are sitting around the table. Natalia smiles thinly at Pierre and taps her fingernails to the red handkerchief cinched around her head.

The candlelight flickers and sways. Jorgen watches her slowly raise her glass to her lips. The glass hits her front tooth, and wine dribbles down her chin. She is deadly still, he thinks, unnervingly so. He waits for her to wipe off the red drops of wine. When she doesn't, he gestures to her, then hands her his napkin.

How was the funeral? asks Jorgen.

Nice, she says, wiping the wine away, then staring down at her place setting. She tells them countless soldiers were buried and the band played the French national anthem five times along with a seventeen-gun salute. Her voice is monotone, filling up the dead air of the room. She doesn't tell them it feels as if the veil of politeness has been torn away, and she sees what she's always sensed. Emptiness. A vacuum of nothingness; everything done from a stiff pose of habit. The evening will be over almost as quickly as it began. Another day. And tomorrow. Soon, she will be gone. There is nothing to love, she thinks, nothing to hate. The only truth: We hover at the cliff of death.

The servant brings out one dish after another: champagne soup, followed by roasted rabbit in mustard sauce, salade verte et fromage blanc, grilled potatoes with rosemary, bread, and bottles of red and white wine.

Look at all this food, says Svensk.

Extravagant, murmurs Natalia.

Yes. *My* extravagance, says Pierre. Even when I throw you a party, you have to complain, don't you? Perhaps mingling with the lower types in the army will teach you something about humility. My dear sister, let me celebrate in my own way. Pierre deliberately pours himself another glass. How about this? Anything you don't eat, I'll give to the beggars outside. That'll make you happy, won't it?

She looks at him blankly. I just don't think—

Stop right there, says Pierre.

I'll eat the leftovers, says Svensk, slurping his soup.

But you were always different, weren't you? Pierre says, his sharp nose twitching. The army, he shakes his head, clicking his tongue. Who would have thought? The army. I've done my part for France, providing the Parisians with food. And Edmond. He did his part. And now you must go to join the army. Have you heard voices calling you to fight for France? Saint Michael or Saint Catherine or Saint Margaret?

She sips her soup, trying not to breathe.

The bells of Saint Denis Cathedral were melted down today so they could make more cannons, says Svensk. He looks at Jorgen. What's wrong? You're not eating?

Jorgen picks up his spoon.

Pierre turns to Jorgen. You were a rich French man's replacement, weren't you? How much were you paid?

Enough.

How much?

Jorgen doesn't answer.

Well, at least he got paid. My sister comes along and joins the army for free. For free!

She rubs her thumb on something stuck on the table.

Pierre sets his glass down and fixes her with a fierce gaze. Can you believe this country was at a peak of splendor a short three years ago? We hosted the Great Exhibition. We were the crown jewel of the world. Everyone yearned to be like France. It was in Paris that Lister introduced antisepsis, and Nobel invented dynamite. Do you remember, my dear, Natalia, what Prussia sent to the Great Exhibition? Do you recall?

A statue of King Wilhelm I, says Svensk, his tone more of a question than a statement.

Yes, but do you remember what was beside it? A fifty-ton gun. There it stood. But did France take note? Did it see this was the largest gun the world had ever seen? No, of course not. The French were too arrogant. They called the cannon grotesque and ugly. The Prussians sent the world's most powerful cannon to the Great Exhibition and Louis-Napoléon sent a statue of a robust nude reclining upon a lion. It was entitled *Peace*. You see, my little sister. I am a man of the world, and that has saved me. My passion is not with France or parochial Paris. My engagement is with the world beyond these borders, with the rivers of money and goods that flow around the globe. It is in my veins. Which you despise. But we are different, aren't we? You made it a point to be different. Some might say strange. Odd.

She clasps her arms around her front. You will soon be rid of me, she says.

He doesn't mean it, says Jorgen.

Of course he does, she says, pushing away her soup.

Svensk points to the butter. Real butter, he says. Not the Central Market's big yellow squares of horse or beef fat.

Oh, yes, Pierre says, you are leaving. Eat slowly, Natalia. You always eat too fast. You should savor your food not consume it, as if there might not be enough. Look at this plenty. There is more than enough. Our family, the Blancs, have always had abundance. Remember the Blancs eat slowly for pleasure. Imagine holding a peach and letting the sweet juice drip into your mouth. He deliberately and ceremoniously pours himself more wine.

Pierre is detestable, thinks Jorgen, and now she is rubbing her eyes, her head in her palm. How worn she looks, how drained. He hadn't noticed it before, but her hair. What did she do to it? Is it tucked underneath her headband? He senses something tremendously awful has happened to her, and not just the loss of her brother. It's as if something has taken possession of her soul, but he can't name it or say what it might be.

I tried to find some clematis for you, Natalia, says Pierre. A flower for dreamers, says Pierre, but couldn't. Only daisies. Too bad. The city is bare. Stripped down. What a horrible state Paris is in. Pierre raises his glass. To your success. Maybe you will save her.

She instinctively bows her head.

Pierre finishes his glass and sets it on the table with a flare. I have one small favor to ask.

Jorgen watches her carefully.

A small request, really.

She lets out her breath. Go ahead.

I'd prefer if you didn't use our last name, he says. It can't be good for my business to have my sister join the army. It is against custom and protocol for a woman of our social class to do such a thing. You must understand, don't you?

Of course. Whatever you want, Pierre.

Pierre feigns surprise. Whatever I want? Whatever I want? Someone, please take note.

Svensk looks up from his pile of food.

Then I want you to change your last name. Use something else. How about Uchard or Zeller or Bocher or Capoul or Bourbonne? Our honorable father is crying in his grave to think his daughter is doing such a thing.

Fine, she says, the slightest irritation crossing her brow. Edmond would never demand such a thing.

No, he was a saint and I am the devil. But you've always thought that, haven't you? So easy to divide the world up into stark contrasts. The mind of a simple girl.

Jorgen picks up his fork and fights the urge to plunge it into Pierre's pudgy hand. Pierre sits there now, smiling sarcastically, while his sister seems to have left the table, flung her spirit far from this miserable dinner. She's going to leave any moment, and why shouldn't she? Jorgen shifts in his chair uncertainly and announces all the lofts are almost done.

Pierre's mood shifts magically, and he is jubilant and triumphant again.

Wonderful! The Danes are good workers, after all. For a while, I had my doubts. Natalia, did you know Jorgen threatened to walk off the job? He was going to try to stop you from leaving. God knows what he planned to do.

I'll be quite fine, she says, her face expressionless.

I told him it was a lost cause. Once you put your terrible mind to something, it is done. Do you know when she was a young girl, she pleaded with my father to give books to the poor children in our neighborhood, but my dear father wouldn't support such a thing, so Natalia took up tailoring, sewing coats and trousers for the people of our small town. With the money she made, she bought them books. It was utterly embarrassing. These people didn't want books. They wanted food or liquor or medical supplies and so they ended up hanging around our Chaumont estate, waiting for handouts. Which she proceeded to give them from the back kitchen door! It was abominable. I charged at those beggars with a pitchfork to drive them away.

Natalia sets down her wine glass, her hand trembling.

Jorgen is the same way, says Svensk, pouring himself more wine and stabbing his dirty fork in the air at Jorgen. Not giving things to people, but putting his mind to something. He was the smartest in our class. The teacher helped him get into the university. Didn't you get some money? A scholarship? But he dropped out or got kicked out, I'm not sure.

Jorgen doesn't say anything.

He could have done anything. The teachers were always praising him. His father was a mean son of a bitch. His mom got sick, and his father was never around—always at work, at the bar, or gambling. Debtor's prison for a while. Everyone thought Jorgen was going to take care of his mother, since his father was no good. But you just took off one day. You just left. Even your mom—

That's enough, says Jorgen, scooting his chair from the table.

Pierre tells Natalia he saw a huge bull mount a cow this afternoon. He's had too much wine, thinks Jorgen, and he's trying to shock her.

Thank you for the meal, she says, setting down her napkin and rising. Now I should be going.

You never forget your manners, do you Natalia? says Pierre. A redeeming quality and it makes it difficult to dislike you completely. Oh, you are
quite welcome. A cause for celebration. Your leaving and all. Before you go,
you must see my newest acquisition. Go and see the birds, the ugly bunch of
pigeons shitting in the backyard.

She hesitates.

It'll take just a moment, says Jorgen.

She follows him out the back door and they stand on the porch. The blackness of the sky is speckled with stars and the melody of gentle cooing comes
from underneath the blankets. They walk to the first loft and peer in. Jorgen
stands beside her. The air is filled with winter cold. Something pools in his
throat and stays there.

They will wither if left unseen, she says solemnly.

He feels flimsy and shaky and she feels so solid, so sure of herself. What
could he possibly say that would make her pause and reconsider?

Look at their wings, he says. Their feathers are so dry and clean. And
somewhere in that body, they know how to fly home.

She doesn't say anything.

I've always thought of them as dirty birds, says Jorgen. Scavengers. Living off garbage and far away from their natural cliff homes, but up close they
are quite beautiful. He tells her this batch comes from Tours.

The thunder of cannons rings in the far off hills.

You didn't eat much dinner, he says.

No.

He means well. Pierre. Giving you a dinner.

No he doesn't, she says, directing her dull eyes at him. He is despicable,
but that is how he means to be. Natalia's hand is resting on the cage. One of
the pigeons pecks at her palm. He gently takes her hand and moves it away
from the cage.

Your hand is cold, he says.

She puts it in her pocket, turns to him, and fastens her eyes on him. What
were you going to say to make me stay?

He leans against one of the lofts. What can he say? What should he say? He pauses. She is standing, waiting. I just want to make sure you know what you are doing, but I guess I already asked you that.

Yes, you did.

You're going, aren't you?

She nods.

She buttons her coat to the top. Her face is blank and steady. He searches for the words he meant to give her. She is shivering now. What can he say?

Your brother Edmond once mentioned someone named Henri.

She looks at him bewildered and slowly begins to shake her head.

This Henri. A boyfriend. Edmond told me. Jorgen says it before he knows what he's doing.

Edmond mentioned him, says Jorgen. Your brother told me about him.

She drops her head down and hugs herself. Henri was never a boyfriend. A good friend, yes, but not a boyfriend. And—she hesitates. He's gone. In the war. Like Edmond. I never told Edmond because I didn't want him to lose heart. She pauses and looks across the dark yard.

Jorgen feels something break inside. He grabs his hands together and cracks his knuckles. Clouds are racing in from the north.

Maybe I shouldn't have prayed so hard for Edmond to live, she says. He was in such pain at the end. Maybe I should have prayed for him to die.

He touches her shoulder and she stiffens.

What else is there? he thinks. What else is there to do? I have something for you, he says finally.

He leads her upstairs through the back door. There, in the corner, his well-kept rifle. He tells her it has a farther range than hers. Better than the majority of guns used by the French, or the Prussians. Along with the rifle, he hands her a bag of metal cartridges.

She lifts the gun to her shoulder, walks over to the window, and aims at the tree. She pulls the trigger of the unloaded gun. He feels the ripple of excitement upon hearing the gun's cocking and firing.

I have come to love the smell of gunpowder, she says, her voice dreamy.

He nods, knowing the intoxication of the smell.

She recocks the gun and fires again. Thank you, she says, and touches him lightly on the forearm.

For the first time all evening, he feels her presence. She is here, he thinks, she is finally here, and he reaches underneath the bed. The laughter of Pierre and Svensk rings up from the first floor of the house. I wanted to show you this, he says.

He sets the painting on the bed and lights another lantern. His heart beats faster. Yes, this is what he meant to show her, not the birds or the gun, but this. She will see and something will shift inside. She steps closer to the bed. He slowly lifts the cardboard covering, and there is the green of the hill and her lacquer black hair, her ivory complexion, and the shading on her face. So much more vibrant than the last time he looked. And look! The dark red leaves glossy and fluttering around her body and his. A wonderful spring day, look at the yellow flowers all around them, it must have just rained, everything shiny and full of color. There, the tiny village down below. Is that a rice farmer with his straw hat and hoe? The air smells of flowers and honey, he is sure, and her kiss, the bow of her pink mouth, so tender. Her feet are bare, and her toes, such small feet. And the way the man is gazing at her, such tenderness, and yes, such love. An aliveness to everything, a vitality uncontained, and not just the man and woman. The trees are singing and swaying and the long grass is rubbing up against the flowers. The sun is melting on the world below and the sky holds everything, a thick, blue container. And there's a small bird. He smiles. A brown bird with a tinge of orange on its wings. He thought the couple was parting. But no, he was wrong. They are in love, they can't bear any part of their flesh not touching. He has never drawn anything in his life, but if he did, if he could, he would want to be the maker of this painting.

Pretty, she says, leaning away from the painting. She pulls out her pocket watch. I should get going.

His soft face tightens and his jaw drops. Her eyes are distant and glazed, as if she's considering something remote.

What? he says.

It's a fine painting, but I've got a lot to do before I leave.

He quickly covers it up again and slides it underneath the bed. She turns to the door. He follows her numbly down the hallway. They reach the top of the staircase, the gun clutched to her side. He keeps following her as she steps down the stairs and outside.

She stops on the front porch and turns to him. Well, I'll be going.

I'm sure you'll be fine, he says. He leans over to pat her, but she steps toward him, into the open arm, and now he is hugging her, she is lingering there, in the nest of his arms. Natalia and Jorgen stand under the burning streetlight. She thanks him again for the gun. What is the scent of birds? she asks.

I don't know. Wind. Air.

That's your smell, she says. I will remember it.

THE AIR BITES AT his ears and exposed hands. The cold freezes his nostrils. He watches her lonely figure walk across the park, the bright gas lights highlighting her slender form, his gun slung on her shoulder. He wants to call out, say something, but instead, he just watches.

His stump aches and he's about to follow her, but he hears them, calling louder, demanding him. He's learned their sounds; this one is hunger.

He steps inside, grabs the feed bag, and heads to the backyard. Between his fingers, he rolls the polished, shiny seeds around and around. He didn't mean to give her his gun. Why did he do it?

They cry again. All right, he says. All right.

One bird has rubbed off a patch of feathers against the metal wiring of the cage. The bird wants to fly, he thinks. He wants out, and who could blame him? So what if his wages are docked; Pierre, so preoccupied, probably doesn't yet know how many birds he has.

He unfixes the metal notch and slips his hand around the body of the bird. Feels its heat, its small heart beating. He stares at the bird's bright orange eyes. Like the color of the bird's wings in the painting. Or the small touch of lichen on the rock by the Japanese woman's foot. Natalia did not truly see the painting. Is it excitement of the unknown that pulled her away, or despair?

He knows the answer. He returns the bird to its cage, pulls out a piece of paper from his pocket, and writes, *Paris will lose, but there is a woman who will fight without fear because she believes she has already lost everything.*

He reads what he's written, shuddering at this bald truth. He rolls the message up tightly and ties it with a thread to a tail feather. Tossing the bird into the air, he watches it flutter against the wind, flying up to the tree branches, up and up, and beyond.

JAPAN

S HE WILL LOOK STUNNING in such a gown, thinks Sato, casting an approving gaze at the picture of the Western-style dress. He sets the picture on the tailor's cutting table and glances around the shop for fabrics. Why shouldn't she have a beautiful gown? Japan is changing, and Ayoshi should shed her dusty kimono and wear this full-skirted dress with the tight-fitting waist.

The old tailor rests his age-spotted hand on the table and shakes his head in dismay. So many curves for everyone to see, he says. He looks again at the picture, then out his storefront window, as if the sight of the Western dress is too much to bear.

Soon every Japanese woman will want one, says Sato, opening his wallet. The tailor refuses until Sato offers him triple his rate.

At the house the old man takes Ayoshi's measurements. She stands atop a small wooden crate in the receiving room, which is covered in ten tatami mats. What if she began the painting with wildflowers? she thinks, searching the swatches of colorful fabric lying on the floor, a palette beckoning for a spring painting. The tailor measures from her hip to her ankle.

Soon, this will be what everyone considers beautiful, says Sato.

Her arms are extended out from her sides. I don't know. Do you really think beauty is so whimsical?

Smart girl, mumbles the old man, a straight pin clenched between his two lips. The tailor excuses himself, reaches for her wrist, and measures the length of her arm.

Sato paces around the room. Japan is in the midst of a great upheaval. And yes, indeed, I think something can come along more beautiful.

She lifts her arms above her head for the tailor. The tailor marks the cloth with chalk. How disconcerting, she thinks, and the more she considers it, the more agitated she becomes. What happens to the old beautiful object? she asks. Is it tossed in the garbage? How horrible for one so easily to usurp the other.

Sato stops pacing. No, no. The old beauty is treated with generosity, he says. Remember when you danced as a girl, you undid your obi so the bottom of your kimono swirled? I am imagining that now. Your dancing in this Western dress in a large ballroom. I'll escort you and when you enter the room, everyone will stop and look at the new beauty.

You wouldn't know what to do with me, Sato, she says.

What do you mean? We'd have a grand time, a wonderful time. I'd show you the marvelous sights.

And if I didn't want to see them? If I wanted to stay in my room and paint all day?

Oh, you wouldn't do that. You'd want to see everything.

I'm not going anywhere with you.

He smiles a secret, knowing smile and resumes his pacing.

Thin, she thinks, studying herself in the tailor's long mirror. Too thin. My face has more angles to it. I am becoming old. She puts her hand on her cheek and pushes down hard. Soon my hair will have streaks of gray. And there, a hint of a line running from my nose to my mouth. She turns away from the mirror.

Hayashi walks into the room. You've ordered a new kimono? he asks.

No, a gift from Sato, she says.

Sato hands him the picture.

Sato, you are too generous, says Hayashi, his brow puckering. Much too generous.

It's the least I could do for your hospitality, says Sato, bowing.

Ayoshi looks at Hayashi gazing at the picture of the dress, his face flushing, his mouth bending into a frown. He's probably thinking it's too revealing. How will someone know the status of a woman? she wonders. Will the dress come in different styles, like a kimono, some with regular-size sleeves to show the woman is married? Will only the younger women wear bright colors? And where will the family crest go?

She'll look lovely, don't you think? says Sato, looking at Ayoshi with admiration.

Of course, says Hayashi, his voice curt.

She sees Hayashi wince. Still not recovered from the night of dancing and the long day of construction work. Today he did not have the strength to work beside the monk.

Go away, she says. Both of you. She steps down from the crate and picks up a blue-and-peach-colored fabric swatch.

We are not worthy of such generous—

Oh, I'll hear none of that, says Sato, interrupting Hayashi.

She picks up a patch of fabric. An abrupt blue, she thinks. This one, she says, handing it to the tailor.

Yes, says Sato, his hands jittery and tapping his sides.

For the first time this morning, she hears the hammering of nails. Her heart pounds. Suddenly nothing in the house or the garden feels right. She walks over to the window and watches a Japanese maple relinquish a leaf. She's growing old and can't stand another minute in this house.

HAYASHI LOOKS DOWN AND without hesitating smashes the left side of the bowl. It's too excessive, this gift of a dress, he thinks. A bottle of sake, sweets from the bakery, those are fine, but this gift costs thousands of yen, he's sure. He pinches the clay and tries to imagine that different bowl, the one Ayoshi said she liked. Did it expand at the midpoint or below that?

Excuse me, says Sato, stepping into the studio. I hope I'm not interrupting.

No, not at all. He punches in the other side. We are surrounded by the gardens from the Heian Period, a time when Japan was seeped in beauty, and I can't seem to make anything that's close to that.

Sato stands by Ayoshi's desk and fingers a piece of blank paper.

From 794 to 1185 there was the development of calligraphy, the painting style yamato-e, and the golden age for poetry, says Hayashi. The most compelling work, Lady Murasaki's epic, *Tale of Genji*.

The clay is now collapsing on itself, returning to its original shape. Sato stares at the dilapidated bowl. Yes, an interesting time, says Sato. I hope you will accept my gift to Ayoshi.

Hayashi mashes the bowl into a lump of clay. It's rather extravagant.

We're old friends, you know. She's my dearest friend. Sato sits in Ayoshi's chair, stretching his legs out in front of him and crossing his ankles.

Yes, says Hayashi, too loudly. You've already told me that. Truthfully, I am partial to the kimono. I think we ought to honor and respect our past. This Western dress seems rather objectionable.

Sato sighs. Japan has grown by seizing things from other countries—China, Korea, India, Tibet, and soon the West. Remember how deftly Japan saddled up to China and took what she needed and desired, writing, philosophy. The entire city of Nara? Modeled after the Chinese capital at His-an with its street patterns in relation to the Imperial Palace.

Hayashi examines Sato's feet. If he had those feet, he'd be outside with a hammer and nail. Please ask if you need anything, says Hayashi, his voice abrupt. We are your hosts. And he can't help adding, At least for as long as you stay with us.

Sato smiles. So Japan will find her way through this Westernization, and Ayoshi will wear a new dress.

Do you know the Heian concept of miyabi?

No, says Sato.

It's something the West, I'm sure, knows nothing about, and you'll never find in their artwork or fashion. He tells Sato a person with miyabi derives pleasure from perfection. It doesn't matter if the object is composed of detailed or simple beauty, it is a perfection of form and color. And that person has an awareness of beauty's inherent sadness.

Sato uncrosses his legs and sits straight up. What sadness?

Hayashi grabs a rag and wipes off his hands. Beauty is fleeting.

Now you sound like that gloomy monk and his dismal views of the world. At the precise moment of beauty, that one singular moment when you see beauty, what happens to you?

Hayashi jabs his hands back into the clay and feels his face become hot. I don't know. It's too quick.

Sato jumps up from his chair. Pay closer attention.

Hayashi stops moving.

Let me be more specific. When you see your wife, her bloom of beauty, aren't you held in a state of wonder? Sato steps toward him.

His wife. The words still sound so foreign. A grim anxiety overtakes him. *His wife.* What is Sato doing looking so closely at his wife? Hayashi's hands grip the clay.

Sato hovers over him. You must feel something.

Hayashi doesn't reply. What did he feel when he looked at her atop the wooden crate? He sits in silence, the world swimming around him. Pin pricks of sweat pop on his brow and temple. The light shifts and the room darkens as rain clouds gather outside the window. What did he feel? He can't say that he felt nothing; that wouldn't be true. Careful? Cautious? Tentative? Do you know when she first came here, she wouldn't eat? says Hayashi, staring out the small window, his voice barely audible. She ran away five times. Five times. She cried and cried; I didn't think she'd ever stop. Most days she wouldn't get out of bed. When I let her use the studio, she'd stay in here for hours, unless I came in, and then she'd flee. She still does that, you know. She couldn't stand to be near me, and now, I suppose she bears it. I've learned to stay away so I don't upset her.

Hayashi turns away from Sato, scraping the extra clay from the top of his wheel and throwing it into the bucket.

Sato sits again.

I suppose I'm not the easiest man to be with, says Hayashi. Quiet, he thinks, I've always preferred quiet, not the company of others. There are times I think I should have stayed at the monastery, he says. Do you know that her father sent a formal kimono dress and hakama, but nothing else?

And they both know what was missing—the long piece of seaweed, the kanji used to signify *seaweed* and also *childbearing woman*. The gift would have held out hope for many children.

Hayashi looks down at his folded hands resting on the wheel. I've come to think, and I can't say why, she removed it.

Neither man says anything for a while.

She is better now, says Sato. Better than when she first arrived, isn't she? He waits for an answer, for a sign, but Hayashi's eyes are away from him now.

AYOSHI GRABS HER COAT and rushes outside. A gust of wind picks up the fallen leaves. Where can she go? She looks at the iron gates. Turns to the lake. To the temple. The monk calls out to her. She walks over to him in a daze. There is the smell of pine from the new deck he's added to the tea-house, and then, unexpectedly, she is struck in the face, like a branch swinging back, by his body's musty scent of manual labor. His black hair is now almost a quarter-inch long. Her stomach shrinks to a small rock. What is he saying? He is pointing to something and speaking. The wood. Yes, he is speaking about the wood and the grain. Light wood. He is saying, Light wood, preferred, and she wants to say, Yes, he is right.

He steps inside the unfinished structure, and she follows him through the doorway, crouching down to half her size.

Here will be the tokonoma, he says, where in springtime, a small vase will sit with a single flower. Behind it, a scroll, with a sutra.

I can't seem to paint today.

He turns and faces her. Maybe you need inspiration.

She doesn't say anything.

A walk in the garden?

No, she thinks. Not far enough. I need to go to town to get some things, she says. Would you accompany me?

He hesitates and looks at the half-built teahouse.

Of course, I can ask the maid to go with me, she says, feeling ashamed for being so bold.

His master would never leave unfinished work. Would not succumb to an arm aching from the hammer, to the boredom of the measured blows. His master would not think these thoughts, or consider the sweet smell of a female. If his master knew how little self-discipline he had, he'd call him unfit to be a monk. And perhaps it's true. He picks up a small piece of wood and runs his hand over the grain. Perhaps he learned all he can, and the rest will have to be learned in another lifetime. He sets the wood down. To go to town and experience the streets and the people. At the thought of going, he feels his life expand in a wonderful way. Yes, he says, yes, he'd like to go.

She hurries inside the house, puts on her walking shoes, a heavier coat, finds her parasol, and heads outside. The monk is waiting on the new porch. He has a long piece of grass between the sides of his thumbs. He sees her, blows air through the makeshift musical instrument, and makes the grass sing.

She smiles at him. Yes, this is exactly what she needs. She opens the big black gate and slams it shut behind them. She peers back at the house, the temple, the cemetery, and a heaviness sloughs from her. Certainly something will inspire her. She turns to the monk. Look at the way he studies the tall trees. He takes such pleasure in being in the world. She imagines that everything swims and glitters for him. The other day she saw him admiring the way the white clouds gathered along the mountain peak. She wishes she'd been stuck in a dusty old monastery and only recently stepped out; the world would be fresh, everything a dazzle to the eye.

I saw the town from a distance, he says. I saw it when I came down the mountain and got lost trying to find the temple.

You've never been to town before?

He shakes his head. There was always a lot of work to be done. The vegetable gardens and the cleaning. We woke every day at two A.M. And he proceeds to tell her his former life: Forty minutes of meditation, a five-minute break, then another forty minutes of meditation, a meeting with my teacher, breakfast, chores, back to meditation, a break, more meditation, dinner, and meditation from seven to eleven at night. Every minute of the day was allocated to some chore, some task.

This was my life for years and years, he says.

It sounds very hard. Very strenuous.

The trees are swaying and bending. She feels his buoyancy, as if he might leap up into the air and swing on a tree limb. When is the last time she felt this way?

Then it's good we're going, she says.

Yes, I think so.

He tells her that although he wishes it hadn't happened the way it did, the time away from the monastery has been good for him. There are a lot of stories of monks achieving sublime enlightenment in strange ways. He heard of one monk who was sweeping a temple courtyard when his broom struck a pebble. The pebble smacked against a bamboo fence, and the sudden sound dislodged something in the monk's mind. He instantly figured out his koan and became enlightened.

So maybe on this walk, it will happen to you, she says. Anything could happen today, she thinks.

Maybe. Or to you.

She laughs.

They walk for a while in silence, but they are connected now from the laughter, and she feels a hint of comfort that comes from knowing someone a long time. She felt it for a moment when she showed him her paintings. He studied them so carefully and thoughtfully. Yes, this was the perfect thing to do today. It all feels fluid, and a new painting will come, she feels certain. Hayashi once recited a line from Emerson and she asked him to write down, she loved it so: *Life is a train of moods like a string of beads, and, as we pass through them, they prove to be many colored lenses which paint the world their own hue, and each shows only what lies in its focus.* It's true, she thinks.

You mentioned you come from the north. Do you ever miss your hometown? he asks.

Which colored beads to look through? She holds all the colors in her hands. Some days, she says. Some days it pulls at me, but not right now. Her lacerated heart is forgetting itself, she thinks, left behind the iron gate, and the day feels like something she's never experienced.

As they head into town, they see people swarming everywhere. The sun has broken through the clouds and shines on the wooden sidewalks, and there are men in kimonos and one or two in smart Western suits. A boy skips alongside his mother. Women carry baskets of vegetables and sugar cakes from the bakery. People are pushing big wheelbarrows of rice and barley in the street and men are smoking long sticks of tobacco. Fresh wood is stacked in piles along the main street. New shops and tall buildings are being birthed, including the one with imposing tall white pillars in front.

Look at that, he says, pointing to a woman balancing a basket on her head. Then to a small boy bouncing a ball and a girl balancing herself on a raised wooden plank. Ayoshi laughs and is taken out of herself.

A man rides by enclosed in a wooden box with windows; he's being pulled not by another man, but by horses. Three of these new carts are waiting in front of the market, announcing that for a fee, you can ride to the new capital, Tokyo, in a little over an hour.

This is what they must do, she thinks. Of course. All morning she felt anxious and suffocated and now this. Travel to the capital. The last time she went anywhere was from her home in Hokkaido to here.

A carriage, says the driver, it's called a carriage. This one from Europe.

The monk's face blooms with color, and his eyes grow wide, alert, and slightly wild. She brought money for shopping and now they will take this new carriage. They step gingerly onto the platform. It wobbles and they grab each other's arm, laughing. They sit up high above the ground on the black leather bench. The driver sits in front of them, cracks a whip, Giddyup, he shouts, and the horses whinny and start and trot by the shops.

The world is speeding beside them, a blurry line outside their wooden carriage. She feels the heat of his thigh pressed up against hers.

The driver says along this road, all the guard stations are gone, and people are now free to come and go as they please. It will happen all over this country, he says. That's why he bought this new cart and two strong horses. There will be more business than he can handle. Look behind you, he says, and they see the town receding, a small dark dot. They turn around; the tall buildings of the capital rise up in the distance.

What are you thinking? asks the monk.

Nothing. Nothing at all. She closes her eyes and opens them again. The world is new, as if it shed its skin and it is gleaming for her.

He smiles and points to a tall gray heron standing in a pond, one long leg raised out of the water, its head tilted. The breeze ripples the surface of the green water and it is hypnotizing, the lines repeated, over and over. Everything is green, a brilliant deep color that her paints can only imitate.

As they come closer to the new capital, they see the gathering of larger buildings. The sound of hammers rings out. There, points the driver, a dormitory for workers who are pouring into the new capital. There, a Western restaurant will open its doors, and there are Western-style buildings made of reddish orange material. Brick, the driver calls it.

They draw into town and people are crowded on sidewalks, carrying bags and more bags of goods. These new carriages are everywhere. The sounds and the flurry of movement—it is daunting and intimidating. They sit in the carriage, amazed, in a half stupor. The monk moves first, as if being pulled along by the swell of people.

Women wearing every color of kimono pass by, some in Western-style dresses, and men in kimonos and tight Western suits. They begin walking and pass a tall wooden boardinghouse. A sign reads, RECENTLY CONSTRUCTED FOR WOMEN WORKERS. She grabs his arm and makes him halt in front of the large structure. A room on the top floor. There, in the right corner with the white shade flapping with the breeze. She'd set up an easel at the window and paint the city. Rise early and paint before going to work. And what might she do? Whatever the girls do. Stitch clothing or calligraphy. Perhaps someone would buy a painting.

A woman walks by, her hair cut short. She's walking up to the front steps of the new building, wearing a kimono, smelling of rose. Yes, she would cut her hair and paint in the morning.

His head feels as if it is going to burst with all the sound and motion. He is dizzy from the horses passing by, the shouting of men pulling rickshas— Watch out!—and the drivers of these new carriages, the people clustered together and gossiping on the street. Everything so fast, it makes him weary. They begin walking again. There is a tea shop with small dishes of food in the window. A window displays a Western-style bathroom. The sign says, THE NECESSARY THINGS, a toothbrush dish, toothbrush, soap dish, and comb.

A mistake to wander around the city; what is the point of this life? People are rushing about with mindless energy. Look at all the bags that woman is carrying. What could she possibly need in all those bags? And he feels so strongly, stronger than he's felt in a while, the longing for the quiet of the meditation hall, the simple task of washing a white dish. He turns to Ayoshi to tell her he'd like to go back. She is no longer beside him. He stops walking. Swarms of people are everywhere. He turns around and around, a small cyclone. A prick of adrenaline pokes at the base of his head. He cranes his neck. His breathing tightens and his mind unleashes a flurry of worries. What should he do? How will he get back? He could beg, but he no longer looks like a monk. Who would give him money? Someone shouts for him to get out of the way. He steps aside and bumps into a woman who's walking with a man. The monk apologizes and feels his eyes tear.

Then he sees her. She's about halfway down the block, staring at something in a store window. He rushes back and finds her fixated on a hat.

I thought I lost you, he says, panting.

I'm so glad you're here. Her voice is tight and her lips compressed. She feels her anger and fear all at once. And for a moment, seeing so much emotion in the monk's face—he looks so thrilled to see her—almost makes her forget her fright. But when the man who has been standing next to her, who won't leave, who pressed his dirty fingers on her arm, begins to speak to her again, her fear returns. They shouldn't have gone on this trip. It was stupid and too daring. She was intrigued by the man's Western-style suit and asked him where he bought it. A dark blue with thin gray lines. The man's face is flared red and his eyes are still roaming over her.

The monk folds Ayoshi's hand into his. Excuse me, says the monk to the man, pulling her by his side.

You've got a beautiful woman here, says the man.

Thank you, says the monk. My wife. She's my wife. We're going now.

You shouldn't leave her standing alone. That's not very gentlemanlike.

Of course not. We became separated for a moment.

I thought I'd wandered into the pleasure quarters. He laughs loudly, then stops and stares. His thick belly falls over the strap of leather wrapped around his waist. Finally the man stumbles away.

The monk leads her down the sidewalk, her hand still clasped in his. When he reaches the entrance of the tea shop, he asks if she is all right. She nods, still shaken. They step inside. The light in the small shop is murky, and they find seats on a wooden bench. Only a few people are having afternoon tea near the windows. He is relieved to be inside.

Thank you, she says.

I should have paid more attention.

The waiter nods to them. She feels as though she walked through a spiderweb, the sticky filaments all over her skin, but the monk grabbed her hand and pulled her through. The man touched her elbow. His acrid breath and the grip of his thick hand on her elbow. She still feels where he touched her. And now there is the heat of the monk's leg searing hers.

Steaming green tea arrives and rice crackers, too.

I got distracted by the hat.

The monk nods and sips his tea, the inflated feeling of heroism fading.

Out the window she glimpses a young couple walking together; the woman's head tilts toward the man, who is saying something to her. She laughs, covering her mouth. I have never had that, she thinks, that open ease with a man. She looks at the monk's hand, the moon shape of his fingernails.

When the waiter comes again, she orders sake. A tall bottle. The small sliver of light through the front door curtain cuts a thin line on the floor. The waiter returns with two small cups and a tall vase of hot sake. She raises her glass, a toast, but to what? His hands are clenched now. She wants this day to be wonderful, the bead through which to look bright yellow. There is a painting on the wall, a waterfall with an old man fishing from a large rock. The monk is studying it intensely.

You said I was your wife, she says, smiling. Isn't that funny?

For a moment, the burden won't lift, but he looks at her and smiles.

Yes.

What would your teacher think?

He'd say I was no good. Which he said all the time anyway.

A bad monk.

But maybe this time I wouldn't mind, says the monk, drinking his sake. Maybe I'd agree.

They laugh again and the lightness is returning. Everything is going to be fine, she thinks, and touches him lightly on the wrist.

He tells her some of the young monks used to get so restless, they'd sneak out at night, climb down the mountain, and go to the brothels.

And did you? she asks.

No. I got drunk instead, he says, pouring himself more sake.

The waiter brings a plate of rice crackers and sashimi and tells them it is a gift from the owner, please come to this restaurant whenever they visit the new capital.

Ayoshi claps her hands in delight. Doesn't the air feel different here, she says. As if you could be anything or do anything? It makes you giddy, doesn't it?

His breathing slows as he takes in the air. Yes, he says, his shoulders unfolding. Everyone is moving, going here and there in a mad rush. It makes you feel as though you're missing something, or might miss something.

That's exactly it, she says, smiling.

He refills her glass.

This rushing around. It reminds you that life is fleeting, so you must try everything, don't you think? he says.

She is beginning to feel drunk.

His cheeks are a bright red hue. Here's to death, which makes us remember to live, he says raising his glass. That, he thinks, is the truest thought he's had in a long time. He brushes his fingers against her thigh. The heat. The heat. This day is unlike any other. He tells her that for generations his family has always given one child to the monastery. He was the one. And now he is a man and he is alive, hearing the people clamoring in the kitchen, throwing wonderful scents wide into the room. He can't possibly go back, he thinks. No, he won't return to the monastery. And he must do what he's been wanting to do—when did he first feel this urge? It seems that it's been there from the moment he saw her—and he leans over and quickly kisses her, catching the side of her cheek.

This is it, she thinks. This is what she's been waiting for. No one is looking, the chef busy with an order, the other couples tucked in conversations. This is what she wants—to be drawn into life, to cross the almost visible line that has kept her out. She turns to him. He kisses her again, this time on the lips.

He is full of attention, sensing the tip of her shoulder forward, finding her hair, brushing long strands behind her ear. His scalp tingles to the touch. The way her lips part halfway, he tastes her moistness. The hairs on his arms stand up, alarmed. He feels altogether changed and different. All the time he has been meditating to dissolve the self, and here, with one kiss on rose-colored lips, he has disappeared completely into her.

She feels an electricity run through her body. Smells his skin, a freshness to it, clean and the hint of incense. The monk's eyes, the streaks of amber. What a beautiful color, and she tells him so, as if he's illuminated within. He touches the inside of her wrist.

Silk, he murmurs.

She moves closer, firmly pushing aside the first pang of guilt, of any thought of Urashi, of Hayashi, as he leans into her, finding a long stretch of warm silk.

THEY STUMBLE BACK INTO the light of the city. It is dusk now, the sky swollen with strokes of purple and pink. As they walk down the bustling sidewalk, he gently takes her by the arm and pushes through the throngs of people. No one looks at them oddly and she thinks, It must be so natural, this pairing. Soon they will return, and she will have not painted. What if she never bothered to paint again?

The monk leans over and whispers his nickname. The name attached because he was restless on the cushion, and he's never told anyone because he disliked it, but now, he rather likes it. The name makes him laugh. She remembers the meaning of the name: independent, outspoken, ready to accept challenges, and also impulsive and prone to dark moods.

Enri, she repeats. Enri. She smiles. Yes. The restless monk.

It fits, doesn't it?

Yes, she says, smiling.

They find a carriage and climb in, leaning into each other. The horse's trotting and the silence of birds blend together. When they arrive home, she will buy some vegetables and green tea and sugar cakes. Shopping, she'll say, and before that, a long, luxurious bath.

As they near the town, there is the smell of smoke in the air. Something burned today, but she can't see the remains of the fire. They sit quietly. He touches her wrist again, as if once the border is broken down, it can't be resisted.

A WHITE CRANE, ITS wings fringed with what? Sorrow? Joy? How would he make a bowl that suggests joy? Light, slender, and delicate. The bowl made of porcelain, or perhaps a vase, not a bowl at all.

The enlightened leaders take their seats around the table and Hayashi steps away from the window. They all wear Western suits, like Sato's. This morning's conversation with Sato still echoes. A dear friend, he said. One of her oldest friends. The bloom of her beauty.

Someone hands him an American cigarette, and the crane keeps rising up in his mind and pulling him out of the room to the lake where he passed by five cranes on the way to town. Perhaps a crane on the side of his next bowl. He's never painted an image, only a glaze. He picks up a pencil and draws a sketch on his notepad. His throat tightens; what is he doing here? It is pointless.

How is your business? the head of trade asks Hayashi.

Fine, fine, says Hayashi, his voice fading, his hand still drawing. Business? So strange to put it that way, he thinks. As if he sits at the wheel for hours and hours, all for the exchange of money.

The head of trade pauses, waiting for him to say more, but Hayashi keeps drawing, and the man turns away.

Shall we begin, says the man at the head of the table.

Hayashi feels the knot in his stomach tighten, his hand twitches. The men fall silent and he sets his pencil down. An agenda is passed out and the room stills as everyone reads.

The men are speaking, and he is back on his walk to town, looking at the land as he descended the hill, spread out before him like a green fan. The rice fields caressed by the sun. The cranes nestled at the lake's edge, and, as he passed by, they flew up into the air, like pearls broken from a necklace. The tall pond grass scraped against the edges of the water, and he desperately wanted to stay and sit at the water's edge. A poem would have eventually taken shape as he watched the birds and listened to the whir of insects.

Shall we begin? says the man again.

Hayashi moans quietly; perhaps today is not the day to make any trouble. What if they demand that he move out of the house and they condemn the entire place? That horrible promise to the monk. He made it on an impulse, out of gratitude for what the mountain monks gave to him, for what the monk brought to his home.

The telegraph system is up and running, announces one of the men. Messages can be sent from Tokyo to Yokohama. The system is ahead of schedule by several months. The men raise their brandy glasses. Hayashi hesitates, his glass at half-mast. What is the meaning of this telegraph? Who would he want to speak to in Kyoto? In Kyushu? As he walked by the lake, the cranes stood calmly at the edge of the water. Then, suddenly, they flew up in the air. Was it a bad sign? Perhaps he should wait for the next meeting to speak.

The train, says the man in charge of transportation. Soon, says the man, the railroad tracks will be crisscrossing the country, and we will permit, no encourage, everyone to travel anywhere. This will help commerce. The man pushes up his eyeglasses and announces, already, carriages are taking people from the town to the capital. They raise their glasses again and Hayashi thinks at least this is a good thing. To Tokyo for a moon-viewing party. And what did the man just say? From here to Tokyo only an hour. They could pack a picnic and stay the night, return the next day. He feels his heartbeat quicken at the thought, then the slow smile droops. She won't want to go with him. She'd want to stay home and paint.

Hayashi reaches down and rubs his feet. The men's voices rumble on; he looks down at his kimono and sees a long black strand of her hair. From end to end, it stretches over one meter.

The man in charge of edicts inquires about the proper attire for a train ride. How stupid, thinks Hayashi. That man is the one who announced several months ago that men must cut off their topknots and samurai can no longer carry their swords. He feels himself become angry at the idiocy of such things and turns again to the cranes. Yes, and by the strength of their wings, you could sense they could fly anywhere.

The curtains are sucked in and out the window by the breeze. Hayashi thinks he hears shouting, but dismisses it. Only birds flying overhead and the sound of dogs barking.

The head of edicts speaks again, and in a flash, Hayashi knows he is the one who ordered the teahouse burned. The head of edicts slurps his tea and Hayashi watches his knobby fingers, his brown teeth. He would do such a thing, he thinks. Such a despicable man would order the burning. There is a pause in the discussion.

Excuse me, but I believe the raids on the Buddhist monasteries and temples are unnecessary, says Hayashi.

The military official's face turns red.

People will turn against the government if they continue. I think we must reconsider.

We are not leading these so-called raids, says the military official. It's the people. The citizens who are sick of the corrupt monks.

Regardless, it can be stopped, says Hayashi. If our army is so powerful, we could stop it.

The military man waves the agenda in the air. This is not a proper subject. It is not on the agenda. Where is it on the agenda? Show me. This man is out of order.

Hayashi's heart races. He clenches the fabric of his clothes. If it were a priority, it could be stopped.

Still waving the paper, the man stabs out his cigarette. Where?

Hayashi begins to sweat. His hands shake.

This isn't your area of expertise, is it? says the man responsible for education, scooting back his chair, his voice cold and calm.

No, says Hayashi, surprising himself at his insistence, but it's a critical issue.

I didn't think so. I believe it's about art or preserving art or some such thing. Perhaps you'd like to report on that.

But it is a concern, says Hayashi. And much of Japanese art is indebted to Buddhism for its influence. But that is not my main point.

Of course. We are all concerned. Very concerned. By the way, haven't you been told to close the temple? I believe an official message was delivered to you. Was it not?

Yes, but—

Good. I'm sure there have been no problems. I'm sure you have turned away any villagers who have come for prayer services.

The room is quiet. Hayashi doesn't know what to say.

The next item on the list is a visit by American officials, says the military man.

It doesn't bode well for the new government, says Hayashi.

The military man waves his smoking cigarette in the air. Next item, he says, his voice abrupt.

Hayashi bows his head, his face filling with shame. He pushed too far and now he's a pariah in the room. Why couldn't he have been more composed? Why did it come out as a burst? They've already moved on to the upcoming visit by the Americans. Nothing will come of it, he thinks, what could come of it? Hayashi calls up his crane, but it wavers and the wings spread so wide, flying far away, no longer visible. His hands long to fall into cool clay. If he could, he'd leave right now.

Finally the meeting is adjourned, and Hayashi rushes down the staircase and steps outside. At the far end of the dusty road, there are shouts from a crowd gathered in front of the rice shop. The shopkeeper stands out front, pleading. Rocks smash against the wooden storefront. They rush into the store and carry out big, shiny bags of rice on their shoulders. They return with wheelbarrows, cleaning out his store.

Hayashi stops a man who is scurrying by. What is going on?

He tells Hayashi about the price of rice. Gone up threefold. Hayashi watches as the angry mob sets fire to the wooden shop and the lips of the flame brush against the old wooden porch. Hayashi hurries by, faster than he's walked in a long time, passing by the rice shopkeeper, weeping on the ground, and Hayashi knows he should stop to help the man, but he can't, he has to get home. He hurries up the hill, with big heaves of breath, his feet screaming, his head tipped down, not stopping at the pond, the cranes now gone.

FRANCE

NATALIA, HE SAYS, RAPPING his knuckles on her door. When there is no answer, Jorgen pounds the door then jiggles the knob. Natalia. Natalia. Please open the door.

Down the hallway, a door creaks open.

My God, says an old woman, her hair a blur of white gray, a red terry-cloth robe wrapped around her doughy frame. Why all this noise so early in the morning? The bombs, the cannons, and now you. Must everything go to pieces at once?

He is sweating from the walk and the long climb up the narrow stairs.

The young lady is gone. She left in the middle of the night. I heard her go. She was wearing those dreadful boots. The old woman stops herself and eyes him suspiciously. Who are you? What do you want?

He is too late, he thinks. Too late. That is it. The pounding of his fist against the door—*too late, too late.*

A friend of hers. He hesitates. A good friend. I thought—before she left, but she's gone—could I see her apartment?

The old woman looks at him with curiosity. Whatever for?

He stands still, repeating the question to himself. What does he think he'll

find inside? The old woman is about to step inside her apartment. I'm thinking of renting it, he says. She loved this place, so quiet and clean, and wonderful neighbors. I'm looking for a new place to live.

The old woman's scowl tips up to a smile. She reaches for her walking
cane, snaps shut her door, and hobbles into the hallway. She tells Jorgen that
Natalia was a good tenant. She kept to herself—she never had visitors, poor
girl, but she was generous. It's such a shame a girl is so alone in the world.

He yanks nervously on his coat sleeve. He had shown her things, hadn't he?
The beautiful feathers on the pigeons and the painting. What did she say
about the painting? A fine painting, or something. But that was not seeing,
not truly seeing, having your whole body soften; he should have shaken her,
taken her by the shoulders, yelled at her dulled face, locked up in numbness,
Can't you see? But how do you make someone's eyes soak in the blues and
greens? Make her see the depth of the shadows and the brightness of the wild
daisies? And from there—hasn't this been happening to him—make her fall
headlong into the world?

The old woman touches his arm.

A young lad, she says, staring up at him with filmy eyes.

Sorry to bother you, he says. And if she looked, truly looked, he thinks,
Natalia would have found her heart quickening, and a small tear in the thick,
gray fog. In the clearing, the world welcoming her, at least in some small way.
That's it, isn't it? That's what he's begun to feel, and something more, something she seems to have lost.

The old woman turns the key. He steps inside and almost gasps. So bleak.
This room with its one dirty window barely letting in the morning light. A
leafless tree branch scrapes against the glass. On the window ledge, leaves,
blackened and rotting. Dust motes congregate in the corners. The room is
smaller than his, except for the tiny walk-in kitchen. Pushed up against the
wall, a single cot stripped of its sheets and blankets, the silver mattress
exposed.

He walks over to her cot. There, a pillow without a casing. He imagines
her curled up there, her fists clutching. Most likely a serious face—of
late, it has been so grim—even in thick sleep. Gently, he touches the pointed

corner of her pillow. He leans over the cot, lifts the pillow, and there is her scent—fresh flowers and something else. What could he have done to stop her? Nothing, nothing, but then, why does it feel so terribly wrong that he is here, standing in her vacated apartment, and she is on the battlefield? He drops the pillow on the cot.

The old woman scrubs the counters, and Jorgen half listens to her speak of the new government, with the emperor living in exile, a quarter of a million French soldiers held captive, and the French army in desperate need of soldiers and supplies. She watched General Vinoy return to Paris with his troops.

They looked like a wreck upon a beach, she says. It was pitiful. Poor Natalia. The old woman rattles on.

What is the scent of birds? Natalia asked. A cannon rings out, shattering the silence of the early morning. The old woman sighs. How much longer? she asks. This dreadful war.

Jorgen sits on the cot and stares at the floor. A single strand of her hair—yes, chestnut brown—stuck in between two wooden floorboards. He carefully releases the hair from its hold and wraps it around his finger. I'll take it, he says, and he doesn't know how he'll pay for it, but there is her smell, her ghostly presence.

Good, she says. If you're a friend of Natalia's, I'm sure you'll be a welcome tenant.

The old woman heads back to her apartment to find an extra set of keys. As he listens to her footsteps recede, he opens the closet door. He steps back aghast. It takes a moment to realize it is only a dress. A light blue dress on a hanger. He holds it up to the light and the color enters a slit in his mind, taking him elsewhere, to the color of a summer sky, the ocean, to the blue wildflowers—or are they tears?—in the painting. He must find her.

He hears the old woman returning. The cloth against his cheek is velvet. Natalia, he whispers. When he walked her outside, she stayed in his arms, as if she never wanted to leave, and he didn't want to feel it, pulled far back from that embrace, but now, his body conjures it up, her cheek resting next to his, her warm breath on his neck, her hands pressed into his back. The woman is almost at the apartment door, rattling the keys. He stuffs the dress inside his coat pocket.

NATALIA HAS BEEN GONE over two weeks and Jorgen has begun to steal more regularly. Whenever Pierre goes out, Jorgen rifles through a box. He does it without thinking, with no sense of guilt. For why should he? He can't stay here. Tonight, with Pierre at some party, he is rummaging through a box, shoving things into his bag, when he thinks he hears someone downstairs. It can't be Pierre. He left hours ago.

Jorgen!

Jorgen freezes. It's Pierre.

Jorgen!

He sets the bag down behind a box. If Pierre says he heard him in the storage room, he will say he had work to finish; and if he heard the tearing open of boxes? An extra inventory check. The carting of a bag into his room? Nonsense. He misheard. He was moving boxes around to make them easier to unload. Jorgen sets his teeth, tightens his shoulders, and walks down the stairs, the explanations bumping into each other.

Jorgen finds Pierre sitting alone at the kitchen table.

Come share a bottle of wine with me! Come, come sit down, says Pierre. I hate to drink alone. It's a miserable thing. There's no one interesting at the café. A bunch of bores whining about the war and I'm tired of it.

Pierre swirls the red wine in his glass, holding it out in front of him. Crumbs stick to the corners of his mouth. While most of Paris suffers, Pierre has managed to acquire a small potbelly.

Drink up, my man, says Pierre. Jorgen sits across from him and Pierre pours him a glass. Pierre tells him the first batch of pigeons are to be released at the end of the week. You'll have to let go of some of your little friends. Oh, don't be upset. That'll teach you to become attached to the dirty creatures. To be attached to anything. Stick with being a shrewd businessman and you'll be safe.

Some part of Jorgen envies Pierre, his peculiar freedom; it seems Jorgen once had this independence, free of attachments and obligations to people, didn't owe anything to anyone, but it seems long ago, so remote, maybe it wasn't ever true.

You've never married? asks Jorgen.

Never married, never wanted to marry. I've never met a woman interesting enough or beautiful enough to warrant spending my entire life with her. In the end, marriage is, after all, an economic transaction. It is best to remain independent and unattached. He dabs his napkin to the corner of his mouth. More wine? asks Pierre, refilling his glass.

The hard rock in Jorgen's stomach turns; no, he is not made for such freedom. Maybe once, but not anymore. He places his palms on the table, preparing to leave.

Pierre stares out the window. Don't go. I'm just a little drunk right now. There is a particularly beautiful pigeon. Have you seen it? Its wings are a soft gray with a dab of purple on the edges. A light green ring around its neck. A lovely bird. Its eyes, a soft orange yellow. When you find it, don't let that one go.

Jorgen feels some of his animosity toward Pierre dissipate. He's never heard Pierre talk with such affection.

Put it to the side. Maybe in its own cage. Yes, build the lovely creature its own home.

They sit for a while in silence. Pierre pours more wine into Jorgen's glass. Jorgen looks into the glow of the candlelight, watching the flame flicker and leap.

I don't think Natalia is well, says Pierre, staring into his glass.

Jorgen abruptly sets down his glass. You've heard from her? What have you heard?

No, I've heard nothing.

What do you know?

I promised my father I'd look after her. Did I tell you already? Well, it bears repeating. A young servant of ours had relations with my father, gave birth to Natalia, and then was sent away. My father, the respectable man that he was, raised Natalia in a formal way. We are distantly related to Napoléon, you know. I know nearly everyone makes that claim, but in our case, it's true. Did you hear of our family name before you came here?

No.

Well, no matter. My father hired a tutor who taught her to read at an early age and she read quite well, very precocious. We thought we had a chance of raising a proper lady. She had some rather uncouth parts. She loved to play the rough games with the boys. We had to drag her inside sometimes, her knees bloody and her frocks dirty. She had a disgustingly deep affinity for the peasants. I told you about the books. We probably only knew about half of what she did.

A group of soldiers in red coats pass by the window singing loudly, their arms linked, leading one another forward, helping one another stay on their feet.

Drunk fools, says Pierre. She was proposed to twice, and she turned them down. They were fairly rich men, too. She could have been dressed in silks and embroideries, lace and furs. She could have had that. I've said before she's not a looker, but her eyes, yes, I'll admit, her eyes, their intense glow. Stunning, really. Not the soft, motherly eyes in the style of our new painters, but the fierce eyes of an Athena or one of the Furies. Some men prefer such a look. You've noticed them, haven't you?

He has; Jorgen recalls her eyes were the first thing he saw when he woke in the hospital from a fitful sleep. She was sitting at Edmond's bedside, holding his hand. Jorgen must have made some sound upon waking, because she turned to him. Her eyes were bright robin's-egg blue with startling clarity and a penetrating force. They seemed to take everything in at once, without flinching. He stared at her, quickly looked away, and curtly dismissed her physical beauty.

It's not right, Pierre says, shaking his head.

What?

To put another human's well-being before yours. That Englishman, Darwin, he'd say it's all wrong. What kind of nature is that? It's self-destructive, that's what it is. Nothing is gained by such behavior. She acts unnaturally.

Jorgen sets down his glass. She probably doesn't see it that way.

Pierre looks at Jorgen with a distraught gaze. Of course she doesn't see it that way. That's the problem. She's never been well. And it's only gotten worse.

Jorgen straightens in his chair. You could find her, couldn't you? I'm sure you have connections.

Such an embarrassment. I can't believe she's joined the army. Damn foolish. I'm a damn fool for making that cursed promise to my father. How can I look after a loony like her?

You could bring her back, says Jorgen, his voice excited, and he scoots to the edge of his chair. If anyone could do it, you could. With your money and the people you know.

Pierre's face slowly brightens. But if my father were alive today, I don't think he'd want me to honor such a promise. No, not at all. Stripped of her senses, he'd say. No daughter of his would do such a thing. She's become a half-wit. We have a family name to protect. The family name is the most important thing, and I believe those are the exact words he'd use, and yes, my business, which I won't apologize for, it should be protected, too. A man has a right to make a good living. He tosses the napkin from his lap onto the table. I worked myself into a fit for nothing.

Pierre stands up, grinning, wavering, hitting his thighs against the edge of the table. He grabs his coat from the rack. Now I've wasted enough time on this rot, says Pierre. I feel fine. Such rot. All of it. The solution is obvious. I have no sister.

THE HOUSE IS SILENT. Jorgen sits at the table and listens to the thumping of his heavy heart, hunting for her light footsteps, her singsong voice, but there is nothing.

He picks up his crutches and walks outside with a lantern. The pigeons call out and the night is still and empty. He lifts the blanket from one of the cages and there are the shiny eyes, alert and intense.

Hello, he says.

He searches for his favorite, the one with silver and peach tips on her wings. There she is, sitting in her nest.

Hello, pretty one, he says. He has named a couple of the birds. This one, Binie, because she was one of the first to come and perch on his finger.

He reaches into the cage and gently clasps his hands around the body of the bird. So light. He weighed her the other day. Almost half a kilogram.

The other birds stir. He sets her down on the bottom of the cage and holds seeds in the palm of his hand. She snaps them up, one at a time, a brush of a beak against his palm.

He climbs the stairs to his room, finds the seaman's journal, and lies on his cot. *Picture,* writes the seaman, *in Japanese means threads meet in picture.*

He reaches for the painting. As the birds settle in, and the city sinks into another night, he sees them, the threads linking everything, the threads of the rice fields below, the threads of the horse's mane and tail, the farmer's straw hat, of white clouds twined into blue sky, of the tree bark and the imagined tangled roots underneath, the long grass, swaying and weaving, the wild-flower stems, and there, the threads of her long dress, of his long dress, his long fingers on her back, his black hair.

This is what he should have shown Natalia, the threads that leave nothing out, her fingers digging into his back. He should have shown her the threads reaching beyond their fleshy limits and into his heart, the threads from her to him.

IN THE MORNING, Jorgen is jarred awake by knocking at the front door. From his second-floor window, he leans out and sees the cap of a National Guardsman. The young man looks up and asks him if he is the master of the house. The man's solemn face is scrubbed clean. It can't be. He wants to hide so the guard will go away, and he wants to know, he must know the news. Jorgen tries to assess the young guard's expression for the contents of the letter in his hand, but the guard, who must have delivered thousands of these notices, gives nothing away. Jorgen hurries downstairs and flings open the front door.

What? What is it? asks Jorgen.

Are you Pierre Blanc?

Yes, of course. What is it?

The guard nods and hands him a thin blue letter.

He frantically turns it over and over. What is this?

The guard points to the address.

A letter from Natalia. It's addressed to Jorgen in care of Pierre.

Thank you, says Jorgen, feeling his pounding heart.

The guard nods and leaves.

Jorgen closes the door. He presses the letter to his chest, then rips it open.

Dear Jorgen,

The women now have proper uniforms, but inferior muskets, which have such a short range. The men say the women will be in less danger of causing accidents, but I am determined to find them better rifles. My rifle is envied by all, and I must thank you all over again for such a generous, valuable gift. I sleep with it; it's never out of my sight for fear of it being stolen.

I'm fine, except for some chills and a recurring cold from the weather. Everywhere I go, dead soldiers are splayed on the ground, as if they had fallen out of the sky.

The other day, I watched from a high tree branch a small parade in the town of Gravelotte, a feast in honor of the Blessed Virgin Mary. Despite the Prussian soldiers who lay on the outskirts of this town, the townspeople marched down the center of their small village with plates of food——cooked squash, a slaughtered sheep, and steaming-hot meat pies——and at the front of the procession was a statue of the Virgin Mary dressed in white, her head covered in a veil. They congregated in the town square at tables adorned in white cloth and dined under the evening stars. You probably think I was deeply moved by the festival, but as I was about to climb down from the tree, I spotted a Prussian soldier prowling around the edge of town. I pointed him out to another soldier, who shot him.

Excuse my handwriting. My first letter, the rain destroyed. This one was rushed. I am wondering if I might trouble you to ask my brother to send money. I'm sorry to burden you with this request, but provisions are very low, and as you can imagine, there is a teeming black market for goods, but at a steep price. If you could convince Pierre to send along a bit of money, I'd be most grateful, and if this war ever ends and I return, I promise to pay him back. Make sure you tell him that. Please send it in care of the 160th battalion.

Natalia

. . .

GENERAL TROCHU REFUSED to let Natalia and the other women fight, so before he could pack them up and send them back to Paris, they splintered off and wandered for days in the woods. Eventually they found their way to the 160th battalion, which had lost a third of its soldiers in a recent skirmish. General Bazaine welcomed them. They've been marching for a week, and Natalia isn't sure where they are going. They seem to be heading in the direction of Metz, though the information is so scattered and unverifiable, no one knows for sure.

When the pale light of dawn comes, Natalia wipes the crust from her eyes, and there is the drab gray of a tent. Her back is so stiff from the hard ground, she can barely pull her knees to her chest. One of the women is still asleep beside her. Natalia tries to move silently out of her sleeping bag, but the woman snaps open her eyes.

I haven't slept all night, says the woman, her eyes wide and anxious. I'm so frightened.

Natalia leans over and smoothes the woman's matted red hair.

I heard the Prussian soldiers have splendid amounts of food. When they wake, the Prussian soldiers rise and shout, Nach Paris!

Natalia has heard the same thing.

And what do we have? Did you know that Bazaine has never commanded more than twenty-five thousand? That's what one of the soldiers told me. The woman rolls onto her side and clutches her stomach. I'm so hungry.

Natalia feels the cramped cold in her finger joints. We'll be all right, she says, hearing the profound doubt in her voice.

The woman moans louder and rolls away from Natalia.

For the past three nights, Natalia served on night patrol in the pouring rain. Last night she delivered a message to the second in command that she saw enemy movement in the nearby woods. When pressed for more information, she said it could have been French soldiers; it was dark and she could barely keep her eyes open. Her three hours of dreams were filled with nothing, only misty shadows and the utter blankness that comes from exhaustion.

A soldier pokes his head into the tent. Get up! We're moving again.

As Natalia packs her gear, her mind blurry and numb, she hears the buzz of excitement in the camp. Finally, something is happening. Perhaps they will get to fight, says a soldier. Natalia wets down her dark stubbly hair, clamps on her red and blue serge kepi, her tunic, and dark blue greatcoat, a clean pair of socks, scoops up her cowhide pack, tucking in her allotment of bread, her mess tins, and poles and pegs of the tent. She feels as though she is moving in a trance. The air is wet and cold. She sits down in front of the small fire outside the tent to warm her chapped hands.

You, says a soldier, pointing to Natalia. Reconnoitering expedition. Now.

With five others, Natalia is sent to scout the outlying area. Low on ammunition, they run from tree to tree to conserve bullets. A hard rain falls and the valleys quickly become lakes. Natalia's worn boots fill with mud. The roads break up and the gutters weep with water.

About an hour later, someone hisses, Get down! Movement to the east.

Belly down in mud, she lies still for an hour before someone finally spots the source of movement. A red fox.

The soldier next to her in the gully sighs, raises himself up on his knees, and looks around. I heard a French unit shot a Prussian colonel who was waving a white handkerchief, says the soldier.

Nothing surprises her anymore. She reaches down to unlace her boots. Her feet are swollen.

The young soldier comes from Lyon and he's taken to Natalia in a brotherly way. He has big brown eyes, and because of shortsightedness, should have been dismissed from the army, but he memorized the eye chart, wanting nothing more than to be a soldier.

Where's the general? she asks. She is so tired she can barely keep her eyes open.

Most likely retired to some restaurant to smoke and drink wine, he says. He stands up to stretch, his long arms high above his head, his front side drenched with mud, his knees cracking, and as he turns to hand her a flask of wine, a bullet plunges into his chest. He collapses next to her, falling on his front, the red of blood spilling everywhere, turning the water red. She can't move, stunned now by the bright blood seeping underneath her, staining her uniform, her hands. She smells its metallic odor, feels it stick to her hands.

She lies there all day, watching the red turn to darker red, then brown and black. Watches his face turn ashen, then gray and slightly green. His fingers look like marble claws. She lies there paralyzed until one of the women comes looking for her, pulls her back into the night air.

She tells Natalia that two more women have died. Natalia drapes her arm over the woman's shoulder. The rain changes to snow and the two women trudge through the night to find the others. Snow blankets her kepi, shoulders, and eyelashes, and when the flakes melt and run down her cheeks, the woman holding her up wipes them off with the back of her glove.

In the morning, they arrive at the new campsite. Natalia is handed a small chunk of old bread, and now she can't get rid of the taste of mold. She is ravenous. Later, when they march by a pile of dead bodies, she rushes over and scavenges from a dead soldier's coat pocket. She hears someone snicker. In it, she finds a bit of pâté de foie gras. She shoves it into her mouth.

When they arrive outside of Metz, they are told to hide in the tall grass and wait for signs of Prussian soldiers. Pulling at the hay grass, she sucks the sweetness from the roots. An hour later, she wakes to watch the sun drop below the low-lying mountains. For a moment, a hint of her former self appears as she marvels at the orange and red glow of the dying sun.

JORGEN SETS THE LETTER down, picks it up, and reads it again.

Damn, he says, smiling. She's alive and brave and heroic. She is perfectly fine.

He sees her scrambling up a bank, the rifle—it was the right gift after all—strapped across her back, then her thrill at raising the gun and peering down the long shaft. From this distance, from this small room in Paris, everything on the battlefield seems grander and more compelling than it was when he frantically ran from tree to tree and found the dying embers of a campfire, nervously fingered the remains of Prussian soldiers' dinner, canned beans and bread, and quickly devoured it before his fellow soldiers found him.

He picks up the letter again.

Svensk walks in the front door, and Jorgen waves the letter at him.

She's fine, he says.

Who?

Natalia. Natalia is fine.

Jorgen reads the letter to him.

She's probably one of the best shooters out there, says Jorgen.

She's doing better than we are, that's for sure, says Svensk. Paris is miserable.

She's got the right temperament for it.

It's become so depressing here, says Svensk. Everyone is starving. You can't find a decent meal, even if you have money. The women? They are complaining and whining about everything.

Jorgen looks longingly toward the front door; he wants to leave right now. To the battlefield. To the 160th battalion. He'll send her the money; Pierre will never do it.

Have you fed them? asks Svensk.

For the first time this morning, Jorgen hears the pigeons calling loudly. Jorgen rushes toward the back door. They are squawking and flinging themselves against the cages. As he prepares the seed, Jorgen folds the letter and slides it into his pants pocket. He hears in the distance the gunfire ring out and feels a wave of exhaustion. He has not slept well in days, and as he reaches his hand into the feed bag, he remembers how tired he was on the battlefield, the edges a foggy blur, his thoughts smeared. But he pushes those memories away, stuffing them into the stack of things he'd rather not recall— the burning hunger, weakness in places he'd never felt, an elbow, the back of his knees.

He stands beside Svensk, leaning his heavy weight into the crutch. The birds are calm again, and the smell of gunpowder wafts in the chilly morning air.

NATALIA SEES A PRUSSIAN soldier. He is walking within her range, dressed almost as she is, with a dark blue coat and a red and blue cap, though he wears gray trousers. The French soldier beside her has fallen asleep, snoring lightly, drunk on wine to ease the pain of an inflamed cut on his upper arm. If she wakes him, he might make too much noise and the Prussian will shoot. The Prussian is now unscrewing the cap from his canteen, tipping his head back to drink. White lines crisscross his dirty neck. She watches his Adam's apple dance. She raises her gun. I am preparing to kill someone, she thinks. I am going to end someone's life. Against God's commandments. Outside of God's rules. How did she ever think she could do this? Every other time she has aimed and fired her rifle, she has been too far away to see whom she hit, if anyone at all. Now the Prussian looks straight at her. She exhales, pulls the trigger. He crumples, a loose collection of limbs. She stares at the spot where he stood. Empty space. The soldier lying next to her rouses from his sleep, looks at her blackened hands, the man folded on the ground, and congratulates her. She presses her dirty hands to her face.

The soldier pats her on the shoulder. You did a good job, he says.

She begins to cry.

Oh, now, don't do that. That was your first one, wasn't it? It'll get easier. A hell of a lot easier.

She hears the wind in the tree branches and underneath that, stillness. Who is she? She has stepped outside of herself; her reference points have vanished. Not long ago, she thought life was precious, and now she has killed a man. The dead man is lying on his back, his face turned up to the sky, as if in desperate prayer. The French soldier hands her a bottle of wine, and she gulps it down. She's no better than this drunk soldier who is belching and wiping his dirty palm against his beard.

I've got some chocolate, he says.

How long has it been since she's eaten? She can't remember. Her mouth waters and she tightens her lips.

Do you want some?

She reaches out her hand.

What do you got in return? he asks.

For the first time she looks at him. He's a large man, his bowl-shaped face yellow pale. His eyes are dark and flashing. She withdraws her hand.

What do you mean? she asks, her voice barely audible.

Got any money?

She feels a sudden spasmodic shudder run through her. How can she feel hungry after killing a man. A young man. But she is no longer herself, and her mind seizes on the sweet, as if it's an answer to an unknown but pressing question. The chocolate, she must have it. But she has no money. Where could she get money?

You don't, do you? Don't got any money, he says, smiling harshly, his face hardening, and his eyes, coy and cool. But I know you want some.

She doesn't move, just stares at the soldier's front pocket where she thinks she spots the sweet.

I haven't been with a woman for a while. How about a trade? How about it?

He pulls out the chocolate from his breast pocket. A royal blue wrapper conceals the long, flat bar; a shiny thin foil lies underneath. She smells the rich sweet fragrance of mocha—how long has it been—and now the saliva pools at the back of her throat. She closes her eyes and breathes it in. He un-peels part of the wrapper and breaks off a square, slowly puts it into his mouth, lets it melt there, never taking his eyes off of her.

I guess you don't want any, he says, grinning at her. He reaches over and pushes his fingers into her cheek.

She looks over at the dead Prussian. What does this life matter, anyway? She has killed a man, and she feels nothing. Even with his dirty hand on her cheek, she doesn't jerk away, doesn't slap it away, or even flinch. The only thing she feels is a pressure in her chest. He reaches over and undoes her top button. His breath smells of chocolate. When she doesn't stop him, he keeps going, until her shirt is open, the cold air raising goosebumps on her skin. He clamps a hand on her back and pulls her to him, undoing her bra. His mouth finds her breast while his other hand undoes her trousers. She closes her eyes, and when she doesn't push him away, he climbs on top of her. When he is done, he rolls off of her and hands her the chocolate bar.

I'll let you know when my brother sends more, he says, narrowing his eyes and laughing heartily.

She buttons her trousers and her shirt, rips off the wrapper, shoves the bar of chocolate into her mouth.

Dear Natalia,
  I'm glad you are doing so well.

Jorgen balls up the paper and begins again.

Dear Natalia,
  I received your letter. A good rifle is crucial.

He throws this one away too. What he wants to say is tangled up inside, not ready to be boxed into words. And if he could unravel the mess? What would the stream of words say? He puts his pen down, rises, and pulls open the top drawer, where he keeps his money. Sitting down again, he stares at the blank paper. He would like to say he feels responsible for her; he taught her how to shoot, gave her confidence and enough prowess that the French army snatched her up. What else? That he cares for her, yes, he does, though he is not sure how that happened, and he wishes he could be there to protect her, to shield her from the danger that is certainly all around her. How could a month of training be enough?

He pulls out her letter again. She is fine, he thinks. She writes that she is fine, even though he feels the pull of doubt.

Dear Natalia,
  Here is some money. Hopefully this helps. From the tone of your letter, you sound well. Soon I will have enough money for a new leg and I will join you.
  Jorgen

This, too, is pathetic, he thinks, but she needs the money and he doesn't want to dally any longer, for there is this sense—why can't he dismiss it—that not everything is right. He gives the envelope to one of Pierre's clerks to deliver to army headquarters. Upstairs in his room, he pulls out the doctor's business card. Dr. Whitbread, he says, turning the card over and over. Dr. Whitbread.

OH, YOU ARE A godsend. Come in! Come in!

Daniel opens the door wide for Jorgen. Stubbed cigarette butts mark the front porch landing, and the small plant in the flowerpot has withered and died.

Jorgen steps into the entranceway. The air smells musty and stale.

Oh, you're wonderful. You're Hermes bearing good news.

Jorgen lugs along a big bag strapped on his back and hauls a second one, pressed against his chest. They stand in the darkened hallway. Daniel tells him he ran out of his last bottle of good wine two days ago, he's down to his last block of cheese, and he's dying for a good steak.

Your friend Svensk is not with you?

No, too busy, says Jorgen, though he didn't tell Svensk he was planning this trip. He can't afford to give Svensk any proceeds from this sale. This must be the last one. He must be on his way.

Under the harsh hallway light, Jorgen sees that Daniel's face is heavily lined and pale. His tall frame stooped. He wears a white shirt with small yellow stains near the pocket.

What has happened? Jorgen wonders, but doesn't ask, not wanting to be the vessel for Daniel's story. Daniel is clinging to his arm, pulling at it, as if he can't wait to tell. Jorgen pretends he dropped a coin so he is released from Daniel's desperate grip.

I've got one of everything for you, says Jorgen, slowly rising, postponing another view of Daniel's face.

Wonderful, says Daniel. Can you sit a minute?

Jorgen clenches his hands. For a moment. Then I must get back.

They walk down the long hallway and into Daniel's office. Daniel's heavy demeanor has stained everything in the house. Even the flowery wallpaper along the hallway walls, the large daisies mixed with roses, seems to be drooping and fading. The smell is the odor of sickness. In the office, a fine layer of dust coats the top of tables. A cigarette mark punctures the green velvet chair; cigarette ashes are everywhere on the rug.

Through the window, there's the dormant garden, and the spindly tree, now leafless. Isn't she beautiful? says Daniel, following his gaze. An apple tree. She is my joy. My one true joy. I think I must have the only fruit tree left in the entire city. In the spring, if all goes well, it will bear red apples the size of a man's fist.

They stand side by side at the window, admiring the one living thing in his yard, and Jorgen wonders if the tree in the painting—if there is such a tree in the Orient—is now shorn of its leaves.

Jorgen opens the bag and retrieves a bottle of wine, canned corn and meat, a garnet bracelet, cheese, and special truffles. He sets them out on the desktop in neat lines, hoping all the colorful and shiny objects will distract Daniel from his sad, lugubrious mood.

Daniel fondles the bottle of red wine. Shall we have a drink? Celebrate that we are still alive? And before Jorgen can protest, Daniel scurries off to the kitchen and returns with glasses. Jorgen stands by the window, watching Daniel pour the wine, Daniel's lips puckering. No, he won't sell the painting to Daniel. He'll triple the price for everything else.

Daniel sinks into his chair behind the desk and swirls the wine round and round, watching the dark red liquid ripple down the sides. They drink and Daniel closes his eyes, savoring the flavor.

It's been so long, says Daniel.

I'm offering a good price, says Jorgen. Now that Daniel has settled in, he can see the story coming. It's tucked in Daniel's eyes, and his pallor is coming back. He clears his throat.

Sit with me.

Jorgen hesitates, then takes the chair across from him.

Something horrible has happened, says Daniel, pulling on his bottom lip with his top teeth. Just this morning, I got word that a very dear friend was killed in the war. He was so young, like you. He loved the opera. A pleasant fellow. Daniel shakes his head. A whole life in front of him. Now he's gone.

There is a long silence. Fix yourself something, says Jorgen. It feels worse when you are famished.

Daniel takes out his pocketknife and slices off a big chunk of cheddar cheese. He closes his eyes and chews. Daniel opens his eyes and looks at Jorgen with a steady gaze. My dear, dear friend is gone, murmurs Daniel. So young. One moment alive, the next, gone. We are sparks so easily extinguished.

Jorgen coughs.

Daniel stares at his row of books on the shelf. What happens to the heart when it doesn't feel safe?

I must leave, thinks Jorgen. Must get out of Daniel's home. He feels his throat tighten, as if hands are choking him. He must leave this house, and not just here, but Paris, and if he sells the painting, he's certain to have enough money, more than enough to buy himself a new gun and whatever other provisions he will need. And he won't have the painting to stir up his feelings. He'll sell it, along with everything else.

How can you stand Paris? Daniel asks. But where would you go? Surely not Denmark, where it gets dark so early in the winter and that endless snow. The horrible pickled herring. And what do Danes have in terms of romance? That tale of the mermaid who loses her lovely voice and tail for love. That's the beautiful part, but the prince marries someone else, and she dies.

No, says Jorgen. She lives.

But something happens to her.

She can't speak and turns into thin air.

How morbid.

It's just a children's story, says Jorgen. We hear it when we're young and then we forget it.

Well, I could see why a young man like you would come to France. To the great city of Paris. What kind of tale of romance is that mermaid? Here there are lovely French women. But now Paris is dreary and sad. My good friend. He was only twenty-two, he sighs, letting out a flood of grief. A brilliant lad. Dead. This city is no longer home for me, but where do I go? What do I do?

I should get back, says Jorgen. I'm sorry to be in a rush. He can't sell the painting, he thinks. To leave it in Daniel's hands, to let them touch it seems obscene.

Daniel steps to his safe, turns the knob, and pulls out his wallet. Jorgen stands near the desk and watches the colorful bills come out of the leather fold. He gathers the money with shy haste.

No, the wine is twice that price, says Jorgen quickly.

Oh, my, says Daniel. We must be fair.

More money comes out of Daniel's wallet, and still it isn't enough. Natalia said a new leg costs twice that amount.

The canned meat, I'm sorry, says Jorgen. I'm sorry, I've had to raise the price for that.

My dear Dane. You are cleaning me out.

Jorgen wipes the sweat from his forehead. Daniel pulls out more money, and still, Jorgen counts, it is not enough. To have the new leg and the rifle and some extra for a new life. He must do it or lose his chance. And this is his opportunity to leave this house, leave Pierre, Paris, to leave all of it.

There is one more thing, he says.

I don't know, says Daniel. You've taken just about everything.

Jorgen slides the painting from his leather satchel. He lays it out on the desktop. The two men stand side by side. Neither one says a word, and in the growing stillness, Jorgen grips the edge of the desk as he falls into the painting. I will never see it again, he thinks, sinking farther into the smooth skin of the woman's face, her hands, and the blue dots are both flowers and tears, not one or the other, but intermingled, sadness and beauty all at once. What else hasn't he seen? He touches the edge of the paper. What is this paper? This paper, like skin.

I've never seen anything like it, stutters Daniel. It's simply exquisite.

Jorgen clasps his shaking hands together and swallows hard. Daniel gently picks up the painting and walks slowly over to the window to the light. Jorgen follows behind him unable to let it leave his sight. Daniel puts his face next to the image as Jorgen has done so many times.

How much? Daniel asks after a long while.

Nothing stirs. The house tilts and settles. The air vibrates, as if more life entered the room. Daniel's breathing turns rapid and short.

How much?

Jorgen gazes at the bare tree outside. He knows what to say, how much he needs, and he's about to speak, but can't. His chest tightens and his throat feels wrapped in taut wire. He pulls a handkerchief from his trouser pocket and tries to relieve his throat with coughing. With a bowed head, he looks only at the painting. He'll always see it, always be able to imagine it. If he must, he could visit Daniel, couldn't he? But why must he lose everything? What is the meaning of so much loss? To have something of beauty. Isn't that what everyone should have? But he can't. If he wants to leave Paris. . . . He drops his gaze to the floor and pushes down whatever rose up. Without looking at Daniel, he gives his price. Daniel walks to the safe, fiddles with the combination, and removes a black tin box. He wordlessly inserts a key into the lock, takes a wad of cash, and sets it on the table. Jorgen snatches up the money and shoves it in his pocket. He feels sick. Gathering his empty bags, he turns to the hallway.

Daniel walks him to the front door. It's simply astonishing, he says.

Yes, says Jorgen, pulling on his coat sleeve. He turns and leaves without saying another word.

JAPAN

WHERE IS HIS FAVORITE? Hayashi wonders, staring at the swirling fish. The fish seem dull, as if the water leached their colors. There, over at the edge, the younger ones are crowding him out. He walks over to his old friend and tosses him a handful of food.

Something doesn't look right. The old fish's eyes are coated with a white film, a spot of dark green on its side. Hayashi crouches down, but the discovery is the same. The fish is sick. It's never been ill. He should go to town and buy special food, but when he thinks of town, there is the rice shopkeeper, weeping on the steps of his store. How could he have rushed by without helping the poor man? And still, he hasn't found the nerve to speak to the monk about the meeting and how badly it went.

In the distance, he hears the hammer. The teahouse is nearly complete, but the monk cautioned him the final touches take the longest. Please don't rush, he told the monk, and the monk smiled in a way that reminded Hayashi of the cherry-bark man, as if his whole being lit up from within.

He stays down by the lake a while longer, hoping by the time he walks up the hill she will have left the studio. Perhaps this morning she will join him for breakfast. If he had the courage, he'd tell the maid not to bring her meal to the studio, but insist that she come inside.

A WHOOPER SWAN RISES and engulfs the whole painting. The bird's black eye, the lacy edge of its wing, the yellow and black beak, its perfectly white body, its rubbery feet. She smiles, a tentative, hopeful smile. The swans' nesting grounds were not far from where she used to meet Urashi. Suddenly the hammering begins. She won't look up. Not yet. It is nothing, she whispers to her painting, trying to coax Urashi out from behind the bird. The monk means nothing to me. But as she listens to herself, she hears betrayal. The monk will leave soon, like the wind, she thinks, and what stain does the wind leave? She holds her brush poised for Urashi's face. It never would have happened if you'd come for me, she pleads. So lonely, why haven't you come?

Their last winter together, Urashi told her he could not live without her. She bit into his shoulder and said, There, you will always bear my mark.

He said he loved the way she would leap from her horse and rush toward him, as if compelled by a strong force that sent her hurling straight into his arms. His hand rested on her neck, the pulse of her ringing through his fingertips. When they lay together, she traced the long scar on the side of his body. A brown bear, he said. A mother and her cubs. I wandered too close to the den. She must have thought I was a threat. The scar felt like silk, a long ribbon underneath her finger. Strange, she thought, how such an injury could leave something so soft.

Finally she sets her brush down.

The hammering sounds as if it's right outside her window, beyond the fluttering bamboo. She feels his gaze on her, like a steady heat source.

She leaves her painting and walks to the window. The teahouse has four walls, and the black tiles for the roof lie in stacks on the ground. The monk is pacing back and forth, his head bowed. He's nearly finished, she thinks, feeling a sense of relief and panic. His neck, a long, lovely line. He is pulling on his knuckles, cracking them.

IF I WALKED INTO her studio and interrupted her work, what would she think of me? He feels the tremendous urge to ask her, Did it really happen? He can barely think the words, barely tell himself that he kissed her. At the same time, he is jumpy, his breathing quick, as if his body is preparing to do it again. He picks up the hammer and pounds in a nail. If he ignores her today, what then? He sets the hammer down, stares at it, and puts his hand to his forehead. He feels as if he has a fever.

There is the top of her head. She is painting. He picks up a tile and wants to slam it on his hand. If he were unable to work, the teahouse would come to a standstill. He'd have to rest; maybe she would take care of him. Step out of the studio and sit beside him for the day, make him laugh like she did in the tea shop in the big city.

He walks over to the porch, dips the ladle in the bucket, and drinks, all the while looking at the top of her head. How can she go about her day as if everything is the same? As if nothing happened? She tempted him, didn't she? Her leg against his in the carriage. Her warmth, her scent. Yes, she seduced him, he decides, feeling better about himself. But as he sets the ladle down, he can't push aside the image of his leg pressing against hers. In the cool corner of that shop, he was the one who leaned over and kissed her.

No, he won't go to her. Won't find some pretext to knock on the studio door. Won't pretend he needs her help holding a board while he remeasures the door frame. He will concentrate on the hammer and nail. He'll even say his midday prayers. How long has it been? His hand is trembling. Perhaps he does have a fever.

SHE WALKS OVER TO her husband's side of the work space. Dried clay chips lie on the floor. Moist, bluish black clay rises up to the rim of a bucket. The smell, it is earth and water and something ancient, tucked away and forgotten. A beautiful color, she thinks, this midnight blue, the heart of night, the depth of still water. She's never touched it before. Taking a bit between her fingers, she rubs and stretches it. Still curious, she plunges her hand into a bucket, up to her elbow, and is astounded by how alive it is, like a body, shifting and moving with her.

As she walks back to her desk, cleaning the clay from her hand, she looks at the floor. A folded piece of white paper, the kanji, beautifully and perfectly designed.

Your thousand colors
a warm coat
on this winter day.

A rush of blood bounds to her face. She stands again and looks out the window. He's carrying a board from the stack of new wood. How gracefully he moves, she thinks. His face, a beautiful calm. When they were in the capital together, he laughed with such ease and honesty. She crumples up the paper, then opens it again. She rereads the poem, and now she cannot focus at all.

SHE STEPS OUT OF the studio. Hayashi went into the house a while ago; by now, the maid must be working on his feet. Sato is probably still asleep. She walks over to the teahouse and picks up a nail. Why does she feel so jittery and awkward?

Good morning, she says.

Oh, he says. He sets down a board, picks it up again. Good morning.

The teahouse?

He lets out his breath, as if sighing. It's coming along.

Are you almost done?

No, he says quickly. I still have a lot to do.

Really?

He is quiet for a moment, then lists all the unfinished tasks—the posts, cross beams, and rafters for the roof, the mixture of clay and chopped straw in which the tile will be embedded, the perfect alignment of tile—that takes a lot of time, he assures her.

Good, she says, and adds quickly, because I'm sure you'll want it perfect. She decides she feels uncomfortable because they are standing too far apart. Yesterday, their thighs against each other, and now cold air is between them. And the kiss. It shouldn't have happened, she thinks, can't happen again. With this distance between them, she wonders if it really did happen. She steps closer, now an arm's length away, and there is his fragrance of pine wood and incense.

Would you like to take a walk in the gardens?

He sets down his hammer. I was about to take a break.

You've been working since dawn.

He nods. But you rose before I did.

She smiles, feeling slightly vulnerable. What else has he seen? How closely is he watching me? When did he enter the studio and leave the poem? With a swift glance, she looks at him, his long eyelashes, the bow shape of his upper lip. As they walk toward the far pine trees, neither one of them speaks.

The new capital, he says after a while.

It's captivating, isn't it? she says, blushing slightly, wondering if she should mention the poem.

Yes, he says. He picks up a twig and snaps it apart.

She laughs lightly.

So much bustling and hurrying.

I never knew so much could occur in one place, she says. And the carriage?

Yes, the carriage, he says, clasping his hands behind him. It's difficult to forget.

She averts her face, not sure what to say. There are the Japanese maples, shorn of their leaves. She never liked them bare, but now she sees their coral-colored bark. Reaching over, she stops and takes one of the branches in her hands.

This color, she says.

They stand there together, looking at the branch. She hears his breathing.

Have you ever painted that color? he asks.

It has been so long since she thought of this painting: Urashi, his finger hooked in the mouth of a trout. On a summer day, she accompanied him to the river, where he caught trout with his spear. He wrapped one in a burlap bag and gave it to her. A gift. He told her the Ainu believe the world rests on the back of a trout. Everything dependent on the fish. When the trout sucks in water, he creates the ebb of the tide; when he sends it out, the tide flows. As I am dependent on you, he said. She could never take it home. How would she explain where she got it? On her way home, she dug a hole and buried it beneath a fir tree.

I think I used that color once, she says, remembering the coral stripe down the trout's back.

I'd like to see more of your work, he says.

You would?

The ones that you showed me, I can't get out of my mind.

She bows her head. Thank you.

You must be cold, he says, pulling out a pair of gloves. Here.

She slips her hands into his gloves. What a thoughtful gesture, she thinks. She could show him more of her landscapes, her pictures of birds. What if she showed him her paintings of Urashi? The thought of doing so fills her with fear and an overwhelming sense of intimacy. They walk farther to the edge of the garden, where a bamboo fence marks the end of the property. She presses her fingertips into the ends of the gloves; his gloves, she thinks.

Thank you for the poem, she says, turning to him.

He nods, his face flushed. His gaze wavers over her, past her. Our visit to the capital, he says, clearing his throat. It makes this life here seem so quiet.

How so?

I don't know. He hesitates. It sounds strange, but it makes me realize there is so much more.

A shadow passes over her face. But I thought you liked it here?

Oh, yes. I do, he says, as if trying to take back what he just said. The temple is beautiful. I feel fortunate. To have come here.

They are at the cluster of pine trees. From here, the house looks so much smaller, she thinks. The front door is barely visible.

Do you think you could live in Tokyo? she asks, thinking again of the women's dormitory, her easel stationed at the window, the morning light flooding the room. And where would the monk live?

I don't know. He pauses and pulls on the rope twined around his waist. Are you planning on going there again? he asks, his tone soft, tentative.

She smiles, with an almost flirtatious glance.

His hand brushes against hers. Her breath quickens. She steps toward him, removes his gloves, touches the nape of his neck, puts her lips to his. His fingers slide inside the sleeve of her kimono and find the inside of her arm. For a moment, she is lost in his embrace.

She steps away from him. We should go back, she says, handing him his gloves.

He nods, looking down at his hand still clutching the cuff of her kimono.

They walk toward the house. As it looms larger, she imagines Hayashi inside with the maid. When is the last time she helped him with his feet? Her step quickens and suddenly her hair loosens from its bun. With one hand, she removes the four-pronged comb, lets down her hair, then twists it round and round, tucking it into a bun. The monk is looking at her, his mouth slightly open, as if he's witnessing a wondrous event.

Sato has gathered them around the table in the formal receiving room. He said he had special news tonight. Ayoshi sits beside Hayashi, with Sato at the head of the table. The monk sits across from her. The maid brings in green tea. As she leaves, Sato calls out they are ready for the first course.

Ayoshi sees Sato watching her, as if trying to decipher the flickering and sparkling in her eyes. She is glowing, she knows, strangely magnetic. She tries to flatten her expression.

I'll help carry the platters, says Ayoshi finally.

She returns with sake and rice crackers, Sato still watching.

Wonderful sake, says Hayashi.

He's always gracious, she thinks. But why are there worry lines streaking his forehead?

She rises again and rushes into the kitchen. More buri daikon. The maid offers to take it out. No, no, she tells the maid. She will do it. When she enters the room again, she wonders if Hayashi's worry lines have deepened; he looks up at her and smiles sadly, his eyes dreamy and glazed. Since she's known him, he's always worn a thin coat of sadness, but tonight, is it more pronounced? How can she know what he is thinking? For so long, he's remained concealed, like a buttercup, its petals folded up for the night. She refills his sake cup.

Thank you, he says.

Sit down, says Sato. You're rushing around and it's making me nervous. I'm the host tonight, and I have a big announcement. Sit. Sit. No, just put that down.

She slides in beside Hayashi. Sato begins talking about his favorite subject, trade with the West, and she nods, not listening. The monk's second fingernail is bruised blue-black, matching his thumb. When did he do that? she wonders. The maid brings in another course. Ayoshi shifts uncomfortably.

I was thinking I could build something else for you, says the monk. To repay you for your generosity.

Oh, what? asks Hayashi.

The monk looks across the table at Ayoshi. Perhaps a second studio.

Ayoshi spends all her time in that studio, says Sato.

Ayoshi drops a chopstick on the floor.

Tell us, Ayoshi, whatever are you painting? asks Sato.

The rims of her ears burn. She feels his searing bite trained on her. Her fingers fumble with her napkin. She tries to remain still, hidden under layers of politeness.

I'm experimenting, she says, her voice measured.

All the hours you've spent on it, I bet it's stunning.

The maid brings in a platter of grilled pink salmon.

Look! says Ayoshi. She feels the air thinning. The steam of the salmon fills the table. Now Hayashi and the monk are discussing the dimensions of the teahouse porch. When there is a lull in the conversation, Hayashi touches her arm.

I'd love to see it, he says to Ayoshi. When you are finished.

What would he do if she showed him? She has no idea.

Maybe after dinner, we can all see what you are working on, says Sato.

Something trembles all around her and her limbs feel shaky.

I don't think so, she says slowly. Not now.

The monk accidentally clinks his tooth against his glass. She regards him quickly. His mouth twitches and he smiles at her. She hears the wind gust outside, tearing through the tree branches. Everyone sits uncomfortably at the edge of their chairs. This must end, she thinks. You had something you wanted to announce? she asks Sato. I'm feeling tired and want to lie down.

Sato opens a bottle of brandy. Expansively, he holds the bottle in the air and pauses, gaining everyone's attention. To Ayoshi's first painting, sold.

Hayashi claps his hands.

A rush of excitement rattles her. The one in the temple? You sold it? she says, her voice an exhalation of disbelief. For so long, she has not painted for any kind of notoriety. Not at all. It is an old dream, a very old dream, but here it is again, revived, dusted off, and hers.

With a broad smile, Sato pours the rich liquid into four glasses, and when he announces the price, she says there must be a mistake. She laughs out loud and finishes her drink. Sato refills her glass.

To many more sales, says Sato.

She tells him it isn't even her best work. Perhaps this man will buy more.

Of course he will, says Sato, grinning broadly.

Maybe she will travel to Europe after all, she thinks. She could go with Sato on his next trip. She will travel on a boat and paint during the entire voyage.

To your next creation, says Hayashi, toasting her with his glass.

She bows her head, her face flushed.

The monk raises his glass.

He won't be your only buyer, says Sato. I'll promise you that.

They linger longer, discussing the sale, and she swirls her chopstick in the leftover sauce on her plate while Sato and Hayashi talk about the West. Mostly Hayashi listens as Sato expounds on all the possibilities, the grand opening of Japan to the world. There is a quickening in the air, she feels it, a chrysalis holding her. The monk smiles at her and nods, as if giving approval to the news. She looks out the window, but all she sees is her reflection, a blur of herself.

AFTER DINNER SATO FOLLOWS her into the kitchen. She is humming, filled with a sense of abundance that she hasn't felt in a long time.

Something is different about you, he says.

She sets the dirty dishes on the counter and turns to retrieve more empty bowls from the table, but Sato stands in her way.

What? she says.

I don't know, he says.

You just sold one of my paintings. I'm thrilled.

No, before that, you felt different. And the way the monk kept staring at you. Smiling at you.

I don't know what you mean. She picks up a bowl—one of Hayashi's, the color of midnight blue—to make more room for the dirty dishes, and it slips from her hands.

Her hands cover her mouth.

Hayashi steps into the room. Are you all right?

I'm so sorry, she says.

It's fine, he says.

She crouches and gathers the pieces in her hand.

It should have been smashed a long time ago, says Hayashi. A small imperfection in the lip.

No, she says.

Please, don't worry.

We can fix it, can't we? It was one of your favorites. Wasn't it?

Hayashi touches her lightly on the shoulder. Sato leans against the counter, his arms crossed in front of him, watching her.

FRANCE

EXCUSE ME, MADEMOISELLE, SAYS Jorgen, fingering the oily money in his pocket. I'm here to see Dr. Whitbread. For how long has he waited for this moment, his pocket flush with money, on the perimeter of Paris, about to plunge himself out of this dreadful place? A new life perched before him, much better than the old one, no longer a clerk in a dusty office; yes, a shiny, brilliant life, and he will find Natalia.

The woman's graying brown hair is pulled into a tight bun and her lips are bluish and retracted, as if she's swallowed something distasteful. Can't you read the sign? she says, pointing to the sign taped to the window. THE DOCTOR IS NOT IN.

Jorgen stands there, half dazed. But where?

He's been accused of being a Prussian spy. The idiot National Guard dragged him away last week. Her face flushes bright red. I've not seen him in a week, she says, her stern voice beginning to break up. I've been waiting and waiting for him. She tells Jorgen they were engaged to be married. Every single day I go to La Grande Roquette, but the idiot guards won't let me see him. It's abominable.

The drizzle that falls onto his cap now turns into a hard rain. Jorgen peers around her. He's waited so long and he won't relinquish what he expects to see, what he must see. Perhaps the doctor is asleep or drunk, or too dispirited to see anyone. The room is dark. He grabs the side of the wet door frame and wipes the rain from his forehead. Slowly, he begins to wrap his mind around her words. Where is he? he asks.

She pulls out a handkerchief and blows her already red nose. I told you. Prison. They took him away.

But—

She shakes her head, pressing tissue to her nose. He's English. He's not a spy. They took him away because he happens to be English. They heard him speaking on the street corner. She looks at Jorgen, as if only now she sees him. She begins to shut the door.

I've got the money right here, he says. Right here. I've been saving it, see, and now I've got it. He grabs the thick bundle of notes and shoves it in front of her. He's never had so much money in his life, and he stares at it, amazed at the amount.

She looks at him perplexed. Have you heard anything I've said? She's about to close the door again. Jorgen puts his hand out.

I must have a new leg.

Her voice hardens. I've already explained, monsieur. And I think I've been very patient, given the circumstances. It's impossible. Now please.

The world is shutting around him, making it difficult to breathe. His leg begins to throb. All around them, the rumbling of the gunboats echoes across the Sevres and Meudon hills, and the cannons on Mont Valérien thunder. The pain shoots to his hip bones. He mutters swear words in Danish and the woman's face softens.

You're not French, are you? she asks. You're Danish. My sister married a Dane. He's a good man. Yes, a good soul.

His eyes brighten. He shows her the money again.

She smiles faintly, the edges of her mouth quivering. I do wish Jonathan were here. He could help you. But then again, it takes many weeks to make a proper leg. It must be fitted right. Even then it doesn't simulate the knee exactly, so you won't regain your natural walking stride. Did someone say you'd walk again with a perfect gait? I hope not. It's a lie, after all.

I'll walk just fine, he says, half listening, his mind fixated on the image of himself striding down the boulevard, slipping through the gap in the barricades, a rifle slung on his shoulder. The air heavy with gunpowder and bitter cold, and there he goes, leaving behind this dilapidated city, tromping through deep snow dotted with blue shadows.

Her eyes soften and her arms drop to her sides. You look like you're in pain. I can help you with that.

She cracks open the door, and suddenly, magically, he is inside. The room is hushed and ice cold, with the smell of medicine and something acidic jolting the air. A couple threadbare couches encircle a scratched wooden table. She tells him to have a seat. He obliges her, stares straight ahead at the dirty white wall, but gets up again, paces the room on his crutches. She steps into the side room. He peers in, hoping to see the doctor asleep in a chair or stretched out on a back couch. Only a table and white cabinets. What will he do? he thinks, beginning to feel the dreary shadow of emptiness that has haunted him for weeks.

Do you know of any other doctors who could help me?

I don't know. Jonathan is superb.

She comes out again and hands him a brown bottle of pills. Tablets of opium, she says, patting down a loose strand of hair. Eases the pain.

He takes the bottle and stares at it. This is not what he came for. He looks at her with bewildered, angry eyes.

Who knows? she says, her voice soft. Perhaps Jonathan will be released this week. He's innocent, of course. The imbeciles just have to take one look at him to know that.

Yes, says Jorgen. Maybe this week. Maybe tomorrow or the next day, he thinks, or even today.

May I take a look at your leg? she asks.

He rolls up his pants.

The cut, she says, it was done well. The skin has grown back thick. No infections. You're lucky. Many men have died of gangrene. You're one of the lucky ones.

Lucky, he thinks, lucky? He laughs out loud. How insane, how utterly insane, he thinks. She looks at him oddly, then shuts the door.

JORGEN RUSHES ALONG THE Rue de la Roquette, passing by a funeral procession of twenty people or so dressed in black, their heads bowed, singing a church hymn as they walk beside a polished coffin. He scurries up the steps to the men's prison and enters the great stone hallway. For a moment, he is blinded by the muted light. The air is freezing and his vision is slow to adjust. The sorrowful cries of men echo and bounce off the stone walls of the chamber. A cavernous hallway of prison cells stretches as far back as Jorgen can see. Jorgen stands waiting for a guard, pressing his coat sleeve to his nose to stem the stench of urine, sweat, and the pungent odor of fear. Some prisoners are pushing their heads through the black bars, as if their cells are so abominable they prefer their necks in a stranglehold. One man closes his eyes, opens his mouth, a black hole, his teeth half gone, and wails. Jorgen shivers, as if the human misery held in the walls of La Grande Roquette is seeping under his skin. What a horror, he thinks, and he feels every muscle demand to leave this frightening place.

Finally a prison guard with deep-set eyes and a large forehead approaches the receiving desk. The guard holds himself squarely, with a disciplined restraint to each gesture. Jorgen tells the guard whom he wants to see.

Are you a relative?

No, sir.

Impossible.

I'm a patient of the doctor's, sir.

The guard's eyes narrow and something behind them hardens.

Jorgen gestures pathetically to his empty pant leg, searching for a morsel of sympathy.

The guard doesn't say anything. A new round of screaming hurls from the cells. Jorgen cringes, glances down the hallway, and watches as two guards drag a prisoner out of his cell, his legs sagging, the heavy chains around his ankles clanking.

The guard waits for the screaming to subside. Only relatives allowed.

But the doctor is here? asks Jorgen.

The guard raises an eyebrow and fixes his gaze on Jorgen. I didn't say that.

Jorgen leans hard into his crutches, frantically searching for something to say that will win this man over. When will the doctor be released? My leg, you see. He was going to make me a new leg, and I planned to return to the war. The guard's face twitches. Now, thinks Jorgen, he has the guard's good graces.

The guard stiffens again. Let me see your papers.

Jorgen clambers in his pocket. He hands over his passport.

The guard looks at the papers, then at him. You're not French?

Jorgen explains his situation, his tone exasperated and desperate. The doctor is a good man. He came here from England to help. He's done nothing wrong.

The guard studies the passport again. To date, twenty-one foreigners have been arrested and are being held here for spying, he says. The city is teeming with spies. I'd say your tone indicates you're not a very cooperative fellow. You don't seem to have the proper respect for French security. We could call you in for questioning at any time. In fact, I could call my supervisor right now and say I've got a fellow here who is causing trouble.

Jorgen's breath quickens. He glances toward the cells and, for a flash, sees how easily he could end up in such a terrible place, languishing in filth, listening to that man down the way coughing and hacking up phlegm.

You'd best be on your way. I've wasted enough time with you.

The odor of fresh urine wafts through the receiving hallway. He feels as if he might retch. Jorgen heads for the front door. As he turns, he hears a bell ring. The guard removes a key from his pocket, enters the long hallway of cells, and with a heavy black chain, swipes at the heads jammed between the bars.

PULLING HIS GRAY WOOL blanket up to his chin, Jorgen nestles into the deep depression he's carved into the mattress and listens to the cooing of the pigeons in the backyard. Four weeks now she's been gone. Four long weeks, and winter is here.

Down the hallway, a new shipment waits for him. He should trudge to the inventory room, but he feels empty and exhausted, and the thought of work tucks him farther into bed. What if the doctor is never released? Nearly nine in the morning, and his room is freezing. His whole body aches. He reaches over, pops open the brown bottle, and swallows another white pill. Three pills should make the pain in his head go away, four could erase the ache in his chest. He pulls his gray knit cap over his ears. Outside, a voice calling, And we must deliver, then the words trail off. A door opens and closes downstairs, but he is cut off from everything, a man floating in the air, untethered, tossed by the whim of a mood. What mood he is riding on, he has no idea. Moaning quietly, he rubs his face with his calloused hands and it feels as if his skin is putty. All around him dreary gray.

He reaches underneath his bed for the painting. His hand scrapes the vacant, dirty floor. How many times has he checked and rechecked? It seems impossible the painting is gone; his mind is a carousel going round and round the question, How could he? In his blurred state, he can't recall how he sold it. As he leans back, his arm knocks over a glass on the nightstand, glass shatters everywhere.

Footsteps leap up the stairs and down the hallway toward his room. Svensk charges into the room. I heard something crash.

Jorgen rolls away from Svensk and feels something squeeze inside. How could he explain it? He doesn't even know how to explain it to himself. It sounds so silly. There was a beautiful painting and now it's gone. Just like everything else. He doesn't recognize himself, this suffering, this loneliness that sits on top of him.

Pierre says you're behind on your work.

Jorgen lies there inert, not saying anything. He went by the doctor's office again two days ago, but the assistant's mournful gaze through the half-open door told him everything he needed to know.

Svensk walks to the other side of the cot and faces Jorgen. You look horrible, says Svensk. Pierre said the only thing you do is feed those damn pigeons. He said he's thinking of firing you. He asked me if I wanted your job.

Jorgen looks through Svensk and stares at the wall. Go ahead, he says. Take the godawful job.

You better get dressed.

Jorgen slowly removes the blankets and glances down. He's in a white bed shirt. Svensk tries not to look at his stump.

I'll get your trousers, says Svensk.

If I left Paris, would you take care of the pigeons? asks Jorgen.

Svensk stops digging through the chest of drawers. Sure, he says. Where are you thinking of going?

You'd take care of them, wouldn't you?

There's no getting out of Paris, says Svensk. He tells him the French are guarding Paris like a precious jewel, and the Prussians have formed siege lines all around the city.

He hands Jorgen his trousers. Jorgen perches on the edge of the bed.

You would, wouldn't you? Jorgen asks.

What?

Take care of the pigeons.

Jesus, I said I would, didn't I?

You must promise me. Say that you promise.

God almighty. What's wrong with you? Where do you think you're going?

Jorgen doesn't answer.

Svensk leans against the wall by the window, watching Jorgen pull on the pants with slow, heavy hands.

PIERRE IS GONE. A letter sits on the table, like a broken wing.

Dear brother,

We are finally at Metz. We marched for ten leagues in one direction. Then we turned around and nearly walked back the distance we came. Needless to say, we are exhausted and hungry and demoralized. Tell Jorgen I can understand the desire to break off into a separate unit, and there are such units, renegade groups of soldiers roaming through the woods.

*I'm sorry to keep asking, but any small bit of money would be most ap-
preciated. I will pay you back. Please keep a record of what you send. Please send
anything.*

Natalia

Underneath the letter on the table, still tucked in an envelope, a note addressed to Jorgen.

Dear Jorgen,

*There are so many things I should have asked you while I could. Your favorite
food. What makes you sing? I never knew it, but I've discovered I love to hear a
man sing. (There was a young soldier who died yesterday who always sang while
we marched.) It seems like years have gone by since I made you sandwiches. Were
they terrible? I was never much of a cook.*

*What would you do differently? Right now. That's something I'd ask you.
When I ask myself, I know I would have discovered more about you. You were the
one person who understood. Edmond was the other. I'm sorry, but I'm feeling sentimental today. Most of the time, I feel nothing.*

*All around me, death. It is possible to die. At any moment. It would be so easy.
A Prussian steps from behind a tree, his shiny helmet blinding. A cannon shell
lands in your trench. I saw a girl killed for standing on her porch at the wrong
time. A doctor, too. A nurse. I have seen it happen all around me. I think that's
what makes it so easy to write the truth. Some part of me welcomes it, this greedy
thing of death. It must take all of us, but here, it is taking everyone with such
rapaciousness. I welcome it, not to meet my savior, the Lord, but to end all this.
There is nothing here but misery and more misery.*

*You once said your dream was to join up again with the war. And now that I
am here, I can only say that your dream is a nightmare. To call that a dream is
insane. (You see how honest I am with death gathered at my feet. Five good
women have died.) If life has not fallen away from you, if life hasn't retracted
from your being, then don't come here. Don't call it a dream.*

Natalia

Clutching the letter with both hands, he reads it again and again. The walls of the room press in. He steps outside into the night, into enveloping blackness, and walks over to the birds. They coo and call out to him, and with soft eyes, he sees them anew.

Listen, he says.

He reads the letter out loud to the pigeons, and they quiet down, held by the deep timbre of his voice. She wants to know these things about me, he says. Things no one has ever asked. What would he do differently? His entire body contracts, as if ready to leap into the air, as if changing, made of some other substance, something elastic and expansive. There is the orange-red eye of a pigeon glowing, holding him in this moment.

Her heart is good, he says. Too good.

He looks to the edge of the yard, recalling a warm day when they sat outside on the porch. He hadn't wanted to go out, but she insisted. She spotted some dahlias and wild red poppies by that back corner, ran down the steps, and gathered a couple to put in her hair. Here, she said, and tried to put one behind his ear, and he had brushed her away. Though he didn't want a flower in his hair, he was glad to be sitting with her outside. Fresh air and a bit of sunshine, so simple, as he thinks it over now, and why hadn't he returned the favor?

Cannon fire booms, shaking the night. Suddenly, he begins to shudder, as if the danger of the battlefield, of what she is encountering, of death gathered at her feet, has laid itself in front of him. Urgency flushes through his limbs. He reads her letter again and tries to release the cold hand of panic gripping his heart. She has his gun and that will save her, he thinks. No, it won't save her. His illusions about her strong will, her fearlessness, quickly crumble. She is in danger. He must help her. He charges over to the back door and stands stock still. What is there for him to do? He is a cripple, only half a man.

Pierre's favorite bird has rubbed off its right wing feathers. Jorgen walks over to the cage and undoes the metal latch. He rolls his message tightly, ties it to the bird's feather, and tosses the pigeon into the gray sky. He watches the bird flutter against the wind, fly up beyond the rooftops, carrying his words, *Natalia, I will soon join you.*

THE OFFICER WHO DELIVERS the mail comes down the narrow path between the pitched tents. Natalia stands, expectantly, hopefully. Perhaps today, she thinks. Please. Please. Please send money. But the officer walks by without even a glance, only a small exasperated sigh. She has asked him too many times if there is any mail for her. She sits down again. Her only thoughts are of home. A beautiful place, she thinks. Home. With wine and pleasant talk and strolls down flower-lined sidewalks. Jorgen, what is he doing now? And she knows how easy it is to fall in love when the distance is great, so much room for the imagination to invent. Her last letter, perhaps she said too much, succumbed to a fantasy, but there is something about him, isn't there?—she'd like to find out.

Bazaine ordered the last of the transport mules killed for food; at least a half dozen of the cavalry horses have been slaughtered. When the soldier comes to her for sex, she's learned to ask for the food first. Too many times he has tricked her, saying he just ran out.

She rips a thread from her coat and jams it into her mouth. Something to suck on. Her mind is endless loops of incoherent phrases. Everything artless and clumsy. She has lost the mind of reflection, left only with these loops, which come seemingly on their own volition, disappear, only to snake back again.

Mouth caked with soil. Caked with. One of the women buried that way. Soil.

Swallowing shadows until we are full.

Caked with. Torn ligaments around the throat.

Later, when she's sent to gather firewood, she stumbles upon two lovers coupling on a slab of hard granite. She laughs so hard she weeps uncontrollably. The couple looks over and goes back to their business. When she returns to camp, there is only the indigestible pâté de foie gras. Natalia sits beside one of the other women and hangs her head, staring at the hole in her boot. She'll have to find some way to patch it, or soon she will be without a shoe. She sticks her finger into the hole and rubs her frozen toes, trying to bring them back to life.

Come on, says the woman. We'll die of starvation if we don't do something.

Together they stagger along the fringe of forest toward the town of Metz. They come to a white farmhouse, the glow of a candle in the window. They walk toward the front door. A man comes out holding a rifle.

We're French soldiers, Natalia calls out, holding up her arms.

We don't got anything, says the man.

They walk closer. The man is tall and so thin, his pants are held up by a cinched rope. He has a long sallow face, his high cheekbones protruding like two round bowls. His eyes are deep, like punched-out holes. Behind him Natalia sees five children, no six, covered in sores, their limbs as thin as sapling branches. They stare at Natalia with big round eyes.

Don't got nothing, says the man. They took it all.

Anything you can spare, says Natalia's comrade.

My wife is dead. Got shot when she went out to the barn to check on the cow. Could have been a Prussian soldier. Might have been French. All the same to me.

A young girl, she can't be more than ten years old, sneaks from behind her father. She has stringy brown hair and a long pale face; her eyes are protruding brown globes, the luster nearly smudged from them.

We got some milk, says the girl, her voice firm.

The man turns to her. Go inside.

We do.

Louise, get inside.

She stands there, not budging. And as Natalia looks closer, she sees the defiant upper lip, the steeliness behind the glazed eye, a certain stony determinism. Natalia recognizes that look, that fierce will. And now Natalia begins to cry. The other soldier nudges her with her elbow.

We'll get something from them, she hisses. Hold yourself together. That girl has something. I heard her.

Natalia remembers how she once tried to do the right thing, to be good, the way Louise is standing there, staring down her father, offering milk that shouldn't be offered. What does she believe in now? What is left? She no longer knows what is good or right, or who she is or what would have become of the Prussian she shot if he had been allowed to live. Or how many more men she will kill, all in the name of France. What is that name? What does it mean? To be French, to kill for France? She touches the cold metal trigger of her gun, as if seeking comfort.

We don't need anything, says Natalia. Sorry to trouble you.

The other woman grabs Natalia by the arm. Are you crazy? She walks toward the man and the children. She's so hungry she can't think straight, she says, pointing to Natalia and laughing harshly. Milk would be wonderful. It's been so long since we had anything.

Natalia follows her. Leave them alone.

Louise rushes into the house and comes out with a bottle of milk. Her father tries to catch her, but the girl darts from his grasp and runs down the front steps toward Natalia and the woman. The bottle is wet, and there is the milk, the precious milk, as white as the moon.

That's a nice girl, says the woman, smiling faintly. Good. Good girl.

We can't take it, says Natalia. She needs it. Her family needs it.

So do we, says the woman. Now shut up or go on your way.

Natalia looks at Louise. The girl is so thin, her arms and legs are wobbly lines. What has she eaten today? thinks Natalia. Yesterday? Louise looks at Natalia with curious cavernous eyes. Louise holds out the bottle of milk to Natalia. It looks like a bouquet of calla lilies.

Take it, says the woman. Take it.

Please mademoiselle, says Louise. You're hungry.

. Natalia no longer feels hunger, only a sinking dread as she reaches for the bottle. If she had any goodness left, she wouldn't be feeling the cold, wet glass underneath her dirty fingertips, or placing the curve of the bottle lip to her mouth, closing her eyes and gulping the thick sweetness. No, if there were anything redeemable in her, she'd walk away, leave this rich sustenance for Louise, her brothers and sisters, her beaten-down father. But the milk coats her cheeks, her tongue, so rich, and her hunger wakes with a fury; she hears herself greedily gulping; she's never tasted anything like it; she can't seem to stop. And the girl smiles gently, all the while watching Natalia, who can't stop staring at the girl. A vision, thinks Natalia, an angel, this Louise, with brown luminous eyes, still holding so much goodness in her small, dying body.

THIRTY PIGEONS ARE TO be released.

This morning, the government delivered the official messages along with personal correspondences. Another thirty tomorrow. They flash shiny bead-like eyes; their feet dance on the metal wiring. Jorgen stands next to the cages and envies their wings.

Svensk steps out on the porch to help. Jorgen looks right through him before he sees him. When he is around the birds now, humans seem almost obscene. The birds coo and jump around the cage, rubbing their wings against the wire. He would release them all, he thinks, in one gleam of gray; he would do it, if they would teach him the mystery of wings.

Svensk pats him on the back. A balloon made it, he says. It caught a favorable wind and landed at Dreux. They say the man stepped out with a handful of the mail in both hands. He waved the letters in the air, then fell on his knees and wept.

Jorgen lifts the metal clasp out of its hole, opens the door, and reaches into the cage. The birds flit around him. He braces his hands around one of the birds, holding down its wings, and slowly pulls it through the open door.

Svensk opens the envelope and pulls out a thin, white note.

Hold him still, says Svensk.

Wait, says Jorgen.

Jorgen puts the bird back in the cage and takes the note from Svensk.

What are you doing? asks Svensk.

Jorgen opens the message. It is addressed to the British ambassador to France who escaped from Paris and is now in Tours. *Bazaine is trapped in Metz. If not assisted by the British, Metz will fall. Then, only a matter of time before France falls to Prussia.*

What does it say? asks Svensk.

Jorgen swallows and tries to control his rapid breathing. He reads it out loud. For a moment, they stand in silence.

Is that where Natalia is? In Metz?

Jorgen shakes his head at the image of swarming Prussian soldiers descending on Metz, the shrills of delight as they fire at any moving thing. French soldiers firing haphazardly, desperately, hidden behind bullet-riddled walls.

If France loses Metz, there's nothing left. The Prussians will come charging to Paris, says Svensk. What other stronghold does France have?

At least she has my rifle.

You gave her your rifle? Geez. Your rifle. You loved that thing. Maybe you should write her and tell her to desert.

She'd never do that. She's too headstrong. Too noble, he thinks. She'll be one of the soldiers fighting to the end. You should have seen her patience at the shooting range, he says. She's a real soldier.

That's where you're going, isn't it? You asked me the other day if I'd take care of the pigeons if you left. You're going to her, aren't you? You gave her your rifle. You wouldn't give it to just anyone. You're going to find her.

Jorgen doesn't say anything.

I won't tell anyone, says Svensk. I don't know how you'll get out of here. Open another one.

Jorgen undoes another dispatch. *Simon being sent to Bordeaux to begin armistice negotiations.*

Svenks stares wide-eyed at Jorgen. France is going to surrender?

Perhaps the armistice will come before Metz falls, he thinks; she could escape unharmed. And the more dispatches they read, the more they understand it is only a matter of time before the Prussians bombard Paris and march down the boulevards in their shiny helmets.

It's over, says Svensk. It's almost over.

They stand there a quiet moment, feeling as if the edges of Paris are disintegrating. The prestige, the glamour, the once strong army of France vanquished. Svensk rolls up a note and ties it with waxed thread to the bird's tail feather. Jorgen tosses the bird into the air and watches the flutter of light gray

wings. A good flight, my friend, he thinks. He follows the bird as it flies beyond the roof of the house, up, up, beyond the tree limbs.

Look at it go, says Svensk.

A strong breeze of optimism blows through Jorgen. The war will be over
soon, he thinks, and he clutches to the thought she's coming home soon.
She's fine and she will be fine. Who knows? Maybe tomorrow she'll be standing at the front door. Jorgen watches until the bird becomes a gray speck
against a gray sky. They stand there watching for a long time.

As easily as it blew in, the optimism drifts away. It's not true, Jorgen
thinks. From her last note, she might be shell-shocked, and in some terrible
way, she's given up. *Death. . . . It would be so easy.* It would, of course. How
many times did he think the same thought? Not only on the battlefield, but
here, in the drab office or his depressing room. A miracle that anything stays
alive.

He looks up at the bird again. How he wishes he could fly.

Svensk releases another bird, then another, and another.

And it doesn't stand up to logic, no, it's quite irrational, but when he had
the painting, Natalia was here. Of course it's not rational, but nothing makes
sense anymore, the war, his ghost leg, nothing. The painting, if he had it—
he thinks of the many times his hand has swept underneath his bed searching
for it, as many times as he has looked out the window in search of Natalia—
if he had the painting, she would return, yes, he feels it. She'd find her way
back to Paris.

Boy, that's a big weight off you, says Svensk, turning to Jorgen.

Yes, it's a relief, says Jorgen, thinking of course she would return. For now
there is something for him to do. He'll get the painting back, and with that,
Natalia will find her way home. The painting, a concentration of such beauty.
How could he have let it go? He had it, he once held it in his hands, as he once
embraced Natalia. She stood in the cup of his arms. He rubs his hand on his
forehead, bewildered and astonished he hadn't seen the connection before.

That's it, then, says Svensk.

Yes, says Jorgen. That's it.

· · ·

A MAID OPENS THE front door of Daniel's house.

The master is out, she says. She is a frail, frightened woman, with worry lines traced over her forehead and around her eyes like an intricately drawn map.

When might I see him? asks Jorgen, trying to keep the frantic desperation from his voice. This afternoon? This evening? I must see him.

The sound of a cannon ruptures the morning air, and she jumps, gives a small shriek, and slams shut the door. He pounds on the door for a while then decides to walk around the block and try again.

Winter nips the air, and everyone is bundled up in layers of scarves and hats and heavy coats. Faces are buttoned down and flattened, no one meeting another's eye, no one wanting to be asked anything, for money, food, lodging, firewood, not wanting to part with anything, too huddled up in a heavy blanket of deprivation. He passes by a bread line. The wind blows and a woman's purple hat flies up into the air. No one moves to retrieve it. She asks the man behind her if she might keep her place to get it; the man considers for a moment and reluctantly consents.

Shivering, he joins the line. A bit of bread will help, he thinks, not remembering when he last ate. He's thinking how he could break into Daniel's house, perhaps climb in through the back window, when he hears something and turns.

What? he asks. What did you say?

Bazaine surrendered at Metz.

Other people wake up from their isolated daze. News is so scarce.

The man says a group of soldiers staggered in last night, emaciated and weary. They walked all the way from Metz. There's a bunch of soldiers at the plaza.

Jorgen hurries along Avenue de l'Imperatrice; cows graze alongside horses and sheep. He passes by soldiers wearing faded coats and dirty boots and playing galline. Beside them, their pitched tents and open fires. Someone shouts to his right; at his feet, an old woman in rags begs; a soldier rides by on a horse, his arm bandaged and his face weary. It all passes by him, around him, a churning of events that have nothing to do with him.

At the Hôtel de Ville a mob has gathered. Rain begins to fall and umbrellas pop like bomb bursts. Jorgen bumps into a National Guardsman. He quickly apologizes in his best French and asks if he's spoken to anyone returning from Metz. The guard tells him to try the hospitals.

Jorgen walks rapidly to the first hospital in view and almost tumbles out, the smell of blood and sweat and fear too sickeningly familiar. The room is spilling with a fresh wave of injured soldiers. Rows of cots, soldiers sitting on the floor, lying on the floor, in chairs. By the door, there's a soldier with a head wound; his bandage is soaked through. It'll be hours before someone has time to take care of that, thinks Jorgen. Jorgen asks him whether he came from Metz. The man shakes his head mutely and points to another soldier, sitting in a chair, his head in his hands.

Jorgen bends down. Excuse me.

The soldier groans and asks Jorgen for a cup of water. Jorgen finds the man's canteen resting on the floor. He tips the man's head back and puts it to his parched lips. The soldier tells Jorgen that Bazaine will be punished for this. He will probably hang.

Did you see women soldiers? asks Jorgen.

The whole thing a mess. A damn mess.

Jorgen asks again.

Women? Several died up there. Can't remember. We didn't have time to bury them. Birds and feral dogs picking away at the dead bodies. Stacks of bodies. No one knew what they were doing. Damn Bazaine.

Jorgen describes Natalia. He's surprised at how many details he remembers. The color of her hair, her face, soft but pensive, as if always thinking or listening intently. Sometimes her face open, like an animal sunning itself. Her eyes, the same eyes, blue and intense.

I don't know. Maybe.

The injured soldier rubs his face with dirty, blood-stained hands and asks Jorgen if he's got any food. Jorgen walks around the makeshift hospital and finds a side room. There are bags and coats. Probably the doctors' and nurses'. He fishes around in one of the bags, grabs an apple and a strawberry scone, and heads back to the soldier. The soldier bites into the apple, closes his eyes, and tries to savor it, but ends up eating it voraciously. Jorgen hands the man the scone. He stuffs it in his mouth.

We ran out of supplies. Days went by without food. Lived on roots, slop for hogs. Sometimes we lay still in our trenches for hours. Didn't have any energy to move. The bastards let us run out of ammunition. Seventy days. Seventy days of battle and not enough guns, bullets, food, or water. That god-damn Bazaine.

She had a powerful gun, says Jorgen. This woman, Natalia.

The soldier drinks from his canteen. Maybe. No, I remember. There was a woman who had a good, solid rifle. Good shooter.

Jorgen grips the edge of his chair. Is she alive?

Last I saw of her she was.

Did she return to Paris?

I don't think so. The soldier slumps in his chair and closes his eyes. Jorgen rises to go; the soldier grabs Jorgen's arm and says he just remembered something. He asks Jorgen to pull out his handkerchief from his knapsack. Jorgen snatches the bag and digs out the blue cloth, tied up in a knot. Open it! says the man. Open it! Inside a last crust of bread. He shoves it in his mouth.

JAPAN

THE MONK STEPS INTO the studio.

She looks up from her painting but is still deeply engrossed in what she is doing. Her eyes widen with alarm and she quickly leans over her painting, concealing it.

He holds up the tray with a teapot and cup. I'm sorry, he says, bowing. The maid was bringing you tea. I thought, he says, then stops. He'll only stay a minute, he thinks, he shouldn't have interrupted her; look at the pained expression on her face. How impulsive of him to barge into her private place. I'm so sorry.

He sets the tray on the edge of her desk. When she reaches for the tray, he catches sight of the painting. A man, a young man embracing a woman who looks like Ayoshi. She's painted a man wearing an elegant blue kimono and the couple is standing under a flowering plum tree. He feels a peculiar fluttering in his chest and doesn't know what to say. He thought she painted seascapes and mountains, jays and waterfalls. Does she spend these hours in the studio painting this man?

It's someone I once knew, she says, darting an anxious look.

He grips the edge of her desk, turning crimson. Do you usually paint this subject? he stammers.

She dabs the edge of a cloth, soaking up a puddle of blue paint on the man's kimono, and slides the painting onto a stack under her desk.

Thank you for the tea, she says, her voice, a whisper. She sits there, her hands folded.

He fidgets with the button on his sleeve and ducks his head to avoid her eyes. I'm sorry I intruded, he says, backing out of the studio.

He looks over at the studio. She's still bowed over her painting. She shouldn't be imagining such things. Such lust-filled images, he thinks. It's not proper, soaking herself in desire. He recalls what his teacher said: Desire is like a drink of salty water, which only causes thirst to grow more intense. Desire for that man. Not Hayashi; the man in the painting, too young, too strong, and his face, open and filled with unmistakable dignity and poise. It wasn't a picture of him either.

She is in there. Painting another man.

He begins pounding in the nails for the wooden frame of the roof. He sets the hammer down and feels a sense of deepening despair. What can he do? He glances up to the top of the mountain. What is up there now? Did anything survive? Perhaps a small statue. Maybe a scroll or part of a hut. By now, the path to the mountain monastery is closed.

He walks over to the temple to pray.

In the morning, the monk's tools are coated with dew, and the garden is emptied of sound. He's finished the roof, everything except the black tiles. She hasn't seen him all morning. After he saw her painting, he looked so flustered, so ashamed for her. She should have immediately slid it under her desk, as she does with Hayashi. Why hadn't she done so? She thought, no she hoped, of all people, he would view it without judgment. But he said nothing and looked at her with what? Disdain? Jealousy? She doesn't know. Didn't his eyes have a sense of disquiet about them? He should have said something. If he had said something, she would have told him she no longer can paint this man, can't find him anymore, the memory nearly effaced. She stands again to look for him from the kitchen window. A woman

and three children are walking down the pebble path, the tallest boy pushing a wooden cart. Ayoshi steps outside. There's something, she thinks, a
spurt of green grass underfoot and the first quake of the bulbs underground.

Hello, says Ayoshi, smiling faintly.

Please, says the woman, rushing toward Ayoshi, a storm of gray and black.
Tears streak her dusty face. Please.

Ayoshi backs away. The woman's eyes are glassy and flaring. Her age, in-
distinct, she is so worn down. Dirt smudges her cheeks and forehead. Strands
of hair have escaped her bun and shudder around her face. And now she is so
close, her knuckles are chapped and red squiggly lines streak the whites of
her eyes. She smells of something kept for a long time in a tight box. The
woman says she's traveled from temple to temple all morning, but they are
closed. No one will hold a proper Buddhist burial for her husband. She grabs
Ayoshi's wrist; her freezing hand singes Ayoshi's skin. Ayoshi yanks her arm
away and stumbles back. She glances toward the house. Where is Hayashi?
He should attend to this hysterical woman.

The woman scrambles over to the cart, her eldest son standing beside it,
a guardian of sorts. Ayoshi doesn't want to follow, but the woman is reaching
in, as if she might lift her husband's body and bring it over. The husband is
wrapped in a white sheet. Around his midsection, the stain of blood. The
woman begins to weep, and the children, crouched in the pebble path, look
up wide-eyed from their game. Ayoshi woozily grips the side of the cart and
stares mesmerized at the red-brown bloom. The sight sickens her, but she
can't tear her gaze away. The woman is saying something, what is she saying?

The temple doors swing open. The monk stands at the entrance, wearing
his old brown robe again, the twist of twine around his middle, as if he had
been expecting this woman's arrival. His face is stern, composed, revealing
nothing.

The woman dashes over to him. He places his hand on her head. Ayoshi
closes her eyes and shakes her head to toss off the memory, rising in sharp
shards.

The old woman's house was tucked behind a tall bamboo fence. Her father
took her there. Opened the gate. Dragged her from the cart. She fell on her

knees in the old woman's front garden. She remembers the wind scurrying dried leaves around her, as if encircling her, holding her there. In the heat of that summer day, the old woman came out and placed her clawlike hand on her head and clutched her arm. Took her inside, a bright white sheet swathed a board. As she listened to the leaves outside, that claw of a hand ripped out her insides; the pain tore off the top of her head. Below her, the red blossoms, fire flowers, slippery, one after another, a never ending emptying. Her thighs covered in them, a whole row, a field, an endless field of fire flowers and the old woman mopping.

Ayoshi. Ayoshi?

Ayoshi turns to the monk. He frowns, steps inside, and returns with a glass of water. With his finger, he places water on the dead man's lips.

Who did it? he asks the woman, his voice formal and commanding.

The woman pulls her two youngest to her side. The oldest son still stands by the cart, staring at his dead father.

Please, she says. Please.

The older boy says his father was involved in a protest against the government over the new land tax. The government no longer permits the tax to be paid in kind with soybeans or other grains. They want money, he says, solemnly. My father said we didn't have any money to spare. A soldier smashed his rifle over his father's head. Then he took a sword and sliced his stomach. I saw it. He fell to the ground, and the soldier took his sword and did it. I saw it.

The woman begs the monk to wash her husband's body.

The grief surrounds the woman as cold as a cave; Ayoshi wore such a mist when she left the old woman's house, her insides on the woman's floor. She grew sick and frail and felt death rapping at her heart. Too many red blooms, the rip too deep, beyond repair. Her mother knew how to help her, but afterward, she refused to look at Ayoshi. Afterward, she walked right past her. What? I have no daughter, she told her husband. Outside her bedroom, Ayoshi heard the women of the village come to their house, seeking her mother's healing hands. In the six-tatami room, they stretched out on the floor, and her mother ran her hands an inch above their bodies, smoothing out their energy. Her mother did this day after day, but never for her non-existent daughter.

The monk is saying something. She looks at him. Please take her over to the bench, he says. She must sit or she will faint.

She must stop staring at the crumpled figure. But there is the red-brown clotted in the white sheet. For weeks afterward, she dreamt of hot red flowing in her veins. How much fell out? Where did it go? Nightmares of swimming in red, viscous flowers, a baby submerged, she kept diving to save it from drowning.

Not long after that, her father contacted the go-between. She was a whisper of herself when Hayashi appeared. In a fresh new kimono, he held out a cask of sake for her family, wrapped in gold-speckled rice paper, a red ribbon around the bottle's neck for good luck, and dutifully long for a long life together. His eyes widened when he saw her. She felt nothing, except her insides gone, an emptiness smoldering. Her bags were packed; she didn't understand; where was she going?

Do you need something to drink? asks the monk. You look pale.

No, thank you, says Ayoshi.

It takes her a moment to understand he is not speaking to her but to the widow.

Here, he says to the woman. She will give you some water.

She stares at the monk. His body is stiff and rigid, like a tight boot.

THE MONK SITS IN front of the Buddha. The woman left her husband's body to be prepared for its passage. As he walked the woman and her children to the gate, he told her to return tomorrow for the formal Buddhist funeral. Hayashi promised he'd speak to the officials, but what has he done? Nothing. He will conduct the funeral, no matter how much Hayashi protests, no matter what harm it might bring.

He hears a tap on the door. His legs tremble, wanting to run to the door and see if it is Ayoshi. Ask her about the man in the painting. Where is this man? Does she care for him? Does he live in the village? Does she kiss this man the way she kissed him? But he won't let himself leave this cushion. He has swung so far from his chosen path, he barely recognizes himself. Who has he become? This new man, thrown this way and that by desire or jealousy; he despises this new man. He tries to meditate, to focus on the serene expression of the Buddha, but his heart aches so.

He stands and looks around the temple, as if seeing it for the first time. The woman's screams are dark rings inside him; she cried out for her husband. And before his life at the bottom of the mountain, he would not have understood the depth of her misery; but now he feels it howling under his skin.

He rushes to the door. No one is there. He gazes into the darkness and feels his stomach squeeze. Who was she daydreaming about today? When he asked her to fetch water for the woman, was she thinking about that man? Then he stops himself. Enough of this, he says out loud. He shuts the door, intending to sit again, but instead, he paces. Her paintings, he thinks, those horrible paintings.

SATO FINDS HER RESTING in the Western room, curled up on the couch. On the table in front of her, her paper and black ink for calligraphy. The light sprinkles on the floor like diamonds. Stripes of shadow lie on the wall. She pulls a thread from the couch and molds it into a ball.

He drags a chair next to the couch.

I'm too tired for whatever trouble you're bringing, she says, propping herself on an elbow.

He studies her.

She dips her brush in the ink, scrapes it against the edge of the plate, and writes his name. She chooses the kanji, a person with a saw about to make something.

Here, she says.

Is that a compliment? he asks.

She shrugs. Depends how you use the saw.

This flirtation with the monk.

She sits up.

Whatever is going on, it must stop.

She looks at her paper, not meeting his eyes.

I don't think you realize—

It's stopped, she says, her voice pinched tight.

The way he broods for you? The way he can't stay away from you—

She doesn't say anything.

And you from him? His tone is threatening and possessive.

That's not true, she says.

He sniffs and looks out the window. The wind wrestles with the trees, and when they hear the hammer pounding, she freezes. The monk is finishing the teahouse. She draws in a deep breath.

Sato's face darkens. I'm worried for your safety.

She laughs unpleasantly. You think Hayashi cares?

Sato is silent for a moment. Some men act irrationally when they discover their wives have affection for another man.

Hayashi searches me out only when his feet hurt too badly.

Sato stands. What does the monk know about the world? What has he seen?

She doesn't answer, but studies Sato, weighing the urgent tone of his voice. He professes to want nothing, but Sato wants something.

Hayashi is not stupid, he says.

She wraps her arms around her shins. No. Not stupid.

He sighs and falls back into her chair. What am I going to do with you?

What would you like to do with me?

You know.

Say it.

I'd like you to come with me when I leave. That's what I want. You're dying here, shriveling into something unrecognizable. You're not the person I once knew. That person was brilliant and talented. She seized hold of life. What happened to her? You've let yourself grow small. You're going to disappear. The next time I come visit, you will have vanished. No one will know whom I'm asking for. Ayoshi? they will say. Who?

It's so easy with Hayashi, she says, before she knows what she is saying.

Of course it is, he says. How does he challenge you? He doesn't. That's why it's so easy.

Who says I want to be challenged? she says.

You used to want more.

With you, I'd have more? she asks, and the moment she says it, she knows this is what she would most like to know.

He considers her critically. I understand you, more than anyone.

Ayoshi doesn't say anything for a long time.

He sighs, gets up, and leaves the room. She sits there, watching the shadows move on the wall.

THE MONK WORKS THROUGH the night to finish the teahouse, five lanterns perched along the edges of the roof. At the deepest part of the night, far past midnight, he finishes laying the final tile.

Sato stands at the window and watches the monk put away his tools. Finally, whispers Sato.

The branches stir, cutting the moon into a series of dark lines. He thinks of all the stories that people tell about the moon, the myths, the dreams, the power that people give to the globe reflecting the sun's light. Under a full moon in Shanghai, a woman read the Chien Tung fortune-telling sticks for him. She stared at him with ebony eyes, her eyelids painted bright blue. There is much more than has been revealed to you, she said. The material world is giving you such abundance, tremendous abundance, but it is sullying your spirit. He laughed, kissed her brown stained fingertips, and slipped her extra coins.

Sato hears a ship call out in the night and imagines it passing through black waters. On that ship or some other, he has boxes of gunpowder and rifles bought in China and sold to the English to be used against a group of insurgents in India.

Strange how much time has passed since he's been on a ship. Usually the waves creep into his body, venture into his veins. Walking on land, he feels the sea and is buoyant, the sea lulling him, lifting him, and he never quite touches down.

But now the rocking in his body is gone, and he's never been so fully weighted on his feet. It is time to leave. He walks back to his bed and lies down. And if Ayoshi comes with him? If she finally gathers the nerve to leave her dismal husband? He could give her so much, show her the red cliffs in San Francisco, take her to Twining at the Strand in London for English tea. He'd sell her paintings, fetch such prices. A perfect fit, he thinks.

IT IS SO QUIET. The monk finished hammering about an hour ago, far past midnight. Now everyone is sleeping. Then why is he so restless? He gets up again and paces. He feels his mind pulling at something. The room darkens, the clouds dashing over the slice of moon, and for a moment, everything feels bleak. The teahouse is finished; there is no further need. It is time for him to go.

HAYASHI JERKS AWAKE TO the sound of a sad, helpless cry. He sits up and looks first around the room, then to the other side of the bed, thinking she might be hurt. There is Ayoshi, curled up into a ball, like something without its hard shell. He waits to see if she called out. But she is sleeping soundly. When has she ever needed him? he thinks. When has she ever asked him for anything? As he touches her arm, he hears the cry again, a ship moaning. Ayoshi stirs. He pulls away his hand.

Ayoshi wakes. Are you all right?

Yes, he says, I'm sorry I woke you. Go back to sleep.

He looks at her in the dim light and sees in her face something he's never seen before, a certain gleam of fright in her eyes.

Shall I get you a glass of water? she asks.

I heard that ship. The horn of the ship. Sad isn't it? he says. The sound of a ship, coming or going. It's just that—I find some sounds haunting.

IN THE EARLY MORNING sun, Ayoshi steps outside to look at the finished teahouse. It is magnificent, she thinks. She slips off her geta, crouches down, passing through the small entryway. There is the scent of fresh pine and spring reeds. From the small window, she looks out onto the rock garden, white pebbles with large black stones arranged by the monk for contemplation. She sits at the tea table and stares at the blank wall. Presses her hands to her face. It is so easy to hate this world, she thinks.

The teahouse door snaps open. The monk stands in the doorway. Her body stiffens. I'm sorry, he says. I didn't know anyone was in here.

You did a beautiful job, she says, half rising.

He bows and turns to leave.

Please stay, she says. A moment.

The room is small. He stands by the door, not moving.

Can't you sit with me for a moment?

He mechanically steps to the far end of the table and sits, folding his hands.

You've been well?

Yes, he says, looking at her, then out the window. And you?

She nods, her throat tightening.

You're probably leaving soon? she says.

Yes.

He says it so nonchalantly, as if nothing transpired between them, she thinks. She feels herself seeking the fire of his skin, the urgent silk of his fingertips, his lips.

He stands. She rises quickly and moves beside him, brushing her fingertips against his cheek. He jerks away, his eyes flickering.

I'm sorry I showed you the painting, she says. She reaches for him. I'm so sorry.

It's what you paint. He stiffens again. You shouldn't apologize. He pauses. You said it's someone you once knew?

A long time ago, she says, startled by her words.

He nods, looking down at her tabi socks.

They stand there, not speaking.

I knew him in Hokkaido, she says. I didn't mean to hurt you.

He waves her off. It's better this way.

What way?

I should go. The family is coming today for a formal burial, he says. I don't care if Hayashi tries to stop me. I don't care if the government sends its soldiers here to kill me. It's what must be done.

Enri—

He rushes from the teahouse. She turns to follow him, but stops herself, listening to his footsteps rush across the pebbled path, until they become fainter and fainter, then nothing at all.

HAYASHI IS ON HIS way to the kitchen when he sees the monk hurry from the teahouse, his face flushed. He must have forgotten something, he thinks. Some final touch to make it perfect. Hayashi smiles knowingly and is about to continue down the hallway when Ayoshi steps from the teahouse. Her head is downcast. And he's ready to erase this—what is this?—not willing to believe what is slowly creeping into mind. Won't let himself think these horrible, blasphemous thoughts, and he casts around for something else. Perhaps the monk wanted to show her a new design of a shelf or the way he wove the floorboards so tightly together. So proud, he is, of his creation. Hayashi presses his fingertips to the cold window. Or maybe during a moment his hammer was silent, she stepped inside to admire the construction, not realizing he was inside.

He treads down the hallway and into the kitchen, and the ugly, intolerable thoughts keep snaking in. The maid brings him a bowl of soup. It isn't clear, he thinks, so why stretch it into something where it shouldn't go? Where it must not go. He is an honored guest.

More tea, sir? asks the maid.

What? he looks at her, baffled.

More tea?

Fine. I'm fine. He focuses on his soup, the long stretch of green seaweed, the small diced cubes of tofu in a light brown watery mix. The maid asks if there is anything else he might need.

What?

Do you need anything else?

No, thank you. He stirs his soup with a chopstick, watching the murky swirl.

HAYASHI SITS AT HIS potter's wheel. Will he let this new shape appear? He stares at the lump of clay in front of him. How long has he been sitting here? He plunges his hands into the lump, closes his eyes, and begins to pull a shape from the thick soft mud. The rest of the world begins to fall away, and then he hears the loud gong of the temple bell.

Oh, no, he whispers, feeling an overwhelming sense of dread.

He quickly wipes his hands and steps outside. He must find the monk. Tell him to stop ringing that bell. The whole town will hear it. There is a woman and her children. She looks like she's dressed for a formal funeral in her black kimono. Dear woman, please go home. He never did tell the monk how badly the meeting went. And that bell is so loud. Like a siren to the government officials, a blatant snubbing of their demand. What if they come charging up here, the army fully outfitted with their Western guns?

The family huddles together, waiting for the monk to appear. The oldest boy, with his hair combed and wet to keep it in place, stands beside his mother, his arms crossed, nodding at something she is saying. The two youngest clutch the cloth of her kimono. He must stop this, but he can't move, can't prevent what has begun, what has always happened after a death, a funeral, a formal Buddhist funeral. And he glides back years to the gathering of townspeople at the temple, this very temple, where the people came to bury the members of his family. He could not attend their funeral, too badly burned, but the old woman who helped heal him went. Wearing her musty kimono, she walked to where the family house once stood, picked through the ashes with chopsticks, and found the bones of his family. Put them in bronze urns and carried them to the Buddhist priest. There were no bodies to wash, nothing to cleanse to prepare for the passage, no placing of a white kimono on top of a body, along with leggings, sandals, and money for the deceased to pay the toll across the River of the Three Hells. Only the blackened bones that the priest scrubbed until they shone almost white. The priest placed them into the tall golden urns, starting with the lower body bones and then the upper and finally the pieces of the skull so his mother and father and little sister were not uncomfortably upside down in their final resting place.

As Hayashi walks toward the family, he's not sure what he's going to do until he's standing in front of the woman, her eyes red from crying, her face soft and tender from grief. He bows low to her and gives her condolences. The monk appears in his robe, his expression solemn and still, and Hayashi sees the slightly raised eyebrow, the monk waiting to see what he'll do. And Hayashi is amazed he is now part of the small gathering following the monk into the temple, taking a seat behind the small family, watching the monk stand at the front, next to the casket, open his book, and begin chanting the sutras. Hayashi floats in the sound, so lovely, and now the boy's voice, so sweet, and the woman's tender and soft, he drifts there, letting the sound, almost, but not quite, smother the increasing panic in his limbs.

Soon the woman will walk back to town, her children in tow, and her step will have a looseness, the blood returned to her face, not quite smiling, but her draperies, her infirmities undoing their hold. Her neighbors will see the relief. And the story will come out she went to the temple on the hill, a monk lives there, a traditional funeral can still be conducted there; the word will spread and more people will come. The officials will hear if they haven't already heard the bell.

It's Hayashi's turn. He stands, balancing awkwardly, chanting louder, louder than the woman, as he walks to the front with his incense, hoping to stem the fear chattering through his limbs.

FRANCE

YES, THAT'S WHAT WE'LL do, thinks Jorgen, feeling the brisk wind from the North Sea. When I find her, we'll travel to the sea. He tugs his collar up to his chin and cinches his hands into the sleeves of his coat. Yes, the sea, the great expanse of blue, and we'll wander along the gray sand, and I'll find her a perfect shell. He blows warm air onto his freezing hands. He looks again at Daniel's house. A figure passes by the window. He's been daydreaming. Daniel is home.

He rings the doorbell. The maid opens the door, and a rush of heat surrounds him. It feels as if he could shape it with his hands. He hears the clink of silverware on plates, the rumble of a man's voice, the laughter of a woman. He inches toward the front room, and there is the smell of garlic and tomato sauce. Daniel bounds into the hallway, his face bright red. He's exhumed his old self and then some, thinks Jorgen, with the making of a jowl, the unpleasant business of death now conveniently behind him. Daniel gestures weakly toward the guests who are dining in the living room.

Perhaps you could come back at a better time? he says, his speech slurred.

Later tonight? asks Jorgen.

Tomorrow would be much better, he says with a tolerant smile. It's so rare these days that I throw a good party. Jorgen smells the liquor on his breath.

Daniel looks at Jorgen's empty hands with glassy eyes. Have you come about something else?

I need to talk to you.

One of the guests yells for another bottle of wine. Raucous laughter follows. Daniel hesitates, then tells Jorgen to wait in the study. Jorgen walks down the long hallway, into the dark room, and turns on a small kerosene lamp. Here is where he sold the painting. He rolled it out on the desktop. Under this light, they both stood stunned. It seems unimaginable that he sold it. Did he think it wouldn't matter? Only another hole in his life amongst all the other perforations? But now he knows he must not leave without the painting, and with it in hand, he can see her coming home, back to Paris.

He sits in the chair across from the desk. What was the color in the painting of her dress? He closes his eyes. Nothing but white dots under his lids. He snaps open his eyes. Flowers or tears or something else he hasn't yet understood? Standing now, he gazes out the window. His hands begin to shake. Her dress, red, but what precise color of red? Daniel's voice drifts from far down the hallway. Where is it? He quickly searches through a stack of large books on the desk, slides open desk drawers, and climbs down on his knee to check underneath the desk. If he found it, he'd steal it.

Did you drop something? asks Daniel.

Jorgen rises awkwardly. Yes. But it doesn't matter. Jorgen gathers himself. I've come to buy the painting back.

Daniel raises an eyebrow, a leer on his lips. In a bit of trouble? Someone discover it missing? You know, Svensk came by the other day and seemed rather surprised to learn you paid me a visit alone. In fact, he seemed rather displeased. He chuckles to himself. I'm sorry, my dear man. I can't help you.

I have the money, says Jorgen, his palms sweating.

Daniel grins clumsily.

I'll pay more than what I sold it for.

I'm sorry, says Daniel. I can't help you. I sold it.

Jorgen leans hard onto his crutch. What?

I sold it. Daniel shifts on his feet and looks down at his desk.

To whom?

A rich French man. He belongs to a prominent literary salon. A very intriguing fellow.

Jorgen stands there, his lower jaw falling open.

Why are you looking at me like that?

But you said you'd never seen anything like it.

Well, *you* sold it to me.

Neither man moves.

Finally Daniel shifts his gaze to the floor, pulls a pack of cigarettes from his breast pocket, removes one, and takes several swipes with a match before he lights it. As he blows smoke into the room, he tells Jorgen the rich fellow offered a good price and, though he didn't want to sell, the man kept raising his offer. Other guests were in the room, and everyone began to laugh, and someone asked, Are you getting sentimental in your old age, Daniel? It made me wonder, was I? It did seem rather odd. All that money for a painting. Daniel smiles weakly. And so I sold it.

Someone begins to play the piano.

I should get back, says Daniel. I'm sorry, my dear man.

Jorgen hears himself breathing rapidly. Where do I find this man?

I could contact him for you, he says, holding onto the desk, swaying slightly.

A tremor runs through Jorgen's body and his leg feels stiff and weak.

Well? asks Daniel, now scowling. What price? What are you willing to pay?

Jorgen pauses. I don't know.

Daniel tells him to think about it and in the meantime, he'll contact the buyer. He tells Jorgen to come back on Thursday. He's having another dinner party and the buyer will be coming. The guests are squealing for Daniel to return. Jorgen walks down the hallway and steps outside into the cold night.

How could he? And who is this rich man now staring at the painting? Jorgen feels his chest tighten. He keeps passing by people, the same words on their lips, The Prussians have refused an armistice. Why should they call a truce when they know they've won, he thinks, and in the same vein, he won't settle for anything but the painting. But what if this man sold it? What then? He trips over a bag of garbage and almost stumbles and falls. But the question is so weighty, the near mishap doesn't infringe on his thoughts. Without the painting, she won't return, he thinks, and then what? The question presses down on him, constricting his lungs. When he looks up again, he's walked himself to the street of the doctor's office, as if this is the answer. The woman flits behind the opaque glass. With a leg, he could go to her. Yes, perhaps that's why he is here, the doctor finally has been released. He knocks and white paint chips fall onto the toe of his shoe. The door cracks open. A narrow band of dark room appears.

Go away. Her voice is stripped of pleasantry.

The doctor, he implores.

Leave me alone.

But I must see the doctor.

Please, she says, the word sliding on her tongue.

He pushes on the door.

She tries to slam it shut. There is no doctor.

Please. I must.

Stop this! The doctor is dead! He's dead. Do you understand? They killed him.

Her eyes are flat. The door slams shut. He steps back, mumbling, Sorry, so sorry, and nearly tumbles down the first stair. He feels a headache crawling around at the back of his skull. Stumbling to the sidewalk, he passes by a young woman roasting a rat. She squats in front of a small fire, a stick pierced through the rat's body, and turns it over and over in the flames, humming a song. The ragged woman smiles up at him with a toothless grin. He pulls back, frightened by the ghoulish look, and rushes down the street. *Dead, dead, the doctor.* What did Natalia write? It is so easy to die. And it is, if everything falls away and you are left, retracted and cold. He must get the painting back. He grabs his hands and anxiously twists his thumbs. Death, he thinks, is the opposite of beauty.

• • •

IN THE MORNING, Jorgen flings another batch of pigeons into the snowy air. He won't watch them go. Too awful to witness their easy departure. A rapid flutter, up, up, into an air current, and then gone. He pulls another bird from its cage, puts it up to his face, and whispers, Go find her, find her and make sure she's safe.

When he steps inside, he hears Pierre call for him. Pierre sits in his dark office, a long candle flickering on the desk.

I think we have a problem, says Pierre. His long face looks haunted in the low light. Jorgen grips his hands to his thighs.

What is it? Jorgen asks, and by the grim look on Pierre's face, it must be news about Natalia.

Sit down. Pierre glances at his calendar. Well, I almost forgot. It's Natalia's birthday today, and she's celebrating, God knows where.

Jorgen feels a rush of panic. This would be the day, her birthday, when she'd do something drastic, he thinks. Throw herself into the heat of battle, surround herself by the spatter of gunfire. Why he thinks this, he isn't sure, but he feels awful dread mounting.

Did you just hear what I said? demands Pierre. We have a leak somewhere in the supply line of goods. Jorgen shifts in his chair. His face remains placid. Pierre twirls a pencil in front of him, pretending to study it. Someone is stealing from me. Not boxes of things, but individual items. They are doing it piecemeal, hoping I won't notice.

Jorgen feels a rushing of his heart. How can you be sure? asks Jorgen. Couldn't it be errors on the part of the seller?

Pierre watches him closely. I'm not stupid. I've set up systems to check what comes in, what goes out. And I've got loyal sources.

They sit there a moment, neither one speaking. Svensk must have made some oblique reference to it, thinks Jorgen. Angry that I went to Daniel's and didn't give him a cut. You don't think I did it, do you? asks Jorgen, trying to sit straight in his chair and look at Pierre without wavering. I told you about the sewer line. I'd hardly be the one—

Pierre frowns. I'm not saying just yet that you did or didn't do it.

Jorgen's hands grope vainly in his coat pocket. I'm concerned about Natalia. Aren't you—

Pierre slams his hands down on the desk. For God's sake. Don't worry about my family affairs. Whatever happens to her, she deserves it.

The pounding begins, the headache rolling in like a thunderstorm. A tremor rumbles through his hands and rattles his spine. People are starving, says Jorgen. They know you are a wealthy man. You're one of the few who is still in business. People like you attract envy.

Pierre sits up in his chair. Their starvation is not my problem. I'm a businessman. He leans forward and looks directly at Jorgen. If I find the thief, I'll have him arrested.

Jorgen presses a finger to his temple and glares broodingly at Pierre. Pierre leans back so his face is half in shadows. Why did you come to France?

What?

You heard me.

I'm a soldier.

You were wounded within the first few months. A great soldier, I'm sure.

Jorgen clenches his jaw, which makes his head throb even more. Around the periphery of his vision, the images are breaking into small dots of color.

You didn't even bother to fight, says Jorgen.

A half-hearted smile breaks over Pierre's lips. I know my limits. A man does not just pick up and leave his family and country without a good reason.

Jorgen looks at Pierre's hands, squished into tight pudgy fists. Long nails, perfectly manicured.

What crime did you commit back in the northern farmland of Denmark, what horrible thing did you do up there that made you leave? If you are stealing from me, I will call the authorities and tell them you are a spy. They will shoot you on the spot. It's been done. I've seen it, and I would not hesitate to see it again.

There is nothing left for him here, thinks Jorgen. Natalia gone, the pigeons gone, he clamors up from his chair. You want to know why I left? he says, his voice hoarse and rasping. I left because I got a girl in a bad way. His voice ends in a choke of distress. Took off in the middle of the night without telling a soul. It was wrong, and I've paid and paid and paid for it and my life will never be the same.

Pierre's face splits open into hard laughter. That's all? You got a girl pregnant? That happens every day in France and a man doesn't think twice. My God. We just pay the girl off. That's all she wants is your money.

Jorgen's eyes flick to the door. He said it, he said it out loud, and now Pierre's laughter hurts his ears. His headache sinks its roots; he walks to the door, barely able to see his way out. He grabs his coat and stumbles onto the front porch. Agneta didn't want his money. She would have refused all the money that now bulges his pocket. The way she clung to him that last time, she knew, her eyes blinking with incredulity; she knew he was going. He tries to walk faster to stem the tears. It's hours before he is due at Daniel's, but he must keep moving.

A light snow falls and small flakes hurl themselves from the sooty sky. The French lost Metz over two weeks ago and still no word from Natalia, and yet he hears her constantly; she has become a ghostly presence, whispering in his ear.

Halfway to Daniel's house, he hears humming. Is that her chestnut hair, grown back to shoulder length, swinging against a blue cloak, bouncing with her walk? Her gait, there is joy in her step. Wait! he calls. If she turns, what will he say to her? Not words, it is his body that aches for her, to hear her voice.

Wait!

A couple people turn.

Stop! Natalia!

The woman glances over her shoulder. The wrong nose, wrong lips, and the woman walks on. The cannons ring in the distance, making everything tremble. He stops and looks up at the sky. A circle of pigeons overhead.

A girl with a basket of dirty turnips stands in front of him and follows his gaze up. Birds, she says. Pigeons, sir. Dirty birds is all it is.

. . .

THE MAN HAS FAT fingers and a butterball of a body. His fine clothes, a silk vest and a white linen shirt, a belt buckle of silver, do nothing to hide what has grown huge with rich food and wine. He is talking loudly about the war.

Jorgen feels the plush carpet beneath his feet. Rose perfume scents the air in Daniel's living room.

The wounded man has become fashionable, he says, and a small gathering nods. Women swarm over him, trying to save him. If you have an injury, now is the time to flaunt it. I am telling the ladies that I have a problem with my goiter; it has thrown off my weight.

The women offer a hushed laugh.

The fat man stops and points a pudgy finger at Jorgen.

This young man, I'm sure, goes over quite well.

Daniel introduces Jorgen and tells the fat man that Jorgen works for Pierre. The fat man's name is Dr. Daudet.

Daudet's eyes sparkle, and there is a light glisten of sweat on his forehead and upper lip. He takes out a white handkerchief and dabs his face.

I've always wondered, says Daudet, stepping beside Jorgen, how does he do it? In the midst of war, Pierre keeps the supply coming. Remarkable. He must be quite a brilliant man or extremely conniving. Daudet's breathing is loud, like a whir of water running. There is laughter in the room. Someone begins to play Wagner's *Tannhäuser* on the piano. What? says Daudet, his voice booms. Wagner?

I thought it might be appropriate to recall the French and German interplay, says a decorated woman in fine jewels. She raises her wine glass.

The French will send off another balloon, says Daniel. Tonight or tomorrow night or the next, depending on the wind. It takes off from the foot of the Solferino Tower on top of the Montmartre. If you've never seen one fly off into the night, I've heard it's quite a marvelous sight.

Daudet leans over to Jorgen. I believe I have something that interests you. The doctor motions toward the back of the house, and the two men walk down the hallway to the sitting room. On the pale yellow walls, on the tabletop and chest, paintings and jewelry and fine marble sculptures.

Jorgen is sure all these fine things have special names and creators, but he knows none of this. He wanders around the room, and Daudet leans against the door frame, picking his teeth with a silver pen. A drawing of a plump young girl sitting in a chair; another of a ballet dancer. A white marble sculpture of an unremarkable face. He does not see it. He's sold it already, thinks Jorgen, or kept it at home for his own. The old grandfather clock ticks, insistently filling the silence with balls of sound. Jorgen feels the tick bounce in his head. Perhaps it is a scam; Daudet will convince him to buy something else, but he won't have it. If the painting is sold, he wants nothing else.

Daudet steps over to the table. I wouldn't keep such a precious thing out in the open for just anyone to see. He lifts up a framed painting; underneath is the Japanese painting.

The woman in the painting stares at him and Jorgen's heart stutters. A trickle of sweat streams down his right side. He closes his eyes; he's turned it round and round, imagined it so many times, and here it is, he opens his eyes, more vibrant, more beautiful. The smooth line of the woman's back, the long sticks of ivory woven into her hair, the shimmer of her lips, the full moon behind them in the day's sky. His body seizes up with a pleasurable pressure that radiates from his belly to his fingers. He can feel the press of smooth silk. The town below turns and sighs as they embrace. The heat of each passes through the membrane of silk and cotton clothing. She is whispering something. The way her head is tilted, the position of her neck, words flow from her fine mouth.

Daudet sidles up to Jorgen. The painting is exquisite. I hate to part with it. I must tell you, I've shown it to a couple of my artist friends and they were duly inspired. They begged me to sell it to them. But Daniel told me your interest, so out of deference to Daniel, I come to you first.

I've got the money, says Jorgen. The words from her lips, if he collects them, what will they mean? Everything he has loved has been taken, but he will have this and then he will have Natalia.

What is your price? Daudet asks.

What price? thinks Jorgen. How much? He knows how much is in his pocket. Some or all; all or nothing; some and everything. What price?

Daudet breathes heavily.

How to price something that rises up to greet you, as if lifting away from a neutral background to welcome you again? What is she whispering?

Sir?

Yes, says Jorgen, sighing. He says a number.

Daudet clutches his stomach and his laughter is thunderous. When he keeps laughing, Jorgen feels his shame turn to anger. Jorgen fights the desire to grab the painting and run. Just take it and be done with this. How much humiliation does a man have to suffer?

Please, says Daudet. I don't mean to offend, but you are joking, aren't you?

His face red and hot, Jorgen shifts on his heel to the ball of his foot.

Don't tell me Daniel bought it from you for such a low price. Is that your gauge?

He glares at the man and leans his hands against the table to steady himself. Maybe if he turns around and doesn't look at the painting, he could walk out of this room, down the hallway, into the chaos of the sidewalk. If he could turn right now, save a bit of his shredded dignity. Just turn his gaze, turn right now, but he can't keep his eyes off it. She is there, leaning into the man's ear, her silks parted, whispering her words, whispering in his ear.

Daudet pulls up a chair and sits in front of the painting. He asks if that is the best Jorgen can do.

In his calculation, Jorgen set aside some money for food. But there are boxes of canned food. He could steal those from Pierre. Yes, he says. I can raise it. Another hundred francs.

Daudet smiles disappointedly. Poor boy. This must be altogether a new world for you.

Jorgen looks at him confused.

Do you know I have someone offering three times that? Daudet sighs loudly and sniffs. Daniel says you've been through a lot. You came here from Denmark to fight for France. Tell you what. You seem like a good man. I think we can put together something.

Jorgen's weight shifts, fresh heat rises from his skin. He will do this, after all. A deal will be made.

In exchange for a map of Pierre's supply route, and your stated price, I will sell you the painting.

Jorgen pauses only momentarily. Yes. Fine.

Daudet pulls out his black book. You can draw it right here.

He hands Jorgen his pen.

He doesn't hesitate, doesn't weigh and ponder the terms or the consequences, though he senses everything is about to change as he grabs the pen and sketches the city and the entry point for Pierre's treasures. And he offers more: when the next delivery is due. At least two or perhaps three loads are being transported tonight, with one box of jade, some bolts of Oriental silk, and that sharp Danish cheese, of which Pierre has grown particularly fond. Daudet says, That will do. Jorgen smacks the bundle of money from his pocket into Daudet's fleshy hand.

I trust you, says Daudet, but to be sure, you will escort me tonight, and together we will watch the first unloading. After that, you may go. I'll handle the rest.

Daudet reaches for the painting.

Jorgen stops the chubby hand midstream. Daudet chuckles. Jorgen carefully rolls up the painting and gently fits it inside a cardboard cylinder.

DAUDET CALLS FOR HIS carriage. Two black horses trot up to the sidewalk, pulling behind them a carriage. The horses stamp and Daudet pets their noses, reaches into his pocket, and flattening his palm, gives them each rolled oats.

The gate to Daniel's house shuts behind them with a finality that only Jorgen hears. As they trot down the street, he stares out the window, the painting across his lap. He turns the cardboard tube around and around. He can't sit still; the painting, he wants to pull it out and look again. He shouldn't have done it, parted with all his money. How will he live? What will he do? Slowly it comes to him. Nothing is the same anymore.

Daudet sighs. The problem with Pierre is that he deals with only a limited clientele, he says. Those with enough money. But there are many more who would do anything for food. An entire bargaining and exchange market to be tapped into. Think of yourself as helping the common man on the street.

The air is cold and has turned the grass into a silvery white glow. He directs Daudet to park the carriage across from a small white house with a large porch. The shades are drawn and the front metal gate swings with the wind. It seems abandoned, except for the red cross hanging out front and the candlelight glowing inside. It appears to be a makeshift hospital. Next to the house on the street is one of the main openings to the sewer system.

A light snow begins to fall and Jorgen puts his hand out and catches a flake. Daudet opens a flask.

After a while, two men come around the back, leading a carriage with horses. Another two men come out the front carrying a coffin. They step into the house and load another seven.

Daudet chuckles and rubs his belt buckle. He lights his pipe and fills the carriage with blue smoke. Ingenious, he says. Who would open a closed coffin?

When Pierre's delivery boys have ridden away, Jorgen clutches the cardboard cylinder and opens the carriage door. I'll walk home from here, he says.

PIERRE WATCHES THE BOXES come in through the front door and smells one wafting of rich chocolate. There is an indescribable pleasure in the boxes, and Pierre loves the mixture of smells and tastes, the exotic meats and the ordinary canned soup from England. The whole array is wonderful: the common bar of soap, the jewelry of rare stones, the rifles, the bullets, the vests and tan trousers, the imported ceramics, and the pickled cucumbers from Italy. With so many goods, it is easy to love life. War, he thinks, is such good business.

He opens the box of chocolate and takes out a bar. Sent by a small manufacturer in Fontainebleu. He bites into it; the rich flavor coats his tongue.

Hurry up, he shouts, and the hired men stomp up the stairs, carrying the boxes.

He follows them up. Twenty boxes in all. They are all here. He opens his wallet and pays the men. In the inventory room, a single candle burning, Pierre rips apart the box from Japan. He unwraps a tea cup, the color of midnight blue. Lovely, he says, crumpling the paper into a tight wad and tossing it back in the box.

JAPAN

*S*TOP. *STOP. STOP, STOP, stop, stop stop stop!*

It must stop, but he can't shout it, not even whisper it, and now midway through the funeral services, Hayashi is trembling so badly from fright that he must leave.

How could—but why and how—and he didn't ask, the monk never asked, no permission for such a thing, thinks Hayashi, pacing frantically around the garden. He stops. Glares at the teahouse, the exquisite teahouse. He heads toward the lake. But I let it go on, never did tell him about the meeting, the danger, the impending danger, the soldiers who at any moment will arrive with their rifles—perhaps now—he stops abruptly and stares at the black iron gate. He rushes back to the temple. He must stop this. As he approaches, the front door opens and there is the monk escorting the family outside. Hayashi retreats, sighing, but there is little relief; the monk is ringing that bell again. Hayashi presses his hands to his ears; still the sound reverberates. Twice in one day. Something horrible is certain to happen.

Hayashi escapes into the studio. Soon this day will be over and there will be the deep hole of night. Will they come again under the cloak of darkness? Burn down the temple this time? Sneak through the front door and kill him with a sword? Kill everyone? He sits at his wheel, picks up a handful of clay, and kneads it. Maybe he should send everyone to town. He'll stay. He should be the one they take. When he thinks of this, there is a certain familiarity to the thought. As if it is preordained, not by some implacable external force, but by a trajectory running through the course of his entire life.

Excuse me, says Sato.

Hayashi jumps.

I'm sorry I startled you, says Sato, stepping into the studio. What's wrong? You look like you've seen a bad spirit. Sato steps inside, sits in Ayoshi's chair, crossing his ankles. I'm surprised they let you hold a Buddhist funeral.

Hayashi can barely speak the words. No, he says. In fact, I'm supposed to close the temple.

When?

A while ago. I was given an official notice.

Sato pauses. I don't understand.

I shouldn't have let it happen.

It's very dangerous, says Sato.

I know, says Hayashi, putting his hand to his forehead. Do you think the bell was heard in town?

Sato raises an eyebrow in disbelief. If not the first time, then the second.

Maybe the officials weren't in town. They're not always there. Maybe they won't know it happened.

Sato shrugs. I was going to stop it, but then I saw you rush over to the temple, and I thought you'd do it. But you let it go on. You are much too lenient with the monk. It's almost as if he runs the house and the temple and the gardens. You've let him take over.

Hayashi stands and looks out the window, watching for a flash of a uniform, the glint of a rifle. The wind of the oncoming evening rattles the door. Hayashi's feet are throbbing. He looks down and sees streaks of dark blue, bright purple, and red.

Maybe we shouldn't stay in the house tonight. The temple probably isn't safe either.

If they come, I'll speak to them, says Sato. Tell them it was a mistake. I'll say the ringing of the bell was to announce the temple's closure.

Do you think it will work? he asks, his face briefly clears of worry. But the overwhelming panic returns. Hayashi sits again at his potter's wheel and drops his head in his hands. I've made so many mistakes.

The evening settles in, the light changes and falls off. I'll speak to them, he says again, watching Hayashi. When they ask, I'd like to tell them the monk no longer lives here.

Hayashi slowly lifts his head. He does feel it, doesn't he? He'd never admit it to anyone, but at the thought of the monk leaving, he feels as if stones are being removed from his chest.

Now that the teahouse is done, the monk should be sent on his way, says Sato. He only brings trouble to your home.

Hayashi twists a piece of towel in his hands, feeling guilty; how could he wish the monk to leave? How could he do that to the mountain monks? They are the ones who sent the monk here.

Sato glances toward the door. You know as well as I do these are unsettled times. It's for the best.

Hayashi sits expressionless, the veins on his forehead bulging. He looks at the floor, trying to find his balance. I'm not sure you know the position I'm in, he stammers. The things I owe.

I have some sense of it, says Sato.

Hayashi reaches for the bucket of leftover clay and buries his feet.

Sato twirls a paintbrush and sets it back down.

The mountain monks, says Hayashi, pulling clay between two fingers, they are my family. He feels a tumult of emotion. Hayashi scrapes away the dried blue clay encrusted in his fingernails. Night begins to saturate the room. He digs his feet deeper into the clay. Hayashi glances at Sato, whose dark eyes dart furiously around the room, then looks away.

Sato tries to control his rising anger. So you would put your entire household in jeopardy because of this monk? What is so great about this man? Surely he isn't one of the mountain monks who took care of you. Sato exhales loudly, filling the room with his disgust. I guess I don't understand, he says. He's tempted to blurt out the true contours of the danger, but there is Hayashi's pale face, his hands, clenching and unclenching. What harm would the truth bring to Ayoshi? He has seen brief flashes of Hayashi's temper.

Hayashi's face flushes and sets stubbornly. I appreciate your help, he says, rubbing his hands back and forth, unable to look at him. He breathes deeply and gathers his strength. It is what he wishes he'd said so long ago. Now it must be said. But I'd rather you not interfere with my affairs.

Sato rises and pulls his hands behind his back. Fine. Fine. Fine. Let's talk about anything else but your affairs.

Hayashi lets his shoulders drop back down, away from his ears. Good, he says, relieved.

The weather? Shall we talk about the weather? How the season seems to be changing? Or what? The rice crop this year?

Hayashi frowns and narrows his eyes.

Or poetry? Perhaps the Heian period?

Hayashi feels his anger rise, and before he can contain it, he flings back, You can be a very disagreeable man.

Sato leaps out of his chair, smiling brightly, and claps his hands. Now we're getting somewhere.

THE CEREMONY ENDED A while ago, and the family helped carry the casket outside to the cemetery, then left for town to receive condolences from their neighbors. The temple is quiet, the scent of incense still heavy in the air. He will have to build the bonfire soon and cremate the body. But not now.

He pulls out the painting. He shouldn't have stolen it, shouldn't have snuck into the studio last night after he finished the teahouse, but there are so many paintings and he wants to know, who is this man who holds her, as if she is his, and he is hers? He told himself as he walked into the studio, he is just curious. He can't stop staring at the blue and red swatches of kimonos splashed against each other, the pale limbs intertwined. He sees so much more this time as he traces the man's hand skating on her thigh. Their thick sensuality, an escape, he knows now. Her hand on his chest and another wrapped behind his back. He knows the racing of the heart, the warm skin, the breath persecuting the ear.

He walks back to the center of the temple to sit and say his prayers, but fidgets and returns to the painting. His throat constricts; fury and despair and humiliation tangle there. Their faces, blissful; and this is what is confusing. This is the most confusing part of all. This is what is tightening his lungs: She seemed this way with him. Her face radiant, and he felt the flush of heat in his cheeks. Her voice swooning. So what does it mean or does it mean nothing at all? He can't separate himself from this heart-stabbing question, but throws himself at it again and again. The first rip in the painting is done without thought. He tears through the clouds racing through blue sky, mutilates the searing sun, he cleaves until he reaches the top of her head, then stops. He drops it on the floor.

He stands there stunned, staring at the ruined painting, his mind lodging into the need to escape. Run to town, to the carriage with the black horses, and ride away from these people, from her; a thickness falls between him and the world, through which he sees that nothing at all belongs to him. In his innocence he has never had that thought, never desired to own anything. But here, in the valley below the mountain, it is different, and in the home of Hayashi, who owns so much, he feels utterly deprived. That wretched feeling burrows down and pulls up another thought, that he is unworthy and that is why he has nothing. He tries to soothe himself by remembering that Hayashi's soul will be assessed after death and his lavishness will relegate him to rebirth as a beast or worse, the demonic regions of Jigoku. But even those thoughts bring no peace. He finishes ripping the painting, right down the middle of Ayoshi and that man. He is astonished at himself, at his actions. He did not know he could destroy so easily. He crumples up the man and shoves the paper inside the opening of a vase. He holds the image of her in front of him, imagining that her loving eyes are for him. But she's not looking at him; her gaze drifts off to the side. He jams her image into a bag of rice.

SHE COMPELS HER HAND to draw his face slowly with a black-inked brush. The forced hand creates the oval outline, the hair, each strand, but even with that much done, she knows it is not Urashi's face, and as she goes on, it's not the line of his nose, the shape of his lip, the curve of an eyelid, the fall of his dark hair; nothing about him rests on the paper. For weeks, she's tried to find his features. Ayoshi sets the brush down. She remembers the woman's face after the funeral service, the etchings of grief gone, a vision of tranquility. The woman walked with her children to the gate, the deep disturbance removed, her shoulders composed, her breathing steady.

She finds the monk in the temple polishing the Buddha statue. He feels the air shift the moment she walks in. At first he won't look at her.

She won't go away.

He finally turns.

She asks him to conduct a burial ceremony. How long has she known?

Of course, he says, his body softening. His eyes brighten. Of course. His tone is warm now, filled with understanding and a tinge of excitement.

There won't be a body to wash, she says, her voice flat and empty. It is for Urashi, she says. The man in the paintings.

Whatever you need. He's about to say more. She raises a finger, turns, and walks out, expecting to fall down.

HAYASHI REMOVES ONE FOOT and then the other from the bucket. He pauses for a moment, looking at his mangled feet, before he wraps them in cool, wet towels.

It can't be that hard. Just tell the monk it is time.

Hayashi gazes at Sato from heavily veiled lids. Hayashi stands. He feels vulnerable and afraid. The thing he's worked so hard to push aside is now in front of him again.

There are some things that can't be ignored, says Sato.

Hayashi, his hands clasped in front of him, looks out the window. Ayoshi is walking briskly across the grounds from the temple to the house.

No, I suppose not, he says slowly.

SHE FINDS HER BLACK kimono made of exquisite silk. She selects a pair of new tabi socks and slips on her new wooden sandals. A virgin, she thinks, nothing worn before. Twisting her hair, she secures it at the nape of her neck with an ivory comb.

She walks across the pebbled path to the small sitting room for prayer. The monk has lit incense and candles. He bows and continues to light more incense. She sits on a long bench, and he stands at the front of the room and begins to read a sutra. Her head bows and the words of the prayer tumble from her mouth. After a while, the monk gives the signal for her to rise. She goes to the incense urn, bows, and offers another stick of incense from the monk's box, lights it, and lets the smoke spiral up to her face, cleansing her as it seeps into the air. She returns to her seat.

Behind her she hears the door open and close, the footsteps of solid feet on solid ground. She keeps her head bowed, the monk still reciting. Before they parted for the last time, Urashi grabbed her wrist, and she searches now for his words, but they too have disappeared.

She opens her eyes. At the altar, Hayashi places a pinch of incense on the smoldering pile of ash in the urn. He bows and drops his head to his chest. What is he doing here? she thinks. She feels a rise of anger. An intrusion, she thinks, interfering in a private affair. To insert himself into this moment, this critical moment when the man whom she loved more than anyone is being buried. Hayashi doesn't look at her as he resumes his place in the back row. She watches him mumbling the sutras as she is doing now. She takes a deep breath. What does it matter, really, if he is here? Who knows whom he is praying for? When she lowers her voice, she hears Hayashi's deep tenor, and even through the prayer, she hears the rattle of sadness.

Kneeling now, she lets her head fall, sliding into the depth of herself, a weeping willow of a neck, and the tears come. When she is done, she looks up. Hayashi has gone. The monk finishes chanting the sutra alone, and she slips out the door, feeling the lightness of relief in her hollow inside.

FRANCE

S HE'LL BE STANDING THERE, he thinks, as he pins the cardboard cylinder to his side, not even a sliver of freezing air between him and the painting. He inserts the key to her apartment and gasps a nervous breath. Exhausted, yes, but a brilliant smile, a smile announcing she's home, there she'll be, a woman shimmering with happiness.

The hinge squeaks as the door slowly opens. He steps carefully over the threshold. The bleak room stares forlornly at him. He stands perfectly still, not certain what to do. It's too soon, he thinks, much too soon, but he can't endure doing nothing, so he sets the painting on the cot and begins to scour her musty-smelling apartment, searching underneath the black metal frame of the bed, along the damp windowsill, behind the drapes faded an ancient yellow, and hasn't he done this before? What does he hope to find? He can't say and he can't stop because there might be something—what? what is it? whatever is he looking for? He peers into the empty kitchen cupboards, nothing, then rushes to the top drawer of her bureau. In his haste, the entire drawer comes out. There, tucked in the back, a torn piece of paper about the size of his thumb. His hand trembles as he feels a quickening in the air. Her handwriting. He has come to know the thin stretch of it, the way it almost refuses to be known. He wants it to mean so much, to unlock the secret to her, so he can save her, and, in some illogical way, though he can't explain it, save himself, too.

And so they went.... And so they went? The rest of the letter is missing. Just this phrase. What more did she write? He rummages through the other drawers. He rakes through the room again, stumbles into the hallway, and digs through a random bag of garbage. The old woman down the hall cracks open her door and peers at him with an incredulous look on her face. He stands up. There is nothing more, he thinks. Only this fragment, this silly, meaningless fragment. He steps into Natalia's apartment, opens the window, and leans his head out. The air is cold, and he watches the white plume of his breath. In the distance, the din of a crowd's voice rises and falls like ocean waves. All of Paris seems to have congregated, he thinks, and why wouldn't she be there? He grabs the painting, hobbles downstairs, and crosses by the Pantheon. Of course she'd be drawn to the sound, as the swell seems to have swept him into its strong current. It's flowing down from the top of Montmartre.

It is near midnight, and Pierre will be expecting the final shipload that will never arrive. With his arms stretched out, Daudet will have a fantastic story, and the dim delivery boys will hand him the boxes. What does it matter which one of them has the splendors? Daudet or Pierre, men who have ravens picking at their hearts, incessantly squawking acquisition and possession, nothing will ever be enough, and in the end, the raven will win anyway.

Near the top of the hill, people huddle, wearing thick, colorful coats and scarves and holding lanterns that light their open, expectant faces. A huge bonfire roars, and from this vantage point, it looks as if they have come to witness the raging flames. Women and children and men too old to fight push to get a better view, the bodies pressing closer. As he reaches the very top, he sees the center of the curiosity, a reddish-purple balloon limping on the ground.

Moving in and out of the weave of the crowd, he hunts for Natalia until he finds himself standing in front of the balloon. A ring of National Guardsmen surrounds the basket fastened to the varnished balloon with heavy twined rope. Another four soldiers feed a gigantic pile of coal to a hungry fire. The gas from the flames is filling up the balloon. Jorgen stands mesmerized.

The balloon leaps off the ground, a fiery animal now, flashing and coiling its dark red skin. A soldier loses his grip on the rope, and now the rope jumps wildly. The gathering *oohs* and *ahhs,* lurches forward, then back, following the beast as it blusters and roars.

Pierre must be craning his neck, looking for the carriages, for the goods stuffed inside coffins, for the things he promised to sell to the Meaux, the Savants, and the Gladstones; the foreigners are always willing to pay double for food from their home country.

What are we waiting for? someone shouts. The purple-red beast glows, hovering above the crowd, rising, rising to its full height.

It wants to fly, says a girl to her mother, tugging on her mother's coat. Why don't they let it go?

Hush, says her mother.

The soldiers are barely holding on, dangling from the ends of the wild, jerking ropes. Jorgen steps closer to the balloon and feels the heat of the coal fire. The throng at once draws closer, as if following some mysterious collective pattern.

Where is he? a woman says, looking around. The balloonist should have been here hours ago.

If he doesn't show up, what will become of the mail? asks another woman. I've got four letters in the stack.

Probably got scared at the last minute, says a man with a black cap.

It's just like our soldiers, says an old woman. The Prussians have surrounded the city. If you climb the slope from Passy to the Trocadero and stand with binoculars, you can see a squad of Bismarck's cuirassiers with their square hats and waving plumes.

I think the balloon is pretty, says a girl.

It is, says a woman pulling her scarf tighter. Look at it. And those gathered hush and tip up their faces to the black sky and the balloon.

Down the hill the carriage is arriving, and Pierre will make his accounting. Will he shout and curse and run up the stairs? Where is the Dane? And when there is no answer, will he run into the inventory room and down the hallway to Jorgen's old bedroom and find his few belongings, a couple pairs of stained pants and shirts, an empty cot. No note. No footprints, no tread of a dirty shoe sole, no fingerprints smeared on the window glass. A thief, he will say of Jorgen, a spy, running to the police.

The balloon has reached its full height and lofts in the wind. The balloon must take off now, announces an official. Do we have a volunteer?

His money is gone. *And so they went.* Natalia is not in Paris, but perhaps she's in the forest just outside the city. She's pitched her tent for the night and maybe she's killed a rabbit for supper. Roasting it now over a small fire of alder branches. He can almost picture it, almost put himself right there, next to her.

Why did he come here if not for this? She must be right outside the city and there is no other way out, except this balloon. What is the crowd murmuring? A communal chant, a nursery rhyme of song. The bodies pressed tight, the chatter forming a single buoyant voice, And so he went.

I'll go, he says, separating himself from the crowd.

The crowd parts and a hush follows.

I'll go.

The National Guardsmen holding down the swaying balloon look at each other with raised eyebrows. Jorgen stands in front of a particularly tall soldier with a long red nose and hollowed-out cheeks.

Let him do it, says a woman.

An old man turns to the woman. What does this young man know about this? he asks. Look at his condition.

Well, who then? You?

He'll be fine, says someone else.

Jorgen looks at the balloon filled with coal gas. Nearly seven tons of coal burned, and it would be foolish to waste it. Why not let me go? he says to the tall guard. He watches the soldier's expression as he struggles to make a decision, and Jorgen imagines him thinking, This foolish man may or may not make it, but the French have lost so many men already, what is another? And the letters, the letters of sorrow, of longing, of business, of hope, of love and official news and love and love, at least they should try to ensure they reach the recipients' hands.

The soldier steps aside.

Jorgen's hand rests on the hard wicker of the basket. He places his other hand on the side of the rim. One of the soldiers hoists his crutches into the basket. Jorgen straddles the basket, his stump in, then his leg, and there, at the bottom of the basket, several stacks of mail and a cage containing five pigeons. Jorgen smiles. Hello, he says, thinking this is a good sign. There is a perfectly white one with a hint of pale blue around its eyes.

There's a bottle of champagne, and a 150-meter trail rope, which the soldier says works as a ballast, and a six-hooked anchor. If you see the big blue ocean in the distance, throw out the anchor or that will be the last of you. If a Prussian starts shooting, duck below the rim of the basket and pray.

Jorgen sets his cardboard cylinder on the floor next to the pigeons.

You'll need another coat and a blanket, says the soldier, handing him both. Jorgen puts on the heavy coat made of virgin lamb's wool dyed black to stay hidden in the precarious basket.

Here's a flask, says another soldier. Pray for a strong and steady eastern wind. He tells Jorgen the pigeons have messages wrapped in their tail feathers. Let them go when you're clear of Paris, he says.

A young woman comes up to the basket, removes the blue paper flower from her hat, and pins it on his coat lapel. She kisses both cheeks, Thank you, monsieur. You have a letter to my mother, who lives in England. The woman says her mother is quite ill. The letter, she says, will mean so much to her.

Another woman, her hair in long brown braids as thick as tree branches, offers him a kerchief of pastries. She bows her head and removes from her neck a gold chain. Her talisman, she says, putting it over his head.

An older man in gray earmuffs steps up and shakes his hand. Good luck, boy, he says. You'll need it.

More women and men line up to hand him their charms and well-wishes, but the soldiers push them aside.

It'll be too heavy, says the tall soldier. Enough. Get back.

Throw out some mail if you need altitude, but not that stack, says a soldier, pointing to the one tied with red rope. It's official.

Be careful, shouts a woman. You have a message to my daughter in Norway.

And one to my husband in England.

Don't throw out the pink envelope, shouts another woman.

He pulls in the anchor and feels the basket jolt and lift up from the ground. The throng cheers again and up he goes. He looks at the faces turned up, filled with surprise and wonder. The pigeons coo and squawk and the cylinder rolls and bumps against the cage. The crowd shouts and the ligaments of the beast wave furiously in the air. He lifts up, up, screeches beyond the dark rooftops, up to the treetops, the balloon brushes through the branches. There are the big towers and church domes, a tall building lit very white and proud. Up and up to the cloud layer; he is so light.

The balloon comes back down and settles at a height where he can see Paris below, the tiny globes of yellow streetlights, the small cooking fires in the park, the shadowy figures, the houses with people sleeping, and he imagines the rooms inside, the photographs and paintings, the stained-glass windows that in the morning will toss warm colorful light, and he feels like crying, and he is crying, not for the loss, but for the delicacy of life, for this small city, for every city dotted with people. And there, as he flies farther, he sees Prussians surrounding Paris, a ring of bonfires, and they are not far away, just beyond the wall. It is only a matter of time. She's out there, he knows it. He can feel it.

Natalia! he shouts. His voice is a pinprick, swallowed by the expanse of night sky. Such a small sound against the vastness.

As HE WAITS FOR the carriages outside, Pierre glances up and sees the garish-colored balloon. My God, he says out loud. One of the clerks comes out on the porch and stands next to him to watch. Whoever would do such a thing is a fool. No steering capability, at the whim of the wind.

Beautiful, murmurs the clerk.

Victor Hugo called these balloon expeditions an example of human audacity, says Pierre, but it's not that at all. It's human stupidity. What are the chances? A death ride, a goddamn suicide mission.

But look at it, sir, says the clerk, his voice full of awe.

Yes, says Pierre, thinking of the letters floating overhead, and he recalls an old friend with whom he'd gone to the university, a smart man, they'd played polo together, and he'd heard the fellow was ill. The man lives in Nice. He often thought of writing a letter, but never did. Now he feels a surprising need to write to the man and see how he's doing. *What do you need? Is anyone looking after you? After this damn war is over, I will be down your way to attend to you and anything else.* He'd tuck inside a few francs.

He looks down the dark alley, turns his ear, searching for the sound of a carriage rolling. Nothing but street urchins playing in garbage bins.

Pierre pulls out a bill and holds it up. The wind turns the money, blowing it east. Right direction, but damn cold, and with the cloud layer, there might be snow tonight. He heard the reports of the men in the balloons, the ones who survived, the sense of awe and wonder from the view of the sky. That is where Natalia should have gone, he thinks, not the land, but up in a balloon to touch the lips of her God. Damn her, he whispers. Damn her for going.

PARIS IS BEHIND HIM, and he rises higher. The air turns bitter cold. He pulls the two coats tighter and drinks from the flask. A hamlet up ahead, surrounded by darkness. Perhaps she is there, tucked away in a warm house, waiting for the right time to return to Paris. Or maybe she's there, he thinks, spotting a white barn, hiding in the loft, sleeping in yellow straw. The pigeons coo, and he crouches down and blows warm air on their wings. As he moves away from the lights of town, hundreds of stars flash against the darkness.

His leg begins to ache so he sits among the cushion of letters. She wrote, *And so they went.* He finishes the line for himself, *for there was nothing else to do.* His hands are frozen and he thinks the pigeons must be suffering. He opens the cage, clutches a bird, and tosses it into the night. He hears the wings flapping, like the sound of a skirt brushing against legs. Another and another, he lets them fly away.

Nestling into the bottom of the basket, he hooks the painting under his arm. He pulls out one of the letters, and with a pencil, he begins to write on the back of the envelope.

My dear Natalia,

I am above the world looking down, and part of me feels as close to God as I ever will get. A vision that each of us should receive at least once in a lifetime, this view of human lives. Such ants we are, swarming the earth, what do we think we are doing? But I set these thoughts aside and think of you. Don't stop thinking of me so I can find you. It is not to sea that I am heading but land, sweet land, and to you.

He stuffs the letter back under the string. The big lofting balloon enters a pocket of cold air, and he wraps himself tighter into his coat. His eyes hurt and even the skin under his fingernails aches. In the air, the smell of cold purity, of nothingness so high in the clouds, buries in his lungs. He shoves his hands into the sleeves of his coat, feeling the smoothness of silk inside. The balloon sweeps through a gray foggy mass. He feels a spray of mist and he quickly wipes his face, for fear the mist will freeze into a mask. He pushes his hand deeper into the coat pockets and finds a hard candy, puts it in his mouth, and sucks sweetness. In his other pocket, he fingers a smooth stone he found by the Seine. An amber color, it caught his eye in the dying sun, a piece of sunlight, he thought at the time; he takes it and rubs it against his cheek. He can no longer see the land below. He has no idea which way he is going or how much time has passed. Even if he stood up and surveyed below, he couldn't tell, land or the deep sea.

He throws out the birdcage and nudges down deeper. His teeth chatter uncontrollably, and he burrows his face into the double layer of thick coats and the blanket, while his mind clenches with fear. He tries to remember the last image he had on earth. What was it? Unhinging the cold crush on his brain, he finds a woman holding the hand of a small girl. And the girl? The girl in a pink coat, cherry-colored cheeks, a white ribbon in her hair, hair the brown of soil after a rain; the woman, her mother, a replica of the girl, in a long black coat with a fur collar encircling her pale neck, a beauty mark above her upper lip.

He can't feel his good leg or his stump, and now his body shakes. It feels as if he has been racing through ice air for hours.

Another image, quick, something to hold onto. He grabs the image of a small-headed man wearing a violet vest and heavy gray coat. He looked at Jorgen as he climbed into the balloon and nodded, as if giving his approval. Behind the man, an ample woman with a pile of gray hair, she leaned toward the balloon, as if she wanted to touch it.

The balloon drifts lower, and still blackness, as if he's entered the interior of a huge animal. His mind clenches and cold slaps against his skin, burrows into his bones. He has never been this cold. His stiffened hand instinctively reaches for the cylinder and removes the painting. Under the stars' flickering light, he slowly unrolls the painting and gazes at it, and not until it begins to happen does he know why he chose to do this. For now he is slipping away from the freezing night, away from the rocking basket, into the expansive blue sky dabbed with white clouds, warm sunlight on her limbs, the tip of her red lips curving into a smile. She is holding him, wrapping him in her elegant clothes, whispering words, taking her fingers and smoothing his forehead, his hair, touching warmth to his cold skin. Slowly Jorgen's heartbeat settles into a regular warm rhythm.

He traces the figure of the woman, a gesture of gratitude.

He stands and looks over the edge of the basket. The balloon has fallen low enough to see the dark body of land. He returns the painting to its cylinder. He is sailing through the freezing air; he should sit down, but he can't stop looking at the land.

The jagged-edged horizon, a patch of forest coming up, and now he is hovering above the tree branches; like arms reaching for him, they almost touch him. What he can't see from the balloon, he imagines: each thread of pine needle, the pale veins coursing a leaf, the dimpled bark, the soft green lichen, the spiderwebs woven between leaves, and there, a small brown bird, perhaps a finch, resting on a branch, its wings tucked tight against its frail body, asleep for the night. And on it goes, from tree to tree and the life below, for he's never felt so in love with the land.

NATALIA LIES FLAT ON her belly, and through the telescopic lens she mounted on her rifle, she glasses a Prussian sentry about a hundred yards away. She's alone now. Most of her fellow soldiers are dead; others turned back or are missing in the nearby town. For days, perhaps more than a week, she doesn't know how long, she has been alone in these woods, not certain which direction to go, so she just waits. The only other person with her, though he doesn't know it, is the Prussian who has just discovered her backpack and is untying it. Her mess kit clatters against a rock, her notebook sprays loose papers and dried flowers, scattering them on the snowy ground. He plunges his arm to the bottom and pulls out her treasure, a hunk of cheddar cheese. She found it yesterday in the pack of a dead soldier. He breaks off a section and as he shoves it in his mouth, she smells its pungent rich scent waft through the air. She jams together her jaws, trying not to salivate.

What makes her glance up? The stirring of tree branches, the call of a barn owl? Through the snow clouds, she glimpses a balloon drifting silently. Ghostlike, haunting, she thinks, and yet moving with such grace. She turns her lens to the balloon and now she can't find it, hidden by a curtain of mist, and she thinks she might have imagined it, so lonely for human contact, just as she imagined God's good graces. She shivers and the cold snakes over her. She's about to put her glass back on the Prussian, but she veers it up again and spots a flash of red and her heart beats faster. Holding it steady in her glass, she watches; unmanned, she decides, but then a shadowy figure appears. A man, by his shape and his size; he must be freezing.

Be safe, she whispers, and pulls her coat tighter around her neck. Be safe and ride far under the night's cover. She prays that the man in the balloon will wake in the morning. Prays he will look down not at the steely sea but at trees and small whitewashed houses with cows and sheep in tidy pastures, the fresh skin of the day laid out shiny and smooth. How long has it been since she prayed? She prays he wakes to see the faint peach glow of another day lighting up the fields. She'd give anything to be up in that balloon, looking down. From up there, the earth must seem to offer herself up again and again with food and plenty; from up there, how stunning the world, the oceans and the green grass.

Which way is he going? She looks at the tree branches swaying. A steady wind east. Perhaps she will find him, stuck in a tree branch or in an open field of wheat; or tucked in a crevice in a mountain or resting next to a campfire. Or maybe she will never find him; he will sail through the skies, never landing. She turns her gun to the Prussian sentry. He's spotted the balloon. He takes aim, holding steady with his gun, waiting until it is exactly overhead so he won't miss. There is the head of the man in the balloon, a perfect target. It must be done, she thinks. She pulls the trigger and watches the soldier fall.

He looks down from the balloon. He drifts along in a sunny, cloudless, morning sky; below, a herd of dairy cows, a man walking out to the pasture, a red handkerchief around the man's neck.

Years from now, on such a clear morning, Jorgen will linger, not wanting to leave the spring sugar beet fields, overcome by a desire to be with her, Natalia, his wife, who saved him twice, and she'll remind him of the way he made her love the world again. Sometimes they stand in front of the painting. Here, she'll say. These many years later, they find something new: in the right corner, pink petals, a rose blooming.

JAPAN

WHAT CAN POSSIBLY BE so fascinating out there? asks Ayoshi. Hayashi and Sato stand side by side, staring out the window at the night sky. She didn't want supper, preferring to spend the evening in prayer for Urashi, but Hayashi came out to the temple and was uncustomarily insistent. You must have supper, he said. But now look at those two, she thinks, as rigid as stone statues, showing little interest in the evening meal.

Everything, says Hayashi, his jaw hardening as he continues to gaze out the window. He turns toward her, smiling faintly. There follows a strange, heavy silence.

Where is the monk? says Sato finally. He turns to go find him.

No, I should, says Hayashi, and he shuffles down the hallway. Sato walks over to the table and sits across from her.

I'll be leaving soon.

Everything seems to be happening so quickly, as if the release of Urashi has shifted her center of gravity—to where, she doesn't know.

A ship departs for Shanghai tomorrow.

Why must you go now?

I've been here far too long. He pauses. Haven't you?

She tugs on the inside of her cheek and feels the color rush from her face. Before she can answer, Hayashi returns to the room with the monk.

The monk gazes at her with soft eyes. Ayoshi quickly looks away, feeling his desire run through her like a wild flame. She turns to Sato, who is watching the monk.

No, no, says Hayashi. Ayoshi, you sit at the head of the table tonight. You're the guest of honor.

Ayoshi looks at Hayashi bewildered.

Happy birthday, my dear. He leans over and kisses her lightly on the cheek.

She examines the table again. At each place setting, a folded colorful silk fan. Her fan, the color of dark-red plum leaves. She opens it, and a snowy owl flies straight at her. Hayashi's signature chop in the corner. She turns it round and round. She hadn't forgotten, but she assumed he had. How did you remember? she asks.

Hayashi smiles sheepishly and bows. We're also celebrating the completion of the teahouse, says Hayashi, a forced cheerfulness to his voice.

That's right, says Sato.

Hayashi motions for the monk to take a seat at the far end of the table, a long stretch from Ayoshi.

We'll have a viewing of the teahouse after dinner, says Sato.

Hayashi sits beside Ayoshi, Sato on her other side. Sato opens a bottle of sake. The dishes of food are passed around and the room grows warmer. What is wrong with Hayashi? He's so jittery, fiddling with his sash and darting his gaze out the window again. Sato is saying something in his offhand, aggressive manner. Hayashi rises again, steps into the kitchen, and returns with another bowl of rice.

Sato stares at the monk's plate. Such a meager serving? asks Sato.

The monk sets his bowl of soup down and taps his chopstick lightly against his plate.

Your self-control tonight is remarkable, says Sato.

Hayashi coughs uncomfortably. Ayoshi glares at Sato and twists her napkin into a knot.

As I understand it, self-control is the usual path of a monk, says Sato, and yet you've shown little of it.

The monk deliberately folds his hands. Sometimes a new path opens, one that could never have been foreseen.

Ayoshi shifts in her chair.

What do you want? asks Sato, turning to Ayoshi.

What? she says.

He points to the dishes on the table. More rice? More sashimi?

She flushes again. I don't know.

He gives her a swift, critical look.

Hayashi sits up and turns his head to the main entrance.

What is it? she asks.

Did you hear something? Hayashi rises and asks Sato to accompany him to the front door.

The monk and Ayoshi are alone. She feels a cold shiver about her legs.

I didn't properly thank you for the funeral, she says.

He bows, nodding. I'm glad I could do something for you.

She leans toward him. Something is terribly wrong. I've never seen Hayashi so disturbed.

The monk rises and comes to her end of the table. The funeral, he says. You've let him go. There is more room. An opening. Can't you feel it?

Perhaps that's why everything feels so different tonight, she thinks. A spaciousness that wasn't there before. So much room; how wonderful and how frightening. Here is the monk, gazing at her tenderly, presenting himself to her, like an offering. Isn't that what she wanted?

Hayashi and Sato return, and Sato is carrying a big glossy box tied up with a white ribbon.

It was nothing, says Sato.

Are you sure? asks Ayoshi.

Nothing at all, says Sato, handing her the box. Your birthday gift. The monk slides down to his end of the table.

She sits there, staring at the box.

Open it, says Sato.

She removes the lid, and there is the Western dress, a beautiful shade of blue. She holds it up against her body; the skirt is full and the neckline low.

Try it on, says Sato.

She is relieved to leave the room. Why did Hayashi remember her birthday this year and not last? she wonders as she walks down the hallway. He's so anxious and solemn, not the least bit celebratory. She pulls on the new dress and, standing in front of a long mirror, smoothes down the fabric. Perhaps Hayashi is trying to figure out how to fashion a new porcelain bowl, she thinks. Twirling around, she sends the full skirt into a wide swirling circle around her ankles. She presses her hand to her exposed neckline and smiles at herself in the mirror. Enough exposed flesh to excite the imagination, she thinks, laughing nervously. Yes, a spaciousness, and now an opening for something else. She smoothes her hand over the flowing fabric of the skirt, and her eyes soften as she recalls the monk's desirous gaze.

Come show us! shouts Sato.

She walks back into the eating room.

Sato leaps up, his eyes filled with delight.

The monk stares glowingly.

You look beautiful, says Hayashi.

It is too much, she says.

Sato bows low. Do you like it? he asks.

I do, she says, laughing with embarrassment at her admission. I didn't think I would, but I do. She spins around and shows off the wide skirt. Sato claps and laughs loudly.

I can see you in a ballroom in London, says Sato.

Or entertaining guests right here, says Hayashi.

She turns to the monk, half expecting him to chime in, but he shifts awkwardly and looks at the floor. Ayoshi glances at the dress and suddenly feels too exposed.

I knew you'd like it, says Sato. You didn't think you would, but I knew it. You should listen to me more often, Ayoshi.

AFTER THEY FINISH EATING, Hayashi ushers them outside to view the teahouse. Hayashi takes Ayoshi's hand, not letting go, and with her by his side, leads the way. They gather around with lanterns and comment on the pine wood, the black clay tiles, glazed and polished with mica powder for better sealing.

I'm sure Hayashi will give you a wonderful recommendation, says Sato. It'll be easy for you to find a job when you leave here.

Of course, says Hayashi.

Is that what you plan to do, asks Sato, now that you've finished here? Become a builder? There is a great need for construction workers.

Hayashi tells the monk the country is busy redesigning itself. In almost every town near the capital, construction is furious and workers in dire demand.

It sounds like a splendid idea, says Sato, his voice filled with sudden insistence. When do you think you might go? Tomorrow?

That might be the perfect timing, says Hayashi.

What? says Ayoshi.

The monk looks pale.

Ayoshi turns to Hayashi, incredulous. What are you saying?

He's been here a while, says Sato.

And so have you, she says.

There is a long, charged silence.

I'm not sure what I'll do next, says the monk. Perhaps go to another monastery. Maybe to Kyoto, he says, looking at her hand in Hayashi's; he hasn't let go of her hand. Nor has she released his. Or maybe back to the mountain. Or who knows? The capital. He holds up his empty hands in front of him, as if considering the possibilities.

THE SCENT OF BLOWN-OUT candles and burned incense lingers in the eating room. Dirty dishes litter the table. After the viewing of the teahouse, the monk abruptly excused himself and left for the temple. Now the eating room feels empty, she thinks. The evening sags into disturbing solemnity. Sato brings out the playing cards and suggests they retire to the Western room.

Ayoshi leans back on the couch and suddenly feels exhausted. She looks at Hayashi. From where is this new wellspring of power coming? she wonders.

Hayashi keeps looking at his cards, as if refusing to meet her gaze. Sato wears a sardonic smile on his face, as if secretly pleased with himself. There is something between them that wasn't there before, she thinks. She picks up her sake glass, looks at it absentmindedly, and sets it down again. The whole evening seems choreographed.

Your turn, says Sato.

What? she says, frowning.

Play your card.

She sets down her cards. Both of you were impolite to the monk tonight, she says, no longer able to stay away from the dangerous edge of the night's strain.

Hayashi flinches and holds his breath.

It's horrible the way you treated him. Sato's behavior doesn't surprise me, but Hayashi, what is wrong with you?

I'm sorry, but I must insist that he leave, says Hayashi.

She crosses her arms in front of her. Why must you insist?

It's my fault. I've put us in danger.

How?

The two men look at each other, and then she knows. Sato has said something to Hayashi about the monk. Not revealed the whole truth of it, but manipulated the situation to convince Hayashi to send the monk away. And with the monk gone, Sato must think he will have her. Sato. Such a selfish, arrogant man, she thinks. Always getting—by whatever means, it's no matter to him—what he wants, but he won't have her. The world may bend for him, but she won't. She sits, transfixed by this new state, only now aware that she still clung to the fantasy of leaving with him.

Hayashi tells her about the demand to close the temple. I shouldn't have let the Buddhist funeral proceed, he says, shaking his head dolefully. I should have stopped it. To let the monk stay puts us in jeopardy.

Well, what has happened? she says. Nothing. Sato has you all worked up for no reason.

I did nothing of the sort, says Sato, his tone weighted with feigned indignation.

Nothing has happened yet, but there is the potential, says Hayashi, pulling at a hangnail.

There's the potential for anything to happen, she says, rising. I'm going to find him. I want you to apologize. Tell him he's free to stay here as long as he wants.

Ayoshi, says Sato. I don't think that's wise.

She fixes him with a fierce gaze. I don't care what you think.

Sato imperceptibly jerks backward and then smiles bitterly. Hayashi hangs his head.

She marches to the kitchen, feeling her cheeks heat up. She steps outside onto the wooden porch and walks to the temple. How dare Sato intrude like that. She won't have it. Her heart beats louder. She opens the door.

Enri?

Only the stillness of the room. She feels herself quiver, her blood loudly pulsing at her temples. She steps inside. Where is he? There is his bedding and notebook. She walks briskly back to the house, feeling irritable, her new dress swishing like a cool wind.

I can't find him, she says, standing in front of them, forcing them to look at her.

Maybe he finally figured out he overstayed his welcome, says Sato.

You never liked him, she says. Where does he have to go?

She turns to Hayashi. What has come over you?

THE MONK RUNS TO the stable and saddles up the horse. He wants to go to town and get drunk. No, he wants her. The funeral ceremony was held so they could be together. How could it be otherwise? He drives the horse harder, digging his heels into its sides, and the horse snorts and stretches out its stride.

As he heads to town, the thought emerges, what if he's wrong? What if the funeral meant nothing? How many other lovers have there been since that man? The way she held onto Hayashi's hand. But that can't be. There is no love between Ayoshi and Hayashi, as distant as two rocks in a pool of white pebbles. As he rides through the night, he gathers her up in his imagination, kissing her, kissing her everywhere, the warmth of her pressed to him. Why should they live without each other, the days slipping by, colorless and bland?

As he enters the town, he sees great flames leaping high into the sky. A tremendous fire is eating away at a building on the outskirts of town. He rides toward the flames, and as he approaches, he gasps. Through the billowing smoke, he sees the familiar tile roof, the tall wood fence. A small Buddhist temple and surrounding monastery. He jumps off the horse and runs toward the fence. A crowd has gathered, some watching, others are scurrying, throwing pails of water at the flames. He grabs a bucket from an old woman and runs to the well, fills it with water and tosses it at the flames. Then he hears the screams.

People are trapped in there? he yells.

Yes, says a man, breathless. They barred the doors, nailed metal bars across the door handles and the front gate.

Who?

Someone said they saw soldiers do it.

Who's in there?

At least a hundred monks.

The monk blanches and stumbles back.

For what seems like hours, they run back and forth, throwing water on the raging fire. And soon the water runs out, the wells dry up. The men chop at the big wooden door and finally break it down. The monk rushes in, but is pushed back by the intense heat of the blaze. His robe catches fire. He throws himself on the ground, and another man beats the flames with a broom. He clutches his arm, scorched by the heat. The night air shudders with screams. He scrambles up again, choking on the smoke, and lunges for the sound.

SHE SMELLS SOMETHING ELECTRIC in the air. A storm, she thinks. A spring storm, with crackling lightning and roaring thunder. She smiles. She's always liked the energy of a storm. And later, she will think back to this day and remember everything about it, the charged air, the anxious quiet of anticipation—waiting for the monk to return—broken by the occasional smack of the window shade against the wall, the unnamable taste in her mouth, her hand fidgeting with the soft fabric of her dress from the West.

The three of them are drinking sake, and Sato is telling them a story about a fortune-teller in Shanghai when the monk rushes into the room. He stands in the doorway, a furious silhouette. His cheeks are smudged with soot, and black stains his hands and robe. One side of his robe is burned into a ragged edge. His eyes, reddened, blaze at her.

She rushes to her feet. What happened?

Hayashi and Sato jolt upward.

Tears have carved white lines through the soot on his face. He can't stop weeping from eyes filled with hate.

You made such promises, he says, now glaring at Hayashi, his voice choked. You promised these new leaders would stop. You spoke of freedom. The beauty of this new freedom. Lies. All lies.

What happened? cries Ayoshi.

He tells them about the other temple and monastery, burned to the ground, monks and priests dead, trapped inside, burned beyond recognition. Buddhist statues smashed and the paintings sliced and torn and the temple bells taken, carried away in carts. He tells them of the pieces, the shards, the screams cutting through smoke-filled air.

He holds up his sooty hand. Covered with burned flesh, he says. He shoves his hand toward them. My friends, he says, now dead. A fellow mountain monk was there, hung from a rafter, his feet swaying. I knew him. I grew up with him.

Hayashi sinks to his knees, moaning, his face in his hands.

He tried to stop the flames, but they ran out of water. They drained all the water. Who thought of such a thing? Who are these men? What kind of horrible world do you people live in?

The bodies burning, Hayashi sees it searing in his mind anew, and the smell, he knows the stench; it is what has filled his air for years.

Do you know why they did it? says the monk. The officials thought the monks held a formal Buddhist funeral. They killed the wrong monks. They should have killed me. He jabs his finger into his chest. I am the one they wanted.

Oh, no, says Hayashi.

I am the one.

They made a mistake, says Sato, subdued.

The monk glares at Ayoshi, as if she were the one who set the fire. She can't speak. Finally, he stalks out of the room, leaving the three of them standing there. No one says anything. They listen to him walk down the long corridor, a steady heavy step, the crash of pottery smashing to the floor, and another, and another, and then the sound of footsteps grows distant, a door slams, and his footsteps are gone.

THE MONK IS IN the temple gathering his few belongings. The door opens.

Enri, she says.

He won't look at her.

Enri, she says, breathless, grabbing hold of his arm.

He stares at her, his eyes hardened.

Please.

He shakes off her grip and looks right through her.

Talk to me. Say something.

He steps back and looks at her with cold dark eyes. She feels his rage and hatred, a slap against her cheek.

Don't go, she says. Her eyes fill with tears. He is shut down to her. She feels the thick cold wall between them. Even if she took his hand and put it on her beating heart, he would not feel a thing. She watches him turn, walk out the temple door, down the pebble walkway, through the gate, into the wooded area through long dew-drenched grass, and to the path that leads steadily up the mountain.

PEBBLES SHUFFLE UNDERNEATH HIS sandals; the monk shivers in the chill. Swallowed up by the dark woods, he heads up. As he climbs, he knows there is nothing to return to, no homecoming, no home, only the collapsed buildings at the top. As it should be, he thinks. My brothers, now skeletons. That will be my home. His mind feels furious and full. On the spot of the massacre at the top of the mountain, he will cut wood and fashion nails, use a discarded pan or stone figure to pound them in. And he will grow accustomed to the cold again. Eating roots and vegetables from a small garden. Perhaps men will hear of him and climb up the mountain, he thinks. He might become a priest of a new monastery.

Panting now as he climbs higher, he thinks, I've grown soft, indulging in the pleasures of the body. Below me, in the town, at the house, it is all worthless and disorderly and so much to tempt and overwhelm and so much violence. The beauty down in the valley is not true beauty, he thinks, trying to soothe himself. Up on the mountain, he will find true beauty, he tells himself, along with his resilience, and his sturdy center. He will sleep tonight in the nave of a fallen tree and use his satchel for a pillow and jerk awake, his head filled with flames.

He stops now, undoes his satchel, and removes the small piece of paper he took from the bag of rice. Don't look at her, mustn't look, and he's about to rip up her image and throw it away, but he glances at the paper, at Ayoshi, and his eyes water. Why does his heart throb so? He gazes into her eyes. Perhaps he won't stay on the mountaintop, he thinks. Maybe his heartache will bring him down someday. Maybe to the capital, where he will meet a woman, someone who will leave an indelible mark. Caressing the image with his thumb, he looks longingly at Ayoshi, and for a moment, he steps outside himself and is overwhelmed by a quiet, almost euphoric sense of gratitude. Before her, he had not known the ways of the heart. He carefully puts the image into his bag.

In the morning, she rises, slips her hands into a basin, and washes her face in cold water. With shaky tentative steps, she walks into the temple; emptiness greets her. She searches for his scent and finds only the lingering smell of wax from burned candles. She steps to the shadowy corner where the monk nested. Nothing remains, as if he were never here. No blankets, no bowl for rice, no books, except there, underneath a shelf, a small drawing book. She opens the book and there are his sketches, a black ink drawing of the monastery, his mountain hut, his beloved teacher, and the teahouse. Careful, precise drawings of the porch, the roof, the rock garden. On the last page, she finds a portrait of her. She traces the delicate lines with her finger, then closes the book, and takes it with her to the studio. She gathers her secret paintings, along with his book, takes them to the back garden, and burns them. As she watches the flickering fire, the edges of her paintings curling and disappearing, she feels a momentary airiness to her being, before it is covered again by heaviness, like a long, sorrowful sigh.

The house is still, except for Sato, who is in his room shuffling through drawers. She finds him in the Western room. He is packing.

The offer still stands, he says. You can accompany me to Shanghai. He hands her official-looking papers. This will allow you to travel anywhere.

She says nothing.

It isn't safe here anymore.

I know.

The government will figure out they burned down the wrong temple. Why are you looking at me like that? I didn't do it.

She walks out of the room, down the hallway, and into the kitchen, where she sits motionless at the table. When Sato has his bags packed, he comes out, touches her wrist, lingers for a moment. Then he is gone.

She steps outside onto the porch and watches his thin back disappear down the dirt road. The morning air is fresh, and the sky a soft yellow. She waits for Hayashi to rise and come out to the kitchen. When he doesn't come, she steps into the bedroom.

We must leave here, she says.

He doesn't say anything.

Hayashi.

Go.

What? she says.

Go. It's what you've always wanted, isn't it?

She feels tears well up. Hayashi.

Go.

You can't stay. What if they come?

I have a duty. My honor.

I can't leave you here, she says. The moment she says it, her throat tightens, knowing she can't stay. Later, she'll comb through this moment, again and again, convincing herself she did the right thing. She will watch the arc of her life, the precise second where it took a different turn, never forgetting the contraction, not just in her throat, but her chest, a constriction of her body at the thought of staying in this house with the dead buried outside her window. Wherever she is, on a boat, in a tea shop, in the company of friends, she will feel it all over again and know she had no choice: If she remained, the small ember would finally and completely go out.

She looks at him now. Such a kind, gentle man. Why couldn't her heart find his? And she knows the question is the same for him: Why couldn't his heart rise up from its ashes and find hers? Just as she knows she can't stay, his gray face, tight lips, and heavy lidded eyes tell her he won't go.

Please, she says. You must leave here.

He stares at the ceiling. I don't want you here, he says. Maybe that will help you leave. I don't want you with me anymore.

She doesn't move.

Sometimes you learn to love someone, he says, sometimes you don't. I don't love you, Ayoshi.

Hayashi. Save yourself. Please.

Go, he says, turning his back to her.

SHE PULLS OUT A suitcase and packs. She changes into a simple kimono and walks to town, stopping at the sushi shop to tell the owner to send someone for Hayashi. She gives him money from the sale of her painting to reserve a room at the ryokan for Hayashi. He won't cooperate, she tells the owner. If you must, drag him out. Do whatever is necessary, she says, handing over more money.

She walks to the port. The ship for Shanghai has departed. There is a ship leaving for America, says the clerk. San Francisco.

She purchases a ticket and perches on a bench in the waiting room. A couple of women in Western dresses walk by, gossiping, carrying bright parasols. Ayoshi hugs her elbows to try and stop the trembling. She has no image of America, no way to picture it. Sato said it was brash and young. But what does that mean? How will she live? Nervous dampness creeps along her palms. Her fingertips, icy with fear. When the sound of a hammer penetrates her thoughts, she quickly stands and looks in the direction of the temple. But he is no longer there, she thinks. There, above the treetops, the black tile of the roof, and above that, the mountaintop. She sits again and waits.

When the ticket clerk calls out, Boarding time, she mechanically steps onto the plank, clutching her sketchbook and paints, her luggage in her other hand. She finds a seat on deck. A young Japanese woman sits across from her, wearing a traditional kimono, the color of a daffodil. Her glossy black hair is parted in the center and pulled into a formal bun. Her lips are colored red, her face painted white. Ayoshi sits perfectly still, and when the breeze flutters across her face, she smells the woman's powdery fragrance overpowering the sea air. Finally, she feels the ship pull away from the dock. She closes her eyes to stop the tears, the splintering into a thousand fragments. When she opens them again, she looks out toward the sea, then back toward Japan, so long tucked away in history. There will always be the residue of the old, she thinks. Soon to be a blend of East and West, but the old will always be woven into the warp of this island. She turns her gaze to the green sea.

Excuse me, are you traveling to America to meet your new husband? asks the young woman.

It takes a moment for Ayoshi to understand what the woman has asked. No, says Ayoshi. She pauses and looks at the decorated woman.

The woman clicks open her purse, pulls out a photograph, and proudly hands it to Ayoshi. She tells Ayoshi her husband left Japan several years ago to set up a tea and silk import company. I am told he is a very intelligent man.

Ayoshi nods numbly and hands the picture back to the woman. She glances at the empty seat next to her and sees a twig of cherry blossoms, its pale pink flowers, delicate, like a newborn. Most likely it fell out of someone's bouquet. She fingers one flower, feels the soft velvet of its petal, smells the strong scent of green and the pure white, the hints of red and yellow, the soft cream along the edges. With a sudden intensity, she pulls out her sketchbook and begins to draw.

Oh, you are an artist. Are you going to America to paint?

Ayoshi pauses, lets the words sink in, the shadow of apprehension slowly dissipating. Yes, she says. Yes, I am.

The woman smiles appreciatively and asks if she might see her work.

All of it was burned in a fire, says Ayoshi, glancing down at her book. She tells the woman she is going to begin all over again.

ACKNOWLEDGMENTS

FIRST AND FOREMOST, I am especially grateful to Professor Phyllis Burke for her thoughtful and careful attention to this novel. Without her, this novel would not have come to be.

Although this is a work of fiction, some of the places and events are based on historical fact. Many books were important to me in my research. *Paris Under Siege, 1870–1871: From the Goncourt Journal,* edited and translated by George J. Becker, was invaluable to re-creating life in Paris during the Franco-Prussian War. Alistair Horne's *The Fall of Paris: The Siege and the Commune, 1870–71* lent insight into the machinations of the war. I'm indebted to *We Japanese,* by Frederic de Garis, for its descriptions of Japanese traditions, ceremonies, and customs; also *The Revolutionary Origins of Modern Japan,* by Thomas M. Huber, put the Meiji Era in context. I also want to thank my Japanese language teacher, Atsuko Sells, who spent many hours explaining Japanese customs as well as her life in Japan.

A thank-you to Peter Allen, Nancy Tompkins, and Hannelore Seeger for their generous comments and suggestions. A special thank-you to Michelle Tessler and Antonia Fusco for their unwavering belief in the book. And thank you, Peter Seeger, my dear husband, for never doubting.